CHAINS OF FATE & FURY

Cover Design: Marina Laurendi

Interior Map: Marina Laurendi

ISBN: 9798991168939

Printed in the United States of America

10 9 8 7 6 5 4 3 2 1

❀ Created with Vellum

Solmead
CASTLE ILLONA
PRAXIAN SEA
VOD
Baegar
TIR
SOLTERRE

NORTHLANDS
SUNKEN SEA
Cave of Manthis
SKULL VALLEY
WILLOWSPEAK CASTLE
Bone Forest
HYRAX
Iaspus
AEGAR
Cardynia
OUTLANDS
BLEAKWATER BAY
STONE BEACH
ROCKLANDS
ISLAND OF ITERRE
AEIX
MYDLANDS
ERASTIN OCEAN
SOUTHLANDS
HIGH SEER

PRONUNCIATION GUIDE

- Zadyn- Zay Den
- Jace- Jay S
- Kylian- Kill Ee In
- Triori- Tree Or Ee
- Sorscha- Sor Sha
- Marideth- Mae Ri Deth
- Dover- Doh Ver
- Cece (Ceec)- See See | Seec
- Igrid- Ee Grid
- Gnorr- Nor
- Prophyria (Furi)- Pro Fury A | Fury
- Ienar- Eye Nar
- Wyneth- Win Eth
- Stryga- Stri Ga
- Aegar- Aye Gar
- Hyrax- Hi Racks
- Aeix- A Ex
- Vod- Voh D
- Tir- Tee Er
- Solterre- Sohl Tair

- Iaspus- Ee As Pis
- Erastin- Ee Ras Tin
- Stygian- St Eye Gee En
- Markade- Mar Kaid
- Illona- Ill Oh Nuh
- Ilayna- Ill Aye Nuh
- Ilspeth- Ill Sp Eth
- Alto Luminaria- All Toe Loo Min R Ee Uh
- Aurea Dei- Or Ee Uh Day Ee
- Solmead- Soul Meed
- Loryn- Lore N
- Alix- Al Ix
- Eaton- Eet Un
- Coyle- K Oil
- Bronyn- Brah Nin
- Celmilline- Sell Muh Leen
- Garron- Gair Un

RECOMMENDED PLAYLIST

Music has been a massive inspiration in shaping this series. I highly recommend listening along with the cues/footnotes to give you the full cinematic experience.

- Chapter 9: *Talk* by Hozier
- Chater 13: *Trouble* by Pink
- Chapter 14: *Black Beauty* by Lana Del Rey
- Chapter 28: *When You Were Young* by The Killers
- Chapter 35: *So Hot You're Hurting My Feelings* by Caroline Polachek
- Chapter 43: *If You're Too Shy (Let Me Know)-Edit* by the 1975
- Chapter 44: *Ruin My Life* by Zara Larsson
- Chapter 49: *Mamma Mia* by ABBA
- Chapter 51: *So Sweet I Could Die* by Lucia & The Best Boys
- Chapter 55: *Funeral* by Phoebe Bridgers
- Chapter 59: *Bike Dream* by Rostam
- Chapter 63: *circle the drain* by Soccer Mommy | *So Hot You're Hurting My Feelings* by Squirrel Flower
- Chapter 64: *back to friends* by sombr
- Chapter 71: *another woman* by Coral Moons

Spotify Playlist: Chains of Fate & Fury: Blackblooded 2

TRIGGERS

- Blood
- Abuse
- Torture
- PTSD
- Violence
- Death
- Grief

For the quiet ones. Breathing fire is perfectly okay.

BLACKBLOODED 2

MARINA LAURENDI

PART I: SPLINTERED GLASS

1

JACE

"Out of my way. Now."

The two wide-eyed bodies blocking the exit remain planted between me and the stable doors. It's a bold move—testing my patience. Even on a good day.

And today sure as all hell does not classify as a good day.

"Jace."

I shove between Marideth and Dover, yanking the reins of the lithe Stygian horse. The sun glares overhead as I fit my foot to the stirrups and swing my leg over the saddle. Marideth dashes in front of the horse again, holding up her palms.

"*I will run you down,*" I growl.

And I will. I don't care who they are—if they don't move out of my gods-damned way, heads are going to roll.

"It will take you too long on horseback. Vod is a two-week journey without stops. Let us help you."

"You can't help! She is *my* responsibility."

And this is my fault.

I should have fought harder. I should have cut down everything and everyone to get to her.

It's been seven days, nine hours, and approximately thirty minutes since Serena was taken during the attack on the final night of King's Fair. Seven days since I watched helplessly as blood ore shackles rendered her powerless, and she vanished right before my eyes. Seven days when I should have been on my way to Vod with Zadyn to get her back.

And every second I stand here talking to *these* two is a second that she loses.

"And she is *my* friend!" Mar insists. "So is Kai. We want them back just as much as you. Now get off the horse and follow me. I have a plan that beats this idiotic one."

"You are wasting precious time! Time she doesn't have!" I shout, the cap on my temper bursting.

"Listen to her, Jace."

Something in Dover's tone hooks my attention. It's the gravest I've ever seen the jovial, even-tempered male. My eyes narrow, meeting Mar's pale gray gaze.

"There's something I need to show you." She stares up at me from the ground, beseeching. I loose a frustrated sigh, sliding off the horse.

"You have five minutes."

"Where in Zed's name are you taking me?"

My fingers twitch impatiently as I follow them around the back of the stables.

"I need water." Mar pauses at the red trough, sinking to her knees before the murky water.

Oh, you have got to be *kidding* me. "Your thirst can't wait?"

Rather than answering, she places her hands on either side of the trough and leans forward, closing her eyes. The water begins to ripple as an image forms on the surface. Before I can ask what I'm seeing, it clears. And my heart stops.

Serena.

My knees sink into the caked dirt below.

She's sprawled out on a black floor, unmoving, blood ore chains clamped around her wrists, dark hair strewn across her cheek. I surge forward, gripping the edge of the metal trough so hard it dents.

"Is she breathing?" I demand.

Mar makes no attempt to answer me. I try to memorize Serena's surroundings. She's somewhere dark—a cell, maybe. Relief blasts through me as she sits up, reaching out to embrace the figure before her. Then someone new enters the space, and her features shift. The brief hope in me curdles as her mouth stretches open and her throat strains. And though the scream is silent, I have no trouble hearing it. It is the sound of my walking nightmares—the sound that haunts my dreams and my days. She thrashes, my fierce little warrior. She fights. She rears against her chains and bares her fangs.

And all too soon, she's gone. The image blurs and disappears as Mar falls back into Dover's waiting arms.

"Are you alright?" he asks.

"How did you—" I glance from the evaporated image to Mar's pale face. A drop of cobalt leaks from her nose. She quickly wipes it away.

Water seer.

"You're a Blueblood," I say, unable to look away.

How? In all my years of knowing Marideth, I never even suspected —never even *saw* her use magic in any capacity. Did Sorscha know? Did anyone know that we had a witch living under our noses far before Serena ever came along?

Focus, a voice inside me chirps.

I swallow back the thousand questions I have, storing them for a time when the love of my life isn't confined to a fucking dungeon.

"I was." She pushes out of Dover's arms and stands, dusting herself off. "I defected. It's a long story. We can save it for the road."

Hah. Right.

"You're not coming with me."

"Like hell we're not." Setting her hands on her hips, she bellies up to me. "I'm a witch. And I can help you."

"You're barely a witch if you defected."

"I found ways to keep my power."

"Your nose is bleeding after one scrying," I point out.

"Do you want to push me? Because I'm happy to share my other talents, *Captain.*"

I don't bother correcting her. She knows full well that the beloved position I once held is no longer mine.

I stand my ground, refusing to be baited. "You said you have a plan. You've got five seconds to win me over."

She jerks her chin toward the trough. "After you."

I blink at her, brows quirked. "Excuse me?"

"I'm good with water," she says smoothly, a challenge blazing in her silver eyes.

Oh, this is going to be fun.

"Get inside."

When I make no move, she brushes past me, stepping into the trough. Water gushes over the side as she holds out her hand for Dover.

"We're going with or without you."

I heave a sigh and grumble, "This had better work," before taking her other hand and following suit. My boots sink into the water as her eyes drift closed.

"Deep breath, boys."

The bottom of the trough gives way to the center of the earth, opening up into a bottomless ocean below. We sink, dragged down by an invisible anchor, and my grip on Mar's hand tightens. I open my eyes to a dark abyss and auburn hair swirling around me like a wild, fiery halo.

My lungs burn in warning. The moment before they burst, we're spit out onto a bed of pink sand.

The sounds of our choked gasps fill the air as I blink away the white spots in my vision. Dover is on all fours, pounding at his chest, vomiting water. Once he catches his breath, he moves to turn Marideth over.

"Mar," he coughs, giving her shoulders a shake.

Blood slides down her chin and neck, staining the top of her bodice a pale blue. Her eyes crack open.

"That fucking hurt."

Dover lets out a weak laugh and dips his head to kiss her. I look away, ashamed of the envy I feel.

I know I shouldn't feel this way. They're just as unlucky as Serena and me—Dover, with his unbreakable engagement, forced to marry despite having found his mate. I think what I'm most jealous of is the fact that they don't care. They won't let something as immaterial as a piece of paper and a couple of rings stop them from the fate the gods planned for them. They are unafraid of the consequences.

I'm not like that. No matter how much I wish I were.

"Where are we?" My hoarse voice slices through their tender moment as I get to my feet, glancing around the unfamiliar territory.

The sun's beams catch on the waves that ejected us—the effect near blinding. Blues, purples, and greens swirl together like a painting before washing up on the sugar-fine sand. Behind us, the beach is lined with vibrant wildflowers and towering palms shivering in the light sea breeze.

Aegar doesn't have beaches like this. My homeland is filled with rolling hills and valleys. Mountains and green forests.

"I don't know," Mar says, wiping the diluted cobalt off her face with the back of her sleeve.

"You don't know?" I explode, my tone vicious. "You transport us to the middle of fucking nowhere, and now you tell me you don't know where we are?!"

Unbelievable.

This. This right here is why I prefer doing things alone.

"That isn't how water walking works," she explains, wringing out her skirts. "Without knowing where she is, I can't get us to an exact location. But I can get close. I don't know how close, but I'm willing to bet we've just cut your travel time on horseback in half. You're welcome."

"I'll thank you when you've gotten us to Serena."

"Everyone relax," Dover cuts in. "We're in Vod. I'd know our beaches anywhere."

"You don't have to be an ass. We're on the same side here," Mar says.

A cloud of shame settles over me. I'm sleep-starved, and from the moment Serena was taken, I have been frothing at the mouth, ready to bite off anyone's head who so much as blinks at me.

"I'm sorry. I'm just—" I squeeze my eyes shut and drag my hands down my stubbled jaw. "I'm losing my mind."

Mar places a gentle hand on my shoulder, her gaze loaded with sympathy. "I know."

Sighing, I squint over her shoulder at the glittering waters of the Praxian Sea.

"She has to be at the palace. How close are we?" I ask Dover.

"Maybe two, three days on foot."

"Two days." I shake my head.

"Beats two weeks," Mar offers.

"Right." I turn to her with a gentle nod. "Well done, Blue."

2

ZADYN

Come *on*.

Show me something. *Anything.*

I've been circling overhead for hours. The ache in my wings has faded into background noise—the only feeling more potent is the roiling fear that I'm already too late.

It's funny. All my life, I thought I knew what fear was. And then she was taken, and I realized, no—I hadn't had a clue in the fucking world.

I swoop downward in the body of a falcon, coasting over the jagged seaside cliffs. The wards buzz beneath my wings, eager to shock me right out of the sky. To even graze that field would mean certain death.

I've been scouring the perimeter of Kylian's keep for days, looking for chinks in the wards. But it's useless. The magic here is airtight. Castle Illona is an impenetrable fortress. I've all but memorized the exterior of the sprawling palace—the dozens of pale marble tiers layered meticulously one on top of the other, the glare of the glass domes, the courtyards fragmented by ribbon-thin streams, the waterfalls pouring from the open archways to filter down the cliffs into the blue-green sea below.

I do another sweep, peering through the endless windows and seeing nothing.

Like I said. Useless.

In the time I've been patrolling, I have not seen a single soul inside or outside the keep. It's some sort of illusion to protect against onlookers, spies, and anyone doing exactly what I'm doing right now. From here, the castle could pass for abandoned. No indication of life or the horrors I have no doubt lie hidden within those walls.

A blur of movement catches my eye on one of the turrets. Before I can even process what it is, I'm speeding toward it, my heart pumping with desperate hope.

Then I see it.

The small gray bird perched on the stone ledge.

Bastard.

The little tease ruffles its wings and jets into the sky, oblivious to the fact that it just butchered what little faith I had left. That one moment of distraction is all it takes for me to get a bit too close to the wards.

Fucking hell.

I jerk backward, plummeting a few feet as the electric shock rips through my wing, radiating up my entire left side. Not enough to knock me out of the sky, just a gentle reminder of what losing my focus will earn me in a place like this.

I change course, landing on the nearest palm to survey the damage. I suck in a sharp breath as I try to lift my wing. The feathered tip is slightly singed and stinging like hell, but I'm already healing.

"Nice going, idiot," I can almost hear her saying.

If Serena could see me now, she'd be cackling—a smile stretched wide across her heart-shaped face. A pang shoots up my chest, making my throbbing wing feel like a paper cut.

Gods, I miss her. And it's making me want to do stupid, impulsive things that are more likely to get me killed rather than get her back.

Patience never goes unrewarded, Zadyn. Be patient.

My father's favorite thing to remind me as a child.

I'm trying, Father. But it's driving me insane—being this close and not being able to feel her through the bond. The blood ore has made it impossible for me to hear her, no matter how hard I strain against that wall dividing us.

This familiar bond between us has been there since before she was born—a tether linking us together, placed there by my mother as her dying act. I knew shortly after finding Serena in the human world that I would have my work cut out for me. As a child, she tried to kill herself at least five times a day, which was concerning. As she grew into a woman, the dangers shifted to external. Men not so discreetly leering at her on the streets of New York, cornering her in bars, thinking they were somehow worthy of her. Enter Annie Arnold—the kind of friend who could make a man's balls shrivel with one scathing look. That was a great glamour. It worked like a charm until I realized I couldn't keep it up.

Because over time, this bond changed into something I can't describe. A crush on my part, turned infatuation, and now...I try not to think of it. Try not to feel it. But it's impossible not to.

I had no idea the space she would take up in my heart. I had no idea that she would consume it completely.

I may not be able to hear her, but I *know* she's here, just on the other side of that alabaster stone. Likely terrified and alone. And I can't do a single thing to assure her that I'm here and that I will rip this world apart to get her back.

Just as soon as I can figure out a damned way inside.

I fly along the shoreline toward the run-down city nearby as the sky turns powder blue, edging an overcast sunset. Through the thicket of tropical forest, I see three heads weaving through the maze of palms and exotic flowers. The sound of bickering floats up to me.

Voices I recognize.

It's impossible.

"...absolutely one hundred percent sure?"

"Yes, Blue. I am sure."

"We've passed the same plant thirty times!"

"Welcome to walking through a forest."

Well, I'll be damned.

My wings rustle the nearby palms, startling the three of them as I soar downward. I shift before I hit the ground, landing on my feet with a thud.

They stop short as I straighten, eyeing me with a mixture of surprise and relief.

"What took you so long?"

3

SERENA

"Again," Kylian chimes from his gilded throne.

I sit on the floor at his side, the blood ore shackles around my wrists bolted to the smooth tile beneath me.

The sea breeze rolls through the open archways lining the throne room, rippling the sheer red and gold curtains. I shiver, naked aside from my tattered, see-through shift and the dazzling ruby collar around my neck.

A gift and reminder of my master.

Of the male on the throne who now owns me.

The sound of a fist smashing into flesh has my head snapping up.

Kai's face is unrecognizable. Purple welts decorate his once-perfect skin. His left eye is swollen shut, his lips cracked and caked with blood. The straight slope of his nose is now separated into two sharp angles, forcing ragged, labored breaths from him.

He teeters on his knees, dancing on the edge of consciousness as his eyes roll back in his head. Just before his face smacks the tile, Mal's fist shoots out to yank him back, baring his blood-streaked throat to me.

I don't scream. I don't thrash. I just stare.

I have no voice left to scream.

11

I have no strength left to thrash.

I have no will left to fight.

So I stare.

Seeing Kai like this never gets easier, despite being forced to bear witness to his beatings on a daily basis. Kylian thought the quickest way to break me would be to turn my friend into his personal whipping boy. His own *brother*. He is beating and brutalizing his own *brother* to get me to comply.

I ripped this world open for you, he had boasted.

As if it were some grand romantic gesture that he hijacked the one portal in Solterre and is now using it to amass an army of undead creatures to aid him in world domination. As if I should ingratiate myself to him by becoming his bride and giving up my dragon's location.

Yeah. Over my dead body.

Today's show consists of Mal, wearing a handful of ruby rings, repeatedly punching Kai until he passes out. When his face is a cut-up, broken, bloody slab of flesh, the healer standing off to the side comes forward and gives Mal a fresh, blank canvas to work with.

It's the same shit, different day. Yesterday, they waterboarded him, drowning him over and over while I watched. I've tried to retaliate, but these chains have rendered me useless.

Powerless.

After the first night Kylian had Kai beat in front of me, a crumpled-up strip of parchment floated into my cell.

He will use everything at his disposal to break you.
Do not give him what he wants. Promise me. Destroy this.

I ripped the note into the tiniest pieces I could manage and let it dissolve under my tongue where no one would find it.

The notes have continued to appear since that day, letting me know he still lives.

Stay strong.
I am with you.
Do not break.
Fight.

I have torn and devoured each one, proof of Kai's strength consecrated inside of me.

But the sound of his screams and cries haunt my dreams. The smell of his sweat, blood, and piss have calcified in me, hardening a piece of my heart that I fear will never soften again.

I am becoming numb, cold, and immune. Like stone.

Movement catches my eye from the far end of the throne room as Queen Ilspeth breezes in, each perfect feature sharp and prowling. Mal turns, her bloodied second son dangling from his ruthless grasp. She pauses to wipe a splash of blood off Mal's cheek, not even deigning to spare Kai a single glance. Then she drifts up the dais and takes a seat on the empty throne at Kylian's side.

I want to vomit.

Sick, sick bastards. All of them.

She has not spoken more than ten words to me, yet she is the reason for all of this suffering.

I will kill her first. Then I will kill Kylian. Then Mal.

The healer steps forward, and within seconds Kai's injuries are reversed, and he looks like himself again. For a split second, his glassy eyes land on mine and become alert.

Then Mal's ruby-studded fist connects with his jaw in a punch that sends Kai sliding across the blood-slicked tile, a few teeth flying out in the process.

I wince internally, still as a statue on the outside. I won't allow Kylian the pleasure of my cries. I won't allow him the satisfaction of my tears. Not anymore.

"Enough," Ilspeth says, sounding bored. "Kylian, there are other matters that require your attention at present."

He waves a hand, and a nearby guard peels Kai off the floor and drags him from the hall with the healer in tow.

Mal steps up to the dais, eyes glued to the queen as he pulls a cloth from his pristine black pants and begins wiping Kai's blood off his fistful of rings.

I jump when a hand lands on the top of my head. Kylian is gazing down at me like one would look at a beloved pet, smoothing my hair in a gesture meant to be caring.

"You barely flinched that time. You're even more ruthless than I gave you credit for, my love."

I duck my head, but his fist tightens in my hair. I let out a hiss as he leans in close, amusement coloring his face. "Is your answer still no?"

I glower up at him with all the hatred I can muster. A slow smile spreads across his cruel, beautiful mouth.

"We'll resume tomorrow," he says, shoving my head away and standing in one smooth motion.

I think I hear him humming as he jogs down the steps of the dais.

Fucking psychopath.

"Get creative, Mal." His dark voice echoes off the arches as he disappears around the corner. "I want to be entertained."

4

JACE

Zadyn steps through the door of the ramshackle apartment, holding it open for us to pass.

"It's not much, but I'm barely ever here anyway."

The single room contains a bedroll, a sack of supplies, a small wooden table, and a fireplace full of ash.

"What is all this?" I mutter, stepping around the maps and drawings carelessly strewn across the floor.

Zadyn pours out some water for the three of us. "Research."

My eyes drift over the charcoal renderings of Castle Illona. Detailed aerial views, depictions from various angles.

He's been here for over a week, and this is what he has to show for it?

"Please tell me you've done more than doodle since you arrived here."

He turns to me, leaning against the kitchen counter.

"No doubt more than you've done sitting in your ivory tower this last week." He extends a glass to Mar, a smug look on his face as he holds eye contact with me.

He's not wrong. Being Hand of the King does not suit me. I'm used to action and battle, not patience and politicizing. When Derek

15

commanded me to stay in Aegar after Serena was taken, it nearly killed me. Zadyn, unbound by title, left that very night.

I don't think I've ever envied him more.

"How did you get here so fast?"

"It seems Marideth has been holding out on us." I give her a pointed look as she slides into one of the worn wooden chairs. Zadyn glances between us.

"I'm a Blueblood," she says offhandedly. "Do you have anything to eat here? I'm starving."

Zadyn's eyes round, his brows leaping toward his hairline as he grapples for words. "Can we maybe…unpack that a little?"

Mar lifts her glass to her mouth and chugs while Zadyn waits, the unmistakable look of shock plastered across his face. She makes a loud, satisfied sound and wipes her mouth on the back of her hand.

"I forgot how thirsty magic makes you." Fixing her cool eyes on Zadyn, she starts, "I defected from my coven nearly two centuries ago and never looked back. No one knew except Dover. And Serena," she adds. "I told her a few days before she was taken."

"How did you retain your magic?" Zadyn crosses to the table, bracing his hands on the empty chair.

"I found a loophole. When I left, I buried a part of it in here." She lifts her hand, flashing him the delicate moonstone ring encircling her third finger. Now that I think of it, I've never seen her without it.

"I could only get away with keeping a sliver, and I haven't touched it in years. I didn't want to risk being tracked and traced back to the clan."

"So you can siphon off that ring?" Zadyn asks. She nods, twirling it mindlessly around her finger.

"I did a scrying and saw Serena chained up in what looked like a dungeon. I water walked us here." She stretches her long legs out, leaning forward to massage her calves.

"We ended up on the southern beaches two days ago. We've been heading toward the castle ever since," Dover says from her side.

"Judging by the lack of Blackblood here, I'm guessing whatever you've been attempting since you arrived hasn't been successful." I toss a nod at Zadyn, not intending for the bite in my words.

I've never been his greatest fan. Partly because for a familiar, I've witnessed him make a lot of stupid choices when it comes to Serena's well-being. And partly because in her eyes he can do no wrong.

"I've been trying to figure out the best extraction strategy."

He runs a hand through his chestnut-colored hair and bends to scoop up a stack of parchment. I move closer as he spreads them on the table, noticing the darkened circles around his eyes, the unkempt stubble on his chin and jaw. He's clearly slept about as much as I have in the last week.

"I've never seen wards so tight. There's absolutely no way to get in unless we do it on foot. And even that presents its own set of issues."

"Those creatures," I mutter, sifting through the sketches.

"The Stryga." Zadyn palms the table as we study his work. "He could have an army of them waiting on the other side of those walls."

Grotesque images of the mangled, half-male, half-beasts flood my mind. Their snarling jaws wet with innocent blood, the curved horns protruding from their lupine skulls, their taloned claws wrapping around Serena's limp form as they disappeared from the hall.

"Dover, you live at the castle. Maybe you can offer some insight," Zadyn says.

"I haven't lived there in years. Kai and I reside at his estate in Malfa. It's been decades since we've even visited."

Helpful.

"Has there been any activity there?" I ask, falling back on my military instincts.

Zadyn shakes his head. "They have an illusion over the entire perimeter. I haven't seen a single soul from overhead in the days I've been scouting."

"No one? Not even going in and out?"

"Not one."

"Fuck," I mutter, turning to pace around the dim room.

Keep it together and think. There has to be a way.

"I could try to water walk us in," Mar suggests, but Zadyn shakes his head.

"Doing so would set off the alarms. So would using any kind of magic to force entry."

"We should have brought the dragon," she says, crestfallen.

"If we had, she would have sensed Serena in danger and would have obliterated the entire castle and everyone in it. We need to do this cleanly, with the smallest amount of bloodshed possible," Zadyn cautions, eyeing each of us.

"Derek is sending troops, but it will take too long for them to arrive," I add.

He had begged me to wait for them, insisting I would need backup. But I don't think he realized that the rage I have burning inside of me would fuel me with the power of fifty soldiers.

"Let's avoid starting a war at all costs. We do that on Vod soil, and we doom ourselves. If we do this right, we can get her out. The four of us."

"Someone has to leave eventually," Dover adds. "That could give us the opening we need."

"We don't have time to keep waiting," I snarl, my patience slipping. "It's been nearly ten days. We can't just sit here twiddling our thumbs while she—"

"Jace."

My name coming from Zadyn's mouth has my attention snapping to him.

"I know. Believe me, I know."

And I do. Because I've seen the way he looks at Serena. It's more than how a familiar looks at their bonded.

It's the same way I look at her.

WE EAT QUICKLY outside a small tavern below Zadyn's flat. The sky above us is a deep red, as if it too is bleeding without her.

I set the pewter mug down and look at the others. "I want to go by the castle and see it for myself."

Zadyn's eyes shift to me. "Tomorrow. You won't see anything at night. Besides, all of you need rest."

"You need rest. You look like shit." I make a face, which he returns with a tight, sardonic smirk.

"Likewise."

Folding my arms over my chest, I say, "And what are we supposed to do in the meantime? I didn't come here to hurry up and wait. I came to get her back."

Zadyn glances between the three of us. "Actually, there is something we can do."

I quirk a brow, slightly intrigued.

Tossing a few coins onto the table, he stands and starts down the cobbled road. We trail him through the maze of crowded city streets until we reach a busy bazaar. He stops before one of the vendors—an old fae with a glass eye and hair like silver string—seated behind a table full of polished apples.

Zadyn pulls a few silvers from his pocket and drops them into her waiting hands. Chills skitter down my back as she assesses each of us with that singular gray eye. She rises with eerie grace and turns toward the sandstone building behind her. After two raps on the door, it creaks open.

We follow Zadyn inside past the old crone, but as I step through the threshold, her bony hand reaches out to grasp my arm with a grip surprisingly strong for someone so frail-looking.

That eye sears me as she croaks, "King of fools, king of bastards. You *are* no king. Do not test the Fates."

What in hell?

I blink and wrench my arm away. Too stunned to respond, I simply stare as she retreats to her post to sift through Zadyn's payment.

"Jace?" Marideth calls a few feet ahead.

I catch up, struggling to shake off the strange encounter as we make our way down a soft, candle-lit hall.

Red brocade curtains line the narrow passage into a parlor of sinful decadence. I take in the velvet-lined booths and daybeds scattered around the room. The low light and the litany of done-up females in heavy makeup and revealing gowns.

I turn to Zadyn, rage bubbling beneath my skin. "You brought us to a *whorehouse?*"

I'm going to kill him. The fucking *nerve* of him to be seeking pleasure at a time like this. When there is everything to lose.

The moment I snatch up his collar, a sweet voice interrupts.

"Zadyn?"

We both turn to see a slight, brown-haired fae with dark bronzed skin and sea-blue eyes watching us.

"Ilayna," Zadyn breathes. I release him and take a step back.

"I didn't expect you back so soon," she says. She reminds me of Sorscha, with the doe eyes and long lashes. The kind of person you feel instantly protective of.

"Things are urgent."

"You brought friends." She nods, glancing at the rest of us as a few females make their way past, eyeing us up with contrived thirst. "Maybe we should speak privately."

We follow the young courtesan through the ornate, if not tacky halls, the whole place reeking of perfume and expensive sex. She closes us inside an empty bedroom and gestures to the small sitting area across from the silk-dressed bed.

"Who are you?" I demand, refusing to sit.

"Please excuse my friend," Zadyn apologizes on my behalf. "Ilayna, this is Marideth, Dover, and Jace. Everyone, this is Ilayna. She's been helping me since I arrived."

Hmm. I'll bet she has. "Helping you what?" I mutter.

Mar slaps my arm. "Be nice."

Zadyn fixes me with a warning look and turns back to the stranger.

"Helping me infiltrate the castle."

5
SERENA

I used to be able to tell when I was dreaming. But now that the nightmares look, feel, and taste the same as reality, my guess is as good as anyone's.

I fight sleep, drifting in and out like a lightbulb on its last leg, even though I want nothing more than to sink into it for days.

It's when my eyes close that I see them. My friends. I see Jace's haunting eyes, Zadyn's warming smile. I hear Sorscha's laugh. I feel Furi nuzzling against my mind. Mar squeezing my hand in solidarity.

I need them to be alive. And I need them to stay away. Because if Kylian gets his hands on them, I will lose everyone I care about. No matter how hard my mind screams for them to just let me go, I know I'm shouting into a void.

They can't hear me. I can't warn them. I can't protect them. Fuck, I can't even protect myself. There is absolutely nothing I can do.

Nothing except for watch as Mal strips Kai nearly naked in front of me and draws a long dagger coated in rust. Kai wrestles with the chains stretching his arms out to a "T". Our eyes link.

I'm so sorry.

Mal grabs a fistful of his dark hair and yanks his head back.

"Keep moving, and this will hurt a lot worse," he murmurs in a chilling voice.

I glance around at what looks like a medieval torture chamber—dim torchlight, a multitude of chains and restraints hanging from the walls, and racks of objects I can only guess were made with a thirst for blood and suffering.

I'm bolted to one of those walls with a chain linked to the back of my choker.

Yes, I am on an actual leash.

"Morning, gorgeous." Kylian breezes in looking bright-eyed and well-slept, his skin luminous and that ever-present ironic smirk pinned to the corner of his mouth. "Sleep well?"

I glower at him. "Not particularly."

"I'd offer you my bed, but seeing how—*oppositional*—you are, I wouldn't expect my invitation to be well received."

Understatement of the year.

He stops above me, hands stuffed into his pockets. "Is today the day?" When I don't answer, he prompts, "The day you finally say yes to me?"

"She's not fucking marrying you," Kai grits, baring his teeth. Kylian turns toward him, chuckling.

"Feeling chatty today, are we? Congratulations, you've just earned a letter." He claps his hands once.

My friend's anguished cries echo through the chamber as Mal lifts the blade to his chest. I bite my lip to keep from howling along with him.

I will not cry. I will not cry. I will not cry.

I will not give these bastards what they want. Mal steps back, and I can see the singular letter etched on Kai's chest—the beads of blood forming a jagged "W".

"Speak out of turn again, and you'll earn a second. Now," Kylian says, directing his attention back to me. "Seeing as I just can't seem to resist you, I'll give you the choice of what you do first. Either you tell me where your dragon is, or you marry me. Tonight."

I don't know what he wants with Furi, but I know it can't be good.

Just like I know he doesn't want to marry me for my devastating looks and scathing wit.

"I will do no such thing."

"What was that, darling?" Kylian cups a hand against his ear and makes a show of leaning in to listen.

"I said I will do *no such thing!*"

A shark smile splits his beautiful face. "A second letter for my brother."

I force myself to hold Kylian's unflinching gaze as Kai's screams puncture my heart.

"The only way I am walking down an aisle is if you drag me, kicking and screaming."

Kylian scoffs. "Nonsense. What would I tell our children?"

I want to laugh. He has zero qualms about kidnapping and imprisoning, but he draws the line at a forced marriage.

"You're delusional."

He claps a hand over his toned chest. "And you are breaking my heart. Listen, I'm more than happy to keep playing this game with you. It's oddly refreshing, hearing the word *no*. But this is a game I intend to win. As for my feeble little brother…I wonder how much a body can take before just"—he snaps his fingers—"giving out."

Another round of heartrending cries. Crimson blood drips from the tip of Mal's serrated knife as I dare to read the three letters imprinted on Kai's heaving chest.

Wor.

Fury tumbles through me.

"You know, this whole big bad bully act is pretty unoriginal. You must be compensating for something." I make a face, nodding toward his groin.

He smirks, giving me a quick once-over. "Come over here and find out."

"Better idea. Go fuck yourself."

A sharp, gut-wrenching cry has my head snapping toward Kai. Mal has his dagger embedded in the fleshy space between his shoulder and neck. His face is pale, contorted in pain, his eyelids twitching as sweat beads on his brow.

"Mind your tongue when speaking to your king, witch."

"Just stop! Stop hurting him. You want someone to smack around? Fine. I volunteer. But Kai has nothing to do with this."

Kylian stoops to me like a god descending to his acolyte. He cups my cheek, his eyes raking over my mouth.

"Give me what I want, and this can all be over."

Temptation—decadent, *fatal* temptation—drips from his smoky voice. Everything about him is designed to compel. His looks, his scent, the melodic, deep timbre of his voice.

"His suffering can end. We can start over, and I will lay the world at your feet," he vows with sober conviction.

"I'm only interested in a world without you in it."

He cocks his head. "Are you really as fearless as you claim to be? Something tells me you're not, yet here you are gambling with my brother's life."

He's right. The longer I put this off, the bigger risk Kai is at. I don't know how much more he can take.

"Just tell me where she is. I promise to keep it between us."

"Prophyria will destroy you on sight. She will obliterate you just like she obliterated Ienar."

"Are you so sure about that?" His fingers toy with my hair. "My love, I have ways of dealing with dragons just like Ienar and his brother before him."

My stomach sinks. I'm not sure what he means by that, but one thing is certain—the only thing powerful enough to destroy a god is dragon fire. Which is how both brothers met their demise.

I pull back to look him in the eye. "You want me to call her? Fine. Unbind me. It's your funeral."

Kylian's features remain the same—impassive, unaffected, slightly amused. But for a moment, his expression flickers. It's brief, but it's there—that small hesitation.

"Oh, I see." My parched lips pull into a tight smile. "You won't do it. You're afraid. Of her...Of *me*. That's why you haven't taken these chains off—not even to call my dragon. You're so terrified, you had to level the playing field with these, you fucking coward."

Anger slashes across his face, and for a moment I think he might actually do it. Might actually hit me. But instead, his expression shifts, and his rich, warm laughter spills out.

"You really think I would put my hands on my own fiancé?" he says, as if reading my mind.

"I'm not your fiancé. And yes. I do."

"Darling," he softens his voice, shaking his head apologetically. "I don't even have to *touch* you to make you hurt. That's what my brother is for. And should that fail, I can simply move on to some of your other friends."

So they are alive. Thank you, god.

"You'll never catch them."

"Who's to say I haven't already?"

My blood heats, boiling to the point of rage. "Don't you dare."

"Haven't you wondered why no one has come for you? Why you remain bound at my side? Perhaps I already have them. Perhaps we should start with that shifter you call yours."

I swing my fists, catching his lip with my nails. Kylian laughs, dabbing the pad of his thumb to the perfect crimson dot that squeezes out.

"Little wildcat, aren't you?"

He yanks me forward and forces his bloody thumb into my mouth. I gag at the metallic tang, wrenching my face away and spitting the taste of him out at his feet.

His cheek grazes mine as he drops his voice to a bedroom-soft murmur. "You endear me, you really do. But mark my words, Dragon Rider, when I am through with them, you will be begging for me to take you. You are mine. Sooner or later, you'll see that. I just hope it's not too late. For his sake. For all their sakes."

Kylian releases me and stands, waving a hand in Mal's direction.

"Finish him off and return my pet to her cage."

I sit in pained silence, chewing my cracked lip as Mal finishes his scraggly writing, using Kai's skin as parchment, his blood as ink.

When he steps back—vivid red streams like veins trickling down the length of Kai's torso—I can read the completed word scored into him with perfect clarity.

Worthless.

WHY AM I HERE?

My eyes frisk over the mass of High Fae scattered throughout the candlelit hall. Nobles and courtiers flit by in revealing fashions, casting me scornful looks and exchanging whispered jeers at my expense. They leer at me like some sideshow curiosity—manacled, dirty, and powerless.

I am in my usual spot—chained to the cool marble floor at Kylian's feet, dressed in rags while the party guests strut around clean, proud, and haughty.

The smell of food wafts toward me on a sea breeze, and my stomach gurgles with desperation, demanding to be fed. I ignore it. I've become well acquainted with the dull ache of starvation since my stay here began. It's fine, I'll just snack on my guilt later.

Grappling for distraction, I glance toward the wall of ivy-covered archways and the backdrop of glittering starlight beyond. The hall looks magnificent at night, like a Tuscan dream, with romantic pillars expertly placed throughout to give it an old-world, classic feel. Past the balconies, the Praxian sea is a dark blanket, drenched in pale moonlight.

Soft, sensual music floats through the air as the guests mingle on the dance floor, next to naked in their paneled skirts and matching bras, the men wearing only lightweight linen pants.

I search for Kai among the sea of heads, but I don't see him. Not that I was expecting to. I just pray he's alright.

A peal of giggles draws my attention toward the dais.

Kylian is seated on the throne beside me, a harem of girls draped around him. They slither over him like snakes, and he laps up their attention like a man dying of thirst.

That's exactly what he is.

A snake charmer.

I make no attempt to contain my disgust.

"Not having a good time, love?" Kylian is too busy staring up at one of his pliant pets to look my way. "I hate it when you sulk."

A litany of hands roam over his impeccable body.

"What gives you the impression that I care?" I mumble.

"You could join us," he offers, nodding to his lap, which is already crowded with courtesans.

"I would rather gouge my eyes out than touch you."

"Oh darling, you are a terrible liar."

I snap my gaze to him. "It's amazing to me that you think I'm lying."

"Your thoughts are loud, Dragon Rider." He snickers, dragging his hand up the bare leg wrapped around his waist. "I know what you really think of me."

I scoff. "You know that I think you are the most vile, abhorrent, soulless prick I've ever met?"

"When you first saw me, you thought I was the most beautiful creature you'd ever seen." He leans forward on his gilded throne, charm dripping from his perfect face.

"I'll admit, I thought the same thing about you. Even though you were scheming the entire time, trying to use those pretty little eyes to ply me for information." He clicks his tongue, a smile coloring his voice. "It was adorable."

I freeze as he continues.

"When I slipped that collar around your neck, you told yourself the chills were from the breeze rolling through the open doors. But they weren't from that at all." His eyes close as the female straddling him works her fingers through his tousled hair.

"When we danced, and you found yourself leaning in, you told yourself it was an act. But I could taste your lie in the air, that little bit of sour edging the sweet truth of your wanting."

Shame washes over me, staining my cheeks red.

How does he know all that?

"You imagined what it would be like. You and me. You thought that I would rip your clothes off with my teeth"—he chuckles, opening his eyes to me—"but that's only the beginning of what I would do to you."

"*Stop.*" The heat in my cheeks grows unbearable. I hug my knees to my chest, turning away as much as the chain allows to hide my humiliation.

"You thought because I was a siren I was charming you. But the truth you may not want to hear is that I didn't use an ounce of power on you. I didn't have to."

"You're a liar," I toss over my shoulder.

He shakes his head earnestly. "Your thoughts were all your own. Your mind was screaming them so loud it was impossible for me not to hear."

Mortified, I stare out at the sea of bodies, biting down on my lip. There's no way he didn't plant those thoughts in my head. He's lying.

He has to be.

"I'll tell you something else," he adds in an exaggerated whisper. "You *still* want it."

"I could never want someone like you."

"There is only one other person like me. You. What shames you more—the fact that you want me, or that we deserve each other, and deep down you know it?"

I say nothing, focusing on barring him from my mind. I don't want him rummaging around in my head.

"The king is talking to you," one of the serpents snaps, preening her head to look at me. She's striking, with pale eyes and olive skin made even more brilliant by the gold body chains fitted to the groove of her waist.

"Really?" I quirk a brow, glancing back toward the crowd. "I don't see a king anywhere."

Before I can blink, she bounds forward and slaps me across the face.

In my weakened state, the stinging force sends me careening into the floor. I snap to my feet, ready to return the favor.

I don't get the chance.

The female's face freezes in a twisted expression, all color leeched from her luminous skin. That's when I notice the fist protruding from her chest.

My brain puzzles to make sense of what I'm seeing. But it isn't until the girl crumples to the floor wearing the same shocked expression, and I see Kylian standing there, blood-soaked up to his elbow with a still-beating heart in his hand, that I register what's happened.

A shrill scream grates against my ears. I realize after a moment that it's coming from me.

"Are you insane?!"

Kylian stands there, his face a mask of calm fury. He opens his fist and drops the fae's heart onto her lifeless body. Blood smears her arm before it rolls onto the ground with a dense thump.

Vomit churns in my stomach.

"Why did you do that?!" I clutch my roots, my gaze glued to the young female lying in a bloody heap at my feet.

Kylian's chest heaves as he steps over the corpse, stopping an inch from my face.

"Because she touched you," he snarls, slow and quiet, rage riding him hard. I swear I see storms brewing in those ocean eyes.

He killed her because she hit me.

She's dead. Because of *me*.

My mouth falls open as I stare up at him, stunned. Then a loud sob bursts from my chest. I clamp a hand over my mouth and turn away, sickened by the sight. The music has cut out. The room has fallen completely silent. All I can hear is the sound of Kylian's ragged breaths behind me.

I feel the ghost of a hand hovering over my shoulder, but when I turn, Kylian is stalking away, his fingers trailing blood across the pristine floor as the hushed crowd parts for him, and he disappears from the hall.

"Are you alright?"

A sweet voice snags my attention along with a gentle touch at my elbow. I recoil, finding a petite brunette with wide teal eyes in front of me, blocking the blood-soaked courtesan from my view. She's one of the serpents—dressed in a red gossamer skirt barely concealing her front and back and a bra made of solid gold.

"No," I croak. She's the first person I've met here to ask that. To speak to me directly. She drops her voice to a whisper and gives me a meaningful look.

"You will be."

Without another word, she rejoins the other females as they follow after Kylian in a neatly filed line.

6

JACE

I expected to storm into the castle and massacre every single bastard standing between me and Serena.

My expectations are shattered as we spend the next week scouting the area, Zadyn overhead, us on foot. He was right. The wards are rock solid, and walking in the front door is not an option. Not when we don't know what or how many are waiting on the other side.

If we get captured, or killed, then there's no hope for her.

Dover relays everything he knows about the castle, adding to Zadyn's sketches, which are now tacked up on the walls of the flat like a massive map.

My eyes slide to Serena's familiar, tapping his finger against the mantel in Ilayna's room. Tracking down someone who could potentially be our ticket into Kylian's keep was clever. Guess there is a brain in that pretty little head of his. I had all but given up hope there was anything but air between those ears.

I'll be honest. Zadyn is much more level-headed than I am when it comes to being patient, and for that, I find myself appreciating the male just the slightest bit. I'm all hot temper—my instinct is to fight

31

and kill, but he is cool in a crisis. Smart, sharp, and analytical. I know he has just as much to lose as I do. Probably only keeping it together for her sake.

Our heads snap up as the door to Ilayna's chamber swings open, and in slips the fine-boned female we met a few days ago.

Finally. I was just about losing my mind.

I quit my pacing as she shrugs off her cloak and—woah, that's a lot of skin. I quickly avert my gaze.

"Just give me a moment to change, and then we can talk," she tells the four of us.

She skirts behind a folded bamboo screen and emerges in a long blue robe with closures down the front. Tucking her long hair behind her ears, she sinks down onto the upholstered bench in front of the bed.

"Well?" Zadyn asks, sliding onto the settee across from her.

"I saw her."

I charge forward. "Tell us everything. Was she alright? How did she look—"

"Let her speak." Zadyn holds up a hand, eyeing the girl with enough patience for the both of us.

With a steadying breath, Ilayna begins, "She was there, in the hall—chained up beside the king."

Her voice drops off, a haunted look crossing her face.

Zadyn leans in. "Ilayna...did something happen?"

My heart starts thundering, anticipating the news I'm certain isn't good.

"One of our girls, Amira..." She swallows, struggling to articulate.

Come on, spit it out.

"Kylian and Serena were going back and forth, and she started mouthing off a bit, and Amira—she hit her."

"She *hit* Serena?" My voice jumps an octave. Ilayna looks up at me, clasping the front of her robe.

"She struck her across the face and Kylian—" She clutches her throat, shaking her head as she recalls the memory.

"What. Happened," I growl.

I swear to gods, if—

"Kylian ripped her heart out. He ripped Amira's heart from her chest and just dropped it on the floor."

"Fuck," Dover mutters. Zadyn and I exchange a concerned look.

"She was defending Kylian, but Kylian was defending your girl."

What the fuck? Why?

Zadyn masters his surprise enough to continue, "Then what happened? Did you get to speak with her?"

"I asked if she was alright." Ilayna hugs herself tightly, clearly shaken by the events of the night. "There wasn't time for anything else. It would have drawn too much attention."

"No, you did great. Thank you. Thank you, Ilayna." Zadyn reaches out and takes her hand, kissing it gratefully.

"Of course," she murmurs. "I have no love for the Trioris. If I can help your friend get away from them, I will."

"I'm sorry about your friend," Mar says softly, imparting her with a tender look. Ilayna gives her a sad smile.

"I wouldn't say she was a friend. But she was like me, like all the girls in this place." She nibbles her bottom lip. "The four of you shouldn't linger. The madame will start asking questions if she spots you here a few nights in a row." Rising from her seat, she heads toward the door. "We can meet next week."

"Do you think you'll be able to get inside the castle again?" Zadyn asks, getting to his feet.

"Kylian has a handful of favorites. I'm one of them," she says, regret lacing her soft voice. "I'll see your girl again."

Ilayna holds the door for us. I'm last out of the room, and as I cross her I can't refrain from asking, "Did she seem—did she seem alright to you? Has he—did it look like he'd hurt her at all?"

I shudder at the mere possibility. Ilayna leans against the door, looking exhausted.

"No, she was not alright. She was thin. And worn. But I only imagine that what she's enduring there goes beyond the physical. I don't think he's touched her. If tonight proved anything, it's that he values her too much to put his hands on her or to allow anyone else to do so."

I nod my head, slightly relieved. But that relief sours into nausea when she continues, "Which may not be a good thing."

She eyes me warily as I wait for an explanation.

"It means he'll stop at nothing to keep her."

7

JACE

"Where in the seven hells are you taking us?"

I glance at Zadyn through the corner of my eye. We're in Solmead, the slums of Vod, filing through the overcrowded streets. The stifling heat mingles with the smell of unbathed bodies, rotting garbage, and utter hopelessness.

"We're going to visit a lead," he says, his focus fixed ahead.

Zadyn leads us into a dirty old tavern sandwiched between a meat shop and what's likely the only tailor in this sad excuse for a village. We slide into a booth in the corner, and I swat away the horde of flies gathered around the ale and crumbs littering the table.

The funny thing is, this feels like home.

I grew up in a village not much better off. After living behind the sparkling walls of Derek's keep for so long, I almost forgot what this was like.

"Your lead is buried in the heart of the slums?" I look around incredulously.

"Who are we looking for, Zadyn?" Mar asks.

"I heard from Ilayna that an old ward mason who helped construct the wards at the castle is a frequent visitor of this…establishment. I'm hoping he'll be able to offer us some insight."

35

Dover waves over a barmaid and orders us a round.

"If Ilayna and the other courtesans are going in and out of the castle, then how are we not seeing it?" I think out loud.

Zadyn answers, "The wards only permit those already approved by Kylian. She's told us all she knows of the entrances. The illusion around the perimeter must span for miles."

"That's insane. Do you know the kind of magic you would need to generate something of that magnitude?" Dover pitches.

"There's only one person who can answer that question, and it's who we're waiting for. The good news is that Ilayna hasn't seen any Stryga buzzing around the castle."

Every time I hear that word, I'm transported to that first attack in the maze. I'm standing in a fountain, bruised and bloody, fighting to get to her in time, praying I taught her well enough to stay alive. And then that scream. That earth-shattering, heartbreaking scream when she thought I might die. The one that decimated those monsters and saved us all.

Serena's magic has always been fueled by her emotions, by anger and fear. But in that moment, it wasn't fear that fed her power. It was love.

"This tastes like actual piss." Mar's face contorts after one sip of ale, trying to clear the sour taste from her mouth. I shrug, having had worse.

"There he is."

Zadyn leans forward, bracing his elbows on the table. I follow his gaze to the male slipping through the crowd to take a seat at the bar. He might have been handsome in his youth, but now his jaw is shadowed with stubble, bags droop beneath his eyes, and his slightly overgrown head of salt and pepper hair hangs limp around his shoulders. He slumps onto a stool, his back to us. Zadyn and I lock eyes and are on our feet instantaneously.

"Let me do the talking," he mutters.

"Fine." I crack my knuckles. "I prefer to do the torturing, anyway."

He shoots me a dark look as we sidle up to the male. "Excuse me, are these seats taken?"

The seats are in fact taken. I reach forward and grab the collars of the two males seated on either side of our target and yank them backward. Their asses hit the ground with a thud.

"Looks like they're wide open."

The old male turns in his seat, glancing between Zadyn and me with a moderately horrified expression. Zadyn shoots me daggers as we slip into the empty seats.

I shrug. He has his methods. I have mine.

The old male looks uneasy, but says nothing as he sips his drink. There's a slight tremble in his hand as he lowers the pewter mug.

"You're Loryn, aren't you? The Blockade." He looks surprised for a moment as he regards Zadyn.

"No one's called me that in a long time," he rasps.

"You built the wards around Castle Illona."

"Rebuilt. But yes." He looks haunted, his eyes sunken in. "Who are you?"

"Your reputation precedes you. They say you're the best ward mason to ever live."

"It was a lifetime ago. I don't build anymore." Something dark shadows his brow as he hunches over his drink.

"Even so, I think it's the Fates' design that our paths crossed today. It just so happens, my friend and I here are in need of a ward mason. Specifically, the one who designed the wards around Illona." A crackle of threat looms behind Zadyn's warm tone and kind smile. The male —Loryn—starts to stand, but I reach out and shove him back into his seat. He has the good sense to look fearful as his eyes dart between us.

"Who are you? What do you want from me?"

"We're the kind of people you don't want to make enemies of," I answer for Zadyn.

"Relax, Loryn, we just want to ask you some questions," he says. Loryn swallows tightly, his throat bobbing as a thin layer of sweat beads on his forehead.

"Settle in. Get comfortable." I offer him a threatening smile.

"We have this friend," Zadyn begins again. "A very powerful friend, who has found herself in a precarious situation at the castle. She requires our help, but the wards—your wards—seem to keep getting in the way of that. We need to get inside."

"You—you want to get inside Castle Illona?"

"Precisely. That's where you come in."

"No, no, no. There's a reason I stopped building wards. I don't work for the Trioris anymore. I don't work for anyone—"

"Oh, Loryn." I chuckle, discreetly drawing my dagger beneath the bar. Loryn freezes, his gaze dropping to the knife now pressed against his balls. "That wasn't a request."

He looses a tight sigh, glancing over his shoulder at the unassuming crowd of wayward drunks. "We'd be better to discuss this in private."

"Here seems intimate enough." My patience is waning quickly.

"Even if I could get you in—and I'm not saying that I can—you'll never make it out alive. No one does."

I give a half-assed shrug. "They haven't met us yet."

"I understand you want to help your friend, but whoever they are, if they've been taken by the king...you'd do best to let them go."

I press the tip of my knife in deeper, and he straightens.

"I speak the truth. I learned the hard way."

"I don't care about your sob story. What I do care about is the female they're holding captive inside their keep. You are trying my temper, and you don't want to know what happens when I lose it," I growl in his face. He shrinks back, and Zadyn claps a hand on his shoulder.

"We don't want to hurt you, but we will if we have to. We need your help."

"It's always a girl, isn't it?" Loryn hangs his head, and I can see the echoes of a man who once held pride and promise. Time has not been kind to him, and from the way his shoulders slump, the deflated air surrounding him, it seems life hasn't either.

"This is no ordinary girl." I eye him sharply.

"The Trioris will kill you both. And then they'll kill me for helping you."

"Let us worry about the Trioris. You don't know us yet. But they've taken something that belongs to us. It's they who should be afraid," Zadyn says.

Loryn chews his lip for a long time. "What do you want to know?"

LORYN LEADS Zadyn and me to an apartment on the second floor of a decaying sandstone building. The space is small—an unmade bed shoved up against a dark green wall, a kitchen table with chunks of wood missing, and a rickety uneven paneled floor. We move to file through the door, but an invisible shield bars us from the threshold.

"Old habits. I never have company." Loryn's hand twitches at his side, his fingers shifting in a quick series of gestures that reminds me of signing.

The barrier falls, and we step through. The mangy dog lounging on the bed shakes itself off and dashes for Zadyn, panting and nearly pissing himself with excitement. Probably sensing his kin is near. Zadyn bends to ruffle the scruffy hair on his flea-infested head.

I roll my eyes.

Loryn moves over to a wobbly bookcase in the corner, its top shelf slanted, resting on the books below. Dust leaps out as he removes the loose shelf along with the stack of books to reveal a small hole in the wall. He dips a hand inside and then sits down at the table holding a rectangular black box. Zadyn takes a seat across from him, and I remain standing, a hand on my hilt.

"What is that?" I toss a nod at the box.

Loryn pries back the lid to reveal a small crystal wand about three inches tall with a tapered point. A powerful aura rolls off its cloudy density.

"This"—he holds it up to the sliver of light pouring in through his shuttered window—"is celmillene. One of the rarest crystals in the world."

"Never heard of it."

"Not many have. It only grows in a few locations. The ancient ward masons used to mine it, but now that they've been dissolved, the whereabouts of the caves have been lost. The only remaining stones are the ones passed down through the generations."

"What's so special about it?" Zadyn asks.

Loryn takes the fraying edge of his tunic and polishes the enigmatic rock.

"It has many uses. With its help, an average ward maker can build an impenetrable fortress. It can disable wards and illusions too, without any detectable sign." He glances at us. "Temporarily."

"This will lower the illusion around the castle?" Zadyn asks.

Loryn nods. "I'll do my best to help you, but it's been many years since I've been near that castle. I don't know what's changed in that time."

"Your best is all we ask." The dog pants at Zadyn's feet, eager for more pets.

"You'll have it. As long as I'm promised protection. I want your word that I will not be harmed. The king will know it was I who helped you."

"Of course. You have my word," Zadyn says. "We'll secure you safe passage from Vod."

"I want his word too," Loryn slides a mistrustful glance my way. I laugh, oddly flattered by his fear.

"Jace," Zadyn urges.

I purse my lips. "Sure, fine, you have it."

"Very well," he says, closing the crystal inside its padded box. He bends to scoop up the dog's empty bowl and refills it with a pitcher of water.

"So this 'friend' of yours," he starts. "Which one of you belongs to her?"

Zadyn and I lock eyes.

"Ahh." The old male straightens, suppressing a smirk. "I see. Never ends well, let me just say that."

"Maybe not for you," I snap.

His loud laugh turns into a wheezing fit. Clapping a hand over his chest, he regains his breath.

"You've got that right." He gestures around the one-room apartment. "Well, whoever she is, she must be a very special girl. To have you both risking your lives for her."

"She is." Zadyn stares at the table. "She really is."

8

SERENA

"Get up."

I blink to find Mal standing above me, holding a small lantern. I scowl up at his ethereal face, those haunting jade irises and that ivory skin. The soulless stare of a traitor.

It took me longer than I'm proud of to figure out that it was Mal who tried to kidnap me at the tavern in Iaspus. I knew that silk-lined cloak of his looked familiar—and if I had checked, I would have found three inches missing from the bottom, where it tore beneath my heel that night.

"Get out," I retort, my voice like sandpaper. It takes effort to sit up and prop myself against the cell wall.

He lowers himself to a crouch, his vacant eyes traveling over me.

"If you've come to torture me at last, then at least spare me the dramatic looks and be done with it."

I cry out as he yanks me to my feet by my hair and starts to drag me down the corridor.

"Get your hands off me, you fucking traitor."

"There has been no betrayal. My loyalty is and always has been to my queen."

"And who is her loyalty to? You don't actually think it's to you, do you? All she cares about is herself, that horrid bitch."

Crack.

My head slams into the jagged stone wall so hard my eardrum pops. I grunt as stars explode across my vision, the entire right side of my face vibrating with the impact. He leans in close, his fist tightening in my hair as I sag against the wall.

"You will mind your tongue when speaking of her majesty. Or I will have it removed."

"Kylian ripped out a girl's heart for touching me," I mumble through the wave of dizziness. "I think he likes my tongue where it is."

Snarling, he rips me from the wall and tows me from the bowels of the keep. Minutes later, he tosses me onto the floor of a damask room with walls the color of dried blood.

The door slams shut behind me as I sit up and look around at the glossy black furniture and massive silk-covered, four-post bed. A flash of gold catches my eye on the dressing table.

A crown inset with rubies.

Kylian's crown.

I'm in his fucking room.

A pit forms in my stomach. I shove to my feet—on high alert—and freeze when I see movement in the gilded mirror leaning against the dark wall.

I look haunted.

My face is a pale sheet between a curtain of dark hair—my cheeks sunken in from starvation, my eyes hollow. All that beautiful, strong muscle I spent months carving with Jace in the training ring has fallen off my bones, leaving behind a skeletal, emaciated shell. My skin is no longer luminescent. As if the blood ore has dulled me from the inside out.

My hand smooths over a bony cheek, and that's when I feel it.

The slight buzz of energy rolling off the mirror.

Its arched frame is smooth and polished, with whimsical curving lines and dips. I step closer, enthralled.

It sings to me—a song both ancient and dark.

Touch me.

Like a moth to a flame, I draw closer, my fingers reaching out to brush the clouded glass. It begins to ripple like the echoes of disrupted water—liquifying around my fingers.

"What are you?"

The door swings open, breaking my trance. I jump back as two veiled maids in dark sleeveless shifts glide toward me, silently taking hold of my arms. I struggle against them as they drag me into a bathroom of floor-to-ceiling gold, strip me naked, and throw me into the pool of fizzling water.

I break the surface gasping before they wrestle me from the tub and into a two-piece gown. The neckline of the red metal breastplate starts where my ruby choker ends, suctioning to my skin and cinching in every part of me. The skirt's sheer red panels leave little to the imagination, exposing the sides of my legs from my hips down to the strappy golden heels laced up my calves. My hair is pulled and twisted, my face prodded with tiny brushes. Every bit of exposed skin on my body is slathered with gold powder. The final touch is a golden tiara dotted with rubies.

The maids exit, never having said a word.

Kylian appears a moment later, the very definition of a siren, his tan chest and washboard abs on display in nothing but a pair of low-slung black linen pants. His hungry eyes appraise me as he saunters over to the dressing table and flings the crown on top of his head, adjusting it in the vanity mirror. His reflection smirks at me.

"That color suits you," he says, walking back toward me.

I cringe as he grabs my hand and tugs me forward. "What happened here?"

His thumb skims over the bruise Mal gave me when he bashed my head into the wall. I wince, recoiling from him. "I asked you a question."

"Your little handyman happened."

He blinks, and a muscle in his jaw flutters. "Mal?"

I nod. His eyes flare, darkening a shade. Letting out a tight sigh, he grips me by the wrist and tows me down the hall.

"Where are we going?"

"I have a surprise for you," he says, leading me to an unfamiliar part of the castle.

"I hate surprises."

He lets out a dark chuckle, and the snarl on his face subsides. "This one promises not to disappoint."

The beauty of this place still floors me each time I'm removed from my iron cage. I expected a palace of dark decay, of death and chaos and evil. I was surprised to find it couldn't be more opposite.

The alabaster palace is a seaside dream, all natural light and open archways that overlook the most incredible pink sand beaches I've ever seen. Streams of seawater run directly through the castle like a network of veins spidering out through the main floor. It smells like salt air and endless summer.

I have no idea what to expect as we tread down flight after flight of curling cream-colored steps and enter a space as large as a Roman colosseum.

"Welcome to my Underground Theatre."

The Underground Theatre is hewn entirely from pale white coral, like a waterless reef. Porous beams are erected throughout the massive space, and seats of matching make are carved into the tiers to accommodate row after row of scantily clad courtiers. I almost gasp at the size and magnificence of the chandelier. The gargantuan dome hangs like a golden sun above the audience, suspended mid-air, lit with thousands of warm white candles.

We make our way up the endless steps toward an opulent box where two thrones wait. Curious stares and hushed whispers follow us, blending with the orchestra tuning up beneath the red-curtained stage.

Ilspeth is already seated on one of the thrones, Mal hovering at her side. Kylian sits me down to his right and slides into the empty throne.

"What is this?" I demand.

"A little performance I put together in honor of my future queen."

His thumb glides over my cheek, and I hiss, bearing my fangs. He snickers, amused, as the lights inside the theatre dim, and the crowd falls silent. Then the velvet curtains draw back as the stage lights flare, illuminating a male form.

I gasp when I see Kai strung up by his arms, barely conscious. His knees sag, his weight tugging at the rope suspended from the ceiling.

The orchestra breaks into a lively fanfare as the audience in all their finery begins to hurl small gray objects of varying sizes at Kai.

Rocks.

The first one strikes his temple with a sickening thud before the stones start raining down upon him like a swarm of locusts. He takes each one, wincing and grunting. The crowd laughs as crimson streams trickle down his head and neck, staining his broken body in their wake.

"STOP!" I cry, lurching out of my seat to lean over the balcony. "Stop it! Kai!"

He thankfully loses consciousness, but as his full weight sinks and his body goes limp, his shoulders dislocate. I scream, unable to look away as his head droops. It's a pitiful sight.

I watch in helpless horror as the stones begin to leave deep gashes and dents in his head and face, and parts of him become visible that should never be visible.

I dash toward the exit and am met with a wall of guards, shoulder to shoulder. I whirl back to Kylian.

"You need to stop this now. You're going to kill him."

Kylian has the nerve to ignore me and laugh as another large stone collides with Kai's mouth, causing blood to pool out from his slack jaw.

I twist toward Ilspeth sitting there, cold and unfazed. Fully unaffected as she watches her son's brains revealed beneath that beautiful head of dark hair. Rage like I've never known courses through me, and I don't need magic for what I do next.

In one stride, I close the distance between us, lifting my heavy, ore-bound hands and bringing them across her face at a downward angle. I barely have time to appreciate her wide-eyed reaction before I'm toppling her back, throne and all. Satisfying red gashes appear on her smooth face as I unleash the feral animal inside of me.

"That is your son, you fucking monster!"

I claw at her, shredding her skin with my nails before Mal has me pinned to the ground by my neck, fangs bared. Kylian's laughter fills the box before Mal's fist connects with my face and bright light explodes across my vision. He pulls his hand back again, but the blow doesn't come. I blink up to see Kylian holding Mal by the throat, suddenly seething.

"Strange. I don't recall giving you permission to touch her face."

Kylian shifts, and then Mal is bent backward over the railing, his feet kicking for purchase. He clutches Kylian's wrist—the only thing keeping him from his waiting death below.

I struggle to make sense of what I'm seeing. Is Kylian actually defending me? Is this some kind of sick, possessive thing? Only *he's* allowed to torment me?

"Kylian." Ilspeth's icy voice is a sharp command. "Let him go."

Kylian dangles Mal a moment longer before wrenching him away from the ledge. Before he can even recover, Kylian snatches up his collar and yanks him forward to whisper something in his ear, his expression lethal. Just like it was when he ripped out that girl's heart for slapping me.

He shoves Mal aside, and without a word, bends to toss me over his shoulder. I scream my head off, shouting Kai's name all the way back to Kylian's room.

"You killed him." He shrugs me off his shoulder, and I fall to the ground in a heap. "You killed him," I repeat over and over, a broken record, unable to rid myself of the image of Kai hanging there, lifeless, brains exposed.

"Oh, spare me the dramatics. My brother will be fine. I can't say the same for Mother's face."

"I hope it scars," I seethe. That bitch had it coming.

He drops to a crouch before me, elbows resting on his knees. His hand reaches toward my face and I cringe back.

"Don't fucking touch me."

"Let me see your face," he snaps, grabbing it and turning it to the side where Mal cold-cocked me.

"Why are you so obsessed with my face?"

He shoots me a dark look before assessing my cheek. It hurts like hell already, and I can feel my eye swelling shut. Kylian cradles the side of my head, smoothing over the growing bump on my brow a few times. Warm light dances around my periphery as I watch him, my chest heaving.

"What are you doing?"

"That should feel better by the morning," he murmurs.

"Did you just *heal my face?*"

He drops his hand. "Have dinner with me."

The request disarms me as I stare up at him from the floor. "What?"

"I said, have dinner with me. Tomorrow." My expression remains embittered. "I'm not a monster."

"That fact remains to be seen."

"I could have killed my brother so many times. I haven't. I could have let Mal ruin this pretty face of yours with no effort whatsoever, but I didn't. I could take what I want from you, but I haven't."

"*Yet.* You haven't yet. That doesn't mean you won't." I steel myself, looking up at him. Those ocean eyes twinkle, flickering over my face with budding curiosity.

"Have dinner with me," he repeats, battling a smirk.

Behind him, candlelight bounces off the gilded mirror leaned up against the wall, its unearthly presence demanding my focus.

Stay with me, its lullaby entreats.

"In here, in your room?" I ask, peeling my gaze from our reflection. He nods patiently.

I want to know what that mirror is and why it trembles in my presence. It wants *me* to know. I shove to my feet.

"I'm only agreeing because I don't know the next time you'll feed me," I bite.

He chuckles before having his guard escort me back to the dungeons.

9

SERENA

Kylian has gone to great lengths to win me over.

I've never tasted food so delicious. The courses keep coming long after I am stuffed. I decline the wine, however, wanting to keep my wits about me. From my periphery, I keep tabs on that strange mirror leaned against the wall.

Is Kylian oblivious to its power? It's draw? Does it sing for him too?

"Did you enjoy your meal?"

He studies me, swirling the contents of his golden chalice. My eyes haven't left him once this whole night, which only served as amusement for him. He ate and sipped his wine, a small bemused smile tugging at his perfect lips as I watched hawk-like from the other side of the table.

This cat and mouse game must really get him off.

"I would have enjoyed it a lot more if it weren't for these." I hold up my shackled hands. "I'm starting to get sores."

"Give me what I want and I'll remove them straight away," he says in a chipper voice.

"Stop torturing your brother, and maybe I'll consider it."

49

The fire crackles from across the room as he leans back in his chair.

"It's going to take more than your mere consideration for me to do that." He smiles flirtatiously, flashing two rows of perfectly straight teeth.

Handsome bastard.

"When will you tire of this game and give in to me?"

I say nothing. He sighs, crossing one muscled arm over the other.

"You and I are inevitable, Dragon Rider. It's odd, though. I invite you to my chambers, I feed you, I offer you kindness and still you do not warm to me."

"Warm to you?" I slam my fists down on the table, causing the dishes and silverware to leap in response. "Tell me how a prisoner should warm to their jailer?!"

He rises, closing the distance between us to perch on the corner of the table. His depthless blue eyes peer into mine.

"Everything I have done—including this—has been for your own good. If you choose to believe nothing else out of my mouth, believe that."

What does that even mean?

"How in hell can you misconstrue all of this as having my best interests at heart?"

"I know you think I take pleasure in this, but you're wrong. I don't enjoy hurting you." It's astonishing how genuine his words sound. So genuine, I almost believe them. He continues in a slow, steady voice, "But I will if I must. Do not force my hand."

"Didn't anyone ever teach you that violence isn't the only method of getting what you want?" I lift my chin, staring at him with cold defiance.

"It's certainly the most efficient. Anyone with real power at their disposal who doesn't use it is just wasteful." I glare at him, itching to punch the cheeky smirk off that pouty bottom lip.

"*But,*"—he sighs, hanging his head—"as much as I hate to admit this, you may have a point. Maybe you and that bleeding heart of yours would be more responsive to other…methods of persuasion."

Kylian's fingers trail down my biceps. I rip my arm away, ignoring the delicious wave of chills that spring to life on my skin.

"Don't even think about it."

"I wasn't talking about sex. But funny how your mind goes straight to the subject," he mutters, eyes narrowing. "What would you propose?"

"A show of good faith. Maybe we can come to some sort of agreement."

"The only agreement I'm interested in is marriage."

I get to my feet. "You know, my cell sounds really appealing right now. I think I'm going to go."

He moves fast—turning and pinning me against the table as his hands reach out to bracket my waist. All the air leaves the room. His presence, his stature, his hands make me feel so small.

"Stay. Tell me what you had in mind."

I swallow hard, looking up at him. "Stop beating Kai."

"Why would I do that when I know how much it unnerves you? Each time I beat that little maggot, you come closer to caving in. I see how it wears on you. On your weak, little heart." He grips the edge of the table with locked arms and leans in dangerously close.

"It isn't a weakness to care," I manage to get out, feeling his cheek brush mine.

"The weakness lies in *having* a heart," he says, his voice softer than midnight rain. My eyelids threaten to flutter at the sound.

Why is he standing so close? And why is it getting harder to think?

"If I left him alone—" His eyes trace a brazen line down the plunging neckline of the flowing red gown he gave me for tonight, slicing into me with perfect precision. "What would I get in return?"

"I'll consider your request. Seriously."

He pulls back, giving me a doubtful look. "Oh, I'll need something more tangible than a flimsy promise."

"Then what do you want? I won't marry a sadistic king who murders females on a whim and beats his own brother to the brink of death. If you can show me there's more to you than that, then I will consider it. But the more you do this, the more you torture him, the farther away you push me."

He looks over every detail of my face as if trying to swallow me with his stare.

"I'll stop."

My eyes almost fall out of my head. I remain silent, worried that even one breath and he'll change his mind.

"In exchange for what?" I force out. I know this won't come for free.

Kylian eases back and walks over to the high-backed leather chair by the roaring fire. He sits down, his posture arrogantly sensual, leaned back, legs spread out before him.

"Dance for me."

Now my eyes really do fall out of my head. "Excuse me?"

"Dance. For me." His lips form each word slowly, decisively. "I promise to keep my hands to myself."

I dare a step closer. "I—I can't dance."

"Try."*

My stomach fills with rocks at his request. But his silken voice wraps around me, tugging me closer on an invisible string.

Nothing good can come from this. But maybe it will protect Kai. Protect my friend, who has already endured such horrible atrocities for my sake.

I can do this for him. I will do this for him.

I glance back at the table, to my untouched wine. Snatching up the chalice, I chug as Kylian looks on with an endeared smirk on his face. I drink every last drop, buying myself as much time as I can.

Wiping my mouth with the back of my hand, I turn back to him and step forward, a little unsure of myself.

He tracks my movements with a hunter's stare. The sound of my racing heart and uneven breaths thunder in my ears, tangling with the snapping fire.

---

* Cue: *Talk* by Hozier

"There's no music," I mutter, holding his intense gaze. He leans forward, power crackling around him.

"Are you stalling, Dragon Rider?"

I suck in a deep breath. "I'm not. Sit back," I command.

Slinking back into his seat, he folds his arms behind his head. I fight the urge to roll my eyes.

I stare at the floor as I start to move. Awkwardly at first, my movements lacking the intended grace and sensuality. I wonder if my inability to be seductive is a good thing. Dance too well, and it will rile him up. On the other hand, dance poorly, and I'll disappoint him.

Either way, I'm bound to lose.

"You can do better than that," he purrs.

This isn't to get him off, I realize. He has plenty of bimbos floating around the castle for that. This is to humiliate me. My anger flares, but I continue to sway my hips and run my hands through my hair.

"Better. But you're still holding back," he coaches.

I bite back my frustration, lifting my arms above my head.

"Closer."

He brings his electric eyes to the floor then back to mine. I reluctantly oblige, slipping between his knees and forcing him to stare up at me.

"Better."

The wine begins to sing inside me, dulling the sharp edge of shame and revulsion that shadows each sway of my hips. With my eyes closed, I can almost forget who it is I'm dancing for. I can almost picture I'm somewhere else, with someone else.

"I want you to dance for me like you would for your little captain."

My eyes snap open, and fury bubbles up inside me. Before I can stop myself, my hand lashes out to slap him. He catches my wrist with little effort as I seethe down at him.

"There it is." He leans forward, bringing his face close to mine and whispers, "I want to see your fire. I want to feel it."

Slipping my free hand into my belt, my fingers close around the dinner knife I stashed there while I drained my wine.

"Feel this, you fucker."

The satisfaction of seeing his eyes bulge as I drive it deep into his gut is like nothing in this world. I back away as he slowly pulls the knife out, and blood pours from the wound.

I race toward the door, but a hand shoots out and grips me by the hair. His granite arm bands around me, cradling me to his chest.

"You little hypocrite," he commends. "You preach peace and practice violence." Cheek pressed to my head, he takes a deep inhale and whispers, "My soap smells delicious on you."

I reach around and dig my fingers into the fresh wound. His laugh becomes a hiss as I dart for the door again. Shadows like swirling whips lash out to slide the locks on the door shut, sealing me in with an angry bear.

"Stay away from me," I warn, pressing myself against the door and inching toward the open balcony.

Kylian ignores my request, taking a gracious step in my direction as his corded shadows retreat and dissipate. The gash on his washboard stomach knits together, sealing itself into a tiny red scratch.

"Let's not fight, darling." He holds out his arms, suppressing a smirk as I near the fireplace. "Truce?"

Snatching the poker from its iron rack, I twirl it once before angling the pointy end his way. He snickers and gives me a patronizing golf clap.

"Well played." He bends over the chair between us, his voice confidential. "But I think your moves could use some refining."

A scream flies past my lips as he appears an inch from me with unnatural speed. I swing the poker toward his head on instinct. He grabs the pole and yanks it, ripping it from my hands as I crash into him, chest to chest, nose to nose.

"Next time"—Kylian snatches up my wrist and places my hand flush against his bare chest, over his left breast—"you go straight for the heart."

"What heart?"

I stare up at him, snarling. He stares back with searing intensity.

He doesn't release my hand. His fingers slide over mine, trapping them there.

My breathing evens out as I focus on his face.

I hate that face.

I focus on his eyes.

I hate those eyes.

I focus on his lips.

I hate those lips.

I don't know how or when it happens, but suddenly his hands are on me, tugging me closer, and I don't pull away.

Not even as they braid through my hair.

Not even as they bring me up to his waiting lips.

Not even as they taint me with sinful pleasure.

10

SERENA

Sleeping beside a monster, a killer, a true psychopath is not ideal for getting a good eight hours in.

But sleeping *with* a monster? That shit will turn you fully nocturnal.

I don't know how this happened. I don't know what I was thinking. I just…cracked. It was like a thousand cuts all at once—I was drowning in fear, in anger, in sadness, and there he was and I just *cracked*.

I don't have the words to describe it. Partly because the shame of what I did keeps hitting me over the head like a hammer, and partly because…it wasn't awful.

And that realization makes my skin crawl.

But he's promised that Kai's beatings will stop. If this is the price, then so be it.

Cuffed and collared, I lie awake beside Kylian, staring up at the dark panels stretched from bedpost to bedpost. He's traded my rags for a cool silk nightgown; the frozen, damp floor of my cell for this cloud of a mattress. But despite the new luxuries, cold guilt nags at me, refusing to let my heavy lids close.

My stomach sinks when Kylian's muscled arm tightens around my torso. He stirs, letting out a soft groan against the black pillowcase.

"Is my bed not to your liking?"

"Your bed is perfectly fine. Present company questionable."

A slow, lazy smirk spreads over his face as he cracks an eye at me. He thinks I'm kidding, flirting. I allow him to read my words as he will.

"Questionable? Tell me, how can I remedy that?" He leans over, planting a lingering kiss over the fabric at my belly button. I fight the wild tingles that shoot through me.

It's just a physical response, I remind myself, focusing on the ceiling.

"A personality transplant would be a promising start."

He gives me a genuine laugh, his thumb smoothing over the dip of my waist. "You are the most maddening little thing, you know."

This dick.

"Why is that."

"Because." His eyes gloss over me. "You're far more dangerous than I gave you credit for."

He runs a hand through his dark hair and flips onto his side.

"Why, Kylian?"

"Why, what?"

"Why do you want this so badly? And don't tell me it's because you're madly in love with me. You want to take Aegar and the rest of the kingdoms? You have an army of undead marching under your banner. What do you need me for?"

He hesitates before answering. "I have my reasons. That's all you need to know."

"What do you plan to do with me?"

His gaze burns into me, an ocean-blue fire. "I plan to make you my wife. That has not changed."

He slides out of bed, the taut muscles in his back flexing as he slips on a pair of low-slung sleep pants and turns to me, extending a hand.

"Come. There's something I want to show you."

WE REACH a long corridor in a wing that looks forgotten about—lost to time itself. I shiver at the draft in the air, staring up at the cobwebs stretched across the high ceilings.

A dark energy rolls through the closed door before us. Something powerful and ancient looms on the other side. I find myself involuntarily clutching Kylian's hand tighter.

He seems to notice, too, glancing down at our joined hands and smiling. "No need to be frightened."

"I'm not," I snap, ripping free. His chuckle echoes down the hall as he pushes the door open for me.

The room is dark and musty, filled with a series of large objects hidden beneath dusty gray sheets. One by one, Kylian undresses them, removing their covers to reveal an assortment of mirrors in various shapes and sizes. They stir from an ancient sleep, each one vying for my attention. In their faces, I can see a thousand of myself, and each time I move, the gaunt stranger in the mirrors moves with me.

The effect is slightly unnerving.

"What is this place?"

"My Hall of Mirrors."

My shoulders leap as his voice brushes my ear. He starts to strut around the room, hands in his pockets, admiring the impressive collection.

"You think a couple dusty old mirrors are enough to make me change my mind and marry you?"

"It's not the mirrors, love. It's what they can do."

My eyes meet his in the glass.

I don't like this place. It feels like a demented funhouse. I turn to face Kylian, but he isn't there. I whirl again, thinking I've caught him only to grasp the air.

"Stop that."

"Oh, lighten up, darling, I'm just having a bit of fun."

His cool breath hits my ear, and I turn, reaching out to make sure it's not just another illusion. My hand lands on his tanned chest and I exhale.

He takes my shoulders and spins me around to face a long, narrow mirror with delicate silver leaves carved into the frame. The onyx glass is nearly opaque—so dark I can barely make out our forms as Kylian guides me closer.

Like the odd mirror in his room, the one before me begins to move, to melt. I stare, transfixed as it gels and swirls like fresh tar being stirred inside a bottomless vat.

It whispers to me.

"What is this?"

"Your future." His fingers slide from my shoulders down the length of my arms. "*Our* future."

My gaze snaps to him, but his profile is fixed ahead, watching the scene forming inside the changing glass. I follow his stare and gasp at what I see.

"This is what happens when you accept your fate."

The dark glass clears to an image of me seated on a glittering throne made of cured starlight. On my head is a crown of the same make, some material not of this world—something celestial and magnificent.

My strange orchid eyes glow with delight as I glance over at Kylian, looking devastating and proud on a throne of his own, his fingers twined with mine.

The scene changes again to reveal a long stretch of pink-sanded beach. My bare feet sink into the warm grains as a light, foamy tide brushes against my ankles. I look up to see two little boys no taller than my hip teetering toward me, kicking up water as they go. Their eyes are ocean-blue, lit with joy beneath tousled raven curls.

I gasp as Kylian enters the scene smiling, carrying another small boy on his shoulder. My hand slides over my belly, where a small bump stretches my fitted white dress.

Oh my god.

I clutch my mouth in horror, but it doesn't stop the choked cry from slipping out.

"It's beautiful, isn't it? The life we could have. You're so happy."

The boys throw their arms around my legs, looking up at me with adoration. Time slows as I tentatively reach down to pet their heads and—

I can *feel* them. I tilt my lips up to Kylian's face in the mirror, and he gives me a sweet, gentle kiss.

No, this can't be right. It *can't.*

"*This* is what happens when you try to run from your fate."

The mirage of the foreign family shifts as the mirror melts, reconfiguring into something dark and horrific.

A battlefield.

The ground beneath me begins to quake. The roar of battle cries turns deafening as waves of soldiers appear from either side of the empty expanse, charging at each other with mad conviction. There are thousands—endless rows that swallow up the entirety of the green hills.

Spears and swords in hand, the soldiers meet. Death greets them one by one in the ugliest of ways.

That's when I see Jace.

His face is contorted into a feral mask of death—his harsh, beautiful mouth snarling with razored fangs. Like an animal.

He *is* destruction. He *is* chaos—soaked in blood, massacring as easily as he draws breath. Each move is smooth and beautiful, like a lethal dance. I'm so mesmerized by him that I barely notice the soldier at his back. Not until his sword appears through Jace's chest.

I wail, lurching forward as he falls to the ground, teetering on his knees, golden eyes rolling back in his head.

"Jace? No, no, no!" I struggle against Kylian, but his grip has me locked in place.

Blood bubbles from Jace's lips, his chest pumping with ragged, labored breaths. Hot tears spill over my cheeks as the vision pans to the rest of the field. I stare and stare, trying to make sense of the scene.

All around are the bodies of my friends. Kai, Mar, Dover, Igrid, Sorscha...then an animal lying still on the blood-soaked battlefield.

An *OrCat*—its brilliant white coat stained a deep red, rusted chains strung around its neck. My pulse starts to thunder.

"It isn't real," I breathe, gripping the roots of my hair. "This isn't real!"

"See for yourself." Kylian releases me with a gentle nudge forward. My fingers brush past the glass, reaching right through it as if it were air. The outside world dissolves behind me as I enter the scene and crawl toward the limp creature.

No. Please, no.

My fingers close on his soft fur as I turn him over and take in his familiar features. Those beautiful brown eyes staring out from a lifeless corpse, unblinking.

I let out an anguished cry.

It's Zadyn.

Spots dance in my vision as I literally start to see red.

I cradle the lifeless *OrCat* in my arms, my tears soaking his soft fur and dripping onto his matted blood.

"It hurts, doesn't it? Knowing that your choice dooms your friends, your loved ones. That it sets in motion a war where thousands will die in your name."

Zadyn's body disappears from my grasp. I whirl around, staring out into a red-skyed wasteland.

This is your fate if you continue to resist, something whispers inside my mind.

The earth is scorched and angry, the vegetation turned to ash, with only a few stubborn tree trunks remaining. I smell decay. The scent of death that accompanies true discord.

It will be a war to end all worlds.

A war over me…

I can feel the emptiness in the air. There is no sign of life for miles. I wander aimlessly through the illusion of the abandoned desert. I wander until I am lost.

And in my heart, I know what I am seeing. I see a future that cannot be avoided.

I see the end of the world.

I NEVER BELIEVED IN FATE.

In predestation. In a map woven from the fabric of life that could not be veered from or altered.

I never believed until I fell into this world. Until I bonded a dragon. Until I looked into the face of a king and saw my father. Until I fell in love and got my heart ripped open.

And now, to see my future played out before me like a movie on a big screen…it changes everything.

Everything.

Refusing Kylian means that I spark a war. One that destroys this world. One that kills my friends.

But if I say yes…if I agree to marry him, to be his queen…then I would be standing against Aegar. Against the people I love. Which means that they'll die anyway.

Kylian was right about one thing—I did look happy with him in the vision. With our…family.

How is that possible?

How on earth can I be happy with him? How can I find a way to love him knowing what he is—a ruthless monster. A beast waiting to destroy the people I love.

Doubt wedges itself between my racing thoughts. It could easily be a trick. Just another bargaining chip to get me to agree.

But, no. It was so *real*. I could feel Zadyn's lifeless form. I could feel the tether linking me to the cherubic faces of those little boys. Their ethereal, hauntingly beautiful faces. Everything I hoped my children would look like one day.

I may not be able to make sense of it, and though every fiber of my being revolts, I refuse to take the risk and damn my friends.

"You'll kill them all anyway," I whisper. "No matter what I choose. They die."

"Aren't we all just players in the Fates' design?" He cups my arms, staring at me through the mirror. "Who are we to resist our roles?"

A wave of chills echoes through my body.

"Promise me you won't hurt them."

"I won't go out of my way to. But if they stand in my way or it comes down to the choice between my life and theirs, I will choose mine without a second thought."

Our eyes lock in the mirror. The shadows swirling around his wrist recede as he holds up a small velvet box. Flipping it open, my eyes land on a ring with a massive ruby rock set in a halo of diamonds. It gleams like a droplet of blood from its satin bed.

"So," Kylian murmurs against my hair, a glint in his sensuous eyes. "Do we have a deal?"

I force a swallow, wondering if I'm about to make the biggest mistake of my life.

"We have a deal."

11

ZADYN

Days pass as we wait for word from Ilayna that she's been invited back to the castle. We are haggard, sleep-starved, and on edge. I watch Jace's sanity withering away with each passing second she remains out of reach.

I know how he feels. I just do a better job of hiding it.

My eyes drift out over the shimmering black ocean as I feed more sticks into the fire. We decided to set up camp here along the shoreline to be closer to the keep. Closer to *her*.

It physically hurts to be separated like this. To not hear her voice, to know she's suffering and I'm not there when every part of me is hard-wired to protect her. To keep her safe, to keep her happy. So far, I'm failing at all three.

The palms part as a cloaked figure steps out of the forest and drops her hood.

Ilayna.

The first time I saw her was in the marketplace. It was late. She was stepping out of a carriage bearing Vod's royal crest. I watched the footman help her down the steps before she disappeared into an old building. I paid off the old fae with the glass eye and followed her as if

guided by the Fates. I didn't expect to find myself inside a pleasure house.

"Why are you following me?" A honey-sweet voice called from behind me.

There she stood, eyes wide like saucers. Trusting. But I could read all the pain and suffering there, all the crushed innocence and stubborn hope in the face of bleak despair.

I could sense the goodness in her.

Before I could respond, I was thrown against a wall.

"We don't tolerate stalkers here." The guard double my size started hauling me toward the door.

"I'm not a stalker, I just need to speak with the lady. Please, it's urgent."

I was prepared to fight, but I didn't have to.

"Holdyn, stop." The guard froze as we both turned to look at her. "You may have five minutes of my time."

Five minutes was all I needed to convince her. She didn't give me her story, but she made her feelings toward the Trioris clear. They clearly harmed her in some way, but I didn't pry.

It's impossible not to feel sorry for her. Someone too kind and beautiful and delicate for such an ugly world. Someone forced to relinquish their power in order to survive. To resign themselves to being seen and used as an object for pleasure.

It sickens me. She doesn't belong in this place.

"Any word from the castle?" I ask as she drops into the sand beside me.

"The madame received a request this morning. A dozen girls in two days' time"—she pauses, nervously glancing from me to Jace—"for a wedding."

My heart rate ticks up. "A wedding," I repeat mechanically.

Jace shoots forward. "*Whose* wedding?"

"I doubt it's Mal and Ilspeth's," Dover mumbles sardonically.

"It's Kylian's wedding," Ilayna confirms.

No.

No, no, no. This cannot be happening. This is why he wanted her? Why he took her? I'm going to be sick.

"Damn it," Jace hisses.

"Oh gods." Mar lifts a hand to cover her mouth.

"There has to be some mistake. She would never agree to it." I shake my head, baffled.

"You think he's giving her a choice? He'll force her!" Jace shouts. Then he turns to Mar. "Do another scrying. We need to see what's going on."

"Now?"

"Yes, now. I need to make sure she's alright."

"She's being held against her will and forced into marriage. I doubt she's alright, Jace," Dover grumbles.

This has to be a misunderstanding.

But no matter how desperately I want to deny it, in my heart I know it's true. It makes perfect sense.

He wants to bind them together using the Bloodfast—the ritual performed by royals and High Fae with powerful bloodlines to keep their lineage strong. If he marries Serena and they complete the rite, he will not only bind them together, but he'll come into his full generational power. *And* gain a dragon in the process.

He'll be unstoppable.

Mar turns ghost white as Jace rears his head in the direction of the sea. "Look. All the water you could possibly need."

A moment later, Mar is kneeling in the shallow tide with us huddled close behind. She dunks her hands into the cool water, and the sea surrounding us begins to bubble and glow. Mist swirls around the surface, then clears to an image of Kai on a stage, arms suspended from a rope, rocks flying at him until he goes limp and passes out. I can barely watch the grotesque display, cringing as a large rock bashes in part of his skull.

"Oh, Kai." Mar gasps, clasping her mouth.

The image pans to a box high up in an odd-looking theatre. My breath catches at the sight of Serena dressed in crimson, wearing blood ore chains and that damned ruby collar. She leans over the balcony, wailing Kai's name. Then she whirls and lunges for Ilspeth, mauling her with the ferocity of a lioness. My stomach curls as Mal steps in.

No.

His punch hits me in the gut, coiling around the white-hot rage burning there. I throw myself forward into the water, snarling.

The image shifts again to a candlelit bedroom. I watch, sick to my stomach as Serena swings an iron poker at Kylian. He uses it to yank her into his chest. His hands slide into her hair, his face hovering near hers as he whispers something I can't hear, and the fury I feel could decimate an entire city.

The image fades as the water returns to its misty, opaque surface.

"No! I need to see more! If he hurts her—" Jace growls.

"That's all I can see right now," Mar murmurs apologetically. He turns on me with daggers for eyes.

"I told you. I told you that he would force her."

"He won't force her if he wants the Bloodfast, which I'm guessing he does. It has to be consensual. He's a power-hungry fuck, but he can't force her into it," I remind him. That is the only sliver of hope I can cling to.

"No, but he can extort her. You saw what he was doing to Kai. You think she's just going to sit by and allow it to continue? No, either he'll force her or she'll be a martyr."

He's right about that. Kylian is using Kai to wear her down. And from the look on her face in those tableaus, I know it's only a matter of time before he succeeds.

Serena's heart is so big. Leave it to Kylian to exploit that.

"Gods damn it!" Jace spits, pacing through the night-cooled sand. "We need to get in there. Now."

I try to remain levelheaded when every fiber of my being wants to put my fist through a wall. To storm in there and massacre everyone on sight. I'm just as enraged as Jace right now. And it is because I feel completely powerless.

I turn to Loryn, who's been watching us—silent and wary. "Loryn. Is two days enough time for you?"

He nods, his gray brows furrowing. "It's enough time."

"So we have a plan." I eye each of them intently.

"Fuck the plan, she needs us now!" Jace snaps, stalking up to me.

"*Careful*, Jace."

In a flash of speed, he has me gripped around the collar. "I don't fucking care if I have to do this alone. I'm going in, and I will kill anyone who tries to stop me."

He bolts toward the forest, but I'm just as quick, latching onto his jacket and slamming him into the nearest tree. His punch hits me in the jaw, but it's not enough for me to let go. He thrashes, fangs flashing, golden eyes empty except for the compulsive need to rip something apart. And right now that something is me.

"Jace, stop!" Mar shouts.

Dover rushes to help restrain him, and Jace breaks loose, nearly biting off his hand.

"I know you love her," I pant, holding up my hands. His crazed eyes slide back to mine. "I get it. Believe me, I do. But if you do this, you will set off every alarm in that castle, and we will be taken. We won't be able to help her if we're in chains. Be smart about this. We will get her out."

"In what state?" Jace seems to slowly inch back to reason, the murderous glint in his eyes subsiding as his shoulders sag. "We are failing her. She is *ours*, and we are failing her. I'm failing her."

He sinks to his knees in the sand, and I've never seen a male so broken. I never claimed to like him, never felt he was worth the breath or tears Serena wasted on him. But seeing him in this state—shaking with desperation—I feel sorry for him.

I know how he feels because it's everything I feel. Everything I am fighting to keep down because I know what's at stake. His head dips, his fingers curling in the sand. I lower myself beside him and brace a hand on his shoulder.

"This is not over. We have a plan. It is not over until she is safe and home. With us. She isn't helpless. She knows how to survive. We will get her back, and they will pay for every hair out of place on her head."

12

ZADYN

Tomorrow.

Tomorrow is the day I see her again. The day I hold her in my arms and can breathe knowing she is safe.

These weeks without her have been the worst torture of my life. It's a feeling no one could understand unless they've experienced it firsthand. It's like trying to live without your heart.

Cool water curls around my ankles as I stare out at the onyx waves. Jace paces halfway down the beach, glaring out into the ocean, no doubt envisioning all the ways he plans on tormenting Kylian for what he's done. He's not exactly what I'd call a friend, but I'll be there right alongside him, waiting for my turn.

Mar sits cross-legged before the dying fire, tracing patterns in the sand while Dover's sleeping head lolls in her lap.

I take a seat beside her. "How long did Serena know? About you?"

"The night she got back from bonding the dragon. She told me everything. She trusted me, so I returned the favor."

"She's lucky to have a friend like you. You coming out here, using your power again even though it could put you at risk...I know how much it will mean to her. And you should know it means a great deal to me, as well." I pause. "My mother was a Blueblood."

Mar looks up at me, surprised.

"She refused asylum to stay with my father."

"I didn't know," she murmurs, studying me for a moment. "I've missed my magic." Her admission sounds almost guilty. "I worried that leaving it untouched for so long, that power would dwindle away to nothing, but it's the opposite. There is no greater honor than to use it to help save a friend."

A sad smile tugs at her lips.

"Why did you leave your clan?"

"I was tired of hiding." She looks away, using the beat to shift topics. "When we get her back, are you going to tell her, or are you going to wait until the next time she's stolen and made prisoner to speak up?"

I shift my gaze back to her. "Tell her what?"

She tips her head, her keen eyes narrowed as the breeze rustles her auburn hair. "That you're in love with her, obviously."

The statement sends a jolt through me. There's no use in denying it— Mar is too smart for her own good. She'd call bullshit in a second.

"I'm her familiar."

"Zadyn, come *on*."

Dover shifts in his sleep. I lower my voice and say, "She's in love with Jace."

"She thinks she is."

It's clear from her tone that she isn't a fan of that particular relationship.

"Right now my sole focus is getting her back. The rest we can figure out in time."

"We will get her back. And believe me when I say she's going to open her eyes eventually. So you'd better be ready."

"Aren't you the nosy one." I crack a small smile, and she shakes her head, returning it with one of her own.

The truth is, I don't know if there is anything to figure out. For as long as Serena has known me, she really hasn't known *me*. She's known the faces I wore, the disguises I took on in her old life. Sometimes I forget that I'm as new to her as this entire world is. Even though I've known her forever, even though I have always seen her, I don't know if she sees me. Even now.

How can you love someone that's invisible?

We fall silent, lost in our own thoughts. Playing out every possible outcome of our rescue mission until a sliver of sunlight peeks over the horizon.

It may be the last one we ever see.

Tomorrow is almost here.

We will get her back. Or we will die trying.

13

ZADYN

"This will keep us linked," Mar explains, taking a dagger and slicing a clean line across her palm. She squeezes a few cobalt drops into one of the six interlocking circles she's drawn in the sand.

"We'll be able to communicate at all times as long as the connection remains intact. I will serve as the anchor."

She passes me the dagger. I barely feel the slice as my blood fills in the circle at my feet. We go down the line until five red circles and one blue enclose the star etched in the center.

Mar's eyes close, and our blood begins to bubble with life. Almost instantly, I feel a channel open up in my mind.

Can you hear me? Her voice is clear and bright in my head.

Yes, we echo as one.

I can hear all of them.

Loryn carefully uncovers the celmilline and turns to Ilayna. She shivers in the early morning breeze, holding herself.

"Keep it on you at all times," he says. "Once you're inside, you take hold of this and imagine the wards easing down. Understand? The rest I will take care of."

She nods dutifully, taking it from him. "I understand. I have to get back. The carriage is picking us up at noon."

"Go. Be safe," I tell her before she disappears through the tall, wild palms.

"How will we know the wards are down?" Jace asks Loryn, adding another dagger to the collection strapped around his hip.

"I'll be able to tell. On my signal, you go."

"Loryn, thank you." I pull the pouch of gold coins from my pocket and press it into his palm. There's enough there to pay for the celmilline and a fresh start.

"I am forever in your debt. Once the wards are down, take that boat, and don't stop until you hit Tir. Gods be with you."

"Good luck." He takes the pouch and casts a wistful look down the beach at the tiny rowboat and supplies we secured for him.

"We ready?" I ask, turning back to the group.

Dover leans down to kiss Mar. Her gray eyes peer up into his, pregnant with emotion. "Come back to me. In one piece, please."

"I always will." He gives her a reassuring smile as he backs away.

And with that, Dover, Jace, and I start toward the castle. Armed to the teeth and ready for the bloody battle that awaits us.

WE WAIT in the brush lining the pebbled drive, listening for the sound of horses. Finally, the rattle of squeaking wheels interrupts the unbearable quiet, and the carriage carrying twelve courtesans, including Ilayna drives by.

Wards are down, Loryn says.

Showtime, boys, Dover replies.

We lurch forward as one, dashing for the carriage before it disappears through the glittering gates now visible to us for the first time. Jace latches onto the back and pulls himself upward, extending his hand for Dover while I shift into a falcon.

We're in, I confirm for Mar and Loryn as the gates close behind us.

Let the fun begin. *

THE WEDDING GUESTS have already arrived. Empty carriages line the perimeter of the massive courtyard, filling in the gaps between fluted pillars.

I expected lines of military poised and ready for intruders. I half expected hordes of Stryga standing guard. I'm shocked to find only a few armored troops posted outside the towering doors.

It's bold, I'll give them that. Either they're negligent, or it means they don't need to be cautious and they know it. Something tells me it's the latter.

I shift, my features rearranging themselves and taking on a new appearance as Dover and Jace leap off the carriage. The females stir within, their concerned voices rising. I reach for the door and swing it open, but it isn't me they see before them. Their eyes go wide as they take in the blue-green irises and unkempt jet-black hair.

"Prince Kai," a few of them whisper, flashing me flirtatious smiles.

"Now, ladies"—I muster up one of Kai's mischievous grins—"no matter what you hear, I want you to remain calm. Trust me when I tell you everything is alright. Can you do that for me? Pretty, pretty please?"

I'm answered with eleven enamored sighs. Ilayna gives me a curt nod.

Laying it on a bit thick, are we? Dover teases.

Better safe than sorry. On my count, I say as the driver and footman dismount, and two guards approach the carriage to escort the girls inside.

One. Two.

Dover and Jace pounce, leaping from behind the carriage like wildcats, attacking the approaching men.

Three, I guess.

---

* Cue: *Trouble* by Pink

Jace takes down the two guards within a fraction of a second, slamming their helmets together with a sickening crack. The coachmen flee the way they came, tearing out onto the path leading up the long drive. That's when I notice the two stable boys trying to sneak away.

"You there."

They freeze, horrified as *Prince Kai* paces up to them. "I want you to park the carriage close by. Then I want you to go to the stables, tie each other up, and gag yourselves so that you can't speak. Wait there until I command you to come out. Understand?"

They nod and start toward the carriage as Dover helps the last of the females down the steps.

"Kinky." He chuckles. We turn to see Jace undressing one of the unconscious guards. "And kinki*er*."

Jace shoots him a dirty look as he slips on the polished golden breastplate and helmet. "Help me get rid of Tweedledee and Tweedledum."

I grab one of the guards, and he takes the other, stuffing them into the empty carriage before the stable boys lead the horses away.

How are we looking? Mar asks.

So far, so good.

Don't jinx it, Jace mutters.

With another flash of light, I shift again—same color eyes and raven hair, trimmed a little neater on the sides. Standing a few inches taller, I shove through the doors in a hunting outfit only Kylian would wear. I strip off the leather gloves and step inside with the ridiculous swagger of a king, announcing my arrival.

Ilayna leads the pack of courtesans away, but before they can veer off in the opposite direction, I take hold of her arm.

"Ilayna, you should go. Now. I don't want you swept up in what's about to happen here. Take one of the horses and ride to safety."

"Zadyn, I—"

Please.

But the girls—

*Will not be harmed. They knew nothing about this. If you get caught...
just go. Please.*

She takes one more look at the courtesans and nods, slipping the
celmilline into my hand and squeezing tight. "Gods be with you."

Servants cower and bow as I stride through the halls as Kylian, my
heels echoing off the marble expanse. No one asks questions. Who
would dare challenge a sadistic king who publicly beats his own
brother for sport?

Let's split off, I say to Jace and Dover. *I'll check Kylian's rooms, you
take the east wing.* Jace nods, his face concealed beneath the golden
helmet.

"Sire."

I freeze at the sound of that voice.

Jace tenses beside me. Before Dover can turn, Jace grips the back
of his neck and shoves him forward, guiding him away. I pray Mal
didn't get close enough to recognize him.

Keep it together, I warn Jace. I can feel his blood boiling like a riot in
my head.

Watch him, is all he says as their footsteps disappear around the
corner.

I turn to face Mal's harsh green-eyed gaze. "What is it, Mal? I've
matters to tend to."

"I didn't expect you to be out hunting this morning."

I continue walking, not giving him the time of day. "A male can't
let off some steam the morning of his wedding?"

"Apologies, my King. I was not informed," Mal says, his voice calm
and removed as he trails me up the stairs.

I've committed the layout of this place to memory from the
renderings Dover helped me map out. I stop before Kylian's door,
praying to find Serena alone behind it.

"If you must bore someone to death with your prattling, save it for
my mother. I'm not interested. Now if you'll excuse me, I've a
wedding to tend to."

"Sire." I pause, my hand on the door handle. "That's a linen closet."

Fuck.

His eyes narrow suspiciously. I get in his face, doubling down.

"I know that, you imbecile. I intend to *bathe* before my wedding, and I do not have time to wait for these useless servants to fetch me fresh towels. Now go make yourself useful before I lose my patience."

Mal looks unconvinced, his stone face unreadable. But then he steps back, etching a deep bow before retreating down the steps.

I wait until his fiery hair disappears before continuing down the hall.

A linen closet? Nice. Really believable, Dover chuckles.

Shut up.

You're two doors off.

I approach the correct door. Hopefully. Pressing my ear against the wood, I wait to pick up any sounds within. Then I burst inside, scanning the empty room for any sign of her. I try every door in the wing.

Nothing.

Zadyn. What in the seven hells is going on? Jace snaps.

She's not here.

I dart back down the stairs to the main hall. But before I can reach the bottom, Mal appears in front of me.

"Hello, my King."

His wicked eyes gleam, and before I can react, a bolt of lightning shoots out to strike me in the chest.

Zadyn? What's happening?

I groan as my back and head connect with the unforgiving stairs. Mal's footsteps stop beside my ear as he grips my collar and yanks me an inch off the steps.

"What do we have here? A crasher? Mind showing me your invite?"

"Sure. Here it is."

Gripping his wrists for leverage, I pitch forward, head-butting him until he tumbles back.

Jace and Dover appear at the bottom of the steps as Mal rights himself. A silver stream of light bursts from his palm, but Jace ducks, tackling him back into the wall.

"Fucking traitor!"

Jace grabs him by the collar and tosses him down the stairs before hauling me to my feet. The three of us race back up the steps and down the hall as the faint sound of music drifts toward us.

It's starting.

We exchange a worried glance.

"Dover, where are we going?" Jace's voice is edged with panic as we careen around a corner.

"The back stairs will lead us to the chapel."

"Wait." Jace skids to a stop, his eyes catching on the exposed corridor across the way.

Through the window, I see a figure in white drifting down the hall in the wing across from us. She moves like a specter—there, but not fully present. Unreachable and unobtainable.

Time slows as she floats forward like an ivory queen in a shimmering silk dress, escorted by two golden guards. My heart hammers. She's concealed beneath the veil, and I pray she turns—pray she can somehow feel me. I need to see her face.

I need...I need *her.*

But she doesn't turn. I watch helplessly as the girl I love disappears down the hall to attend her own wedding.

Come on! Dover shoves us forward, breaking our trance.

We hurry down the steps, the chapel doors coming into view across the way. But as we reach the bottom, a line of golden soldiers is waiting to greet us. I manage to break through, twisting back to see Jace and Dover caught in the madness. I freeze, my hand on the door.

"Go!" Jace shouts. "Go now!"

A twinge of guilt tugs at me as they hold the line. But I can feel her on the other side of this door. I feel her in my blood, in my bones, calling to me. So I don't waste another second before turning and throwing open the chapel's heavy doors.

14

SERENA

Something old.
Something new.
Something borrowed.
And something blue.

I've pictured my wedding a thousand times. Dogeared countless magazines, filled Pinterest boards with white gowns and floral arrangements. I've fantasized about the exact lilac shade of bridesmaid dresses I would choose. I imagined smiling as my dad walked me down the aisle, getting choked up as he gave me away.

I imagined this day being the happiest of my life.

Instead, it is a nightmare come true.

Forced to marry a man I loathe with every fiber of my being on the off-chance that I can find a way to keep my friends safe from his relentless, destructive ambition.

I stand facing the mirror in a large, empty bedroom. Inside the glass, I see a version of myself that is a stranger. A hollow husk of a woman hidden beneath a silk train fifty feet long, blue flowers woven into her hair, and a line of rubies around her neck like a blood-drenched noose.

Who are you?

79

The door swings open, and Kylian enters without so much as a knock. I track him in the mirror, looking devastating—his hair swept back off his face, sea-blue eyes twinkling. For a moment, I'm struck speechless.

He pauses, letting his eyes trail over me. "You look—"

Then, as if remembering himself, he clears his throat and continues toward me.

"I know it's bad luck to see the bride before the ceremony, but," he starts, slipping a hand into his pocket, "I have a gift for you."

I turn as he pulls out a small black box. His fingers tug at the ribbon, discarding it on the floor without shifting his gaze from me.

Inside is a small gold locket—pretty, if not a bit plain. But when he flips it open, out bursts a blinding little light. I squint as it dances around the room like a firefly, so fast I can barely keep track of it.

"What is that?"

"It's a star fragment. It's been in my family for generations."

Kylian turns my palm up to the ceiling, and the sliver of starlight darts into my waiting hand, bouncing with frenetic energy.

"Keep it on you at all times and you will never be lost. It will always guide you home."

My mouth parts as I glance up at him. I want to be suspicious. I want to throw the star in his face and run. But I just stare.

He lifts the locket, snapping it closed as the tiny star dances back inside. Then he leans in and plants a lingering kiss on my cheek. Warmth spreads down my neck.

"I'll see you at the altar."*

I stare after him, stunned, before dragging my eyes back to the locket.

So he gave me a heartfelt gift. It changes nothing. He is still a monster and that will never change.

But for reasons I can't explain, I slip it around my neck, tucking the pendant into the scooping neckline of my dress. I study myself in

---

* Cue: *Black Beauty* by Lana Del Rey

the mirror one last time, already hating myself for what I'm about to do.

They will hate me too. Zadyn and Jace. They won't understand why I had to do it. To them, I will be a traitor.

But I stand at the center of this knot. And I'm the only one who can untangle it. My hands are stained with blood that hasn't yet been spilled.

But it will be if I refuse Kylian.

If this sacrifice makes me a traitor, then so be it. I'll be the bad guy. As long as it keeps them safe.

Something old.

Something new.

Something borrowed.

And something blue.

The blood ore around my wrists is old as time itself.

The ivory dress is new.

My love was borrowed.

And inside I am blue.

The blue of ice, the blue of death. The blue of a bloodless body rotting beneath the earth.

When the guards appear at my door and usher me from the room, I don't resist. Each step I take feels heavy and thick, like trudging through quicksand. Like a funeral dirge.

The sunlight pouring in through the open archways feels too bright. The rusted bands around my wrists are too heavy, even without the chain linking them together. The silk against my skin is too tight, too constricting.

But none of it fazes me. My emotions have been sanded down to apathy.

I don't care what happens to me. I only care about protecting the people I love for as long as I can.

I can't let Kylian get to them. I can't let him torture Kai until his body gives out for good. And I can't let him grow more powerful by marrying me.

That's what I remind myself as the towering doors of the chapel yawn open to an ivory fever dream. It looks like the happy ending to a fairytale. Something triumphant and glorious, meant to be ever-lasting.

Only the white roses smell sour. The pristine silk carpet awaits my first steps like the tongue of some beast waiting to swallow me whole. It stretches past the endless rows of fae, past the floating orbs filled with tiny candles, past the overhead loft where a choir of angel voices echoes through the rafters. Leading all the way up to the stunning male at the altar, in a sparkling golden crown and epaulet of ruby-studded suns.

I don't hear the music as I'm nudged forward, carrying a massive bouquet to hide the heavy blood ore cuffs still encircling my wrists. No one walks beside me as I make my way toward Kylian. He beams, bright as the sun itself. Bright as the light filtering in through the stained-glass dome stretched high above the altar, casting the room in brilliant rainbows.

I wish he were different. I wish I could love him. I wish he were a better male.

But things are not different. And neither is he.

Numbly, I drift past row after row of wedding guests, whom I've never even seen before today. I don't even feel the blinding need to claw Ilspeth's perfect face again as she oversees the ceremony contemptuously from her gilded throne.

Kai stands beside her, a golden guard looming at his back. The shadows beneath his eyes are a deep purple as he stares at me, horrified.

There is nothing he can do. There is nothing any of them can do. It's up to me.

I'm sorry, I murmur to him in my mind. *I'm sorry, all of you. Zadyn. Jace. What I wouldn't give to say goodbye to you both.*

To tell you that I love you.

Kylian extends a sun-kissed hand to guide me up the two remaining steps to the dais where his High Priest waits. Behind him, the cathedral ends in a delicate sheet of glass. Just a thin, transparent wisp standing between the wedding and the cliff-lined sea. Between confinement and freedom.

So close and yet so, *so* fucking far.

Kylian lifts my veil, tucking it behind my head and allowing me to see the space with more clarity.

Such a waste, I think, taking in the wild splendor of the room. What a gloriously beautiful wedding, wasted on the two of us. Wasted on what will never be.

The High Priest recites a prayer in Ancient Fae as he hands Kylian an ornate dagger. Dragging it across his palm, he squeezes a few drops into the depths of a golden chalice. Then it's my turn.

With steady hands, I accept the dagger, sunlight glinting off the silver blade.

Two futures stretch before me in this moment: the choice to finish what I started today on this altar and the choice to thrash against my chains.

Against fate.

But what if there were a third option? One carved from love and selflessness and sacrifice. One that guarantees to alter the fixed destinies that await my decision. One so great it would be impossible not to have a rippling domino effect on the future.

I don't accept my fate.

Instead, I tell fate to go fuck itself as I plunge the dagger into my waiting heart.

15

ZADYN

There she is.

The sight of her steals my breath and fills me with something far more potent.

Maybe it's relief, maybe it's hope. But no words could describe what I feel as my vision narrows to her and her alone.

I decide two things in this moment.

One: I want that. One day when we've rid this world of our enemies and set everything right, I want her walking down an aisle to *me*.

And two: If I have to wait for it, I will. But I want her to choose me.

To choose us. Forever.

I'm halfway down the aisle, my mouth forming her name when Serena lifts the dagger into the air and drives it through her chest.

My entire *world* stops spinning to shatter into a million pieces.

"NO!"

Crippling pain slams into me, taking me to my knees.

Kylian staggers back, clutching his chest as if she'd struck him instead. Someone is shouting her name from somewhere in the room, but I can't tear my eyes away.

84

Can't make sense of what I'm seeing.

If I ever doubted hell was real, this just proved me so sickeningly wrong.

Chaos erupts around me. Kylian lunges forward as Serena collapses, catching her head and easing her down. I grip the edge of the nearest pew, dragging myself upright. I try to run, but all I can do is stumble forward through debilitating pain, each step like trudging through a nightmare.

I'm too slow. I need to get to her.

Damn it, why can't I move!

"You stupid, stupid witch," Kylian says, smoothing back her hair. He rips the dagger free, sending it clattering to the marble floor. Black blood spreads like spilled ink over her ivory gown.

A fist tightens around my heart, unrelenting and brutal as I make it to the altar.

Serena is dying.

I've never known such pain as I do now. Such horror as our bond is stretched to its limit, her soul threatening to exit this world and leave me behind. The pain of that stretch, the fear of it snapping and splintering for good, makes it impossible to breathe.

With all of my strength, I knock Kylian backward and pull her into my lap. She sucks in slow, labored breaths.

"No, no, no. Don't do this to me. Don't you dare leave me."

My hands cradle her face, leaving ebony streaks over her porcelain cheek. She's so fucking pale. Her glazed eyes link with mine for a brief second.

"She's dying," Kylian rasps, dragging himself back to her side.

It's fear I see on his face—genuine fear. He reaches out a trembling hand, and I snarl, shoving it away as I bare my fangs.

"Don't you fucking touch her."

"Let me heal her. I can heal her." His wide blue eyes plead with me.

More shouts from behind. More blood spilling out of her, soaking my clothes, my hands. I glance up at Kylian and nod numbly. Light flows from his palms as he presses them to the gaping wound on Serena's chest. But her eyes still, and I can feel the last of her life slipping through my fingers like sand in an hourglass.

"It's not working," Kylian growls, staring at his hands in disbelief. "Why isn't it working? Damn it!"

I add to the effort, using what little magic I have left and funneling it into fixing her ruined heart.

"What happened."

Jace is suddenly on the ground beside me, his face drained of color.

"She stabbed herself."

"No," he whispers. "*No.*"

"Help me." I shoot him a desperate look. He nods, bringing her hands up to his lips.

"Come on." I give her a light shake, pounding on the sealed partition separating me from her mind. "Come *on.*"

What did you do, Serena? What did you do?

I thrash against it over and over, but it's useless. She's severed the line between us and left me here alone. In a world that holds no meaning, no light without her smile, without her warmth.

"Please," Jace groans, burying himself in Serena's lap.

My stomach churns as the pain subsides, releasing its grip on me. Leaving only ice in its wake.

The absence of that pain can mean only one thing. I slowly regain the ability to breathe, and I know that nothing—*nothing*—can stop me from ripping out Kylian's throat with my bare teeth.

Serena goes absolutely still.

Jace's wails rebound off the chapel walls.

I drag my gaze up to Kylian.

Then I leap forward, sinking my teeth into his throat.

16

JACE

I have been stabbed before. Many times in many places. But this…this is a different kind of pain, concocted of my own worst fears—my own worst nightmares.

This is a shot of venom to the heart.

Something pierces my chest. A sharp, paralyzing pain. My knees slam into the hard marble tile.

What's happening to me?

There's this sickening feeling coming from Zadyn. His thoughts are racing so fast I can't even comprehend them.

"Jace!" Dover drives his foot into the chest of a golden soldier.

Get up, I tell myself. *Get up, or you're dead.*

"Come on!" Dover wrenches me upright, and I'm ashamed at my inability to lift a sword. We back up until we fall through the chapel doors, sealing ourselves in.

And that's when I see her.

Serena.

My little witch, lying in a heap in Zadyn's lap, Kylian's hands pressed to her chest. I struggle to make sense of the tableau.

Her white gown is stained tar-black, blood seeping from the

87

gaping wound on her chest. A few feet away lies a dagger slick with that same blood.

The room starts to spin.

I'm vaguely aware that I'm moving—no, *dragging* myself—closer. But it all feels like a blur. A nightmare and not reality. This can't be happening.

We can't be too late.

Flashes of gold rush at me from all sides. My gift pushes out, wrapping invisible tethers around the necks of each assailant as they fall to the ground choking. More come at me from every angle, and I feel my magic falter and escape me altogether.

I cut through them despite the agony slowing my steps, my sword hacking through the crowd like a field of thorns. I can feel the slices of their blades, I can feel the blood trickling down my skin, but I keep going.

Keep pushing.

The floor rises up to meet me, and I crawl the rest of the way to her side.

"What happened?" I choke.

"She stabbed herself."

What? Why?

"No," I breathe. "No."

"Help me." Zadyn's composure has snapped, and before me is a male just as desperate and terrified as I am. Even Kylian is distraught —pouring over her with panic in his eyes.

I clasp her hands, hurling out my efforts to heal her—to stop death in its tracks.

"Come on," Zadyn curses under his breath. More guards rush toward us, but Kylian stops them with a warning look.

"Please. *Please.*"

Don't let her die, I beg, crushing her fingers to my lips.

In my head, I make all kinds of promises. Thoughtless vows, empty trades to gods who aren't listening—who don't care.

Fool's bargains, I know. But it doesn't stop me.

Tears roll down my face and onto her dress, soaking through the silk of her gown as I bury my head in her lap.

Come back. Please come back. This cannot be our ending. I cannot lose you. This cannot be over.

Her eyelids flutter a few times before she goes still.

Still as death.

Something in me snaps. My heart rips open as my anguished, choked scream fills the expansive chapel. The pain reaches a crescendo, swirling with the torment of her loss.

I barely even notice as Zadyn lets out a battle cry and tackles Kylian backward, latching onto his neck. They go flying back into the altar, taking out the long table and golden candelabras in their wake. Fire catches, eating its way across the dais.

I have no idea why Serena stabbing herself is affecting Kylian this way, this heartless, cold monster. But I couldn't care less if the two of them kill each other. I don't plan to stick around much longer if she's not here.

I can't live without her. I can't breathe without her.

I will find you, I vow.

My fingers trace over her face one last time before I reach for the dagger.

The chapel doors fly off the hinges and the Stryga burst into the room with Mal at the helm. The wedding guests cry out and scatter like ants. Then I feel something that can only be described as the greatest relief of my entire life.

Her finger squeezes mine.

Faintly, so faintly. But undeniably.

I let out a strangled laugh.

"Jace!" I turn to see Dover and Kai holding open a door off to the side of the dais.

"This way!" Kai shouts over the chaos. I scoop Serena up into my arms and race toward them. Dover pauses in the doorway, glancing back toward Zadyn.

"We can't leave him."

"He's already dead," I spit.

That's when Serena stirs in my arms. She coughs up some black blood, her eyes still closed. I stagger back, my heart leaping in response. At the sound of her choking, Zadyn whirls, stunned.

In that split second, Kylian's guards are on him, Mal in the lead. I shove Serena into Dover's arms and, with a growl, lunge straight for him.

Sparks fly as our swords meet, colliding in a lethal kiss. I drive my foot into his chest, sending him back into the wall. Marble crumbles beneath the force. Whirling to Zadyn, I shout, "Time to go."

"Not before I kill him." He steps toward a still-recovering Kylian, but my fist wraps around his arm.

"Let go of me."

"She's alive. And if you die, she'll hold me responsible."

Recognition registers in his eyes as he inches back to sanity. We sprint toward our friends, spilling through the door as Kai slams it behind us, shutting out a wave of bloodthirsty beasts.

"We need to get to Mar. She's posted up on the shore," I tell Kai.

"Going out the way we came in is out of the question," Dover says.

"I have a better way out." Kai hastily leads us down a dark corridor through a hidden door in the wall.

My eyes are fixed solely on Serena, stirring lightly in Dover's arms.

We make it to a decrepit part of the castle, and Kai ushers us inside a room filled with antique mirrors. I can sense dark, seductive magic rolling off of them. Kai moves around at a brisk pace, feeling the glass surface of each one as I shrug out of the remnants of golden armor. I stand ready by the door, sword in hand, listening for attackers.

"Which one is it?" Kai mutters to himself.

"What is this?" I ask, though deep in my bones, I fear I already know.

"Our ticket out of here alive."

"They're magic mirrors," Zadyn pants as Serena goes into another coughing fit.

Both of us wheel toward the sound.

"Put her down," he commands Dover, who gently lays her on the drafty floor. Zadyn rips the ridiculous veil from her head and smooths back her hair. I take slight comfort in the gentle rise and fall of her chest.

Alive, I tell myself. *She's alive.*

Serena's eyes fly open and she shoots up, gasping for air.

17

SERENA

This is nice—death.

So quiet. So peaceful.

There is no pain here in this kingdom of nothingness. There is no suffering. There is just—nothing.

Sweet, blissful nothing.

I am weightless, floating through a timeless, matter-less void with no evil kings, no disastrous fates, no ultimatums. All that I was so desperate to hold on to—all those names and faces I remember wishing I could take with me into the next life—they're getting quieter. I try to fight it, try to cling to them, but their edges are fraying.

I know I should be concerned, but I'm not. I'm just here. Wherever that is. Or wherever it's not.

Something ancient yawns in the distance, glittering with promise. It beckons me with a voice so smooth and inviting, it's hard to resist. I don't know what awaits me there, but I'm eager to find out. A sense of calm washes over me as I strain toward it.

But that peace is quickly disrupted. I try to fight it. I try and I fail.

Something yanks me backward on an invisible string, and I begin to fall.

92

Back to my body. Back to panic. Back to fear. Back to chaos.

Back to the overwhelming gravity of life.

I suck in a gasp, racing to catch up to each breath I missed.

But that first breath after sleep? It doesn't feel like salvation. It feels like the beginning of the end.

"Open your eyes."

My blurry vision gives way to a male form hovering over me. I blink up at the mess of caramel hair and wide brown eyes.

Wow. He is gorgeous.

The handsome stranger stares down at me, scanning my face. His mouth begins to move, and I realize he's speaking out loud.

"Serena." His voice is so familiar. "Say something."

Serena…Serena, Serena. Oh! That's me. I think.

He's staring at me with this *intensity*, his hair disheveled and his clothes bloody.

Why is he bloody?

The fog in my brain makes thought difficult and memory near impossible.

"Serena."

He reaches for me (Serena), confusion etched deep in his brow, and I recoil, pedaling backward on my hands. Hurt flickers over his face as he tries again and I scramble to my feet on unsteady legs.

"It's me." He lifts his palms.

I stare and stare at that face I know from *somewhere*. Then it hits me.

Oh my god.

"Zadyn?" I croak through the lump in my throat.

Before I can get myself to move, anxiety sinks its claws into my back. "No. I'm—I died…this isn't real. This is wrong…this isn't—"

He surges forward and takes hold of my face. I gasp at the sudden movement.

"This is real," he whispers.

I try to wade through the layer of mist clouding my mind. I remember screams. Tears falling onto my skin. Warm, white light pressing against me. I glance down at the black blood drying on my ivory gown. My hand flies to my chest, finding only a raised, textured line there. A fresh scar.

I blink, shaking my head.

"No," I breathe. It's just another nightmare. Just another cruel trick of the mind.

"Look at me, Serena. Look at me. Feel me. I'm here, you're here." He takes my hand and places it over his heart. "You're alive. This is *real.*"

His chest pulses beneath my palm—all the evidence I need packed into that violent, sporadic heartbeat. I glance up into warm brown eyes that threaten to melt me down to nothing.

"Zadyn?"

His shoulders relax, but his grip on me doesn't, not even when I sag in his arms, taking us both down to our knees.

He's here. This is real. And I'm not dead.

"Hey," he whispers, lowering his face to mine.

"How are you here?" I sob, taking him in through blurry eyes, gripping him by the arms, the shoulders, the face to make sure he's real, that this isn't my mind playing nasty tricks on me.

"It doesn't matter. You're safe, that's all I care about."

Another flood of memories hits me, threatening to drown me like a tsunami. Images of me crying over Zadyn's dead body. Images of Jace slain on a battlefield.

I slam my fists into his chest and he stumbles back, shocked. "You should have let me die. I was supposed to die!"

"Don't you dare say that," he hisses, gripping the back of my neck with startling ferocity.

"You shouldn't be here. If he finds you—"

I start to hyperventilate, sucking down shallow breaths, the tightness in my throat becoming unbearable.

"Serena, breathe. Hey, hey, hey. Focus on me. I'm here. I'm not going anywhere. I'm here," he repeats, nodding and holding my gaze until my breathing slows and I regain control of my muscles.

"I know what you've been through has been traumatic, but right now I need you to come back to me. I need you to fight your way out of that darkness and come back to me. Just for a little while, I need you to fight. Alright?" Zadyn's stare is the only thing holding me together.

I nod numbly, straining to find myself beneath the ashes. Beneath the dirt and worms and decay. Beneath the rot.

I'm here! a voice inside me screams. *I'm here, let me out.*

I reach for her.

And when our hands meet, a fire ignites.

Zadyn pulls me into his arms, and I breathe him in, squeezing tight enough to crack his ribs.

Scuffed black boots step into my line of vision, stopping a few feet away. I follow the length of them up two long legs, stopping when I reach a set of cutting golden eyes.

He stands there unmoving, his expression guarded.

Zadyn tracks my gaze past his shoulder.

The boots step closer. And I stop breathing again.

"Hello, little witch."

18

JACE

I feel such loathsome envy as I stare at them.

As I watch my little witch crumple at her familiar's feet, clutching him for dear life, struggling to breathe. I take a cautious step forward, pushing out a scrap of my magic and forcing a gust of air into her lungs. Zadyn guides her through it, soothing her in that way of his until her sobs ease and her throat relaxes.

I study the two of them locked together. They seem right. They make sense. He's the better male. He's the one she should be with—the one she deserves. Someone who will never hurt her the way that I have. The way I always seem to.

But that doesn't stop me from wanting. From this inexplicable notion that she is mine, and I am hers.

Her lavender eyes find mine, and my body goes cold. Nothing can lay me bare except that gaze—that unnervingly beautiful gaze.

"Hello, little witch."

We stare at each other unblinking as she extricates herself from Zadyn and stands. Her mouth parts.

A thousand thoughts blast through me. A thousand emotions. I want to scream at her. Ask her what the fuck she was thinking trying to put death between us.

96

But there will be a time and place for my anger later. Because right now, beneath the weight of her bewildered eyes, I'm melting.

"Not to cut the reunion short, but we should really be on our way."

Serena whirls and launches herself at Kai, nearly tackling him back into a mirror. He catches her and holds tight, an unsteady laugh bursting from his dry, cracked lips.

Gods, he looks terrible.

"I'm so sorry, Kai. I'm so, so sorry." Serena's voice is muffled against his chest.

"You should be. That stunt with the dagger? You almost made me sweat." He draws back, bracing her shoulders. "Don't worry, I'm already thinking of all the ways you can make it up to me."

"Kai, what are we looking for here?" Dover says, glancing at the assortment of mirrors.

"Dover," Serena breathes in surprise. "Is Mar—"

"She's here, she's safe," he assures her.

Turning from Serena, Kai resumes surveying the collection.

Everyone thought these mirrors had been lost to time. But no. These ancient objects with great and terrible power have been under the possession of Vod for gods know how long. As if they really needed another advantage.

"One of these," he murmurs, "is a traveling mirror."

"It's this one."

Serena stops before a tall, thin mirror with a rusted frame carved with suns and moons. A piece in the bottom right corner appears to be missing.

"How do you know?" I ask.

"Because it told me."

"The mirror spoke to you?"

"Kylian had one in his room. That one sang."

I slide a wary glance toward Zadyn. But as Serena's fingers reach toward the mirror, it comes to life, the glass giving way to a starry, dark vacuum of glittering night.

That's when a loud crash sounds from the door. Chunks of splintered wood rain down on us as we form a blockade in front of Serena.

Kylian steps over the shattered door, a line of Stryga at his back and a murderous glint in his eye.

"My runaway bride."

19

SERENA

"Feeling better?" he taunts.

A shudder forces its way through me as Zadyn pushes me behind him. The five of us huddle close together, weapons drawn and teeth bared. I back up an inch toward the mirror, tugging on Kai's jacket with one hand and clasping Zadyn's free hand with the other.

"You saw what happens to them if you keep up this little game of resistance."

"What's he talking about?" Jace barks.

Kylian sighs, completely disregarding him. "I thought you a modern female. Playing hard to get is so old fashioned."

"So is chaining me to your side until I agreed to be your little woman," I hiss, venom coating my tone.

He takes a step and our huddle backs away.

"Step away from the mirror or your friends are dead." Smoky shadows spill into the room, coiling around Kylian's ankles. The Stryga begin to march forward on those thick, matted horse legs, saliva leaking from their snarling mouths.

We back up again as a unit.

99

Kylian tenses, but he keeps his voice steady. "You don't want to do that, darling."

"Oh, I think I do. *Darling.*"

His expression turns lethal, hitting me like a thousand-pound boulder.

"There is *nowhere* on this earth you can go that I will not find you. You belong to me."

The threat hooks around my bones as I tug Zadyn and Kai backward. Dover and Jace latch onto us at the last second before we fall through the mirror. The last thing I see is Kylian darting toward us, hands outstretched, face twisted in rage as we slip away into the void.

Time stills as if we've entered a vacuum. All I see is stars forever and ever. No end and no beginning.

A moment later, we're spit out onto the grounds in front of the castle. Zadyn helps me up as a line of soldiers bursts through the gates and charges toward us.

"Get to the beach!" Dover shouts.

We break into a sprint. A tidal wave bursts from Kai's palms, quelling the first line of soldiers. But they're quickly replaced by more. I hold my gown in my hands—it's impossible to run in this damned thing. My foot catches on the massive train and I collide with the hard dirt.

But Zadyn is right there, flipping me onto my back and shredding it, leaving a jagged hem mid-thigh.

Woah.

Our eyes lock as he discards the fabric and hauls me to my feet.

Another wave of guards flows from the castle, threatening to cut us off. I'm slow, Kai is slow. We're holding them back.

As if reading my mind, Zadyn shifts into his *OrCat* form and nudges my thigh. I swing my leg over his back, latching onto his long, silky coat.

"Kai!" I shout over my shoulder.

"Serena, get out of here! Now!" he bellows, sweat beading on his brow as he pushes his magic to the brink. Jace and Dover launch into action, swords clanking as they meet the golden soldiers.

"Zadyn, stop! We can't leave them!" I protest, but he's already taken off. I have no choice but to hold on for dear life.

With his animal speed, we reach the start of a tropical forest in no time. I can no longer make out the forms of my friends among the sea of gold.

I slide off of Zadyn's back, and he shifts instantly, gripping my shoulders as he pants, "Go. Through the trees. Mar is waiting."

"Don't go—"

But he's already gone.

I debate running after him, but with these cuffs I'll be more of a hindrance. I can't just leave, though. I can't get my feet to move.

A furious wind picks up, tossing my hair around my face. I squint up at the sky. The tiny black speck grows closer and closer until its shadow eclipses the sun.

Then I hear it. A dull whooshing sound. For a moment, I think it's a dream. But there is no mistaking that sound as it floods me with relief.

Wingbeats.

"Oh my god," I whisper.

Furi bursts through the clouds in all her ancient majesty, weaving purple streaks across the sky as she beelines for me. I let out a wild cry, flailing my arms above my head.

She's alive. And she's *here*! My heart feels like it's about to burst.

How did she find me?

Her wings slice through the air, and the power she exudes has every tree, every palm, every grain of sand bowing to her. She looses a battle cry, followed by a puff of blue fire.

The ground trembles beneath her as she settles and lets out another loud howl. I race toward her and throw myself down around her thick leg, tears bursting from my eyes.

"I can't believe you're here," I cry.

Her purr reverberates through my bones as she dips her head, and tucks me beneath her chin. Nuzzled against her, I feel a sense of completion. Of hope.

Her barbed tail curls around me, thumping against the ground and melting my heart. I can't hear her because of the damned blood ore, but I know she is feeling all that I am right now. I peel back to look at her, stroking my hand over her sloped nose.

"I've missed you so much, girl. Feel like saving the day?"

The challenge registers in her cat-like eyes, and I swear to god, she's smiling. When I scale her back and take my place on her worn-out saddle, she lets out a howl to rattle the earth. Her head tips back as she flaps her wings, and we blast into the sky.

JACE

Outnumbered and fully fucked.

That's what we are.

Lines of soldiers pour from the gates until they surround us on all sides. To make matters worse, the Stryga have now joined them.

Zadyn dashes back in his *OrCat* form, shredding men to bits left and right. But there are four of us and far too many of them.

Years of battles, years of victories. I've never lost a fight. But I don't know that we'll walk away from this one.

Any minute I expect Kylian to storm out of the castle and decimate us all. It would be nothing for him. He's powerful in the same way all High Fae kings are. And that's without the Bloodfast.

I don't even know where Serena is—if Zadyn got her to Mar safely. The second I think her name, the sky becomes overcast. A heavy wind picks up as a dark mass comes into view.

"Perfect timing," I mutter to myself.

The majestic dragon swoops down, her wings blocking out the sun and bathing us in shadow. Some of the Vod soldiers stagger back, retreating toward the towering gates.

Fucking cowards.

Furi makes a sharp dive toward the tangle of fighting on the ground, and I catch a flash of movement between the dip in her shoulders. A banner of long dark hair, shivering proudly in the wind.

My heart lodges in my throat.

Serena.

Alive and whole. Sitting atop her giant dragon like the queen that she is—face set in fierce determination, a sparkle in those lilac eyes visible even from here.

She lives for this. It's what she was made for. She was a warrior long before I taught her how to fight. A warrior by blood.

The lines of soldiers split as a round of blue fire erupts, scorching the ground along with some of the gold-armored guards. Screams of agony rip through the mob.

This is our shot at escape.

"Go!" I shout, racing toward Dover. He's on the ground, leaning over a frighteningly pale Kai.

"He's losing a lot of blood," Dover says, bracing the deep gash in his best friend's thigh. Blood pulses out around his fingers.

"Fuck. Grab him, and let's go. Now!"

Staggering from his own exhaustion, Dover hoists Kai over his shoulder and we bolt toward the trees.

But Zadyn is not giving up.

He's on a rampage, refusing to slow even as the next round of dragon fire erupts in a mesmerizing and gruesome display that leaves men scorched of armor and skin. The smell is foul.

Zadyn, now! I shout into his mind.

It's futile. He's so far gone, he can't hear me.

Serena swoops through the sky again, sending more soldiers skittering back. She gives Furi another second to play with her food, then steers her toward the nearest line of trees. Clawed talons sink into the ground in a concise, graceful landing.

"Get on!" Serena yells.

I sheathe my sword and help Dover load Kai onto Furi's wing. Then I climb the chain until I can use her spikes to hoist myself up behind Serena.

"Call him before he loses himself completely," I pant, sliding my arms around her waist and settling into the saddle. I don't even have time to enjoy the flood of heat that bursts through me from being this close to her—from touching her again.

"Zadyn, come. Now."

The pure command that laces her voice is both shocking and seductive. And even among a crowd of burning soldiers, I find myself strangely turned on.

Until I see the massive ruby on her finger.

My desire is quickly replaced by white-hot rage.

Zadyn's lupine form freezes as if hearing her voice over the roar of the crowds. He snaps into a sprint, shifting between strides and swinging himself onto the rusted chain as Furi begins flapping her wings.

We're twenty feet up when the first round of arrows is launched.

They rain down like a dark meteor shower, whizzing past us from the direction of the palace. When I look back, golden guards line the entire upper perimeter of the castle, bows and arrows in hand. They stand along the highest walls of the keep, on every turret and bridge.

"Stay low!"

Before my words are even out, another round spears toward us. This time Furi's wing takes a beating as a cluster of arrows lodge inside her dark, leathery flesh. Some even sail clean through it. Her gut-wrenching roar rips through the air. Serena screams as if she'd been hit.

"Are you shot?" I grip her tighter from behind.

She turns back to me, horror sprawled across her face as we plummet a few feet.

"She's hurt."

"Blood ore arrows," Zadyn calls up to us. "We need to land!"

I use the scraps of my magic to throw up a shield, sending the next round of arrows bouncing back the way they came.

"We're almost to the camp."

Furi takes out a good amount of trees as we careen into the beach. Water sprays from every direction, rushing up to soak us. We slide down, Zadyn and Dover dragging a limp Kai up the beach toward Mar and Ilayna.

"This is bad! She's in pain," Serena cries, studying Furi's arrow-stricken wing. "Help me get these arrows out. Now."

Furi's head rears as Serena coos to her and smooths her scales.

"If I pull them out like this, shards might be left behind."

Her vicious gaze slams into me. "It's better than leaving them in and letting them cripple her wing permanently."

Feeling around for the last of my magic, I lift my hand and wrap invisible tethers around each arrow before pulling them out in one fell swoop. The bloodied sticks drop into the water and drift away on the tide just as I hit the bottom of my reserve.

Furi's cries start to ease up.

"We can't stay here long." I head toward the beach, water sloshing around my boots. "Kylian will track us right here."

"She can't fly yet, Jace," Serena snaps, following after me. "Her wing looks like a slice of Swiss cheese."

So much for a pleasant reunion.

"Oh, little witch, how I've missed your big mouth."

She shoves me hard, taking me off guard so that I fall into the shallow tide on my ass.

"Do not fuck with me right now." She glares down at me, rage simmering in those wild lavender eyes, and I feel my cock twitch behind my leathers.

Damn her.

I ignore her seething, stalking forward until I'm hauling her against my bloody, cut-up chest and inhaling the scent that has haunted my dreams ever since she was taken.

Her arms slowly wrap around my waist as I breathe in her hair and then freeze.

"You smell like Kylian."

She goes absolutely still and extricates herself from my hold, saying nothing as she jogs up the beach.

"Mar!" Her voice is filled with relief as she takes in the sight of her friend hunched over Kai's body.

Mar glances up, offering her a wry smile. "Nice dress."

Serena musters up an empty laugh. "How is he?"

"Not good. I put him to sleep so I can work on him. Whatever cut him was laced with some kind of poison. I'm doing all I can."

Serena sinks into the sand and takes Kai's hand. He looks like absolute shit. Pale and gaunt, eyes sunken even in sleep. The wound on his leg is a disaster, oozing thick white pus.

I don't know what horrors he endured on Serena's behalf, and I'm guessing it was bad, but that doesn't quell the envy in me at seeing her hands on him.

I'm engaged. To the princess of Aegar, no less. I know I have no right to feel this way, but I am possessive over her in a way that is fully foreign and inexplicable to me.

Every male is a threat. Every male she looks at, talks to, touches, or breathes on—I am constantly fighting the urge to rip their throats out.

Even those who have clearly been to hell and back for her.

She makes me dangerous. The only thing on my mind, day and night, is her. And now even the king knows it. Father figure or not, there will probably be hell to pay when I get back.

But I don't care. I will gladly pay it.

Dover slumps down at Mar's side, sprawling out on the sand. "How bad are your injuries?"

"Already patching myself up," he huffs, resting his eyes.

"I know you." Serena's stare cuts toward Ilayna, wrapping the slice on Zadyn's arm. "Who are you?"

The courtesan freezes, letting her hand fall. "I'm Ilayna," she murmurs, shrinking from Serena's intense gaze.

Zadyn glances between them. "She helped get us inside the castle."

Serena crawls through the sand to sit beside her familiar, his mouth still covered in the blood of the men he ripped apart. She reaches out to clean it away with her hand.

"Are you okay?" she asks quietly.

His eyes are cold and distant. "I'm fine."

Another swell of envy flares up in me. He's a good male. The kind that understands the worth of every life he takes, even if he takes them for good reason.

It makes me hate him all the more.

"We need to find a way to get these off." Serena holds up her shackled wrists. "I need to heal my dragon."

The silky fabric of her dress is now torn, revealing a ridiculous amount of leg. I can also tell she's not wearing anything underneath from the way the material flows over her curves and dips low on her chest, leaving her breasts nearly exposed.

I don't like that. Not at all.

"Blood ore is spelled shut," I grind out.

"I need to heal my dragon," she insists, and I swear I see a flash of Prophyria's blue fire explode through her blown-out pupils.

It's a little unsettling.

"We'll figure it out," Zadyn says. Her eyes snap to him like two sharpened daggers. She blinks, and they slowly soften, her pupils reverting back to normal.

"Jace is right. We shouldn't linger," Mar adds. "There's no hiding a dragon. Kai is stable for now. Let me take a quick look at Furi and see if there's anything I can do."

As Mar follows Serena down the beach to her dragon, I take a breath for the first time since entering the castle.

We're safe. For now.

21

SERENA

Every little noise, every breeze rustling the palms has me looking over my shoulder.

I'm wary of everything. Unused to conversation. Unused to the sun's unfettered beams on my pale skin. The influx of fresh air, the humidity of the sea—it all seems too extreme to handle.

I know I haven't seen the last of Kylian. He won't let me go. Not without a fight.

Jace placed a shield around our camp so we should at least be safe for the night. But it's only a matter of time before we meet to finish what we started.

Once the fire dwindles, Mar and Dover retreat into one tent, Ilayna into another. Mar was able to take away some of Furi's pain, but until I have my own magic back along with a direct link to her thoughts, I won't know the extent of her injuries. I feel useless. I wait until she's asleep, snoring lightly, her tail curled around our camp like a protective watchdog before I slip inside the tent that houses a sleeping Kai, still unconsciously fighting for his life.

I shift his head into my lap and stroke his hair, listening to his even breaths. Thank god he's not awake to feel the pain anymore.

Zadyn joins me a moment later, stretching out on his side.

"So? Are we going to talk about what you did?"

His eyes search mine. I avert my gaze. "I don't want to talk about it."

"Serena—"

"I wasn't suicidal, alright? I was trying to protect you. All of you."

"From *what?*"

He waits for me to elaborate. I draw in a long breath.

"Kylian showed me this mirror—a mirror into the future. If I were to keep refusing him…you all would have died. Hell, you still might," I mutter, defeated. "That's why you should have just let me die. I could have protected you."

He shakes his head. "You can't trust anything he showed you."

"I saw you all die…I felt you. I held your body, Zadyn." I look over him, cringing at the memory of his lifeless weight in my arms.

Zadyn props himself up on his forearm. "Serena, he has an entire room full of magic mirrors. You don't think he has one for illusions?"

"No." I shake my head, something in my bones warning me. "No, it was real."

Those visions were so visceral. I could feel everything. I could feel those beautiful boys with the dark hair and eyes the color of the Praxian Sea. I felt a sense of completion—pride and joy.

I felt all of that in a scenario where my friends were dead.

The guilt of that unborn future haunts me.

"He was manipulating you. Everything he did was to force you into marriage—into performing the Bloodfast with you." Anger laces his every word.

"The Bloodfast," I repeat. "Why?"

"Because"—he sighs—"it would have given him access to his full power. And if you were married, any offspring of yours would be considered legitimate, and therefore eligible to inherit both your power and the power of his entire bloodline someday."

Wow.

"Those visions were just another way to terrorize you, to scare you. It was all just part of the plan."

I let the possibility of what Zadyn is suggesting seep in. Kylian *is* a liar and a deceiver. Could it have been an illusion? I guess. Though I'm not willing to risk their lives on a possible falsity.

"You don't know that for certain."

"I don't care! Don't ever do anything like that again. I could feel you dying." He brushes his hand over my cheek. "I've never felt anything that excruciating. Sacrificing yourself…it's out of the question. Do you understand me?"

I nod reluctantly as Jace slips into the tent. Zadyn drops his hand.

A light breeze rolls through the flap, and Jace catches me shiver. He ducks out and returns a minute later, holding a bundle of clothes.

"You'll freeze in that thing," he says, looking over my torn, blood-stained dress with disdain.

"Where did you get these?"

"Ilayna packed a bag for you," Zadyn answers.

Careful not to jostle Kai, I gently set his head down and stand with my back to them. "Could you undo this?"

"Yes."

Two voices answer me.

I twist to find them both on their feet, motionless, glancing from me to each other. Jace steps back first, giving Zadyn an opening to start on the small buttons down the length of my back. His fingers graze my exposed skin, sparking up a fresh wave of goosebumps.

"There you go." His soft voice hits the back of my neck.

I shudder, feeling the ghost of a touch over my shoulder blade before he drops his hand and steps away to give me my privacy.

The two of them face the other way while I throw on the blousy top and fitted black pants. I discard the dress in the corner, fighting the urge to tear it into tiny pieces and set it on fire.

"Decent."

A quiet moment passes as I settle back on the ground, absorbing the weight of their stares. Something in me feels settled with the two of them near. Centered, even in the face of this shitstorm.

"What's with the choker?" Jace asks, slinging his arm over his knee.

I keep my focus on Kai's heavy lashes, twitching periodically.

"He made me keep it on."

"And what else did he make you do?"

"Jace," Zadyn warns.

"I need to know so I can decide which form of torture to start with before I string him from a tree and gut him with the dullest knife I can find."

His murderous eyes lock on mine.

"You don't have to talk about anything until you're ready," Zadyn says.

I toss him a thankful look before turning to Jace, who clearly doesn't share the same sentiment as my familiar.

"You might want to talk to Kai. He's the one you should be avenging," I mutter, not in the mood for the alpha male threats.

Jace leans forward. "He forced you to wear his gods-damned ruby collar and that gaudy ring. I hope that doesn't mean what I think it does."

"It doesn't mean anything. He was going to kill Kai. I'd wear both for an eternity if it meant keeping my friend safe from him."

"Did he hurt you?"

"He never hit me. And anyone who did was punished severely." I choose my words carefully. But he must pick up on something in my tone.

"Did he do something *other* than hit you?"

I roll my eyes up to the ceiling. "What is it you really want to know, Jace?"

"Did he make you fuck him?"

My mouth falls open. "I don't want to discuss this right now."

"So he did." Jace's hands curl into tight fists.

"She said she's not discussing it."

"He didn't force me. It was my choice."

Their eyes hit me like two sets of darts. I stare at the ground, my face on fire.

No one speaks.

I shouldn't have said it. But right now, I just don't have the energy to dance around it.

"Serena." Zadyn packs so much sympathy into those three syllables, it forces me to look up at him. Then to Jace.

His entire face falls. "You didn't."

"What was I supposed to do?" I whisper.

"Anything but that!" Jace explodes, slamming his palm into the ground so hard I flinch. "I should have murdered that bastard when I had the chance."

"You weren't there."

I keep my voice steady when all I want to do is fucking cry. I feel shitty enough as it is—I don't need the looks they're giving me on top of it.

"You don't know what it was like, what I watched him do to Kai."

"I don't care what he did to Kai—*how could you?*"

My cheeks sting at the accusation, the pure revulsion in his tone.

"*Jace,*" Zadyn repeats, but Jace ignores him, leaping to his feet.

"You are *mine,*" he snarls.

I laugh. "You sound just like him."

"Like Kylian?"

"Yes."

"Funny. Except you seemed pretty into the idea of fucking me the night you bonded the dragon, and it didn't take any coercion on my part."

A deadly silence creeps over the tent as my eyes narrow, and I'm almost certain whatever Jace sees in them makes his hand twitch toward his sword.

"How dare you," I seethe. "How dare you even think that after everything. I am not yours, and I never was. What's *yours* is back at the castle you abandoned, probably worried and devastated that her betrothed is off chasing after someone else."

He crosses the tent to stand over me.

"Don't minimize this. I came here for you. Because I couldn't live with myself if I stayed behind and you...Didn't you know I would come for you? I came here consequences be damned, only to find you'd whore yourself out at the first sign of trouble."

Zadyn is up in an instant, his hand wrapped around Jace's throat, fangs bared and ready to do some serious damage.

"Let him go," I command, my voice cold as ice. Zadyn slowly releases his hold, staying planted between us. I keep my voice low as I address Jace.

"Don't you dare judge me. I did what I had to do to keep his attention off of Kai. I did what I had to do to keep my friend *alive*. To keep you and the rest of the people I love safe from being used against me. You have no idea what he would have done to you and Zadyn and Mar if he had gotten his hands on you, you idiot. I did what was necessary. And I will not be ashamed of that. Don't you *dare* call me a whore. Don't you *dare* judge me."

And with that, I storm out of the tent.

I STAND BAREFOOT in the water, the tide kissing my ankles as the night breeze plays with my hair.

My toes are bordering on numb, but I don't flinch at the cold. I need to feel something.

Footsteps sound from behind me. I don't turn. I already know it's Zadyn from his scent.

Staring out at the gentle waves, I reach around my neck and unclasp the heavy ruby choker. Something in my chest eases as it falls into my hands.

I can breathe again.

I suck down a greedy lungful of air, feeling over the smooth skin of my neck. The rubies glitter beneath the moonlight as I turn them over in my fingers.

I hurl the choker as far as I can into the distance where it lands with the quietest splash and sinks to the bottom of the ocean.

Then I slip the ring off my finger and with one final look, I do the same. I don't touch the locket full of secret starlight. I allow it to remain around my neck. Just in case I need it.

We stand there in silence.
Zadyn doesn't say anything. He doesn't have to.

2 2

JACE

ice.

Real fucking nice, Jace.

Once again, my talent for saying the wrong thing has proven itself undefeatable.

No, not just the wrong thing. The *worst* thing a person could possibly say.

Don't get me wrong—I'm so relieved he didn't force her. That fear was always in the back of my mind, eating away at me. But for her to have agreed? To have consented?

This I could have never seen coming.

I know my reaction was uncalled for, but honestly? I'm heartbroken.

So I do the only thing I can possibly think of.

I get drunk.

Or as close to it as I can get off the flask in Dover's bag.

The look on her face in that tent keeps replaying in my mind. How could I have said those things to her?

She sacrificed so much for Kai. To keep him safe, to keep Kylian from hunting us down and killing us one by one. She was brave. Selfless.

All the things I admire about her.

And yet, I called her a whore.

I finish up whatever vile liquid was in that flask and toss it on the ground, knocking my head back against the palm tree.

I keep fucking this up.

I don't even know how or when it happened, but at some point over these last few months, I have come to belong to her in a way that I still can't even fathom.

That pull to be near her is present even now as I glance down the beach toward the camp. She's become my everything. My true north.

Dragging myself to my feet, I start down the stretch of sand.

There were so many moments that should have told me what was happening. I denied it and denied it until I no longer could. Until the need for her overrode everything in me—my will, my sense of duty, my entire essence.

Maybe it was the sound of her laughter that cracked my shell, or the sound of her breathing beneath me in the training ring. Maybe it was that first time we kissed, on solstice when the veil between her pride and her desire thinned just enough to have her racing into my arms. Maybe it was after she bonded Furi. When she leapt onto the ground and something shifted. The earth's plates clicked into place.

Why did I spend so much time treating her like the enemy? Being angry? Trying to get her to hate me. Trying to hate *her*.

All that time was wasted. Because I was always meant to love her, and she was always meant to destroy me.

And gods, do I love her.

I turn my back on the black waves and slip inside the tent. Lavender eyes stop me dead in my tracks.

"You smell like a bar."

Zadyn is asleep beside her, an arm slung over her lap while Kai snores from her other side.

I try to keep my voice soft. "Can we talk?"

She stares at me for a long moment. I stare back, willing my racing heart to stand down. With a sigh, she slides Zadyn's arm from her waist and steps outside to stand by the dying fire. Her posture is standoffish—arms crossed, staring into the embers—and I don't blame her. I stuff my hands in my pockets, letting the quiet wash over us.

"Don't look at me like that," she finally says. "Like I'm damaged goods."

"I don't think you're damaged goods."

She hits me with an incredulous look.

"I don't think you're damaged goods," I repeat. "Look, I'm—I'm sorry for being an ass."

The words of a poet.

Her expression turns pained. "I never expected you to be angry with me for doing what I had to in order to survive."

"I'm not mad at *you*," I whisper, turning her to face me. "I am *livid* with myself for letting this happen. I should have gotten there sooner, I should have never let you be taken in the first place."

"None of that was in your control," she protests, lowering a fraction of her armor.

"It should have been." My fingers brush over the scratches on her cheek and my heart clenches. "So many things should have been different."

I lose myself in those eyes as they coax the truth from my unwilling tongue.

"I should have told Derek I couldn't marry Sorscha. I should have stopped pushing you away at every turn. But the worst thing I did, the thing that haunted me every second since you were taken"—I step closer, gazing down at her—"is that I never told you I love you."

A single tear slides down her cheek and I catch it with my thumb, erasing the evidence.

"If you had died not knowing—"

"I knew." She shakes her head, her fingers sliding into the crooks of my arms. "I knew."

I slip my hands into her hair and almost groan as my lips brush against hers.

Finally.

Furi chooses that moment to release a loud, disgruntled sigh. Our muscles lock, freezing us in place. Narrowed green orbs track me from behind Serena, filled with judgment as I wait for her to decide where we go next.

"We should get some sleep."

Disappointment floods me as she draws back. I nod and follow her back into the tent, cursing the dragon in my head.

I watch the even rise and fall of Serena's chest as she sleeps and allow myself to think of what might have been if I had just stopped fighting.

If I had realized in those moments of quiet solitude when her image danced across my mind—when I found myself following her scent without meaning to, when I couldn't stay away, or worse, that I didn't want to—that something in me was shifting, melting.

If I had just accepted that she would be the unraveling of my life's design, maybe I would have had a fighting chance.

She is a storm. I would have been safer in the eye than trying to outrun her.

23

SERENA

I'*m a vile, wretched creature.*

My lips sink into his.

I will my tensing body to relax, reminding my nervous system to breathe through the kiss. My frozen lips open for him. He tastes like salt air and the promise of ruin.

I try to detach from my body.

I try not to feel it as his tongue slips into my mouth, learning my insides by feel.

I force myself to lean into his touch and let his hands wrap around me. It feels easier than it should. We fall onto the bed, and I stare up into heavy ocean eyes.

When he starts to undress, I bite my lip so hard I taste blood.

I SPRING out of the nightmare, drenched in sweat. It takes me a moment to realize where I am—to register the strip of light filtering in through the tent. Kai sleeping soundly at my side. I lift my fingers to my mouth and glance down at the drop of black staining my fingertip.

120

This is real. Our friends came for us. My dragon came. We made it out.

Tossing off the thin blanket, I stand and make my way down the beach. Mar, Dover, and Zadyn are plopped down in the warm sand, speaking quietly while Jace stands with his back to me, arms folded over his chest. Zadyn is the first to notice I'm awake, dropping off mid-sentence as the rest of my friends turn toward me.

"There are some things I need to share with you all," I say, planting my bare feet and locking eyes with each of them.

"The Stryga didn't kill those Guardians at the portal. Kylian did. He somehow gained control of it and has been using it to amass an army. No creature can pass through without swearing allegiance to him."

Zadyn mutters a curse, shaking his head as I go on, "His goal is, you guessed it, world domination."

"Surprise, surprise," Mar mutters sardonically.

"And if I had to bet his army is going to consist of the Stryga and others like them." I pause. "He's going to attempt to conquer the remaining four kingdoms, starting with Aegar."

"He could have a whole other arsenal of creatures at his disposal if he's controlling the portal," Mar says. I nod, already having considered that possibility.

"Exactly. And the Stryga have no problem breaching our wards because they aren't from here. We have to figure out how to close the portal before anything else can get through," I continue. "I say we head home to warn them and muster up all the military strength we can. Then we head to Hyrax."

My friends gape at me. Jace seems to be suppressing a small smile. I tweak my head.

"What?"

"Nothing." He inhales loudly. "I've just never heard you speak like that. Like a Dragon Rider."

"Desperate times." I shrug, though his comment sends a swell of pride through me.

"Could Kylian be working with anyone else? Did he mention having the support of any other kingdoms?" Jace asks.

I shake my head. "No, none that I know of."

Zadyn glances at Jace. "I doubt any would align with him, certainly not Berringer."

"There's something else. Kylian was clear that he wanted Furi, but he wouldn't say why. There was something he wasn't saying."

"Well, whatever his intentions were, I doubt they were pure so it's a good thing he doesn't have her."

"If he had shot her out of the sky, he would have. I didn't realize that blood ore worked on dragons."

"It works on all creatures of magic," Zadyn explains. I shudder at the thought of anything hurting my dragon ever again.

"We need to fly home. Tomorrow," Jace says, brows set firmly over his stunning golden eyes.

God, I forgot how intense his stare can be. I hate how much he makes me want to punch him in the face and kiss him raw at the same time.

He's engaged to Sorscha.

He may have come to my rescue, but nothing has actually changed here. I pry my eyes away from him before my mind can be sucked down a rabbit hole of all the things I want to do with him and will never have the chance to in this lifetime.

"If Furi's wings are healed by then. But either way, I'm going to need my hands free."

I hold up my cuffed wrists. Everyone continues to stare at me, saying nothing.

"Guys. We need to take care of this now rather than waiting until we're up shit's creek without a paddle. Kylian could be hunting us as we speak. We need every weapon we can muster."

"We don't have the spell to undo them. Only Kylian does," Zadyn points out.

"I know, so we need to start brainstorming."

Jace props his hands on his hips. "There is nothing to be done. You can't just slice through them with a sword. They're not coming off short of melting them off your skin," he tosses out, carelessly.

A lightbulb goes off in my head. He catches my eyes and shakes his head vehemently.

"Are you *insane*?!"

"It's the only option!"

"You want to burn the shackles from your wrists? Melt them down to ore?"

"If you have a better idea—"

"This masochistic streak you're on is getting old fast. They will burn through to the bone and you will lose your hands if you don't bleed out and die first," Jace explains heatedly, coming too close to maintain a normal heart rate.

"He's right," Zadyn says, getting to his feet. "You can't do this."

"Mar is here, she can siphon off her ring and heal me as we go, can't you?" I glance down at her and she grimaces.

"Serena, the kind of pain it would cause... and I don't even know if I'm strong enough to do this without it killing you."

"There are ways to protect my hands." I snap my fingers. "A shield! Jace, can't you throw one around my wrists while Mar works?"

He looses a long exhale. "I can try, but with margins that thin... I've never done anything like it. And I'm not going to lie, the second you start screaming, I'm going to lose it."

Zadyn looks like he's going to be sick as he huffs a breath and stares up at the sky.

"This is a bad idea. A very, *very* bad idea." He slides his eyes toward me.

"We have no other options. I need my power back. I'm a liability without it. If there is no getting these off without Kylian, then we're doing this. And we're doing it now."

24

ZADYN

This better work.

I mean it should, but then again, I don't think a single one of us has ever attempted to *burn* off magical shackles.

There's a massive pit in my stomach as we make the preparations. The heat of the fire mixes with the thick humidity, turning the air oppressive. It's an effort not to take a step back, but I know what Serena is about to face is going to be ten times worse.

Yes, this is an insane plan.

I would stop her if I truly believed there was another option short of marching straight back to that bastard and asking him to kindly hand over the spell. But if this starts going south, I'll put an end to it. I won't let her mutilate herself just so she doesn't feel like a liability.

I stuff a few dampened cloths under the chains, spreading them out over Serena's wrists and forearms, her palms and delicate fingers.

"I need you to keep going, even if I pass out," she says to Mar, who nods grimly.

"Here." Jace holds out a thick twig. "You're going to want something to bite down on."

She opens her mouth and he places it inside. Moving in front of her, I cup her cheeks, earning her wide-eyed stare.

124

"I'm going to ask you one more time. Are you sure you want to do this?"

Please just say no.

She nods, her lavender eyes determined.

Fuck. My chest deflates and I drop my hands. *Here goes nothing.*

Mar squeezes between us, bumping me behind Serena as Jace comes around her other side. He brings his eyes to the fire and the wild flames are tamed into a narrow column, like they're being contained inside some invisible tube.

"When you're ready," Mar says, bracing Serena's bicep with both hands.

Without hesitating, Serena sticks her hands into the line of fire.

I cringe. It takes mere seconds for her to start whimpering. The whimpers turn into cries then into screams that will haunt my dreams until the day I die. Each one rips through me, spearing me straight through the heart.

I know, sweetheart, I know. It will be over soon.

I hope.

I brace her hips, sending my magic through the point of contact, but her wrists are burning faster than Mar and I can heal them. Her skin is hot to the touch, crocodile tears streaming down her pink cheeks.

Come on. I fix my gaze on those damned cuffs. *Fucking melt already.*

"It's taking too long," I snarl, panic edging my tone. "The fire isn't hot enough to do this."

I watch as the flames eat away at Jace's margins along with the wet towels. Sweat is beading along his forehead and not from the proximity to the flames.

"I'm healing her as we go," Mar forces out, hands still braced on Serena's arms.

But she's in pain! Every fibre of my being is straining against this, begging me to intervene.

Jace is concentrating harder than I've ever seen, trying to contain the fire and also keep a barrier between the shackles and her wrists. Meanwhile, the cuffs don't look like they're even close to liquifying.

"It's not enough," I breathe. *"It's not enough!"*

Serena's screams intensify and her pain becomes this tangible thing, hitting me from all sides.

No, this is over. Finished.

"Take her hands out. Now," I snap.

I can't take it. I can't stand the sound of her muted screams, can't take knowing what this is doing to her. When no one moves, I drag her back, away from the fire. She collapses into me, and I take her down in the sand between my legs.

"What the hell are you doing?" Jace shouts.

"We can't do this," I pant as Serena's tears soak my shirt. She's shaking like a leaf, moaning, her eyes squeezed shut.

"Well, we've got to do something!"

Think, Zadyn.

"Mar, can you burn them off any faster than the fire would?"

She looks stunned by my question. "I—I can try. But I won't be able to heal her as we go. The pain will be—"

"I can't watch her slowly suffer like this. If you can do it quickly then we can heal her afterward."

At this point, I don't know which is the lesser evil. I just know that the sooner this is over with the better.

Gods, I hope I'm right.

Mar lowers to her knees before us. Serena nods her head as much as she can.

"I've got you," I tell her, shifting us onto our knees and propping her up against me. I hold her arms out in front of her so as to not burn her legs. Mar hovers her hands above the two cuffs. They turn white within seconds. Serena writhes, slamming against my chest, but I don't so much as teeter behind her.

I've got you.

Her heart-rending screams as the white metal begins to drip from her wrists along with her skin, are the stuff of nightmares.

I'm going to fucking kill Kylian for this.

Jace is full-out crying at this point, tears of anger and frustration streaking his cheeks as he grits his teeth and sends a cool, soothing breeze to wrap around her ruined wrists.

The shackles are all but molten pools mixed with her blood on the sand as she goes lax against me.

"Lay her down. Now," Mar says, immediately shifting into healing mode.

Serena's face is leeched of color. Mar makes fast work of replacing skin that a second ago was not there, until the whites of her bones are no longer visible. I watch in horrified awe as the skin regrows, sealing in the leaking veins and tendons. The skin looks new, but her forearms and the tops of her hands are bad—bubbled and red.

"Jace," Mar signals. He sends another wave of air to kiss her extremities.

Serena's head lolls against my thigh as she dances on the edge of consciousness. Smoothing her hair off her clammy forehead, I send out my energy to help Mar heal her. The blue in her blood makes her healing abilities ten times what I can do. But there's no way I can sit here doing nothing.

"I need a second," Mar breaks off, gasping for air.

"Mar?" Dover kneels down beside her a second before she falls back into the sand, nose leaking blue.

<h1 style="text-align:center">2 5</h1>

<h1 style="text-align:center">SERENA</h1>

A familiar thrum beneath my skin tickles me awake. The sweet sensation of pinpricks along my legs and the back of my neck. I know that feeling.

My magic.

My eyes fly open to a tangle of dark hair and a perfect profile seated beside me.

"Kai?"

His head whips toward me. "Serena?"

"You're awake," I breathe in relief.

As I move to sit up, my hands come into view and the flood of memories whooshes back in.

Burning flesh. Horrible, searing pain. The feeling of fire kissing bare bone. I shiver, trying to blink away the image of my skin melting off. The smell of it.

My hands are wrapped in pink-tinged cloth, but the flesh around my forearms is badly singed.

"Just when I thought you couldn't get any crazier. What were you thinking *burning* the chains off?"

"What were you thinking almost dying on me?"

He helps me sit up and I throw my arms around him, ignoring the burns.

"I'm so sorry, Kai. I'm so, so sorry." The floodgates open and I sob into him. He holds me tightly, burying his face in my neck.

"Don't you dare apologize to me. None of this was your fault."

I pull back to examine him, the tears making my assessment a bit more difficult. His color is better, his eyes not so sunken in. There are a few scars on his forehead from where the rocks pelted him.

"It was, though."

"Serena, he stopped the beatings." He wears a somber expression as he searches my face. "What did it cost?"

I give him a mournful look. "Not nearly what I would have paid to make sure you were safe."

"No one"—he breaks off, eyes filling with tears—"has ever done anything like that for me. No one."

I look him dead in the eye.

"You are my friend. There is nothing I wouldn't do for you."

"Ditto, savior."

He cracks a beatific, watery smile that melts my heart and I pull him into my arms again, needing to convince myself that we both survived the horrors of Kylian's captivity.

We survived together.

"Pardon the interruption."

Mar breezes into the tent with two tiny strips of cloth stuffed up her nose. I raise an eyebrow as she plops down in front of us.

"The things I do for you."

I give her a smile. "Thank you, Mar."

"Yeah, yeah, yeah, thank you Mar for agreeing to burn my limbs off. Let me see."

I place my grizzly hands in hers.

"Kai, is your leg—" I glance down at the gauzy bandage wrapped around his thigh.

"Loads better, thanks to Mar. Still a little sore, but I'll be back on my feet in no time." He pats his leg emphatically, then winces.

I have to hold in my gasp as Mar unspools the bandages around my wrists. They look even worse beneath the cloth, but at least the cuffs are off.

"Your body should start to heal itself without the constraints of the blood ore. That combined with my healing should fix you up almost as good as new."

"Mar, you should be resting. You've used more power in the last few days than you have in decades."

She shrugs, waving me off. "It feels good to flex the old muscles."

Tingles work their way up my arms and I pull forth my own healing energy to mingle with hers.

"Does that thing ever get tapped out?" I nod toward her moonstone ring—the one that stores her remaining magic.

"It will never dry out completely. But it does deplete the same way all of yours does. The nosebleeds tell me when it's running low."

Zadyn ducks into the tent, pausing in the entrance.

"You're awake." There's a hint of a smile on his face, but it doesn't reach his dimples. "How are you feeling?"

"Not bad, all things considered." I hold up my scorched hands in explanation. He takes a timid step closer, pointing to the space beside me.

"Can I sit?"

"Why would you even ask that? Of course." He settles in next to me. "Hey, you okay?"

"Me?" He sounds surprised. "I'm fine, it's you I'm worried about. I'm so sorry, Serena."

"For what? I made you all promise to keep going if I passed out."

"I had Mar stop healing you so she could speed up the removal."

I vaguely remember him pulling me out of the fire and shouting orders at Mar as I thrashed and wailed in his arms.

With my magic back, the channel between us is now clear. Another huge relief. I can almost see the memory through his eyes. I can feel everything he felt—regret, shame, anger, fear, frustration. Helplessness.

"It was hurting you to see me in pain. You did what you thought was best."

I look over his face and tap my forehead knowingly. His expression warms as I lean my head against his shoulder.

"Where's Jace?" I ask.

"Off brooding, I'm sure," Zadyn mutters.

Mar and I burst out laughing.

We sit there another hour or so, healing my hands, and by the end of our session, the bubbles have vanished from my skin, leaving behind a smooth surface. Still red and irritated, but manageable, thank god.

As Mar helps Kai out of the tent to exercise his leg, I feel something stirring in my mind. And then a soft little nudge.

Blackblood.

Relief slams into me as the channel clears and that silky voice fills my head.

Furi!

Our bond shimmers as her emotions slam into me—her joy at my safety, her seething rage at those who have hurt me. I push to my feet to go to her, forgetting about my hands until pain lances up my wrists and forearms and I fall back on my ass.

Zadyn steadies me, concern tightening his voice. "Shit, are you okay?"

Fresh tears spring to my eyes and I let out an unsteady laugh. "I can hear her!"

I know she's right outside and we've already had our reunion, but it sucked not being able to talk my dragon at will. There's so much I have to say.

I can hear you, I repeat for her. Our minds mingle into an embrace.

You must rest, she scolds.

Are you alright? Are you in pain?

I am healing. You are safe now.

Thanks to you. You came for me. How did you even know where to find me?

I followed the scent of your bond.

My bond?

Your familiar.

Zadyn? You followed Zadyn all the way here?

I knew he would lead me to you. He stopped outside my cave while you were gone. He left squirrels.

I glance at Zadyn, stunned.

"What?" he asks, giving me a perplexed look.

I throw my arms around his neck, catching him off guard and taking him down to his back. He laughs breathlessly, holding me against his chest.

What was that for? His chocolate eyes gleam up at me.

You checked on Furi for me. You fed her, made sure she was safe.

Of course, I knew that's the first thing you would do.

My heart melts.

She followed you to me. She found us because of you.

He breaks into a smile, his thumbs smoothing over my back.

Happy to help.

We stare at each other for a moment, exchanging silent gratitude. I open my head to him and he does the same.

In that quiet conversation, more is said than either of us could ever put into words.

26
JACE

I drop into the hot sand, my heart throbbing in my ears.

It's been a long time since I've pushed myself like this. The heat doesn't make for the best running conditions, but I was in dire need of a distraction.

Laughter has my head snapping toward the tent up the beach.

She's awake.

But I make no move to go to her.

I don't know if it's shame I feel or regret, but hearing her screams yesterday, watching her thrash against Zadyn as her flesh melted off—it's fucked with me.

Badly.

I can't go near her. I can't look at her face. I can't even breathe without feeling so many things all at once.

I don't do emotions. I don't do tears. I don't do…love. And yet the love I feel for this little witch is so big I feel like I'm walking around with a ticking time bomb in my chest, ready to burst at any given moment.

I know I'm not entitled to her, and I know I don't deserve her, but we belong to each other. It isn't a feeling, it's a fact. Like saying the sky

is blue or the grass is green or Kylian is going to fucking die at my hands.

I hear Kai's voice coming from inside the tent and another round of laughter breaks out.

I've never lumped him in with the rest of his vermin kin. Even when we were boys, it was clear that he was the black sheep—the outcast.

I was probably seventeen or eighteen years old when Kai and a newly crowned Kylian arrived at the castle for Ilspeth and Derek's wedding. Kai was a few years younger than me, Kylian a few years older. Derek suggested Kai join me for training. I wasn't his biggest fan because of who his family was, but I was cordial.

Kylian spotted us and insisted on sparring with his brother. It quickly became clear that by sparring he meant beating him unconscious until he had three broken ribs, a bruised tailbone, and needed five stitches on his head.

I intervened on Kai's behalf once I realized that this was no brotherly competition. This was a cocky young king drunk on his own power.

If Sorscha hadn't appeared when she did and distracted us, either Kylian or I would be dead.

She and I brought Kai to the healer together. He was in such bad shape, he missed the wedding altogether.

That was the day we became friends.

It makes me sick to see that Kylian's old habits still rage as hard as ever. He'll never admit it, but Kai is a threat. He just doesn't know it yet.

Grains of sand cling to my back as I sit up and wipe the sweat from my eyes. I push to my feet and start running again, simply to avoid cuddling up with Serena, Zadyn, and Kai.

There's no room for me in there.

And that's fine. I prefer being alone.

27

SERENA

"We need to get on the road." Jace stands above me, blocking out the bright sun at its midday peak. "We're pushing it by staying here any longer."

"Furi isn't ready to fly yet."

I squint down the beach toward my dragon, lapping up saltwater from the ocean. Sometimes I don't know how a creature so ancient and wise can be so dumb.

"My shield is thinning, Serena. We need to move."

"I can't leave her, Jace. It's out of the question. Where will we even go?"

"We could head back to the city," Zadyn suggests, his eyes linking with that female—Ilayna—who's rejoined us. "I've been renting a place for us. We can hide out, just for a day or two until she's ready to fly again."

I frown, making my way over to Furi's side to smooth her warm scales. "Where will she stay?"

Here. I will stay here. You must go.

No, Furi.

I will be fine, Blackblood.

I don't like leaving you like this.

135

She blinks a giant green eye at me. *I can protect myself. I've been doing it in my sleep for two thousand years.*

I roll my eyes. *I don't trust Kylian.*

I can hear you now, wherever you are. You must go. Stay hidden. When I can fly, I will call.

If you hear so much as a tree rustle, I want you to call me. Okay? Promise. I will rip Kylian apart if he touches you.

So will I. Now go.

Her head swings, nudging me forward with her snout.

"Well?" Jace prods.

Furi gives a light growl in response to his voice. She's never been his greatest fan.

"She said to go. She'll stay here until she's fully healed, and then she'll call me."

"Alright. Good. Let's move."

We pack up the camp and make our way through the forest, toward a run-down city that smells like absolute shit.

"Where are we?"

"Solmead," Zadyn says, close by my side.

"The glittering gem of Vod," Kai pipes, leaning on a broken tree branch we fashioned into a walking stick for him. I hang back to keep his pace as he limps alongside us.

I was worried he would never smile, never joke again after Kylian all but wrecked him with his brutality. I thank god his spirit isn't broken after all.

Zadyn leads us toward a decrepit building that looks like it could collapse at the drop of a sneeze. The wooden stairs groan as we make our way up to his apartment. But when we reach the door, we find it slightly ajar.

Heavy boots sound on the other side.

Someone is here. And they're looking for something. Or someone.

Zadyn freezes, his hand coming out to block me from taking another step. I hold my breath as he lifts a finger to his lips and Jace sneaks around his other side, silently drawing his sword with the onyx hilt.

Zadyn cranes his head to peer through the door and turns back to us.

Go, now, Zadyn mouths.

We retreat silently the way we came, bursting out into the hot sun. Zadyn's hand wraps around mine as we fly down the rat-infested alleyways.

"This way!"

We follow Ilayna onto a narrow street lined with trade booths, past an old female seated behind a cart of crimson apples. As we pass, she stands, clamping a crinkled hand around Jace's arm with shocking strength.

"Heed my warning, boy," she says to him.

He wrenches free and marches away.

"What was she talking about?"

He shakes his head, ignoring my question. But I've studied and dreamt of that face enough to know what the strain in his eye means.

"Zadyn, can you glamour the six of you?" Ilayna asks. "It's best if no one sees you come in."

He nods. "Is this safe?"

Her eyes dart around the empty corridor. "Safe as you'll get right now."

"Come on." He urges us forward. "No one say a word."

Under the invisibility of Zadyn's glamour, we make our way down a long, red-tinged corridor and into a perfumed parlor with luxurious curtains and daybeds. Beautiful females in expensive-looking dresses strut around on the arms of well-kept males, fawning over them flirtatiously.

Is this a brothel?

No one says a word as Ilayna turns down a few hallways and holds open a door for us.

"Okay," she says, closing us in.

"Where are we?" I ask.

"A whorehouse," someone answers mildly.

Ilayna looks at the ground. "These rooms are usually reserved for our highest paying patrons, but there are no reservations today. I doubt anyone will come snooping. It's a suite, there's another room through that door. You should be safe here for a while."

"Thank you, Ilayna," Zadyn says sincerely. He turns to me. "Stay here. I want to go see what those men in my flat were up to."

"Don't go alone," I protest, wrapping my bandaged hand around his arm. Jace takes a step toward the door.

"No," Zadyn says. "One of us should stay. Just in case."

"I'll come with you," Dover volunteers.

"Stay out of sight," Mar warns him with a quick peck on the lips. "Don't go picking a useless fight."

I pace around the room after they leave, too restless to sit. Peeling back the curtains, I scan the pitiful streets. When a flash of gold appears in my eyeline, I gasp, yanking the drapes closed.

"What's wrong?" Jace is beside me instantly, his brows threading together.

Shaking my head, I move away from the window and sink into a seat. "Golden guards."

He cracks the curtains the tiniest bit to peer out.

Getting a whiff of myself, I mutter, "God, I need a bath."

"I can show you to the baths. The girls should all be heading to dinner now, so it should be empty." Ilayna looks around awkwardly.

"Mar?" I ask.

"I'm going to take a look at Kai's leg." She settles onto the bed beside him and helps lift his leg. He sucks in a sharp breath through his teeth as she stuffs a pillow beneath it.

I follow Ilayna from the room, surprised to find Jace suddenly beside me. "Oh, you think I'm letting you out of my sight? With golden guards scouring the streets?"

"I'm going to take a *bath.*"

"Don't worry, witch, I won't peek."

Great.

"There are towels and robes here. I'll try and bring you all back some dinner," Ilayna says, lingering in the threshold.

"Thank you," I say to her.

"Thank you, Ilayna," Jace echoes as the door closes behind us, sealing us in with an air of finality. We stand there beneath the sensual low light, the steam curling above the circular pools creating a delicate layer of haze.

Jace and I lock eyes awkwardly as he steps forward. I hold my breath, my stomach doing little somersaults. With excruciating care, he begins to undo my bandages, unspooling them as I study the severe lines of his face, the permanent tension between his brows, the curve of his beautiful mouth, and the thick downcast lashes that shadow those high cheekbones.

The cruel things he said before still linger in the back of my mind, but I know he didn't mean them. And besides, it's hard to hold any kind of grudge when all I want is to crash into him.

When my hands are bare, he glances up at me.

"Thank you," I whisper, my voice like gravel.

Without a word, Jace puts his muscled back to me.

Warm steam kisses my naked skin as I slip out of the borrowed clothes and into the inviting waters. I dip my head beneath the glassy surface and come up feeling renewed.

"You can turn around now."

Slowly, Jace turns and sits down at the edge of the bath.

"What are you thinking?" he asks, drawing his knees up to his chest.

"Honestly?"

"Honestly."

"This feels so good I could cry."

He lets out a chuckle, shaking his head.

"What are *you* thinking?"

"I'm thinking if you ever try to leave me again for the afterlife, I'll lose my mind."

Oh.

"I was just trying to keep you all safe." My voice is a feeble murmur as I stare at the blue tile lining the bath. He reaches out a steady hand and tilts my chin up.

"I don't care why you did it. Just tell me that it will never happen again."

I nod and swallow, reaching for the bar of soap on the ledge. It slips out of my grasp, hovering in the air.

"Say it. Say it will never happen again."

"It will never happen again."

I watch him force a swallow and drop his eyes to the tile.

"I missed you," he says. The candid admission leaves me stunned. "I thought you were dead."

"Nah. Got at least eight more lives in me."

Twin rings of golden light flicker up, full of regret and reckless hope. A gentle breeze sweeps my hair to the side as the bar of soap drifts behind me, brushing over my shoulders in small circular motions. Jace watches, his molten stare intense as he uses his affinity on me. I let my eyes close, feeling those invisible hands roam over every inch of my body, massaging the tension from my shoulders, neck, and calves.

One degree of separation is all that stands between his physical hands on me. But this is toeing the line.

The soap continues to do his bidding, disappearing below the surface to clean my legs. It inches higher and higher on my thighs. I hold my breath, my body clenching in anticipation, wondering if he'll dare to go further.

"I'll let you do the rest."

His raspy voice makes my eyelids flutter open. He's holding the bar of soap out to me, his gaze ravenous, chasing my heart into a sprint.

I reach for it but he's not done teasing me. He grins, pulling his arm back. I lurch forward, water sluicing over the edge of the bath and soaking his pants. For that brief moment, we share breath. Then he surrenders and I retreat back to the water with the soap. He tracks my hand as it dips beneath the surface.

"Close your eyes," I whisper. He does and I can hear his heart beating so loudly. Or maybe it's my own. I don't know.

"You can open them."

"All clean?"

I nod as he twists to pick up a towel.

"When was the last time you had a bath?" I ask.

He laughs, scratching the back of his neck. "I don't remember."

He looks so good in the low light with the mist swirling around him like this. So—

Nope. No. We are not going there.

He's still engaged and that isn't changing. I need to establish some boundaries. Being alone with him is not wise. Being alone and *naked* with him is even more not wise.

Not when I'm fantasizing about dragging him into this water with me and devouring him.

He leans down. "You're thinking dirty thoughts, aren't you?"

"What?" I laugh. "No."

Yes.

"You're lying, little witch."

"How do you know that?"

"Your scent."

"What about it?"

"It shifted. I can tell you're…aroused."

"Ew. Please. Even if was aroused—which I'm not—you using that word just un-aroused me."

"Then why are you still turned on?"

I open my mouth and then close it. Oh, hell. What's the use in lying?

"You're not turned on right now? By this?" I gesture between us.

"We're not talking about me, we're talking about you." He braces his hands on the edge of the pool, a cocky smirk on his face.

"Right. Of course, we are. Jace Fallyn, Ex-Captain of the Guard, current Hand of the King and pillar of morality is above such carnal desires."

I make a serious face, folding my arms over the ledge

"I can assure you," he breathes, eyes tracing my bare shoulders. "I am far from above carnal desires."

"Then I guess I just don't do it for you."

"You know what would do it for me? Having you alone, uninterrupted for the rest of eternity. That bar of soap included."

I bite my lip.

"Don't bite your lip like that. Not unless you want me to do something about it."

"Why, what will you do?"

"You don't want to test me. Not right now."

"It's my lip. I'll bite it if I want to." And since I can…

Suddenly his hands are in my hair, angling my head up so that our noses are pressed together and I can almost taste his lips.

"Serena," he growls.

I draw in a breath, rising up out of the water. Tiny beads skate down my body, but his eyes don't wander. They remain glued to mine, golden and scorching.

An inch away. Less than. An inch away from the relief of his scalding kiss.

My lips ache to close that distance.

So I do the only thing I can think of to keep from sinking them into his.

I clamp my fingers around his collar and haul him into the water beside me.

He falls in head first as I cackle. I almost forgot what it was like to laugh.

Jace breaks the surface with a loud gasp.

"You. Little. Witch," he breathes, his hair plastered to his face. He shakes his head, trying not to smile, but I can see the corners of his mouth tugging upward.

"You needed the bath more than I did," I say, ascending the two steps to the ledge, baring my naked back to him.

I wrap the towel around myself and glance back. It's him who bites his lip now. Bites it until it turns white.

"Are you coming?" I ask, nodding toward the door.

He grimaces. "I think I need a second."

I cock my head.

"To cool off."

Shit. *Why is that so hot?*

"Think you can make it back to the room without running into trouble?"

"I thought you didn't want me out of your sight."

"That. And I just wanted an excuse to see you in the bath."

He flashes me a boyish grin. I dip my foot into the bath and kick some water at him. One of those rare, unguarded laughs slips out of him and my chest aches.

God, I missed him.

I start toward the door, grabbing a cozy-looking robe off the rack by the wall.

"Just—give me a second." His voice is pained as he emerges from the water, clothes clinging to every inch of his chiseled body. He flips his hair back, sending tiny droplets flying through the air, as he comes chest to chest with me. He leans down, a determined look in his eye.

I know that look.

It's his *I'm about to kiss you* look.

I hold my breath, waiting, but he reaches behind me, snatching a towel and shaking the water from his hair.

Idiot.

His arm wraps around my shoulder, pulling me into his side as he walks us out the door.

"You're evil," he murmurs, kissing the top of my head as we step into the hall.

2 8

ZADYN

It takes less than an hour to hunt down the intruders, following their scents from outside the apartment building. Even from a healthy distance, that gold-plated armor is unmistakable.

They're already on the hunt.

The Vod soldiers make their way down the streets, peering into windows, kicking down doors, and prying screams from the innocents inside.

The pleasure house probably is the safest place for us right now. Ilayna once told me it's warded due to its high-profile clientele. The gatekeeper is the old fae with the glass eye. Behind that frail, haggard facade lurks a creature of nightmares—a monster wearing the skin of an old maid, bred to destroy anyone with ill intent.

We make our way back as the sun is setting, sticking to the shadows of the foul back alleys. When I enter the room to find Serena missing, my heart speeds up.

"Where is she?"

"Relax, Zadyn," Mar says, turning to me. "She's taking a bath. No need to have a conniption."

"Where's Jace?"

"He's with her."

144

My entire body tenses. She gives me a withering look and turns back to Kai's swollen leg. "Not like that."

What other way is there?

I slip from the room, tugging on a glamour to conceal myself. Following her scent to the baths, I place a hand on the closed door and freeze as it cracks open a hair.

A loud splash sounds from within, followed by Serena's laughter.

"You. Little. Witch," I hear Jace say.

"You needed the bath more than I did."

She *giggles*. Actually *giggles*.

"Are you coming?"

"I think need a second." Jace pauses. "To cool off."

I grit my teeth, only imagining what's going on behind this door. My instinct is to rip it off the hinges, storm in there and tell him to get his filthy fucking hands off of her. But I remain frozen in place.

"Think you can make it back to the room without running into trouble?"

"I thought you didn't want me out of your sight."

"That. And I just wanted an excuse to see you in the bath." *

Deep, hideous jealousy eats through my stomach. I shake my head, scowling, and force myself back from the door. My feet carry me away before I can even register what I'm doing. Where I'm going.

I find Ilayna alone in her room. My name hasn't even fully left her tongue before I lunge forward, slide my fingers into her hair, and kiss her deeply.

I pull back to study her expression.

Her eyes flicker over my face once. Then she leans in, slamming the door shut behind me as I walk her back into the room. We fall onto the bed, a tangle of hurried limbs. Undressing quickly and artlessly, I bury myself inside of her, purging my desperate longing for a girl that will never be mine.

A girl that I am stuck with for all eternity.

---

* Cue: *When You Were Young* by the Killers

I KNOW I have a tendency to act out where Serena is involved.

I did the same thing with Cece. Desperate for release, desperate for *her*, I end up chasing after the easiest bet. Whatever is ready, willing, and accessible. It's a fact that shames me.

A flaw that makes me even more unworthy of her.

It wasn't always like this. The ache to love her wasn't always there. Neither was the *other* ache. That one came later. But it's been that way for at least a decade now, and I don't remember what it was like not to be in love with her. Not to think about her every moment of every day—the need to be near her far surpassing my need for air.

I re-dress in a hurry, keeping my eyes downcast. Ilayna sits up beside me, slipping on a silk robe. Getting to my feet, I dig into my pocket, reaching for some gold coins. Her hand stills my arm as she shakes her head and stares up at me from the bed.

"Please don't."

I give her a pleading look. "I don't want you to think I'm taking advantage of you."

"You weren't. It's been so long since I…was able to enjoy myself with a male. Not a patron. I wanted to. I don't want your money."

Guilt pools in my stomach. I just used her for sex. I'm just as bad as the rest of the males that darken her doorstep.

I look at her for a moment, in her beautiful, vulnerable innocence, then shift my focus to the floor. "I should go. Check on everyone."

She nods without speaking.

I open my mouth to say more, but nothing comes out. So I turn and duck out of the room, nearly colliding head-first with Serena in the process.

"Hi," she breathes, startled. Her head tilts to the side as her lavender stare strips me down to the bone.

"What are you doing out here?" I snap, not intending to sound so defensive.

"Mar said you were back, I came looking for you."

"You shouldn't be out here. Someone might see you."

"Why is your face all red?"

I shrug.

"Were you just…" She motions to the door before lifting her brows. "Wow. Okay. Good for you."

She turns on her heel and starts the other way. I catch up to her with little effort.

"Oh, just say it," I mutter under my breath.

"Say what?" Her focus is set straight ahead, her lips pressing together like they do when she's withholding a big, fat opinion.

"Whatever it is you're thinking."

"Nothing," she says nonchalantly, lifting one shoulder. "I just didn't know you were into prostitutes."

"She's not a prostitute, she's a courtesan. And a good person," I counter. "She helped us get you out."

"I'm sure she is. I guess I'm just surprised."

"Careful. You almost sound jealous." My voice contains a sliver of bitterness as she matches my stride.

Her eyes roll. "Not this again. I told you in the past and I'll tell you now. I'm not jealous and I don't care who you fuck."

Smirking, I lean toward her ear. "Say that with your fingers uncrossed next time."

Her mouth pops open in surprise as she skids to a stop. "Oh, grow up."

"Live another two hundred years, and *then* tell me to grow up."

"You're unbelievable."

"And you're a terrible liar."

"Not lying. God, you are so—"

I turn to face her head-on. "What, hmm? What am I?"

"Annoying."

"*I'm* annoying?" I bark a laugh as she nods.

"Yes! It's like if you're not getting enough attention, you have to run off and have sex with the first female you see. Not to mention, your timing could not be more inappropriate. Can you ever just keep it in your pants?"

"Do you ever stop to ask yourself why what I do bothers you so much? Why you get all weird after you find out I've gotten off with someone?"

She stares at me blankly.

And before you answer, know that I can tell when you're lying, I add silently.

Fine. I don't like it when you run around fucking other people.

As opposed to fucking who?

As opposed to fucking—

She cuts off her thought abruptly and gives me a death glare. But I know how that sentence was about to end.

I catch the shift in her scent. The shift that hints at desire.

And now I'm fucking hard.

"You know what, it's been a long day and I don't even know what I'm saying so I'm going to go to bed—"

I catch her arm as she walks past, earning a stunned glance from her.

"Maybe one day, when you're not so tired, you can finish that sentence."

She squirms uncomfortably as my eyes lower to her thighs, clenching together.

Good gods have mercy on me.

"Yeah. Maybe." She jerks her arm away and stalks off. Catching the scent of her wet hair as she tosses it over her shoulder, I groan into my hands and lean back against the wall.

I might just die of wanting before I ever get the chance to tell her how I feel.

2 9

JACE

"Rise and shine, little witch."

Serena rolls over, reaching her stiff arms into a long stretch. The sheets pool around her waist and I give myself until her eyes crack open to appreciate the body I got to know so well during training. The curve of her hips, the dip of her lower back, the smell of her hair—her skin.

I want to be waking up next to that body. Waking it with my hands, my mouth.

Fuck.

I clear my throat, shifting on the edge of the mattress. "Heard from your dragon?"

"I just woke up." She digs her palms into her eyes, rubbing away the sleep.

"I was just out scouting the area. There are soldiers everywhere. They know we're in the city."

She curses, pushing onto her elbows. Her hair is a disheveled mess. I love it.

"Where is everyone?" she asks around a yawn.

"Next door, eating breakfast."

"Furi says she's a lot better today. She can get us out of Vod. But we

149

might have to make a few pit stops, Jace." She lays a hand on my arm, and my entire body tenses, honing in on that touch. "I don't want to push her just yet."

Anything you want.

"I understand. We can stop however often she needs to." I stand, offering her my hand. "You should eat something. You need to rebuild your strength."

"Yes sir." She gives me a sardonic salute as she takes it and slides off the bed. I follow her into the adjoining room, where Ilayna has smuggled an assortment of fresh fruit and pastries.

"How are your hands today?" Dover asks around a mouthful of food.

"Good." Serena examines them. "A lot better."

"They look better," Zadyn notes, watching her sink onto the empty loveseat beside me. I pour a glass of water and hand it to Serena, then start filling up a plate for her. She drinks the whole thing down in one go.

"I forgot how thirsty magic makes you," she says in explanation.

Mar nods in agreement. "Right?"

"So I talked to Furi. She said we can head out today."

"That's great news," Mar says. "I've missed my bed like you wouldn't believe."

"I've missed your bed too," Dover agrees.

"Me three." Mar turns to smack Kai on the arm. "Hey, watch it. I'm wounded."

Serena laughs, wrapping her lips around a crimson apple, driving my mind to some dark places.

Stop staring at her fucking mouth. Focus.

"We need a plan," I blurt, effectively squashing the mood. "Kylian's guards are outside, swarming the streets. Our faces are plastered on every wall, window, and lamp post for miles. We're officially wanted persons."

"I was thinking about that earlier," Ilayna says, lingering by the door.

I feel a kind of sympathy when I look at her. Zadyn's done his best to make her feel welcome with us, but I haven't seen him so much as look at her since we walked in.

Interesting.

Taking a tentative step forward, she goes on, "A carriage is coming at noon to take a few of the girls to the dressmaker. Her shop is closer to the edge of town."

"You want to smuggle us out?" Dover asks incredulously.

"What are we going to tell the other girls when the six of us cram into the carriage with them?" Serena asks. "The six of us whose faces match those flyers?"

"Leave that to me, sweets," Kai drawls, folding his arms behind his head.

As PROMISED, a carriage pulls up to the front of the building at noon.

We silently make our way down the halls into an impressive foyer with checkered tiles and crystal teardrop chandeliers. This entire time, Ilayna had been sneaking us in the back to avoid traffic.

"This is…not what I expected," Mar says appreciatively, glancing at the rows of sculptures and expensive-looking art on the walls.

"The madame is all about running a tactful, high-class business. We don't deal with riff-raff here," Ilayna explains, holding open a door off to the side of the entrance.

"Why are we in a coat closet?" Dover asks as we slip inside.

"Wait here. When it's time, I'll knock twice. Alright?" Ilayna says, then shuts us inside.

Kai hums. "Closets are no fun with this many people. I like to limit it to two or three. Females, preferably."

"Kai," Mar and Serena chide in unison.

I can't see her, but I can feel her brushing up against me, her scent pervading my senses, urging me, *begging* me to touch her. This nagging, insistent need is wearing on me. I shake my head, trying to clear the thoughts as we wait in silence.

Thankfully, two raps sound on the door and we follow Ilayna into the waiting carriage full of pretty females.

Kai leads the way. "Ladies, how are we today?"

"Prince Kai." They regard him with whispers and sweet looks.

"You know what would make me so, so happy?" Kai flashes them a roguish smile, his eyes twinkling with siren magic. "If we could all just squeeze and make a little room for my friends and I?"

Giggling, the females readjust so that we have room to cram inside. I take a seat on the floor. It's a tight squeeze, and I almost groan when Serena is all but shoved onto my lap. Dover pulls the door shut behind us. I'm worried it's going to pop back open with the amount of bodies stuffed inside.

"Jesus, it's like a clown car in here," Serena mutters. Zadyn laughs from the other side of the carriage, nestled on the floor between two pastel-colored skirts.

Sometimes it's like she's speaking another language. A language that only Zadyn understands. It gets under my skin to no end.

Each bump in the cobbled road has Serena bouncing on top of me. I have to grit my teeth and clutch the handhold with a white-knuckle grip to keep my erection down. Finally and mercifully, the carriage rolls to a stop.

"Now, my angels—" Kai turns to the courtesans with a honey-soaked voice. "I was hoping we could keep this ride our little secret. We were never here. What do you say?"

He earns a collective lilt and a carriage-full of eager nods.

Dover tugs on the handle and falls out onto the pavement. We empty out one by one, stepping out into the warm sunlight. Across from us is a field bordering the start of the tropical forest where Furi waits.

We're one step closer to home—and with that, the dread of facing Sorscha and our impending nuptials.

30

ZADYN

We step out of the overcrowded carriage parked on the outskirts of town and breathe in the salt air rolling off the sea. I'm relieved to find the color gold absent from my vision. Serena stands a few feet away in the field, talking to Mar, sunlight dancing off her dark waves.

"She's beautiful."

Ilayna sidles up to me, her eyes on Serena, who stands there oblivious to her own beauty. To the effect she has on everyone who meets her.

"I can see why you're so taken with her. Both of you," Ilayna adds, nodding toward Jace. I turn to face her.

"Ilayna…I'm so sorry for the way I behaved."

She laughs. "Zadyn, you've been a perfect gentleman. You were kind to me. And you showed me something that no one has in a very long time."

"What's that?"

She leans in, taking my hand. "Respect."

My heart warms at her bright smile. It's the first time I've seen it reach her eyes.

"Go," she says. "You don't want to be spotted here."

153

"Come with us," I blurt.

Her expression shifts into something I can't read. She drops her gaze to her feet. "I can't."

"Ilayna, you deserve more than this. You don't belong here, with a bunch of—"

"Whores?" she supplies, glancing up at me. "It's okay to say it. It's the truth."

"That's not what I was going to say." I shake my head earnestly. "We can help you start over in Aegar."

A subdued look settles on her heart-shaped face. "That is kind of you, but my home is here. It's the only one I've ever known. The madame and the girls are my only family. It may not be glamorous, but at least I belong. Be well, Zadyn. You're a good male. You deserve someone just as good."

"So do you, Ilayna. We could never have done this without you."

I lean forward and kiss her on the cheek. There's a soft smile on her face when I pull away—one that's taken effort and practice to perfect.

It's the saddest thing.

My heart clenches as I drop her hand.

She's the kind of person I could see myself with. Someone with a pure heart and an innocence that is so rare in this world. And maybe if I hadn't been given to Serena at birth, things would be different. I would be with someone like Ilayna.

But things aren't different. And my heart belongs to Serena completely. I will love her until it destroys me.

So I turn my back to Ilayna, making my way toward destruction herself.

"Tough goodbye?" Serena teases as I reach her side.

"Don't be a dick," I snap, trudging ahead through the tall grass and wildflowers. "Did you even thank her for her help?"

"I did," she says defensively. "If you're so in love with her, why not bring her along?"

"I asked her to come. She said no."

Serena's eyes shoot to me. I avoid looking at her.

I don't know what surprises her more. The fact that I invited Ilayna or the fact that I'm defending her the way I am.

We fall silent as we make our way to the giant purple dragon on the beach. She's right where we left her, roaming the sand, chomping the leaves off the towering trees.

Serena preps her for flight as we climb onto her back, settling in the best we can. There's no real method to staying on top of her. We just have to grip the spikes and hope for the best.

"Are we ready?" Serena says, taking her place in the saddle.

The five of us nod in confirmation.

"Alright. Let's go home."

DEREK'S KEEP FINALLY COMES into view between the mountains, flashing its sparkling glory up at us through the breaks in the clouds. We veer toward it, clinging to Furi's back as she dips down.

And that's when we see it.

The hordes of gold-armored troops surrounding the perimeter, already lodged in battle.

Shit.

31

SERENA

hit.

No other word comes to mind as we circle the castle to get a better view of what we're dealing with. There are so many golden soldiers. They outnumber our armored guards by double.

No, triple.

I expected Kylian to come for me, but I didn't think it would happen this soon. The fighting is already well underway, shouts floating up to us as we coast along the treetops. I turn back to Jace.

"You're the Ex-Captain. What's the order?"

"If we use dragon fire, she'll take out half our armies, and you've never tried to wield before," he responds over the roaring wind. "Have Furi drop us inside the gate and tell her to stay close by. We need to make sure the king and the princess are safe, then round up everyone we can and get them out. Kai, Mar, and Dover—stay with Furi. We don't know if the walls have been breached yet."

"I can fight," Kai protests.

"No," Mar and I say in unison.

"You're not back to full strength, and you can't push it. Not today," I finish.

Furi, did you get all that?

156

Yes, Blackblood. She veers down at a sharp angle.

Be careful, girl.

Jace, Zadyn, and I leap off, the dirt ground of the outer court-yard meeting us with a thud and stealing our breath. It hurts like a bitch, but we're up in a matter of seconds, Zadyn immediately shifting into the biggest beast he can muster. I'm well stocked on knives thanks to Jace, who opts for his usual swords and skilled phantom hands.

Stop thinking about his skilled phantom hands.

We cut our way to the towering doors, hurling out our gifts to take down every golden soldier in our way. The halls are pure chaos, bloodied servants running, tripping over the bodies of nobles scattered across the floor.

We burst into the council room to find bloodstains all over the table. Jace shifts the massive hunk of wood aside in an impressive show of strength and heaves open a trapdoor in the floor. We peer down into a black hole, and I breathe a sigh of relief when Sorscha's big doe eyes peer up at us. She holds a trembling blonde female in her arms. Cece.

"It's you! Oh, thank gods." She clasps her chest, and the horrified look on her face recedes. Her gaze shifts to me. "Cousin."

"Are you hurt?" Jace pants, cutting off my response. The princess shakes her head. "Where is your father?"

"He made us promise to stay here and not to come out."

Jace and I exchange a look.

Then a crashing boom rips through the air. I'm momentarily blinded as shards of stained glass rain down on us. The girls scream as Jace and Zadyn both leap for me. Jace gets there first, tackling me to the ground and covering me with his body.

Black smoke rolls in, letting us know that the castle is now on fucking fire.

I scan the room for Zadyn. He's in one piece, still in *OrCat* form.

Jace scrambles off me, reaching down to pull Sorscha and Cece out from their bunker.

"Get them out of here," he says to Zadyn. "Get to the edge of the woods and have Furi pick them up. Serena, tell her they're coming and to be ready."

I nod as Zadyn nudges Sorscha's leg. When she doesn't move, Jace picks her up and plops her on Zadyn's back, then does the same with Cece.

He hesitates, looking back at me. Jace places his hand on Zadyn's furry head and says, "I've got her. Now go."

I watch him disappear through the blown-out window with the girls.

Furi, we've got an incoming. Zadyn's on his way with the princess and Cece.

On it.

"Oh my god." My breath catches when I see the massive army in the distance, charging over the hill.

The rising smoke. The field turned battleground. The bodies littered across the lawns.

Kylian's vision is coming true.

I grip Jace's sleeve. "We have to find Derek."

He nods, taking my hand and pulling me into the smoke-clogged hall. We're holding our breath, pushing through the thick haze, when a body slams into me full force.

I blink and stumble back a step. "Igrid?"

She stands before me, frantic and disheveled, tears streaking her freckled face.

"Oh gods, you're here!" She throws her arms around my neck. It's then that I notice the cluster of terrified women and children behind her.

I pull back. "Are you alright?"

"It happened so fast, I rounded up as many people as I could—"

"We need to get them out of here," I say to Jace.

"The tunnels are the safest place for them."

She shakes her head. "I couldn't get to everyone—"

Before I can respond, a cluster of golden soldiers bursts through the smoke and charges at us. Igrid's huddle shrieks as Jace shoves me behind him and lunges forward.

"Serena go! Get them out of here!"

"I can't leave you!"

Jace's sword slashes through the air, burying itself in the neck of one of the soldiers. I cringe.

"I could do this in my sleep, now go," he shouts.

A few of the soldiers fall to their knees, clutching their necks and gasping for air. Jace whirls to me, clutching my arms, his voice urgent. "Get to the kitchens. There's a trapdoor inside the pantry. Go now!"

I don't budge.

"If you don't, they will die. Please. I'll find you."

He jerks me forward, pressing a lingering kiss to my forehead. Then he shoves me toward Igrid and turns back to his fight.

I swallow my panic as I stealthily lead the group down the steps toward the kitchens. We're almost in front of the throne room when I see the Stryga materialize before me. There are four or five of them heading right for us.

I pivot to Igrid. "Run. Take them and don't come out."

"Serena, no—"

"Go!"

She breaks away from me, cerulean eyes torn and brimming with tears as she and her group steal around the corner.

I race into the throne room, luring the Stryga in after me. A line of fire shoots from my palms and slams into them, but they don't stop. I reach for my dagger, slicing a clean line through one's throat. Hot blood sprays across my face and pools on the polished marble tiles. I take an involuntary step back.

Razor-sharp pain slices across my arm. I glance down at the four symmetrical slits on my leather sleeve and the blood welling beneath. The creature swings again. I duck just in time to sink the knife into its back.

Hurried footsteps sound down the hall. I whirl as Derek appears beneath the archway, followed by a few of his guards.

"Serena," he breathes.

And in that moment, it's not the king standing there. It's not Derek.

It's my dad.

I can't help it. I do the thing I've been dying to do since the moment I arrived in this strange world, since the moment I saw him on his throne of diamonds, regarding me with violent distaste.

I rush toward him and throw my arms around his neck. He catches me, staggering back a step. Instead of shoving me off like I expected, he hugs me back. His familiar scent washes over me, and my throat seizes up.

"I prayed to the gods for your safe return."

I pull back to look at the perplexed expression on his face as he reads the emotion striking me stupid.

Blinking back tears, I say, "I'll catch you up on everything over dinner tonight. If we survive this."

He breaks into a wide grin, crinkling his kind eyes. "I look forward to that."

Together, we turn to face the next round of Stryga as they pour into the room.

I fall into a killing trance, my motions fluid and streamlined as I cut through the wall of horrific creatures. Derek wields his power in an impressive display, alternating between his sword and the spears of ice shooting from his palms.

I dance around a beast double my height, matching it stride for stride. It knocks the dagger from my hand as I skirt around the marble pillar, swiping the flagpole from its place and snapping it over my knee. I ignore the pain radiating up my leg as I come around the other side and drive the jagged end into its gut.

Metal clangs against marble. I spin toward the sound. Derek's sword is on the floor. His boot catches on the dais and he falls backward. The beast before him lifts its lethal claws.

No.

I grip the other half of the flagpole and hurl it forward like a spear. It flies through the air in a smooth line, finding its target. The Stryga freezes, then hits the ground with the pole protruding from its chest.

Derek glances at me, stunned, as I bend to scoop up my dagger and his sword.

"Jace is upstairs." I jog over and help pull him up. "We need to get to him."

Derek nods. We race out of the throne room and up the steps. My heart locks in my throat as we pass a window in the hall and I see Jace facing off with a golden soldier on the thin ledge between towers.

I clutch Derek's arm, pulling him to a stop. His eyes widen as he sees what I'm seeing.

"This way," he says.

Derek leads us onto a bridge running parallel to Jace. He hurls out his power from across the way, sending a spear of ice into the chest of Jace's opponent. Screams fill the air as he plummets to his death. Jace wheels toward us, dark hair beaded with sweat. He makes an impressive leap onto our bridge, and Derek folds him in an embrace, clapping him on the back like a proud father.

"Jace." I tug his arm as another cluster of golden soldiers spills onto the bridge after us.

He tosses his sword in the air and sends it slicing through our assailants, freeing his hands to draw two daggers.

The way he fights is beautiful. Easy in a way it shouldn't be. Everything about him is calm and deadly.

Shards of ice continue to spray from Derek's palms, skewering the golden soldiers as they topple back over the stone ledges.

I think we're actually doing pretty well.

Until a dozen Stryga arrive on the bridge.

I'M FLOODED with relief when the falcon circling overhead drops down beside me and a certain familiar *OrCat* pops up in his place.

Zadyn takes out two or three Stryga at a time in his lupine form, which would be super useful if they would just fucking stay dead.

"Serena, one of those banshee screams would be helpful right about now," Jace tosses over his shoulder as he lifts a Stryga into the air and impales them on a spike.

"I'm not exactly sure how I did it last time without killing you all," I quip, my voice sing-songy.

"It's easy. Just open your big mouth and let it rip." He grunts, thrusting his blade through the horned skull of another grizzly creature.

"Cover me."

Closing my eyes, I plunge into my well of magic.

The banshee in me is buried in a dark, deep place that I don't like to touch often. A place that houses every bad thing that's ever happened to me—every heartbreak, every grudge, every scrap of pain and grief I have ever endured.

She is made of shadows. Of despair. Of rage. I've never attempted to summon her at will.

But right now, I need her. We all do.

Fire kisses up my throat, narrowing into a soul-deep scream. The castle trembles—pebbles and towers collapsing in on themselves as I rain chaos and destruction down upon us. I lose myself in the peace of death, purging my buried pain, and the world around me disintegrates.

It's uncontrollable. I can't rein it in. It's going to consume me.

Someone is shaking me. Calling a name I forgot I had.

I blink, jarred out of my trance and spit back into my surroundings.

It is deadly quiet.

The Stryga are gone.

I look from Jace, clutching my arms with wide eyes, to Zadyn, now in his fae form, crouched over something.

Someone.

The world shifts into slow motion as I approach him, pulling his shoulder back to let me through.

The king is dead.

PART II: DEVIL'S BARGAINS

3 2

SERENA

I never thought of grief as a privilege. But it turns out bereavement is a luxury only afforded when you're not under siege.

The council room is eerily quiet.

I stare blankly out the shattered stained-glass window, trying to make sense of the last two hours.

Everything happened so fast.

I can't scrub the image from my mind no matter how hard I try. Every time I blink, I see Derek's brown eyes, the eyes of my father, staring up into the sky, frozen and unseeing.

An old wound opened up in that moment. One I'd almost forgotten about until now. Until once again, Death came to collect her due.

I wanted to know him. I wanted to be close to him. But we didn't have enough time. We never do.

"Lady Serena."

My eyes slide to Lord Gronwen, Master of Coin and one of Derek's closest advisors. He stands across from me, fingers steepled over the table, blue-black hair streaming past his shoulders.

"I'm sorry, what?"

He sighs through his nose. "How did this happen?"

It's Zadyn who answers for me. "Right before Serena decimated them, one of the Stryga lunged for Jace while his back was turned. Derek threw himself between them."

Jace sits in the seat designated for the Hand of the King, to the right of Derek's seat.

But he isn't there. He never will be again.

Jace's face is vacant as he stares into the gouges in the wooden table and the freshly dried bloodstains across its surface. He hasn't said a word since it happened. I know the guilt is eating him up inside.

Gronwen runs a hand over his face, looking exhausted. The High Priest and Lord Conwell, Derek's Head of Records, exchange a grave look.

"Who knows about this?" Gronwen presses.

"Our friends and the people in this room," Zadyn responds.

I finally locate my voice. "Sorscha doesn't know yet. We have to tell her. She should be here for this."

"We tell no one else until we've agreed on a course of action."

I cock my head at the finality in his voice. "You want to keep his death a secret? From his own daughter?"

"Until the right time, yes."

"I think that's up to the Hand, don't you agree?"

Gronwen bristles at my challenge, then gives me a sympathetic smile.

"I've been around for the changing of kings before. I've seen enough to know that information like this is delicate. In the absence of a ruler, it is easy for things to fall apart, for empires to crumble. I will not allow my friend's legacy to collapse due to such a grave oversight. Emotions have no place inside this room. If you cannot accept that, Dragon Rider, then by all means, you are dismissed."

I open my mouth, and then close it. I've never liked this male—never trusted this male. But I can feel the sincerity of his words, read the underlying twinge of pain in his eyes that he's trying very hard to repress.

So I sit down and shut up.

He inhales slowly, turning to pace around the room. Broken glass crunches beneath his boots.

"In his absence, the king has named the current Hand, Jace Fallyn, as his regent."

Jace blinks up at him. His eyes are glassy and far-off, though I haven't seen so much as a tear from him.

"But Sorscha is his heir. She's of age."

"The princess is not capable of running this kingdom alone. It was a decision we discussed at length. You are to rule in his late majesty's stead until her coronation."

Jace shakes his head. "I...I can't. I can't be king."

"King *regent*. Until you wed the princess. Then you will ascend as king consort." Going off Jace's horrified expression, Gronwen softens his voice. "This was the plan all along."

I look at Jace. The hard lines of his face, the crease between his brows, the clenched fists that have seen more battle and bloodshed than I could ever fathom.

He is a warrior. And right now, he is lost. Afraid.

"You can do this." Jace's molten gaze lifts to mine. "He trained you for this. He chose you."

What if he chose wrong? Jace's expression says.

I shake my head, wishing I could jump across the table and shake away all of his doubt. Tell him that he's perfect and that choosing him could never be wrong—could never be a mistake.

He turns his tormented eyes to Gronwen and nods.

"Then that's settled."

"But I'm not keeping Derek's death from Sorscha. He's her father. She deserves to know."

"And the public?"

Jace pitches him a dark look.

"If word spreads that the attack was successful and that the king perished at enemy hands...well, you can see how the optics are less than desirable."

"What would you have people believe?"

"Leave that to me. With the proper frame, the picture won't appear so bleak."

"Fine. Do what you will."

"As you wish, Sire. Now," Gronwen continues, his voice perfectly diplomatic, "it seems that war is upon us."

"What does Vod want?" Lord Conwell asks.

"Me."

Every head swings in my direction.

"Kylian is coming for me. And for Aegar. He wants all five kingdoms, and now he has control of the portal. Those creatures can pop up here anytime."

"The castle is secure. For now. The ward masons are working on repairs as we speak."

"How many dead?" Lord Conwell turns to Sir Max, standing behind Jace, bruises and cuts scattered around his face and neck.

"So far the body count is near two hundred. We lost a good deal of men, but we were able to get most of the servants, the females, and children to the tunnels before they breached the keep."

My heart flutters. I pray Igrid made it to the tunnels alive.

"I'll alert the nobles. Tell them to ready their armies," Conwell says, scribbling across his stationery.

The High Priest's age-weathered voice spreads through the room. "The portal presents a pressing issue."

"I'll go to Hyrax." I rise.

Zadyn joins me. "We'll gather support from Berringer and figure out a way to stop anything else from crossing over."

"I'll go with you," Jace offers, but Gronwen shakes his head and taps the table.

"You are needed here, your Grace." Jace blanches at the title. "If it's the Dragon Rider Kylian is after, we can certainly expect more attacks."

"What are you suggesting?" I ask. "That this won't stop until I give myself up?"

Jace's body goes rigid.

"What I'm suggesting, girl, is that you take the head start on offer and get as far from here as you can. This place is no longer safe for you. Or that dragon of yours."

A chill skates down my spine at his unfiltered warning. I find Jace looking at me, his expression forlorn.

Turning to Zadyn, I say, "We'll leave tonight."

"I'll pack a bag. Meet you in your room in ten," Zadyn says as we bustle down the hall.

I try to stay focused as we split off. I can fall apart later. But for now, I have to stay strong. For Jace. For Derek.

"Don't go."

I freeze, neglecting the heap of clothes I was stuffing into a sack. Jace is leaning against my door frame, his face hollow.

"I have to."

"Serena." He shakes his head, closing the gap between us. "I just got you back. I don't want you out of my sight. Not now."

He has no idea how badly I want to be here to help him through this. Because I know what a loss like this tastes like.

Ash and nightmares.

And no matter what there is between us, this undefined thing hanging overhead, I wouldn't want anyone to go through this alone.

But I can't stay. Not even for him.

I turn back to the bed to finish packing. "Jace, I have to do this. That portal has to be dealt with. And Aegar needs a king. You're the only one Derek trusted enough to lead. You belong here."

He moves in front of me. "I belong wherever you are. Nothing matters as much as this. Not anymore." His hands slide into my hair, and I involuntarily breathe in his smoky scent. "Let me keep you safe."

"You know I don't want to leave you."

"Then stay. Fuck the consequences. Just be with me."

"What are you saying?"

"Tell me not to marry her."

My heart stops.

"*What?*"

He waits, knowing full well I heard his words clear as day.

"Stay with me. *Marry* me."

I blink up into eyes I have known in another life. My human life. But here I am in a new world, and still, I can't stop history from repeating.

I push him away like I did Jack.

I deny myself.

I deny him.

"I can't."

"You want to be with me. I know you do."

"It doesn't matter."

"Of course it does."

My heart lodges in my throat. "Jace, I care about you, I do. But nothing has changed here."

"Everything has changed. You were taken, and I—" He cuts himself off, shaking his head. "I'll go to Sorscha right now and tell her I can't marry her."

I take a step back, putting some space between us. "She just lost her father, Jace. You don't know what you're saying, you're in shock right now. We both are—"

"I've never had more clarity in my life."

I give him a look. "You know it's not that simple."

"What if it could be?" His golden eyes are filled with frantic, desperate hope. He moves closer, crowding me, making it hard to think.

"This is the only thing that has ever made sense to me, and I can't fight it any longer. I'm yours. I was yours before I ever knew it."

"Jace, you know how I feel, but I—we can't. You can't."

He dips down and guides me forward until our foreheads meet. "The only thing I can't do is live without you."

I give myself two seconds to savor this. Him holding me. And in those two seconds, I realize something.

One: It took him coming all the way to Vod, bringing me back from the brink of death, to realize what I mean to him.

Two: It's too little. Far too late.

The door swings open, and Zadyn appears. "Time to go."

I pull back to look at Jace. We search each other's eyes for what feels like an eternity, his question lingering like mist in the air. My answer dies on my tongue.

I pull his hands from my hair and plant a kiss on his knuckles.

Then with my heart stuck in my throat, I turn my back on him.

On the new King of Aegar.

And I don't look back.

33

ZADYN

"Stop!"

Halfway down the lawn, we turn to see Mar jogging toward us, a shadow in the darkness.

"Leaving without saying goodbye?"

"It's not goodbye. It's see you later," Serena clarifies.

"Potato, potahto." Mar slows to a stop as she reaches us. "You're going to Hyrax, aren't you?"

Serena nods, looking somewhat numb.

"I'm coming with you."

"I don't know if that's a good idea, Mar. Things are a mess right now, Derek is—" Serena shakes her head, unable to complete the thought.

"I know. But there is nothing I can do here. I can help you find a way to get this portal closed. We can end this. For Derek." She takes Serena's hands.

I sling my bag higher across my chest, anxious to get on the road. My only concern right now is getting Serena out of here as quickly as possible after that attack. It's not safe for her here. Not right now.

"Come on. It can't hurt to have another witch on the job. One who

is, you know, older, wiser, more beautiful." Mar tosses her auburn hair over her shoulder.

A crack appears in Serena's frown, but she still looks torn. And we don't have much time to debate this.

"Sure you're up for this? It could be dangerous," I inform Mar. She should know what she's getting herself into.

"Even better." She shrugs, crossing her lithe arms.

Serena looks at me. I know she wants Mar to come. And the truth is, we could probably use her help. She's just afraid of putting her friend at risk and doesn't want to be the one to decide.

Fuck it. I'll decide for her.

"If you can be ready in ten minutes, you can come."

"I'll be ready in nine."

Mar claps her hands together and disappears into the warm light coming from the castle. The ward masons worked fast, mending most of the exterior of the keep and wiping away the debris on the lawns.

"Are you alright?" I lay a hand on Serena's shoulder. She shakes her head, casting a wistful glance toward the keep.

"It's not me I'm worried about."

Of course. Jace.

Always Jace.

No matter how many times he hurts her, she finds a way to forgive and forget. And he *knows* she always will.

Finding them the way I did in her room, my envy was second only to my sympathy. I can barely tolerate the man, but the way he clung to her, his face addled with desperation, with loss…I know what it's like to lose a father. So does Serena.

This is a mess. The last thing she needed right now was to lose Derek. Just as she was starting to heal, starting to flourish. I'm worried about what this will do to her.

I wish I could somehow fix it. Somehow fill all the holes in her heart.

"Serena—"

"No, don't give me that look. I can't do it right now. If I let myself think about it...I'll fall apart, and right now all of us need me together."

I nod, dropping my hand.

We wait in somber silence, listening to the cicadas sing in the trees. Furi circles overhead, her silhouette zig-zagging across the full moon.

Mar reappears after a few minutes with a bag thrown over her shoulder and two males at her side, one of them limping.

Why am I not surprised?

"You know what they say," Kai breathes as they make their way down to us. He's slightly winded by the time they stop. "Two is company, three's a party."

"And five is way too many," Serena scoffs.

"I tried to say no, but they insisted." Mar holds up her hands, casting a look at her mate.

"Kai, I don't think it's a good idea. You should be letting that leg heal."

"Serena, don't baby me, alright? We're in this mess because of my scum-lord brother. This is the least I can do. Let me help. Please."

"You've already helped. You've done more than enough, I can't ask you to—"

Kai steps forward and pinches Serena's lips together. "It's not up for debate."

She swats him away. "Fine."

Tipping her head up to the sky, she lets out a loud whistle. Furi stops her path mid-loop to land beside us. I settle into the saddle behind Serena, going rigid when she reaches back to slide my arms around her waist.

She turns over her shoulder to look at me. "Comfortable?"

"As I can be," I breathe, my skin prickling at her touch.

She gives me a small smile. "You can get closer, Zadyn, I'm not gonna bite."

I scoot forward until her back meets my chest. She's fitted flush against me, basically in my lap. The scent of her hair washes over me, and I want to bury my face in it.

This is going to be a long, torturous ride.

A moment later, we're airborne, disappearing into the stars.

"WHY IS IT FUCKING FREEZING HERE?"

I can hear Marideth's teeth chattering from across the fire.

We're nestled inside a glen of white-dusted evergreens just over the Hyraxian border. Snow-capped mountains surround us as we sit around the fire, watching the black smoke dissolve into the night sky.

The wind kicks up the snow clinging to the fir-lined boughs, sending soft wisps swirling around us. Serena shivers beside me. I slide my jacket off and sling it around her shoulders, then tuck her into my side.

"Body heat." She gives me a grateful nod.

Yeah, keep telling yourself that, bud.

"So do we have a plan, or are we just going to wing it?" Kai drawls.

"I have a friend here who might be able to help us," I respond.

We fall back into silence. Derek's loss hangs overhead, consuming every bit of air in the glen. I can feel the sorrow rolling off Serena, dimming the light that always seems to hover around her.

"Maybe we should say a few words," Dover suggests, glancing around the fire. "For the king."

Everyone is quiet, staring into the flames.

"I'll start." Kai presses to his feet, struggling to balance on his good leg.

"Derek was a good male and a strong king. Far better than my mother deserved. I wasn't always his favorite—in fact, I don't think I *ever* was. But the day we met, he clapped me on the back and looked me in the eye. It was the first time someone had done that in years. Looked me in the eye and actually saw me. And he said"—Kai smiles to himself— "'I'm sorry for your loss. But know that you always have a home here. And a father if you so desire. My door is always open.'"

He lets out a bleak laugh. "With that one line, he was more of a father to me than mine ever was. I regret not taking him up on it. The open door. The fatherhood. I regret not being his son."

Kai lifts his flask, takes a sip, and pours some of its contents onto the freshly fallen snow. "Long live the king."

"He was kind," Marideth murmurs, her hand twining with Dover's. "Fierce. And generous. He loved his kingdom, and he died defending it. There's honor in that."

"He welcomed all of us. Depraved as we are," Dover says, a nostalgic smile on his face. "How many times he could have tossed us out and banished us for corrupting his daughter."

Kai snickers. "She corrupted us first, and everyone knows it."

"He was a friend to my parents," I find myself saying. "He loved them. He didn't know me, had no reason to put his faith in me, but he did. Trusted me to be on his council. He's probably half the reason I'm here today."

The last link to my parents may be gone, but if not for Derek, they would never have bound me to Serena in the first place. I could have gone a lifetime not knowing her. A lifetime missing someone I'd never met.

I guess I have him to thank for that.

"I was too slow," Serena blurts, lost in the fire. "I was too slow. If I had screamed sooner, he might still be here."

I angle myself toward her. "This was not your fault. Alright? This is on Kylian and those monsters," I tell her, but I don't think she hears me.

"I could have stopped it. Derek—" She breaks off.

Then the flames begin to swell, blasting upward with a loud rush. All of us amble backward except for Serena. She doesn't move. She stares, entranced by the flames, and that's when I realize she's the one doing it.

"Serena." I clasp her shoulders, shaking her. The flames burst higher as she watches, a slave to her own magic. "Serena, the flames. You have to calm down."

Furi lets out a whine, shifting around in circles, tail tucked between her legs. Serena trembles as her knees crash into the snow.

"Serena, look at me."

"It isn't fair. Twice. I had to lose him twice. How is that—how is that fair…" She shakes her head as the flames surge again. I take her face in my hands, sinking down in front of her.

"It's not, sweetheart, it's not. But you have to breathe. You have to leave that fire alone."

Leave it alone, I urge.

Finally, her eyes snap to me, some awareness budding there. The flames recede to normal magnitude, and her face goes blank like she just woke up in an unfamiliar place. She opens her mouth, but something draws her attention upward, and she gasps.

Above us is a myriad of colors painting the starry sky every color of the rainbow.

"What is that?" she asks in wonder.

"The Alto Luminaria. Northern lights," I translate, following her gaze upward.

"I've never seen anything so beautiful."

I have.

"It's rare to be able to see them this clearly from across the sea. They're supposed to be a harbinger of good luck."

"About fucking time," Dover mutters.

Serena watches the lights wave through the sky like a color-changing flag. She blinks as something wet lands on her cheek.

Then it starts to snow.

Grief paused, I catch her smile—actually smile—stretching her palms out to catch the flakes. The others stare at her like she's crazy while I fight the urge to grab her and put my mouth on hers.

"Fucking fantastic," Mar drones.

"You guys don't like snow? What's wrong with you?"

"I don't like to be cold and wet," Mar says, staring up at the flurries with contempt.

Serena scoops up a handful of snow, patting it into a tight ball. It smacks into Mar's back with a satisfying thump.

Mar whirls, silver eyes blazing. "I hope you find hypothermia funny!"

Wasting no time, she packs together a ball of her own. Serena cackles as it hits her sleeve and crumbles. Mar's stone face cracks, and a reluctant giggle slips out.

"Well. It's official." Kai leans back as white flakes begin to dust his raven hair. "They've snapped."

His face lashes to the side as Serena pelts him with a wicked throw.

Then it's war. We fight until our faces, our fingers, our toes are numb. The flakes continue to fall in thick clumps, dusting our heads and soaking through our clothes until the whole forest is covered in a smooth white blanket.

I sink down, breathless, beside Serena, who's splayed out in the snow, arms spread wide like an angel. Her head falls toward me, frost turning her cheeks the perfect shade of pink.

"Hi." She smiles, and it knocks the wind from me.

She has the best smile. Her entire face lights up, and it's just stunning. I have to look away before I can speak.

"Mar was right. One of us is bound to lose a limb if we stay out here any longer."

We find a cave not too far away. Furi curls up at the mouth, blocking out some of the harsh wind. Serena sparks another fire, and we huddle close to the flames, Dover spooning Mar and Kai spooning Dover.

And me spooning Serena.

Because that's not awkward at all. Though she doesn't seem to mind, fitting herself against me as if it's the most natural thing in the world.

I'm finally starting to doze when I feel her shudder against me.

"Are you still cold?" I ask, leaning over her. She shakes her head, eyes squeezed shut, tears glistening on her cheek. "Serena."

He's dead. Her lip trembles despite how hard she's clamping down on it.

My shoulders sink. *I know.*

It felt like I had just gotten him back, you know? Even in my mind, her thoughts are a whisper. *I thought we'd have more time. I thought maybe he could know me. I didn't get to say goodbye. I didn't get to say anything.*

I cradle her face, feeling her pain, her sorrow wash over me like a tidal wave. She rolls over to face me and buries herself in my chest. My heart comes apart for her.

What I wouldn't give to be able to absorb all that pain, to take it from her. Yet for all the magic in this world, I can't do anything but hold her while she cries herself to sleep.

I wake with her still tucked against me, her head lolling against my bicep. Rather than jostling her, I accept that I might lose the limb and lower my head back down to rest beside hers.

This feels so right—waking up to her curled against me. But then those long, heavy lashes lift, and I come crashing right back down to earth.

I'm still thinking about it as we load onto Furi's back and sail into the frigid skies.

"Head northeast," I say from behind her in the saddle. Furi glides onward until the dark iron spires of Castle Bellsphere come into view.

"This is where you want to land? Are you sure?" Serena shouts over the wind, twisting to look at me.

I nod. "Trust me."

She chuckles. "You're lucky I do."

34

SERENA

When one finds themselves flying through a winter-wonderland, one expects the local castle to be a replica of Elsa's ice palace.

My hopes and dreams are crushed as I stare down at what looks like a fortified prison.

Castle Bellsphere has all the makings of a war academy—cold, dark, and fucking terrifying—crafted from iron and stone. To make matters worse, it's situated at the very peak of a mountain, and the temperature is just *rude*.

We circle overhead while Zadyn shifts into a white falcon and flies down to the gates. Once we get the signal to join him, Furi deposits us on the other side of a crumbling stone bridge arching over a heart-stopping drop into a rushing river below. Brawny guards patrol the perimeter—their fur pelts the only thing standing between their naked backs and the icy wind.

"How are they not freezing?" I ask Zadyn as we make our way past.

"They're raised from childhood to withstand the temperatures. Elemental training."

I quirk a brow. "That sounds insane."

"Hyrax is known for its indomitable military. They're trained

179

young to be ruthless and relentless, more beast than fae. Did you see those massive tents set up in the mountains as we flew in?"

I nod.

"Those are training camps. They span for miles. The best soldiers, the best killers come from there."

I shudder. Not from the cold this time.

"Why are we here, Zadyn?"

The portcullis rises with an ancient groan as we cross the snow-dusted courtyard.

"The prince and I are old friends. He may be able to help us. Besides, I want to give him a heads up about Vod invading. Aegar could use all the aid it can get, and this will give them time to prepare for any possible attacks."

There is no element of luxury to the castle as we make our way through the dim, torchlit halls. It's all bones, no flesh—everything a wash of slate gray. Archaic stone and crumbling pillars bracket the walkway as a pair of hulking guards lead us down the corridor.

The wind howls, snapping at us through the open arches. Why in god's name would they have windows here that don't close? In temperatures that have to be below zero?!

Mar and I huddle close together, shaking like leaves behind Zadyn.

A handsome male in a simple crown fashioned from iron appears at the other end of the hall. Like the guards, he wears a fur pelt slung over one bare shoulder.

"Well, well, well." He holds out his thick arms when he spots Zadyn. "What's it been, a century?"

"Not nearly long enough," Zadyn jokes.

The Prince of Hyrax is a strapping, blonde-haired, blue-eyed golden boy. He greets Zadyn with a bear hug and a hearty clap on the back. Spying us over Zadyn's shoulder, he steps back, hands on his hips.

"Lord Rhodes, please introduce me to your friends." He flashes us a lopsided smile that makes him look positively up to no good.

"Prince Eaton Berringer, I'd like you to meet Marideth, Dover,

Prince Kai of Vod—" Zadyn's hand lands on the small of my back. "And this is Serena."

Eaton glances between us a few times, looking intrigued.

"Za-dyn," he sings, breaking his name into two syllables. "Is this… your *bond*?"

Zadyn nods. Prince Eaton breaks into a loud laugh, smacking Zadyn's back so hard he coughs.

"Well, shit. Lucky dog. Pleased to make your acquaintance, all of you. You are very welcome here. Come."

He waves us forward in the direction he came.

"Had I known you'd be joining us, I would have had a feast hot and ready for your arrival." Eaton casts a pointed glance at Zadyn.

"Where's the fun in that?" he says, smiling. "I know how much you love surprises."

Eaton laughs again, a deep, resonant sound. "Alix will be happy to see you."

Zadyn blows out a long breath. They exchange light banter as I watch from behind. I've never seen Zadyn bro out like this before. It's kind of adorable.

Prince Eaton leads us to a line of rooms, offering one to Mar and Dover and one to Kai. Then, opening the door to a cozy room with a massive bed and roaring fire, he says to Zadyn, "You two can share a room. You don't mind, do you, old friend?"

Eaton gives him a shit-eating grin.

"Of course not," Zadyn says through a gritted smile. "The daybed is fine for me."

"Thought so. I'll leave you to dress. Dinner's in ten."

Zadyn and I quickly change into the clothes hanging in the wardrobe and make our way toward a set of tall wooden doors. He pushes them open, and I blink at the revelry within.

"If this is dinner, then what's a feast like here?"

"You don't want to know."

The hall is loud, lit with a thousand tapered candles and filled with boisterous fae in fur pelts and no-nonsense clothing. The females are robust and sturdy in practical wool dresses, some even wearing tight pants tucked into riding boots.

"There you are!" Eaton calls from behind the head table. "I thought Zadyn would need more time to primp. Come, sit." He pats the empty seats beside him.

"Where's your father?" Zadyn asks, pulling out a chair for me.

"Hunting retreat, where else?" Eaton rolls his eyes as a servant pours wine into his waiting cup. "Alix will be down soon."

I slide Zadyn a curious look.

Alix?

Just another old friend.

"How do you two know each other?" I venture, leaning around Zadyn to glance at the prince.

"I rescued Zadyn from a pack of thieves about a million years ago." Eaton takes a greedy sip of wine, wiping his mouth on the back of his hand.

"What he means to say"—Zadyn gives him a stern glance—"is that I rescued *him* and his entire caravan from a pack of thieves."

"It was love at first sight." Eaton flings a chiseled arm around Zadyn's shoulder and gives him a shake. "Our dear Zadyn has a savior complex, if you haven't noticed."

I laugh, taking a sip of wine. Eaton bends to whisper something to Zadyn, then slumps back, a knowing look on his face. Now I'm curious about what couldn't be said for the entire room.

Zadyn clears his throat and continues, "I traveled with Eaton and his siblings for a few decades."

"Oh." I nod.

Mar slips into a seat beside me, Dover on her other side, and Kai near the end of the table, charming the hell out of a female with a wedding band around her finger.

Lively music picks up from a few minstrels in the corner, and some of the fae break from their dinner to dance. The wine and beer keep flowing, everyone here at ease, merry, and unapologetically down to earth. It's nothing like the polished, carefully cultivated court of Aegar.

"So," Eaton says to Zadyn, "to what do I really owe this surprise visit? I know it's not because you couldn't live without me."

"It's a little heavy for dinner conversation," Zadyn warns. Eaton shrugs and waves a hand for him to speak. "The portal."

"What of it?"

"Well, for one thing, we know what happened to it. To the Guardians."

Eaton looks up, suddenly alert.

"The King of Vod somehow destroyed them and gained control of the portal. He's amassing an army of foreign creatures who have sworn obeisance to him in exchange for passage into our world."

"How do you know this?"

"Because he told me," I answer.

For the first time, Eaton seems to notice my eyes. He leans closer, his brow creasing as he studies me. I allow my pupils to constrict, narrowing into black slits and then back into round dots.

He nearly falls out of his chair.

"Mother of Zed." He swallows hard, his sun-kissed face paling a shade. "You didn't tell me your bond was the last Blackblood."

"What kind of familiar would I be if I had?" Zadyn says. "Serena was being held captive by Kylian. He tried to force her into marriage so they could perform the Bloodfast, but we got there in time."

Eaton's eyes narrow, shifting down the table to Kai. "And you're running around with the bastard's kid brother?"

"Kai is nothing like his family," I say defensively. "He did everything he could to keep me safe there. He's on our side."

"And what side is that?"

Then it dawns on me. Eaton is *afraid* of me. He thinks that with my power, I might be a threat to his home. To his kingdom.

"The side that wants to keep Kylian from conquering this world," I say earnestly.

Eaton sucks in a long breath, swirling his empty chalice. "I am far too sober for this."

The towering wooden doors to the hall swing open, pausing our conversation, and in walk three striking fae with hair the same shade as the prince's.

The first is a male, slightly taller than Eaton, veins bulging on his shredded arms and pecs. That one looks like Zeus and Chris Hemsworth had a baby. The male beside him looks more adolescent—shaggy curls, not quite as tall or bulky as the first. And then there's the female.

Nearly as tall as her brothers, she is statuesque and severe like an Amazon, clad in tan-colored leathers with a white fur pelt thrown over her back. Her blonde hair is plaited into an intricate braid that falls to her hips, swaying as she walks with all the cocky confidence of the males at her side.

Zadyn stands and walks around the table to meet her. My eyes narrow in confusion.

"Hello, Alix."

Alix greets him with a punch to the face.

35

SERENA

The sound of her fist meeting Zadyn's jaw is enough to make me cringe and to send him stumbling back into the table. I shoot to my feet as goblets of wine teeter over, soaking the tablecloths and linens.

My fingers start sparking at my sides.

Zadyn lets out a laugh, brushing the caramel hair out of his face as he straightens. "I probably deserved that."

"Probably?" The female cocks her hip, giving him a vicious once-over.

"Definitely."

Eaton bursts into a loud guffaw, holding his gut and stomping his foot under the table. The two males beside Alix break into handsome smiles and clap Zadyn on the back. My shoulders slowly relax, and I unspool my clenched fists.

"Brave male to show your face back here. I admire your balls," says the bigger one, his voice a deep rumble, like thunder itself.

"I thought it was time," Zadyn answers warmly.

The younger of the two leans in. "I wouldn't get too close. She's still got her hunting knife on her."

185

Zadyn ruffles the boy's shaggy blonde hair before slipping back into his seat.

"It's a long story," he says to me.

"Apparently so."

We're briefly introduced to Eaton's siblings as they plop down across from us. I try not to stare, but my curiosity has me sneaking glances every so often.

The princes make light conversation, catching up with Zadyn, while the princess stabs at her food like a psycho killer, eyes burning holes into her plate. I can't help but guess she's picturing Zadyn's face on that meat as she rips it apart.

Mar and I exchange a knowing look and decide to keep our mouths shut for now.

Dinner stretches on far longer than I want it to. I'm exhausted, and my thighs are screaming from hours of riding. That bed with the fur throws is calling my name.

Finally, Eaton stands, tossing down his napkin and turning to us.

"Come on. I'm taking you all out."

"No, no, no." Zadyn shakes his head. "We didn't come here to party."

"Yes, you did. Don't lie to me, Zadyn, I know you. Up you go." Eaton hauls him up and walks over to his siblings, popping his head between his brothers' shoulders.

"Care to join?"

They turn, their mouths full and fingers greasy from tearing apart their dinner with their bare hands. "Where are you going?"

"Black Rabbit."

"Hah!" Alix's bark has each of our heads snapping toward her. "Typical."

She pops a green bean into her mouth. To her credit, she is a more delicate eater than her brothers.

"You're welcome to join, as always, but I know how you hate fun," Eaton quips. She slides her brother a death stare. For a moment, I wonder if she's going to punch him too.

"Thank you for the warm invitation, brother, but I'd rather stick pins in my eyes."

"Well. You can borrow my sewing kit," Eaton says brightly, turning on his heels and clapping for us to follow.

"Don't push it, I think it's her *female time*," the younger brother, Landyn, murmurs to Eaton.

"Pfft," he scoffs. "Is it ever not?"

"Hey." I tug on Zadyn's arm and drop my voice. "How do you know we can trust the princes?"

He gives me a soft smile. "Well, for one, I've known them a long time. They're good, loyal people. And of course, it helps that Eaton's always been a little in love with me," he boasts.

I can't help but chuckle. "One of the many, I'm sure."

We drop by our rooms to grab cloaks, and then we're filing out into the freezing night and loading into a carriage. The mountain roads are bumpy, jostling us every few seconds as we wind down the narrow path.

"So." Eaton bumps my arm, waggling his brows.

"So what?"

"Did you bring her?" He lowers his voice and leans in. "The dragon," he all but mouths.

I snicker. "Yes."

"Can I see her?"

I have swam in rivers of blood and feasted on the bones of my enemies. Please inform the boy prince that I am no sideshow curiosity to be ogled.

Ignoring Furi's homicidal commentary, I answer, "Yes, you can see her tomorrow. But just to warn you, she only allows Zadyn to pet her. And me, of course."

"Of course." He cranes his neck to peer at Zadyn, who rolls his eyes.

The carriage slows to a stop, and we step out into a village teeming with life. People bustle down the busy avenues and torchlit bridges, bundled in fur-lined cloaks and tightly wrapped scarves. A light dusting of snow covers the homes and shops lining the uneven cobblestone streets, their curtained windows lit from within. The city is quaint and charming in a way I'd expect the North Pole to be.

We stop before an unmarked door. "Hoods up," Eaton says, a wickedness in his voice.

I glance up at Zadyn. "Where are we?"

"You're about to find out."

Eaton knocks twice, and the door creaks open. Warm candlelight pours out as a voluptuous redhead appears in the threshold, eyeing us up one at a time.

Eaton holds out a small velvet purse, which she dumps into her palm. Seeming content with the silvers, she gives us a toothy smile and holds the door for us to pass.

Long gauzy curtains are staggered throughout the space, creating a depthless illusion. Bodies move between the suspended panels, and from their silhouettes, it is very clear that they are very naked.

I clap a hand over my mouth. "Oh my god, this is a pleasure hall?!"

Zadyn chuckles and nods.

"The one in Vod didn't look like this."

"*That* was not a pleasure hall. That was a high-end brothel with a very specific clientele. This place is more like…a local dive."

Arms linked, we make our way into the endless maze. The shadows dance behind the low-lit strips of cloth, intertwining in time to the music. The cloying scent of sex and sweat rolls over us. It's palpable.

I sneak glances at the shadowy figures in various states of undress. Limbs entangle, writhing on velvet settees. They kneel on soft throws and floor pillows, locked in intimate embraces. My cheeks heat, the urge to cover my eyes growing with every step, but no one else seems to bear the same sense of shame. Instead, they look on unabashedly, their gazes returned by hungry, lust-ridden eyes.

We approach a wall of thick crimson curtains, rhythmic music thumping from the other side. I cling to Zadyn.

"You okay?" He smirks down at me.

"Yeah. Just not used to this sort of thing. I've never even been to a strip club."

His laugh reverberates against me. "It's not so taboo here. People come here to express their deepest desires—to live out their fantasies. Everyone has them. The fae are just less—"

"Prudish?"

"Inhibited." He leans down, murmuring softly in my ear, "You don't have to look away. That's kind of the point."

"To watch?"

"Watch, join, whatever piques your interest."

"I think it's going to take some time to become accustomed to how, uh, free the fae are."

"We have all the time in the world."

The princes sweep back the curtains, and darkness devours us. Red light pulses in time to the hypnotic music, illuminating a cluster of dancing bodies in the center of the space. Tall exotic plants line the walls, their branches dangling overhead.

I think I just stepped into my first faerie rave.

We form a daisy chain, squeezing through the tight-pressed crowd. A pair of tall, statuesque females work their way over to us, stripping off our cloaks and offering us shots from a tray. Aside from the swirling paint transforming their bodies into ethereal works of art, they're not wearing a stitch of clothing. And every male in our group —including Zadyn—is quick to notice.

I fight back an eye roll as Kai passes me a shot of sparkling green liquid.

"Do you think this is smart?" I call to Mar over the music.

"Probably not, but we did recently escape death for about the hundredth time," she deadpans.

I look from her to the shot. "Fuck it."

"Fuck it," she echoes as we clink glasses and toss them back. The sour taste hits my tongue, making me shudder. My friends instantly give in to the music, but the buzz is slower to hit me. I stand there awkwardly, feeling like the odd man out.

"You're tense." Kai is suddenly at my side, speaking over the noise.

"I am not."

I'm just not in the mood for a party. Wonder why.

He purses his lips at my standoffish posture. Tossing him a boastful look, I grab two more shots off a passing tray and throw them back, one after another. He breaks into a pearly smile, satisfied with the results of his peer pressure.

The red strobe flares, and for a moment, it isn't Kai standing there.

It's Kylian.

It's *his* eyes peering down at me in a darkened bedroom. It's his mouth taunting me, reminding me of my betrayal. Turning my desire into a dagger. I stumble back a step.

"Savior?" The lights shift, and Kai is himself again.

"I'm okay."

I'm okay. I'm okay. Just breathe.

Distraction. That's what I need.

I pull Mar from Dover's arms. "Let's dance."

Kai has no trouble finding a partner, instantly surrounded by women. Neither does Eaton, who's sandwiched between a male and female who look about ready to devour him. I try to find my groove with the strange, foreign music, but I can't catch the beat or figure out how to move my body.

"Relax," Mar says, shaking my shoulders.* I nod stiffly.

She takes hold of my hips and steers me like a puppeteer. Once I get familiar with the motion, she lifts her slender arms above her head in slow, languid strokes—moving as if submerged in water. I mirror her, easing into the melody.

She twines our fingers and twists around, putting her back to me and drawing me closer. The liquor begins to take effect, warming me and melding us together until we're one sensuous wave moving in tandem.

My gaze lands on Zadyn across from us, his arms wrapped around a pretty fae in a plunging, skin-tight dress. His nose grazes the smooth line of her neck as she tilts her head to allow him better access. I can't bring myself to look away as he traces her curves, mapping out each dip, each hard line and soft patch of flesh.

---

* Cue: *So Hot You're Hurting My Feelings* by Caroline Polachek

It's mesmerizing.

Zadyn's eyes snap up to mine as if I'd called his name.

The drums pound in the background, shaking the floor and echoing deep in my bones. I can feel them everywhere, pulsing in me, throbbing in time to my rapid heartbeat.

I trail my fingers over Mar's shoulder. Zadyn's heavy-lidded gaze tracks the movement before flickering back up to mine.

He looks so good.

Maybe it's the alcohol. Or maybe it's *not*.

He takes hold of the female's neck, slowly lowering his mouth to it. It's quite possibly the sexiest thing I've ever seen.

The veins in his arms go taut, flexing around her waist as she gives him her weight. But his eyes are on mine.

Locked.

The heat rolling off him transfers to me, making me feverish.

I told you it can be fun to watch.

His voice is a velvet-soft brush against mind. He clutches her skirt, planting slow, agonizing kisses up the column of her throat, and I can almost *feel* them on me.

"Now you've got the hang of it." Mar slips behind me, a sleepy smile on her lips. With a gentle nudge forward, she says, "Go play."

Her warmth disappears, leaving me cold and exposed on the dance floor. Zadyn looks me up and down, a hunger like I've never seen turning his eyes glassy. His stare strips away layer after layer until it feels like I'm on display. Being watched. Being seen.

It's both terrifying and invigorating.

I want to look away. But I can't. Not as he releases the girl and starts walking toward me, his stride magnetic.

"You once warned me about the kind of dancing they do in pleasure halls."

"I remember." His voice carries no amusement as he peers down at me, searching my face.

I give him a shrug. "Show me."

Definitely the alcohol.

He glances up at the ceiling and lets out a laugh. "I don't know if that's the best idea."

God, I hate it when he's responsible.

"It's just dancing." But he doesn't budge. He stares at me, torturing me with his silence. "Alright, well, I'm sure I can find someone else to ask—"

I'm halfway turned when he snatches up my wrist and yanks me back against his chest. My breath leaves my body.

"One dance."

I twist my head to look up at him. *Yes, sir.*

Without breaking eye contact, his hand slides from my ribs down to my hips. He holds me tighter, fusing our laps together, then traces a line up the center of my body starting at my belly button and blazing a taunting trail between my breasts.

My entire body ignites.

I let my head fall back onto his chest as he palms the base of my neck. That simple touch holds so much power over me it's concerning. I'm glued to him, feeling parts of him I never have before—our movements slow, sensual. His free hand glides up my side, leaving little fires in its wake. I circle my hips deeper, grinding against him in the process.

"Serena," he growls.

"Zadyn." I intend to mimic his stern tone, but instead, it comes out like a breathy, need-filled plea.

Maybe *not* the alcohol? Fuck, I really don't know.

All I know is that I want him to do what he did to that female. I want his hands on me. His mouth.

I twist around, raking my nails down the nape of his neck and watching his eyes close. Another swirl of our hips has his length nudging against me, letting me know he's enjoying this as much as I am.

But then I remember.

Zadyn is my familiar. My friend. Have I no self-control? He'll do anything to please me, to make me happy. To go there with him would be taking advantage. I'd be abusing our bond.

I can't do that. Because if I ask or push him the way I did at solstice, I don't think he'll deny me—even if it isn't what he really wants.

He tugs me closer, and I fall into him, gripping his sturdy arms for support. I'm rummaging for the will to put some distance between us, but then his fingers slide into my hair, and my whole body aches for more. More of this side of him—this primal, dark hunger.

My breath becomes ragged as he leans his forehead against mine.

This will ruin your friendship, a tiny voice pipes from inside me.

But I want him.

Do I want him? Or do I just want to try him out? There's a big difference. And Zadyn is the last person in this world that I would want to play games with. He deserves more.

My muscles lock as I push out of his grasp, shaking my head. He blinks, his expression clearing as he tries to read me.

"I'm sorry," I whisper before darting into the crowd.

What am I doing?

I've always known Zadyn was beautiful. It just never fazed me before. Never made my heart lodge in my throat, never made me nervous. But lately, I've become hyperaware of him.

So what? Maybe I have a little crush.

One day I'll grow out of it, and in a decade we can look back and say, "Oh, remember when I wanted to eat your face and swallow you whole?"

It'll definitely be worth a laugh. I think.

God, this is confusing. Not to mention everything that's happened with Jace. My feelings for him haven't just gone away. Knowing I can't have him doesn't stop me from wanting him in a way that physically hurts.

Why is it so hard for me to just let him go?

Our last conversation has haunted me since I left. Asking me to marry him like some Hail Mary had hurt. Just like it had two years ago when Jack asked me to marry him because he thought I was pregnant. And I had run from him too.

The symmetry of that is just too perfect. Too cruel.

But now is not the time for any of this. Now is not the time for mixed feelings and boy drama. For horny dancing and green drinks and indecisiveness. Now is the time for problem solving. For portal closing and serious hats and mustaches.

God, I'm drunk.

I weave through the crowd, not really sure where I'm going until a hand clamps around my wrist, pulling me to a stop.

"What's wrong?"

"Nothing," I say to Mar. "Everything. I can't think in here."

"Let's go get some air."

She shoves me through the nearest door, into an empty hall painted the color of fresh blood. I slide down the length of the wall, taking a deep breath.

"Is this about Zadyn?"

I snap my gaze to her.

"I saw you two in there." Mar slumps down beside me and elbows me in the ribs. "Getting cozy."

"Stop, it's not like that."

"Well, if it was like that, let me just say…I approve."

"He's my familiar, Mar!"

"He's gorgeous, is what he is. And he will do everything in his power to make you happy. I am really not seeing the issue here."

"He's my best friend."

"Your *second* best friend," she amends, knocking her knee against mine.

"I'm just…so confused." My head flops into my hands.

"What is the damn problem?"

I usually appreciate Mar's no-nonsense talks. Sometimes I need someone to tell me to pull it together, but right now, it feels like I'm crumbling.

There is so much I haven't even begun to process. Like my almost-marriage. Like sleeping with my mortal enemy—a male who would kill my friends with a smile on his face. Like seeing a future in which I am married to a monster, carrying his little monster babies.

I haven't told anyone about that. I really don't think I can.

Fighting back tears, I say, "We are so far off track right now. We're clubbing while Aegar could be under another attack. While Derek is dead. We're supposed to be closing the portal, and we're just raging until the sun comes up."

"Listen." Mar lays a gentle hand on mine. "When you live as long as we have, you realize that moments are all you have. Sometimes it's easier to laugh and smile through the hard times than it is to wallow. It hurts a hell of a lot less. One night is not going to make a difference. We'll get to work tomorrow."

Two large bodies crash through the door, banging into the wall. Our heads whip up to Zadyn and Eaton, cackling, arms slung around each other's shoulders. Their laughter cuts out at the sight of me blubbering on the floor.

"What's wrong?" Zadyn asks, dropping his smile.

"Serena's drunk and having a mental breakdown," Mar answers.

"I'm not drunk, and I'm not having a mental breakdown. I'm just… tired!" I cry, and *boy*, do I sound wasted.

Zadyn is there in an instant, crouching in front of me, his hands on my knees. "I should take her back."

"No, you should not," I slur.

Drunk bitch.

"You just said you were tired." Zadyn stifles a laugh. I am immediately offended.

"Hey!"

"I'm sorry—I'm sorry." He tries to bite his lip, but I can tell he's had a few more shots, and he's not very good at concealing it. "You're just so…"

"So *what*?"

"So—"

"You make a cute drunk! That's what our dear old friend here is trying to say. Isn't that right, Rhodesie?" Eaton kicks him on the butt.

I set my jaw. "I *hate* being called cute. It's degrading."

I agree, Furi announces, though I don't remember asking her.

My three friends burst into laughter, and I truly don't know why. I shove to my feet—a little too fast—but the wall is there to catch me.

"Okay, come on." Zadyn reaches for me. I try to rip my arm away, but I'm too slow. "We're leaving. You can yell at me the whole way back, let some of that anger out."

"There are far more effective ways of relieving anger, in case you didn't know," Eaton crows as Zadyn tries to corral me.

"Oh, Zadyn is well aware," I spit, wriggling against him. "He's an expert at relieving anger. He relieves it all the time, with any female who looks at him, right? He's just a fucking *machine*."

"Alright, I really need to get her back," he says to Eaton.

"Take the carriage. I'll call for another." He winks.

"Are you staying?" Zadyn asks Mar.

"I think you can handle this one on your own, don't you?" She smirks at me.

"Oh, don't give me that look, Mar," I growl. Then Zadyn is scooping me up in his arms and carrying me out the door. "If you don't put me down, I'm gonna torch your ass."

"You'll thank me tomorrow."

"Good night, dear! See you in the morning!" Eaton says with a wave.

We get to the carriage, and Zadyn tosses me inside like a sack of potatoes.

"I hate you right now."

He shuts the door and slides in across from me. "Good. What else?"

"*What else?*" I sputter.

"You want to get some things off your chest? Go ahead. I'm all ears."

"I don't know what you're talking about."

"Bottling it all up isn't going to do any good."

"Neither is blubbering about it."

"Serena."

"Alright! You want me to spill my guts? Fine. How about the fact that I'm a complete mess right now, and I can barely hold it together? How about the fact that I almost married my arch-nemesis? Or how I was dead, and then I wasn't, and now reality seems all fucked up? I don't know what the fuck I'm doing, and my feelings are in knots, and I just want to…I just—"

"What?"

"*I just want it to stop.*"

His eyes soften. "I know."

"Please don't try to make me feel better right now—"

"I'm not. I'm saying *I know.*"

I turn my face toward the window. "Who's Alix?"

"Eaton's sister."

"I mean, who is she to you? Did you have a thing?"

"Yes, you could say we had a *thing*. Briefly."

"What happened?"

"We were…spending time together—"

"You were fucking."

"Okay"—he sighs—"we were fucking, and then this happened."

He pulls his jacket aside and taps his finger against the tattoo over his heart. Two interlocking circles with a star in the center. The mark of a familiar.

"And I left. Without saying goodbye."

"And now?"

"Now she hates me." He shrugs.

I let out a scoff, staring out the frosted glass. "I bet. Do you want to be with her?"

"No. Why would you ask that?"

"Because after she punched you, I thought you were either going to fistfight or screw right there on the table."

"First off, I'd never hit a female. And second—would that have pissed you off?" A slow smirk tugs at his lips.

"For the last time—"

"You don't care what I do, blah blah blah, you're not jealous—"

"You know what, Zadyn?"

"What, Serena?"

"I'll admit that I'm jealous when you admit that *you're* jealous."

"Of what?"

"Of me. And Jace." I cross my arms. "You were jealous."

He stares at me for a second, then leans forward, resting his elbows on his knees.

"Yes. I was jealous. Insanely. Still am."

Heat floods my face. I open my mouth and then close it, stunned by how easy that was for him to confess.

"Fine." I stick my chin in the air, refusing to look at him. "So was I."

He leans back, fighting a smug little smile. It takes me a minute to realize I'm doing the same.

36

SERENA

Silk sheets slide between my legs.

Calloused palms glide over my shoulders and the ruby choker at my throat. It begins to constrict, cutting off my air supply. I choke, clutching at the smooth, cold gems with skeleton hands. I try to scream, but nothing comes out.

Ocean eyes hover above me, glowing in the dark as Kylian's soft lips ghost over mine.

There is nowhere on this earth you can go that I will not find you. You belong to me.

His whisper slathers goosebumps over my skin.

He smiles a wicked, cruel smile before I take my final breath.

"SERENA!" Someone is shaking me. "Wake up! It's just a dream. Look at me, open your eyes."

I fly awake, finding Zadyn leaned over me.

"What happened?" I croak.

"You were screaming. I woke up, and you were covered in shadows. I think you were about to shadow walk in your sleep." Zadyn's

grip on my shoulders loosens. He sinks onto the bed beside me. "What the hell were you dreaming about?"

I sit up, clasping my neck.

I'm free. That collar is buried in the depths of the Praxian Sea, along with its matching ring.

"I've been having nightmares."

"For how long?"

I shrug. I can't remember the last time I slept without them.

"Why didn't you tell me?"

"What could you have done? Fought them off?"

"If that's what it took." I'm surprised at the earnestness behind his statement.

I swallow the pins in my throat, staring straight ahead, seeing something that isn't there. Lost in the memories of Kylian touching me, holding me until he fell asleep. Of his fingers weaving through mine as he ground them into the mattress. Of how my body responded to him against my will.

I blink, and the images clear like smoke.

"You don't have to talk about it unless you want to. But you need to know that I don't fault you for what you did. You were surviving."

"I said I wasn't ashamed of what I did. And I'm not," I start, trying to find the right way to express the complicated knot of feelings I have over what happened with Kylian. "But I do feel ashamed of how I felt."

The instant the words leave my mouth, I want to suck them back in. Zadyn studies me, waiting for me to elaborate.

"How did you feel?" he asks without a hint of judgment.

"I hate him. And I hated the thought of doing what I did. I *should* have hated every second. It should have made me physically ill." I stare at the bed, feeling like I could burn a hole through it.

"But you didn't hate it."

I shake my head, holding in tears, but my stupid lip trembles.

"He wasn't rough with me like I expected. He didn't force me. It just…happened. He never actually hurt me, not physically." I swallow.

"I found myself thinking about how much I should have hated it, and I…"

A choked laugh escapes me as I hug my knees to my chest.

"What kind of sick monster enjoys being with another monster? There's something so, so wrong with me. I'm fucking sick in the head, I'm so demented."

My chest tightens. My mouth races to catch up to my mind—spewing words until I run out of air. Zadyn slides closer, cupping my cheeks.

"Stop, stop, stop. Breathe." He grounds me, holding my gaze until the panic subsides and my breath returns.

"There were moments I felt sorry for him. Moments I actually forgot how horrible he really was. Moments he made me…even knowing all the things he'd done, after witnessing him nearly kill Kai day after day, and then I just go and fall into bed with him."

I bury my face in my palms.

"I don't expect you or Jace to understand—I don't even understand."

"I *do* understand. I understand that whatever happened between you, whatever you did to survive, resulted in a lot of complicated, conflicting emotions. That's only natural. You are not a monster, Serena. You are not a monster for *feeling* things."

"Yes, I am! I felt things for my enemy. For a murderer, for my captor!"

"Do you love him?" Zadyn asks, cutting me off. I open my mouth, a bit stunned by the question.

"No—"

"Then there's nothing to worry about. We're talking about sex under duress here. It's all gray area. There is no right or wrong to whatever feelings came with it, even positive ones. Not to mention, he's a siren—who knows what he could have planted in your head."

"He never used his magic on me." I wait for his horrified expression. But it doesn't come. He just stares at me, his face concerned but unmoving. "Everything I felt, everything I did and even initiated was real. I was the one feeling those things, doing those things—oh my *god*."

I'm going to be sick.

"You're not going to convince me you're a monster. I don't care what you initiated, I don't care what you did and how many times, I don't fucking care if you liked it. All I care about is that you are safe right now in front of me, and that I can make sure nothing like this ever happens again."

His fingers thread through my hair, and those brown eyes thaw some of the ice in my veins. I nod as a charged moment passes between us. Then he looks away, easing back from me.

"I understand if you don't want to be touched right now."

"I'm okay," I assure him, glancing at his biceps. There's nothing quite as comforting as being locked between them.

As if reading my mind, he gives me a reluctant smile and opens his arms. Tucked beneath his chin, his hands linked around my waist, I feel small and warm and safe.

I feel at home.

"I'm sorry I let this happen," he says. "He's going to pay for ever hurting you."

"Please stop apologizing, and just hold me."

"I can do that."

His warmth envelops me, and I fall asleep with no more night-marish interruptions for the remainder of the night.

37

ZADYN

I wake early to Serena's steady sighs, each exhale breezing over my bare chest. She's sprawled out on her belly, half of her body draped over mine, an arm slung around my waist and a thigh hooked over my hip. I'd find it amusing if I wasn't so damn worried that with the slightest shift in movement, she might wake to find me hard, pressing against her leg.

I ease out of her grasp with glacial slowness, careful not to jostle her. Moving to the bathroom, I splash some cold water on my face, hoping it will cool me down enough to stop the thoughts that flood my mind every time I wake up with her body tangled around mine.

So completely inappropriate.

But as I grab a change of clothes, she rolls onto her back—dark hair fanning out over the pillow—and groans in her sleep. I have to bite my lip and clench my fists.

She's so fucking perfect.

But if last night proved anything, it's that she isn't ready for this. She may never be. All I am to her is a friend. Her familiar.

I'm one hundred and ninety-eight years old. I've had almost two centuries of experience with females, and not one has given me the

203

trouble this girl has. Not one has had me tongue tied at every turn. Not one has had me awestruck and so pathetically whipped.

I used to think I felt this way because I'm her familiar. But I've done my research on the subject, and what I feel for her is something else entirely.

Once I change, I scribble a note for Serena and head out.

Eaton is exactly where I expected to find him. Holed up in his sanctuary.

Despite being a fierce warrior prince and second in line to his father's throne, Eaton is actually a skilled historian. His family's library is double the size of the one in Aegar, with family trees and records of magical objects dating back to the beginning of Solterre. Even hungover, he's seated beside the crackling fire, feet propped up with a heavy tome on his lap.

"Enjoy the rest of your night?" he mutters without looking up. I slip into the seat beside him.

"Subtle."

"No one's ever accused me of that before." He snickers, sipping his tea.

"We need to finish our conversation from dinner last night."

He glances up at me and sets the saucer down on the wooden side table. "All ears."

Eaton listens as I explain our predicament.

"You need to tell your father to prepare."

"I'll write to him today. He'll send troops to Aegar. Or he'll send fleets straight to Vod to crush them on their own turf."

I nod.

"As for the rest—" He stands and moves over to the nearest wall of records. "There has to be something in here to help with the portal."

We spend the next two hours sifting through texts and translating the ones in Ancient Fae.

"This might be something," he mutters, sliding the thick tome from the top shelf and passing it down the ladder to me.

"What is this?"

"It's a grimoire, recovered from one of the first Blackbloods."

The wrinkled spine looks ready to disintegrate at any given moment—its leather binding almost completely faded. I move to flip it open, but it refuses.

"It's spelled. Never could get it to open."

I glance at him. "This could have our answer."

"Maybe your witch is the key."

My fingers ghost over the surface, so thin and worn I'm afraid if I touch it, it might crumble. The grimoire is charged, like all magical objects. They teem with life, even in their ancient state.

Eaton sinks into a wooden chair, and I do the same, pushing my hair out of my face.

"You need a haircut."

"Thanks."

He kicks back in his seat, drumming his fingers on the table. After a moment, he says, "You know what she is, don't you?"

I drag my eyes up to him. "How could I not?"

"Does *she* know?"

"No. And I don't plan on telling her. Not right now, at least."

"Gods, Zadyn. Any fool could read the writing on the wall. Why does she think you can peer into each other's minds the way you can?"

"Because I'm her familiar. She thinks nothing of it. She's not from here, she wouldn't know the difference."

Serena is too new to magic to understand our connection—the direct link we have to each other's minds. I didn't want to overwhelm her by letting her know that, unfettered, I can literally read her mind.

Not that I would. But sometimes her thoughts are so loud, I can hear them even when I don't want to. Even when it feels like a knife to the gut.

"You're more than her familiar, Zadyn. You're her primary. Do you know how rare that is?"

I do, actually.

"It's worse if you don't tell her. She's going to find out eventually, and then you'll have to lie about knowing, and it will be a whole mess that could easily have been avoided if you'd just gazed into those pretty lavender eyes, and said, '*Serena, darling, you're my—*'"

"Stop, Eaton. Just stop."

"What are you afraid of? That she won't accept it?"

"I'm not afraid of anything. And that has nothing to do with why we're here. I'm not telling her."

Eaton lifts his hands in surrender.

"Not telling who what?"

I turn as Serena breezes into the library, her dark hair still damp and clinging to her shoulders. I wave a hand and dry it for her. She smiles in thanks and plops into the seat beside me. Eaton appraises her with no attempt at discretion.

"Nothing," I mutter.

Miraculously, she doesn't press the question.

"What's that?" She points to the grimoire on the table.

"This is a grimoire. It belonged to one of the original Blackblood witches."

Eaton nudges it toward her, and she pours over it, transfixed. "We were hoping you might be able to help crack it."

She glances between us. "How?"

He reaches out and takes her hand, laying her palm flat against the binding.

As soon as her skin meets the book, she gasps.

3 8

SERENA

If I were a library in a spooky, stony castle, where would I be?

I collide with a body as I round the corner and rebound off a pair of rock-hard boobs. Alix stands before me, her harsh blue eyes pinned on mine.

"I'm sorry, I should have been watching my step," I mutter, half expecting her to rip my head from my body. She's got a good five inches on me and was raised with three brothers.

"Have you seen Zadyn? He said he'd be in the library, but I have no idea where that is," I blurt, eager to break the uncomfortable silence.

"Is that a serious question?" She snorts, crossing her arms. "Library is that way. Don't be surprised if he's not in there. He and Eaton practically lived at that whorehouse before he left to find you."

My stomach turns to lead. Alix angles her head, her long braid falling over her back as she takes an intimidating step closer.

"Just between you and me, Zadyn's not the type to stay. Even if—" She breaks off.

"Even if what?"

"Oh, wow. You really don't know, do you?" She looks at me with sardonic pity and brushes past, knocking my shoulder in the process. "Clueless."

207

"I'm sorry, *what*?" I call after her, but she's already halfway down the hall with her annoyingly long legs. I heave a frustrated groan and continue my quest.

"…not telling her."

I follow the faint sound of Zadyn's voice, feeling a bit of relief as I step into my version of heaven.

The library is stunning—dark, warm, and full of rich texture. It's even bigger than the one in Aegar, with hanging tapestries, lacquered wood and leather furniture, and a blazing fire beneath a stony mantle to offset the snow and mist swirling outside the arching windows. It smells just right—like old parchment and endless wisdom.

"Not telling who what?"

Zadyn twists around in his seat, his cheeks flushing pink when he sees me. He waves a hand, and my hair is suddenly dry. I love it when he does that.

"Nothing," he says quickly. I'm about to push for an actual answer when I notice the thick, dusty tome on the table between him and Eaton, and I can't look away.

"What's that?"

"This is a grimoire. It belonged to one of the original Blackblood witches."

"We were hoping you might be able to help crack it."

"How?"

Eaton grabs my hand and presses it to the worn cover. A jolt of electricity zaps through me, wracking me with violent tremors.

"What's wrong?" Zadyn grabs my arm, and jerks back with a loud hiss.

I rip my trembling hands from the book, stumbling out of my seat. "You felt it too?"

Zadyn nods, revealing two singed palms.

The grimoire flies open. Words in another language flood my vision, swirling around the room like a tornado—so fast and dizzying that I reel back into the table. Zadyn is calling my name, but I can't respond. Even closed, the writing remains pasted behind my eyes in vivid script.

I turn and slam the book shut.

The room stops spinning. With measured slowness, I pull back the cover.

"What the hell?"

The faded words on the page are gradually replaced by perfectly inked text. The volume is fully restored—its weathered binding now a sharp coal-black with gold foil running down the crisp edges.

"You and old books," I say to Zadyn. "Bad combination."

"I knew it. It must be keyed to black blood." Eaton sounds as awestruck as I feel.

A shimmering aura coils around the grimoire, calling to me.

Hello, my Queen.

I recoil at the words—the same ones whispered to me by the traveling mirror in Kylian's collection.

"Oh, I'm not—"

"Who are you talking to?" Zadyn asks.

"The book. The book was talking to me."

Zadyn and Eaton exchange a look.

"This is incredible. Can you feel that?"

Zadyn's chest brushes my back as he grazes the page with his index finger. "It's magnetic."

You come seeking answers.

Yes.

They will be yours, my Queen. You need only ask the right questions.

Is there a way to close the portal?

I'm met with silence.

Show me, I press.

In answer, the book slams itself shut.

Rude.

"Okay." I roll my neck. "Let's try this again."

Show me something useful. How can we defeat our enemy?

A beat passes. Then the pages begin to flip, landing on a passage I can scarcely read. A drawing occupies most of the page—silver lines connected by dots, creating an interesting shape across the parchment like some kind of zodiac constellation.

I gloss over the scribbled words that look like they'd been written with thoughtless haste. "What is this language? Is this Ancient Fae?"

Zadyn reads over my shoulder. "Some of it, but there are a lot of words here I don't recognize."

"Do you think you can interpret it?" I ask Eaton.

"May take me a few days, but I'll do my damndest."

"What did the book say to you, Serena?"

I swallow before answering Zadyn. "It told me our answers are in here—that I just need to ask the right questions."

"I'm sure this thing is full of valuable information. Besides. It technically belongs to you," Eaton points out.

And as the book hums in approval, I can tell that it agrees.

WE SPEND the next two days surrounded by towering mahogany shelves, scouring the library for any sort of lead. Eaton works on interpreting the passage, comparing it to other lost languages while we read up on spells and enchantments to offer any kind of solution, temporary or otherwise. But nothing we find can draw on enough energy to manipulate the portal.

"I think I've got some of this worked out."

"What have you got?" I move around the table, peering over Eaton's shoulder.

"It's some kind of spell. Well, more like notes on a spell. But it's confusing. A bunch of gibberish. It's like trying to solve an equation with numbers you've never even heard of."

"Does it say anything about the portal?"

"No." I frown as Eaton continues, "It's all coordinates and random notes. There are pages of them here." He flips onto the next one. "I can't quite figure out what they were attempting to do, but whoever wrote this was very interested in astrology." His finger plops down on the sketch weaving between the words. "This constellation in particular."

"Do you recognize it?"

"It's called the Aurea Dei. Translates to *Halo of the Gods*. It originally consisted of seven stars, but two have gone dark, so now there are five."

"What could that have to do with defeating Kylian or closing the portal?" Zadyn says.

"I have no fucking clue." I sink onto the table, exhaustion tugging at me. "Hey book?"

Its ears perk up at the sound of my voice.

Yes, my Queen?

"What does this have to do with the portal?" I ask, hoping this time it just spits out the answer like Siri and makes everything a hell of a lot simpler for us.

But the book seals itself up again, spitting dust at me in the process.

"Cool. Thanks so much."

It's dark by the time Eaton leads us to the empty kitchens, slipping into a large pantry and emerging with his hands full of snacks. Tragically, none of which include a Butterfinger.

"Damn it," he mutters. "I really thought that grimoire would be the key."

"I did too." Zadyn sighs, slumping back against the counter where I'm perched. "There's got to be something we're missing."

"I think that's a given," Kai says around a mouthful of grapes. Zadyn shoots him a dark look.

"Do you know who it belonged to?" I ask Eaton.

"Not sure exactly. My grandfather once told me it belonged to one of the first Blackbloods, but he never figured out who."

"One of the High Queens?"

"It's possible."

That would explain the book mistakenly calling me queen.

"Maybe if we could figure out more about the portal, then we might be able to understand the science behind it."

Eaton shakes his head. "That's where you're wrong, sunshine. It's not science. It's magic. And it doesn't always tend to make a lot of sense."

Propping his elbows on the butcher block island, he starts, "From what I've read, it dates back to the beginning of our world. No one is certain how it came to be. Some texts say it was a natural perforation that occurred during the forming of Solterre—making it easier for those with enough skill and power to walk between worlds that shared similar rifts. The High Queens began to worry about the kind of creatures that were passing through and decided it needed to be regulated. So they installed the Guardians."

Kai holds up a hand. "Random thought, but how could my brother have actually gained control of the portal?"

"I think the bigger question is how was he powerful enough to kill two Guardians?" Dover points out.

"It doesn't make sense. You'd have to be god to manipulate the portal like that. Even the witches couldn't." Eaton rustles his golden curls, his eyes landing on me. "Hence the Guardians."

"So just to be clear—the portal was essentially a gate?" I confirm. "Well, doesn't every gate have a key?"

"If there were a key, then why wouldn't the High Queens have used it themselves instead of sticking the Guardians out there?" Mar says.

Furi? I ask. *Your previous rider...did she ever mention anything about the portal or a key?*

I do not know of any key, Blackblood.

"There could be a million explanations for that. Maybe they didn't know about it or never found it," Dover suggests.

"The only ones who could answer that question are the witches," Eaton says.

"But the Blackbloods are all dead. Except for Serena."

That *does* present an issue.

"What if we…" I trail off because the idea is just absurd.

Zadyn turns to me, his big brown eyes turned the color of whiskey by the fire in the hearth. "What if we what?"

"I was going to say—what if we try to contact them?"

"The witches?"

I nod.

"You want to have a seance," he says evenly.

Silence.

"I can't tell if you think it's a terrible idea or a genius one."

My friends exchange a wary glance. All except for Eaton, who chuckles.

"That is absolutely horseshit insane. I love it." He claps once, his blue eyes sparkling. "But why stop there?"

"What do you mean?"

"If you're going to do this, you might as well go straight to the top of the food chain."

"You think we should try to contact the *dead High Queens*?" Dover gapes at him.

"No." Eaton walks around the counter and stops in front of me. "I think you should try to contact their goddess."

39

SERENA

"You think we should try to contact Silva, the Mother of Witches?" I squeak, trailing Eaton up the stairs. It's hard to keep up with him in his state of excitement.

"It's worth a shot."

He shoves open the library doors, striding toward the large floor globe as we pour into the room behind him.

"No one has managed to summon a god in centuries. *But* there also hasn't been a Blackblood witch for centuries. I'm curious to see if she answers you."

"How are we even supposed to attempt this?"

"You'll need an obscene amount of energy." He gives the globe a spin, stopping it with his pointer finger.

"Aeix," I read. "The Outlands?"

"The Burning Tree." He nods. "Where the witches fell. It's an energetic hot spot."

I glance at Zadyn, who's gone pale.

"Maybe our answer is there. Or a clue at least," Eaton presses.

"Are we really about to raid an ancient witch gravesite?" Mar asks from behind me.

214

I look at her. "We're really about to raid an ancient witch gravesite."

"Great." Kai hops off the armrest he was perched on and dusts himself off. "I'll grab my shovel."

WITHOUT TIME to second guess or decide that this is a very bad, very *horrible* idea, we're on Furi's back, flying toward Aeix. The journey takes two days. I'm insanely grateful when the frigid cold of Hyrax gives way to the southern heat—that is, before breathing becomes difficult.

Aeix has all the heat of Vod, except with air dry as ash.

The desert is bare beneath us, nothing in sight as far as the eye can see. Not a plant, not an animal, not even an insect. It's like we have entered a space void of all life, only sky and flat dirt like the deserts out west back home.

I slide down Furi's warm scales, my feet touching down on the dusty ground.

Hey, are you okay? I ask.

I can feel her fatigue echoed in my bones. She's wary of this place. It's making her…sad.

I have not been here in two thousand years. Since that day.

I can't believe I didn't realize that this might be difficult for her. We are standing in the place her first rider fell to Ienar. The place where she watched as her mothers and sisters were slaughtered by an angry god.

Furi, I'm so sorry, I shouldn't have brought you here. I wasn't thinking at all.

No need for apologies, Blackblood. It was a long time ago.

But her mind's voice is laden with sadness, grief. I place a gentle hand on her leg.

Why don't you take off? Maybe find some water or a place to rest for a little while. We've got this.

Her peridot eyes blink at me, looking a bit glassier than usual.

I will not go far.

I watch until she becomes a blip in the sky, then disappears altogether. The sun is so bright I have to use my hand as a visor. But even against the blinding daylight, it would be impossible to miss the glowing white mass in the distance.

As we grow closer, that mass becomes the largest tree I've ever seen. Thick, corded roots wind up the sturdy trunk in spirals. Its circumference is at least the size of four regular trees put together. The branches are solid, fanning out over the land, with exotic ivory flowers lining each crooked limb. But it's the snow-white flames engulfing the entire treetop like a blazing halo that have me enchanted.

We pause at the base, staring up at this strange, beautiful tree that, against all odds, exists—defying the laws of nature.

I step closer, my eyes closing.

The land around us is supercharged. This is where the witches fell. I can feel them around me. My mothers and my sisters. Thousands of souls released with their dying breaths, returned to the land with the magic that birthed them.

I can hear them whispering in my ear, speaking words I don't understand. Their presence is overwhelming, coaxing my own magic to the surface, urging it to come out and play.

Mar stops beside me, her face reverent, and I know she feels it too.

"So should we just spread out and start calling Silva's name? See if she pops up?" Kai prods from behind us. Dover elbows him in the ribs.

"Have some respect, Kai. You don't want to piss them off," I warn.

Kai tickles his fingers along the back of my neck, like a spider. I swat him away.

"Afraid of a few bones, savior?"

The air itself seems to narrow at his joke.

"The witches don't find you funny. You might want to quit while you're ahead."

Something is pulling me toward the tree, to the dark, hollowed arch within. I follow the call as if entranced.

"Can you guys give me a minute, please?"

"Serena, be careful," Zadyn warns.

Everything behind me seems to fade away the second I cross the threshold. I keep my hands outstretched as I walk, waiting to hit the back of the tree, but I don't. I keep going, the daylight behind me growing dimmer until it's extinguished completely, leaving me alone in the dark.

But the witches are with me, and I am not afraid.

I press deeper into the infinite space.

Here.

They want me to stop here.

Blood of my blood.

The voice is pure moonlight, cool, smooth, and bright.

And then I see her.

I know who she is without having to ask. Every part of me knows, though I have never seen her before.

It isn't Silva.

It's Queen Arden.

Words don't do her justice. She *is* starlight. Silver-white hair that falls to the ground like a sheet of pure silk, irises the same searing blue as the dragon she bonded. Her beauty is almost too blinding to face head-on.

I fall to my knees, the full weight of who I am hitting me.

Up until now, I don't think I fully understood that I am not a child of Earth—I never was. Or that I was born from the magic and the will of the Blackbloods who died on this sacred ground. But kneeling before this apparition, feeling the eternal souls around me, I am humbled and whole.

I am home.

"Daughter of my daughters," Arden says, her voice warm and smooth. "Stand, child, let me see you."

I rise, trembling and speechless.

"You've come home at last."

"Yes," I whisper.

"What heaviness weighs on your heart?"

"My kingdom is in trouble."

"Which one?"

"Aegar. My kingdom is Aegar."

"They are all your kingdoms. You belong to them all, just as they all belong to you."

"I don't understand."

"This world will bow to none but you."

I fight the urge to laugh in her face.

"No, I'm just a Blackblood—just a Dragon Rider."

"*Just* a Blackblood? *Just* a Dragon Rider? My child, that is nothing to downplay. You are extraordinary. You have the blood of gods within you, the blood of true royalty in your veins. You are the last of us. You may yet be without your crown"—she drifts closer on an ethereal wind—"but you have been queen from the moment your soul was made."

A queen?

"No," I say reflexively. That's absurd. "I'm just here for Aegar."

"This is greater than Aegar, my warrior. The last Dragon Rider is no errand girl for warring kingdoms that seek to tear each other apart. Your fate is much bigger."

"I don't know if I can handle bigger right now," I admit.

"Not today. And not tomorrow. But one day. The kingdoms are stronger united, and you must be the one to do it."

"Well, today my focus is on stopping Kylian."

"Your fight is not with Vod. Your fight is for the preservation of this world. You will need the young king to do what must be done."

"What—"

"When you ascend and take your place as High Queen, he will be there beside you. It is already written. Your fate is to lead by his side, and he at yours."

"No." I step back. "No, there has to be some mistake."

The wasteland I saw in that mirror, that war zone—all those

deaths flash through my mind like a flipbook, growing more horrific with each new page.

Kylian had told me that if I refused him…No. That can't have been real, it can't—

"He did not deceive you. What you saw was correct. Fight against him, and you and your friends will die."

"No. We can't just let him—this isn't right. He can't win," I trail off, my mind spinning.

"His triumph is your triumph."

"What?" *How?*

Have I had it wrong this entire time? In thinking that good always wins? That love prevails? It's what every fairy tale preaches.

But maybe it doesn't. Look at history. Filled with tyrants and conquerors. Corrupt kings and fallen empires. Wars. Death.

This isn't a storybook, this is real life. Maybe this is a fight we don't walk away from. All I know is that, fate or not, I refuse to be on his side.

"I have said all I can say. The rest is yours to discover."

Well, that's helpful, thanks.

"Please just tell me how to get the portal closed. Is there a key?"

Her brows thread together. She pauses, her eyes falling to the locket around my neck. "Where did you get that?"

"Kylian." The name tastes like ash in my mouth.

Arden stares at it, puzzled. "A word of advice. Keep that star close to you at all times. Guard it with your life, and never take it off. In the wrong hands, it will cause catastrophe."

"I won't let it out of my sight."

How did she even know it was a star?

"Queen Arden, the fate of Aegar, possibly of all of Solterre, depends on me stopping Kylian."

"I cannot say more, my daughter. I will leave you with this. Open your mind to the possibility you fear the most. You cannot move forward without facing it first."

What I fear the most? What do I fear the most?

"Wait—"

But Arden is gone, leaving me inside the hollowed-out tree. When I reach out, my fingers finally hit the trunk. I turn, and the opening to the hollow is a foot away. I step back into the daylight, feeling even more confused than I did before.

My friends surround me with expectant eyes.

"I just saw Queen Arden."

4 0

SERENA

"You just saw the dead witch queen inside that tree?" Kai sputters. "Are you sure you didn't hit your head, precious?"

I smack his arm.

"What did she say?" Mar asks, ignoring Mr. Wise Guy over here.

"Did she tell you how to close the portal?" Eaton presses.

"No. Nothing she said made any sense. She told me Vod is not our enemy, that Kylian will be High King, and I'll—"

"What?"

Be his queen.

The words lodge in my throat. My eyes link with Zadyn's.

Tell me, he entreats.

Unable to voice it, I let him peer into the memory of my conversation with Arden and hear her message firsthand. He gives me a long look, his brows threading together.

"What?" Mar repeats.

I shake my head, at a loss. "I don't know. I'm just as confused as you are."

Kai's face hardens, his posture going rigid. "We can't let that happen. Kylian cannot be High King."

221

As the words leave his mouth, I feel a twinge of panic latch onto my chest. "She said that if we fight against him, all of us will die."

A tense silence falls.

"I think we can all agree that letting Kylian conquer the world would be a fate worse than death," Dover says, his voice subdued.

"Which is why we are not going to let that happen." Zadyn glances around at each of us, saving me for last. "Any of it."

I know he's talking about the part in the story where I marry our enemy. A shudder ripples through me as I force Arden's warning from my mind.

She's wrong. She just has to be.

"Come on. Let's walk and talk. We need to find somewhere to camp before the sun sets. I don't like being out in the open like this," Zadyn says, scanning the expansive flat land.

"It's all desert for miles," Kai protests.

"I sent Furi off. She needed a break. We've been pushing her hard these last few days, and this place was making her edgy."

"Let's head north," Eaton says. "There's a small river there. We can make camp and start back in the morning."

The walk is going smoothly until I hear Mar scream.

I turn to see Mal standing there, his fist clamped around her arm. Behind him are ten golden soldiers.

Where the hell did they come from?

I force my shock to wait as they charge at us, hurling out their magic before they get close enough to strike a blow.

Cowards.

The moment I feel the pain, I crumple to the ground. Something sharp jabs at my chest over and over, leaving me breathless. I scan myself for the arrow or dagger I'm certain has pierced my heart. But there's nothing there. That's when I see one of the soldiers standing still, his arm cast out in my direction.

He's using his affinity.

My magic kicks in, reflecting his power back at him in a jet stream of fury. He flies back, taken to the ground by the gift I've just deflected. The second he's up, I hit him with a line of fire and watch him dance around, desperate to extinguish the flames.

A flash of white whizzes past my head. I turn to see Zadyn leap through the air in *OrCat* form to take off the arm of the soldier whose sword is arcing toward my neck.

Mal materializes behind me, landing a stunning blow to my cheek.

Can't say I've missed his punches.

A metallic tang fills my mouth as he reaches for me again, but a tidal wave shoves him backward.

Kai bends to help me up.

"I don't know what gutter you crawled out of," he calls to Mal, "but in these parts, traitors are generally disliked."

Mal laughs, getting to his feet. "You're the only traitor I see here, *Prince*. Your mother is worried sick."

"I think you have her confused with some other cunt, which is surprising given how much time you've spent plowing hers. Too soon to start calling you 'Daddy'?"

That does it. The rage on Mal's face causes me to take a physical step back, pulling Kai with me as he sends out another powerful rush of water. Mal tosses his hands out at the same time, his fingers trembling and glowing white.

Mal's gift is lightning.

Fuck.

"Kai, no!"

I shove him out of the way the moment the water and lightning meet, absorbing the full weight of the fallout. The electric current eats through me so fast and violently, I hit the ground, convulsing. It's too overwhelming to even deflect. My vision darkens as I jerk and writhe, eating dirt and spitting blood.

I decide then that I want Mal to die first. Ilspeth can watch. Kylian won't give a shit about either of them, so where he falls on the list is not really important as long as he's dead.

Then it stops. The pain, the seizing. All of it. I can see again. Kai is leaning over me, a horrified expression on his face.

"I can only hold them for a minute. Think fast, people."

In my periphery, Mar staggers back a step, nose leaking blue. The soldiers around us are frozen, even Mal. Suspended mid-stride. She's siphoning.

Zadyn shifts back into fae form to pull me into his lap. I don't have the voice to ask how bad my damage is. Not yet.

I can feel Furi rioting in my head, her rage flaring as if she'd been scorched herself. I wish I could tell her I'm alright, but I'm struggling to breathe, and that sucks up all my focus.

"Kai, I need you to make a pool," Zadyn directs, his eyes never leaving mine.

"What?"

"A pool!" he bellows. "A small body of water. Make one right now."

"Fuck." Dover and Eaton pop into view, blotting out the sun.

Kai gives Zadyn a confused look, but obeys. Water flows from his palms, creating a small pond inside the barren desert.

"Mar, get inside," Zadyn snaps, murderously quiet.

"She can't walk all of us, Zadyn," Dover says. Zadyn whirls, snarling at him. "She can't fucking do it!"

"Get inside," Mar commands, sounding winded. "Now."

My voice is still lost to me as Zadyn scoops me into his arms like a rag doll.

"Take a deep breath. You're going to be okay," he vows, gazing down at me. I think I nod.

Then I'm sucked into a whirlpool. My lungs start screaming.

I can't help it. I open my mouth. Maybe my brain is fried from being electrocuted.

I'm still choking as I'm laid out on solid ground. My jacket and shirt are ripped open. Large, cool hands press against my chest, just below my neck. It isn't until I feel them that I realize I'd been burning. I probably look like a charred steak from the outside.

I mumble something.

"What did she say?" Zadyn asks, his voice tight.

"I don't know."

"She doesn't look so hot."

"I think she's in shock."

"She's not healing. *Fuck*."

"She needs to drink."

Then something smooth and cool touches my lips, and a coppery liquid slips onto my tongue.

Mar is giving me her blood.

I want to fight. I want to spit it out, but the moment it slides down my throat, a new feeling replaces the dread. My resistance fades as her blood erases my pain and replenishes me.

"How the fuck did they find us?" Eaton breathes.

"Do you think—"

"They're tracking us," Mar says. "They have to be."

"How?"

"Either they're tracking the dragon or Kylian must have a Hound."

A Hound. Fancy speak for a magic tracker.

"But how did they just appear like that? I've never heard of High Fae being able to do that. Those beasts Kylian brought over did the same thing," Dover says.

"Kylian's mirrors. He can transport them anywhere," Kai answers, a darkness shadowing his tone. "That's how he's been moving the Stryga."

I finally open my eyes, my lashes fluttering up at Zadyn. His entire face transforms from deadly to relieved.

"Hi," he says, flashing a brilliant smile down at me. It's like another bolt of lightning, but this time it's a good one, striking me right in the heart.

I mumble again as he cradles my face.

"What?"

"Ow," I finally croak.

"I know." Zadyn breathes a grateful laugh, tipping his head down to mine. "I know."

41

ZADYN

A fucking Hound.

We need that right now like a hole in the head.

"No magic from here on out. Everyone. Do you hear me?" I don't dare take my eyes off Serena, monitoring her healing. Mar's blood seems to be working fast.

"We don't know if they've been tracking Furi or one of us. After this, no more. We need to move, and we need to do it fast."

"We're not getting anywhere fast on foot. We used magic to get here. And you're using it right now," Kai counters.

"Do you see much of a choice?" I snap.

Smartass.

"My point, *Zadyn*, is that they could be on our asses in a second."

"So we only use it when absolutely necessary," Eaton cuts in.

I smooth Serena's hair back off her face, thankful to feel that she's cooling down. Dover bends to Mar, wiping the blood off her chin and wrapping the slice on her palm with a scrap of his shirt.

"Don't ever push her like that again." He casts a seething look at me.

I know I was asking a lot of her, but what could I do? We had no other option.

226

"Dover, stop." Mar slumps back and dips her head to his shoulder. "She needed it."

"No, Mar, look at your nose. Siphoning that much isn't good for you. If something had happened to you—"

"What did you want me to do, let her die? Nothing happened to me. I'm fine. I just need to rest."

Once Mar is strong enough to walk, we head toward a port town on the coast of Bleakwater Bay. Serena dozes in my arms as we check into a rustic inn off the main road.

Exhaustion nags at me as I carry her up the stairs and tuck her into the bed beneath the slanted ceiling. Then I collapse into the low-backed leather chair, keeping tabs on her breaths until my tired eyelids win and fall closed.

4 2

SERENA

"Wake up," I sing, tickling the tip of Zadyn's nose with my finger. He twitches in his sleep, and I bite back a laugh.

He is out *cold*.

I lean in close, bracing my hands on my knees, and blow on his face. He jerks awake at long last, clutching his heart.

"What the hell?"

I flop back onto the bed, laughing. "I'm sorry, I had to. You were sleeping like a baby."

"Is your first instinct to wake a sleeping baby?" He sits up, smoothing his blousy shirt. "How are you feeling?"

"I feel good. Really good."

"You look a thousand times better. Mar's blood worked almost instantly."

"I'm guessing it was pretty bad?"

His grimace confirms. "You don't want to know."

I shudder and move to the mirror. My skin looks amazing, and my irises are an even brighter shade of purple.

Who knew blue blood was Solterre's best-kept beauty secret? They should put this shit in creams.

I turn back to Zadyn. "I want to go for a walk."

228

His brows lift. "A walk?"

"To clear my head. There's just been a lot thrown at us, and I need some time to just…process."

Zadyn stands to his full height and stretches, his head nearly touching the angled ceiling. "I'll go with you."

I sigh. "Zadyn, really, I just want to be alone."

"Being alone while we're being hunted by Kylian is the worst thing you could do right now." Grabbing his jacket off the armrest, he holds it out for me. "I won't say a word. You can pretend I'm not there."

I want to argue, but he has a valid point.

"Fine. I'll allow it." I slide my arms through the jacket and lift the collar to my nose to inhale. Zadyn clocks the move as he holds the door open for me.

"What? I like the way you smell." I shrug.

He presses his lips together, stifling a smile as I duck under his arm.

THE PORT TOWN is small and charming, centered around a busy square. Zadyn and I walk the cobbled streets, passing shops and bakeries, peering in windows and keeping a leisurely pace. The silence is a welcome change after the week we've had.

"Are we ever going to talk about what Arden said to you?"

Welp. Spoke too soon.

I swing my head in his direction. "Oh, Zadyn. The key to a peaceful walk is *ignoring* your problems."

"You can't run from them forever. She called you a queen."

"I've been called worse."

He slides me a reproachful look. "Are you taking this seriously at all?"

"Not really."

"Serena."

"What? Nothing she said made any sense. All that stuff about me and Kylian ruling together? It's insane."

Zadyn's jaw clenches. "The part about you being queen I can buy. There's not a person alive who wouldn't follow you to the ends of the earth." I glance at him, surprised. "The other part—not so much."

I decide not to tell him about the vision I saw of Kylian and me, happily married with children. Or that I would have died to prevent that from happening—from risking my friends' lives.

"Say we did believe her—what are our options? Either let Kylian take over the world or get ourselves killed trying to stop him?"

Shaking his head, he says, "We can't let him get any more powerful. We'll find a way. No one is getting themselves killed."

I let out a long breath. "She said the kingdoms are stronger united."

"United against what?"

"I don't know, she wasn't exactly forthcoming in her revelations."

"The only threat we're facing right now is Kylian. I don't know how much worse it can get."

"Yet she insisted that I have nothing to fear with him." I groan, racking my brain. "It's absurd. He's a monster. We know what he's capable of. So to answer your question—no. I guess I'm not taking her advice seriously."

We fall silent again, walking until I get the sense that I'm being watched. My awareness ticks up, the hairs on the back of my neck rising.

I turn. That's when I see them.

Golden soldiers. Behind us and more up ahead. And if they're here, then Mal is probably not far behind.

"Zadyn—"

"I see them. Don't panic and don't touch your magic. Just keep walking." He takes hold of my hand, twining our fingers.

The guards up ahead are stopping people on the street, holding up flyers. Flyers with our faces on them. I watch them roughly grab the arm of a brunette around my same height and build. She gasps, cowering and trembling until they realize she has the wrong face and eye color, and release her.

We need to get out of here. Now.

"You!" someone calls from behind us. I jump, but Zadyn doesn't let me turn back, forcing me to keep up with his brisk, steady stride.

"They're right behind us." I glance at him in my periphery, panic gathering in my gut. "*Zadyn.*"

I don't have time to breathe before he has me pinned up against the nearest building. My mouth parts as he grips my face with unwavering hands.

"I'm going to kiss you," he warns.

I nod, stunned as he lowers his lips to mine, shielding me from view of the soldiers.

The kiss is slow and sweet, and he tastes like something familiar and lovely.

"Excuse me," the guard booms from behind him. My heart does a nervous dive. I fight the urge to open my eyes, knowing the color will be a dead giveaway.

I rise onto my toes and snake my arms around Zadyn's neck, pulling him closer, praying the guard gets the hint and moves along.

A throat clears, and I hear a metal gauntlet land on Zadyn's shoulder.

"We're busy here," he mumbles against my lips.

His hands slide around my waist, pulling me flush against him. Something stirs in my stomach as his tongue slips into my mouth.

I really have to fight to keep my eyes closed now, surprised by the kiss.

"We're looking for someone. A female. Dark hair, purple eyes. You seen anyone who looks like that?"

Zadyn shakes his head, keeping his mouth close to mine. "Hard to say—I haven't really been looking. I've got my hands full at the moment."

I fake giggle as Zadyn clamps a hand on my ass and squeezes. A surprised yelp escapes me as he kisses me again.

Sorry, he says into my mind.

It's fine.

I decide to refrain from telling him I kind of liked it, worried that might be weird.

The guard gives an annoyed sigh and leans closer.

"You know, there's an inn around the corner. Hourly rates. You might want to explore that before you end up fucking against the wall."

I have to bite my lip to keep from bursting into laughter, but as my teeth come down, I catch Zadyn's lip. Hard. He lets out a guttural sound and crushes me against the building. The jagged stone digs into my back, and a little gasp slips past my defenses.

For a moment, I forget the soldiers completely as Zadyn and I continue to kiss, a strange hunger building between us. He tilts his head, deepening the kiss, and I let my tongue collide with his.

It's just acting. To an outsider, I could safely say that we are giving the performance of a lifetime. But for that moment, that's all that exists—our mouths, our tongues, his taste and smell, his fucking hands—

A warning bell chimes in the back of my mind. This is dangerous territory.

So what? I throw back, sucking his bottom lip into my mouth. *We're making out. What's a casual makeout between friends? It's harmless. It's like the time in college me and Annie lost a game of flip cup and...*

Oh, shit.

This is *not* the first time Zadyn and I have kissed.

My brain begins to turn over the events of that drunken night, and boy, do I have questions for him. But the way he's kissing me right now is making it hard to form rational, coherent thought and is quickly grinding my morals to dust.

After another moment, he breaks away, breathless.

"Do you think they're gone?" I ask. His forehead tips against mine.

"I think so." Feeling him nod, I crack my eyes open, staring at his swollen bottom lip as his heart thrashes against my palms.

"Do you think they bought it?"

"Honestly?" he breathes. "I don't really care."

I laugh against his open mouth, and we stay that way for a prolonged second, our upper lips just *barely* touching—waiting to see who bites first. I hold my breath, thinking he might kiss me again.

Hoping he might kiss me again.

What is that all about?

Instead, he pushes away from me—the portrait of restraint.

He's always so good with that. I wonder what he's like when he's out of control.

Unrestrained.

He searches my face, and for a second I worry he might be reading my mind in that strange way he does. Instead, he tows me toward the inn at a hurried pace.

As we pass by a storefront window, two strangers mimic our movements. I lift a hand, and the blonde, plain-featured female in the glass does the same.

I sneak a look at Zadyn.

He glamoured us.

That kiss was completely unnecessary.

But as I fight back a smile, I realize I don't mind. Not one bit.

43

ZADYN

Fucking idiot.[*]

   That's what my head screams as I bury my lips in Serena's like a dying man.

She tastes just as good as I remember. But to her, this is new.

I could melt. I could die here and now.

Instead, I slip my tongue into her mouth, unable to control myself, like I've never kissed a girl before. Way too eager.

Calm down, Zadyn. You're in public, and this is just for show. This is a safety measure. Show some fucking restraint.

But then she bites my lip and makes this...this *noise,* and something in me just snaps. I need to hear it again. I shove her back into the wall, allowing the length of my body to press against hers.

I lose myself in the mouth that haunts my dreams, taking as much as I can and still needing more. When the sound of the soldier's boots dissipates, I break away, gasping, praying she doesn't look down.

My eyes peel open. She's staring at my mouth, wearing the glamour I cast on her, speechless for once—which feels like a victory in and of itself. But I'm already mourning the loss of her lips on mine.

---

[*] Cue: *If You're Too Shy (Let Me Know)-Edit* by the 1975

234

I could kiss her again. I could make it very clear that I could do this all day long and never be sick of it.

But something—the very last of my reasoning—forces me to back away and lead her to the inn.

Where we are sharing a room.

Wonderful.

I can't be alone with her. Not right now, not until I've had a chance to…calm down.

I tug her through the streets, saying nothing because what can you really say when you've got a Hound tracking you and you're not supposed to be using magic but you do anyway because you love the girl they're after but then for good measure you decide that making out against the side of a building with a raging hard-on would be a good cover?

I deposit her in Mar's room, leaving her with some wimpy excuse she can undoubtedly see through.

"I'll be right down. I just have to grab something from upstairs."

She nods, briefly meeting my gaze. I'm dying to know what she's thinking. Dying to take a peek into her mind. But I refrain.

I take the steps up to our floor two at a time. As soon as I've closed the door behind me, I lean against it, taking deep breaths, palming my cock through my pants to fight the growing ache.

Get a grip.

I push off the door and move over to the desk, gripping the edges until the base urge within me lets up, and I can think past my raging lust.

This is *so* not normal.

And I know exactly why.

4 4

S E R E N A

"Why are you all flushed?" Mar asks as I slip into her room.

Because Zadyn just backed me into a wall, groped my ass, and kissed me, and now all I can think about is doing it again.

"Soldiers," I flub, pointing toward the door. She arches an auburn brow. "There are Vod soldiers out there with wanted signs."

"Ugh, not again."

Kai and Dover are in the middle of a chess match, Eaton caught between them.

"Where's your boy?" he asks over their bickering.

I freeze. "What?"

"Zadyn?"

"Oh, *that* boy!" I force a laugh. "He's upstairs, he'll be down soon."

Nice. Not obvious at all.

Eaton redirects his attention to the board, shaking his head like I'm a basket case. He's not wrong.

"What is the matter with you right now?" Mar mutters, drifting past me to join her mate.

"We should probably pack up and leave, right?" I pivot, trying to force the feel of Zadyn's hands from my mind.

236

"Maybe wait until nightfall or early morning," Dover says, knocking one of Kai's pieces from the board. "It's not wise to flee while they're buzzing around."

"Cheat," Kai snips. Eaton snickers.

"How are they tracking us?" I move to the window, absently toying with my locket. Then I remember it's from Kylian and drop it like a hot cake.

I still don't know why I decided to keep the damn thing. I've been telling myself it's just because the gift is really cool. I mean, there's a *star fragment* around my neck. How many people could say that? Or maybe it's just a physical representation of my trauma.

And we all know how much I love to cozy up to that late at night.

The door opens, and Zadyn steps through, eyes going right to me.

Act normal, act normal, act normal.

"I told them," I blurt.

He turns bright pink.

Oh, he thinks I'm talking about the *kiss*! I burst into laughter.

"About the soldiers," I finish.

"Oh." He clears his throat, making his way to the boys.

Dear gods, *Blackblood,* Furi groans. I can *feel* her rolling those giant green eyes at me.

What? I retort, trying to keep from looking at Zadyn again. It's not easy, let me tell you.

Eaton shifts his gaze between the two of us. Probably picking up on the awkward tension sucking all the air from the room. "I agree with Dover. Stay another night, head back before the sun comes up."

"Good plan." Zadyn keeps his head down as he sinks into a chair, his knee bouncing with nervous energy.

Mar's silver stare burns into me from her seat on Dover's lap. And judging by the diabolical smirk on her face, we're not fooling anyone.

ZADYN DOESN'T COME BACK to the room.

He stays downstairs with Eaton, drinking well into the night as I toss and turn upstairs. Annoyed because he kissed me and groped me and now he's acting weird.

Typical. Fucking. Male.

I toss back the covers and pad into the hall, making my way down to Mar's room.

"Move over," I hiss into the dark. Mar sits up, squinting at me.

"What in hell?" Dover grumbles as I slide under the covers beside his mate.

"I need to vent."

Mar casts him a pleading look. He groans, scooping up his pillow and stumbling from the bed. "I'll be in Kai's room."

"I love you!" The door slams shut. Mar turns to me. "This better be good."

"Zadyn kissed me."

Her eyes gleam. "Oh, it's good. Tell me everything."

When I'm finished recounting our makeout session in the town square, Mar slumps back against the headboard, looking pleased with herself.

"I *knew* it," she gushes.

"But now he won't even look at me. You know what, though? It's for the best. Things with Jace are complicated enough. To even add someone else into the mix, let alone my familiar—" I shudder.

"First off"—she holds up a finger—"Jace is not a factor in this equation. He is still engaged."

"Yet he still came all the way to Vod to help rescue me. I know you want to keep minimizing things with us, but Jace loves me. I know he does."

And if I'm being honest, there is this stupidly hopeful part of me that still loves him.

Kissing Zadyn had felt good—like a cool salve on a fresh burn. For a moment, I almost forgot about that dull ache in my chest. The one Jace left there. I forgot about missing him. And I'd be lying if I said I didn't feel a bit guilty about that.

But Mar is right. He's not a factor here. And he never will be again.

"That has never been up for debate." She sighs. "I just want what's best for you. Someone who won't hurt you. Intentionally or unintentionally."

"I know."

When I finally drag myself upstairs, Zadyn is sitting in the wide leather chair across from the bed, a glass of whiskey in his hand. He stirs when I shut the door.

"Didn't mean to wake you," I say, slinking back into bed.

"You didn't." He lifts the glass to his lips and takes a long pull.[*]

I nestle into the pillow, facing him. We outright stare at each other as he sets down the drink and drags his pointer finger along the rim of the glass. My breathing quickens.

"Listen," he finally says, glancing away from me. "I'm sorry if that made you…uncomfortable earlier."

"It didn't."

His gaze flickers up to mine.

"You glamoured us. Were you just taking extra precautions or something?"

"Yeah. Or something."

The air around us grows thicker, making me aware of every minuscule move he makes—the twitch of his finger against the glass, the pulse of blood flowing through the veins in his neck, the slight darkening of his eyes.

I reach out to pat the space behind me. Without breaking our stare, he climbs onto the bed. We match postures, an inch of space between us. I can smell the whiskey on his lips. I think about leaning forward to taste it for myself.

"What are we doing?" His voice is barely a whisper.

"I don't know, you tell me."

He gives an exasperated sigh and closes his eyes. "I don't think I have to. I think you know."

I study him, contemplating. Then I slide a touch closer. He cracks his brown eyes to peer down at me. "It's a bad idea."

"What is?"

---

[*] Cue: *Ruin My Life* by Zara Larsson

"This."

"This?" I prod. "Why don't we stop talking in riddles and actually say what we mean?"

"You sure you're ready for that?"

"What's that supposed to mean?"

He hits me with a lopsided grin, flaunting a single dimple that makes my heart catch.

"I have no problem saying what I want and what I mean. But only if you're ready to hear it."

"Then say it. What you want and what you mean."

He leans in, his next words a tease. "I don't think you can handle it."

Pfft. "Try me."

Alright. What I want—

He slides closer—close enough for me to feel the heat rolling off his skin, his slow, even breaths on my lips.

Is to shove you up against that wall and kiss you until your knees buckle. And I don't mean the kind of kissing we did in the street. I want to take my time getting to know every single inch of you, every patch of skin. I want my hands buried in this hair. I want them all over your body until you combust.

Oh. My. God.

Somewhere during that startlingly hot confession, his fingers have found their way to my face, hooking over my jaw and tugging my bottom lip down like this body of mine belongs to him.

My mouth goes dry as I stare at him, unblinking. He chuckles, releasing me and falling onto his back. "Told ya you weren't ready."

I force myself to swallow. "That doesn't count. You thought it. You didn't say it."

He laughs up at the ceiling. "Still a bad idea."

"*What* is?"

"Kissing you again."

"You're right. It's probably a terrible idea."

A secret dare slips into my voice, hooking Zadyn's attention. He flips back onto his side, eyeing my mouth.

"Probably."

"There's really only one way to know for certain."

"You're not wrong."

"Yeah. I mean, we should just see. For—for science."

"Right. For Science." He nods, staring as if hypnotized by my mouth. I'm not sure he's even conscious that the following words slip out. "And because I really want to fucking kiss you again."

A flare of warmth licks up the wall of my stomach. His hand slides over my waist and scoops me closer. Then with torturous, painful slowness, he leans down, dipping his face to mine.

That's when the door flies open, and Zadyn whirls so fast he falls out of the bed. I bolt upright.

Eaton and the others are standing in the doorway, eyes wide.

"The inn is on fire. They've found us. We have to go."

45

SERENA

I heave open the window and stick my head out into the warm
night air. Thick smoke clouds float toward us from the lower
floors. I can see the flames licking up the side of the building,
hear the screams as people flee out onto the lawn and the street
beyond, choking and gasping.

A pack of golden soldiers waits below, dragging people out by the
hair, thrusting the wanted flyers in their faces.

"Call your dragon," Eaton demands.

I am here, Furi answers.

No, Furi. Stay away. It's dangerous.

Says the witch dawdling inside of a burning building.

"No," I say forcefully. "They have arrows. Probably blood ore. I'm
not risking her."

You need me.

*I need you alive, and after what happened in Vod, I'm not taking any
chances. If you get injured here, we're fucked.*

This is not negotiable. I am your defender, she insists.

And I am your rider. Now scram.

She whines, pushing against my command but finally relents.

"Do you have a better idea?" Eaton presses.

242

"I do," Kai says. "I can get us out. Just stay close behind me."

Heat smacks into us as we spill into the hall. Kai forges a path, dousing the flames with his affinity just enough to make it down a flight of stairs. We cling to each other as he blasts down the door of a second-story bedroom and throws open the window.

"Coast is clear," he says, peering down.

That's when a deep roar rattles the burning building, followed by shouted orders and commands to open fire.

"Fuck!" I hiss. Zadyn's eyes lock on mine as he registers what's happening.

What are you doing?! I told you to leave!

It's called a diversion, Blackblood. Trust the process.

God damn it, Furi.

Off you go.

"Go," Zadyn urges our friends. "Hurry."

One at a time, we climb out the window, making the leap onto the soft ground below and breaking for the field ahead. I catch a flash of Furi's wing sailing over the inn. My heart lodges in my throat as she swerves, evading the arrows shooting through the sky in pursuit of her. My friends have already scattered into the brush when a small voice rings out, freezing me in place.

"Daddy?"

A little girl wanders around the corner, covered in soot, tears soaking her face as she frantically scans the field. My stomach twists.

I rush to her, falling on my knees and gripping her by the shoulders—very aware that at any moment, the golden soldiers could appear and snatch me up.

"Where is your daddy?" I demand, brushing the flaky ash from her blonde head. "Can you show me?"

She lifts a trembling hand. I turn, following the trajectory of her finger.

"Serena—" Zadyn calls, one foot in the field, no doubt reading my mind.

"I'm sorry."

Then without thinking, I sprint headlong into the burning building.

"Serena!" Zadyn's voice chases me through the door as I plunge into the thick billows of smoke. The heat is stifling as I search the first and second floors and come up empty. I dart up the stairs, carefully dodging the flames, checking every room.

"Hello?" I call out.

Damn it. He's not here.

As I reach the steps again, the inn is transformed into the stuff of nightmares. Everything is black except for the deviant flames devouring everything in their path with an insatiable hunger.

I hear Zadyn shout for me again. As I open my mouth to respond, the floor beneath me gives out, and I fall.

I groan as my back takes the brunt of it. Rolling off the piles of splintered wood, I bury my nose and mouth in my arm to keep from inhaling the smoke. A flash of movement catches my eye in the corner of the room.

Someone tries to stand and collapses.

Scrambling forward, I'm seized by a sharp pain in my shoulder. I look down at my arm dangling awkwardly at my side. I try to lift it and let out a loud cry.

"Fuck."

It has to be dislocated.

Gritting my teeth, I haul the half-conscious male to his feet and sling his arm around my good shoulder. It takes three kicks for me to get the door open and peer out. The fire in the hall is low but manageable as we miraculously make it to the bottom floor.

Which is entirely engulfed in flames.

"Zadyn!" I shout, glancing around.

I burst into a coughing fit as my eyes sting and tear, turning my vision blurry. Everything is disorienting, covered in thick smog and rippling fire. Around us is a labyrinth of fallen beams and burning furniture.

We don't have much time. But this girl isn't losing her father. Not tonight.

A loud crack sounds, and I jump back in time to dodge the falling beam. It hits the ground with a roar, scarcely missing us, blocking the only path in sight.

I can't see anything. I don't even know what fucking room I'm in. I can't see the exits, can't see the windows, I can barely see my own feet.

Keep it on you at all times, and you will never be lost. It will always guide you home.

Kylian's words echo in my mind as I reach for the locket.

Worth a shot.

I rip it open, allowing the star to burst from its cage. Its glow puts the fire to shame. It takes all my effort to haul the male through the ash and debris to follow that brilliant little beam toward the most beautiful door I've ever seen. Sweet relief tumbles through me as I push forward through the blistering heat. Just a few more steps. I can almost feel the reprieve of fresh air.

That relief is replaced by a sinking feeling when the door flies off the hinges, blasting us backward, and Mal steps through the threshold.

46

SERENA

Rage floods through me at the very sight of him.

He charges at me, his fiery hair blending in with the surrounding flames. I have no weapons on me, which means this will be a fight of fists and magic.

Fine by me.

In the split second it takes to scramble off the floor, Mal tackles me back through a wall. I groan at the impact as he lands on top of me. He's strong and heavy, pinning my arms above my head and trapping me between his legs. Searing pain radiates through my dislocated shoulder as he reaches for the blood ore chains at his side.

"NO!" I screech, writhing against him.

I manage to wedge my knee between us and slam it into his groin. His reaction gives me all of two seconds to get out from under him and on my feet. Icy fingers wrap around my ankle, and then I'm flopping onto the ground face-first. Mal ropes my hair around his fist, wrenching me a few inches off the floor.

"You should have stayed dead," he whispers in my ear.

Then he kicks me in the ribs so hard they crack. I roll onto my back, gasping through the sharp pain. He bends toward me as my fingers close around a splintered plank of wood. I swing with all my

246

strength, whacking him in the face with it. The rusted nail jutting from the scrap roots in his cheek as gravity takes him down over a busted chair.

I ignore my pain, throwing my leg over his hips to punch his face with my good hand. Once. Twice. Three times as blood sprays from his nose and mouth. Just when I think I've got the upper hand, he grips my wrists, yanks me forward, and headbutts me so hard I see stars.

Blackblood! Furi's shout adds to my already pounding headache.

Mal flips me on my back and slams my head into the floorboards, making me groan. Then he does it again. Crack after sickening crack, my skull thuds against the floor until I'm nauseous.

Everything blurs.

Then Zadyn is there, gripping Mal by the throat and lifting him off the ground. Mal gives a haunting smile as his lightning shoots out to shock Zadyn. He falls back, seizing. I scramble toward him, fighting through the intense dizziness. The heavy smoke adds to the assault, making it hard to breathe, hard to stay awake, let alone put up a fight. Mal darts for me again, and I flip onto my back, landing a hard kick to his face.

His nose gives a satisfying crunch.

"I thought people could use some help telling you and Max apart," I goad.

Blood gushes from his nostrils as he straightens. Without flinching, he pops the bone back into alignment. I shudder, throwing myself over Zadyn.

"Wake up," I beg as he comes to. But not quick enough.

Mal grabs me around the waist and pries me off the ground. I shriek and claw like a wild beast, but his grip is unrelenting.

I can't be powerless again. I can't go back there. I can't.

The panic latches on with razored teeth, but as my adrenaline pumps harder, my fingers start to prickle. My magic is there, gathering—coiling. I dig my nails into the door frame as Mal tries to get me past the threshold. The flames around us shrink and grow faint. The smoke starts to clear. And I realize I'm absorbing the fire.

The flames are bowing.

To *me.*

I release the door frame to clamp down on Mal's arm, hurling all the gathered heat into my touch.

He roars, releasing me, and as I turn, he goes up in flames.

But he's not done with me. And I'm not done with him.

He hurls out a bolt of lightning. My hand comes up to stop it midair and redirect it toward him. He blasts through the gaping doorway and hits the ground, seized by his own power.

I wave a hand, and the flames disappear from his body. He glares up at me, his teeth chattering with the electric shocks. If he could move, I'd be a dead woman. But now he's got a taste of his own medicine.

"This is for Kai, you piece of shit." I dig my fingers into the fresh burns on his neck. He cries out, his eyes clenching shut.

That taste of anguish has me hungry for more. I ignore my screaming shoulder as my hands lock around his throat and squeeze, my mind recalling every time he hit Kai, burned him, branded him, every rock that was thrown, every cry, every tear, every scream—

"Serena!" Zadyn tugs at me. "Stop, you'll kill him."

"I know," I growl, some demon taking hold of my body and refusing to let go as Mal's life slips away. He's turning the most wonderful shade of purple.

Just as his eyes start to drift closed, Zadyn hauls me off him.

"What are you doing?! I had him! I had him!" I shriek, thrashing against him. He drops me onto the scorched grass a few feet away, beside the little girl's unconscious father.

"Trust me, revenge doesn't always taste as sweet as you think it will."

"Daddy!" The little blonde head bobs toward us, throwing herself on top of her father.

"He deserves to die!" I snarl at Zadyn, still bloodthirsty as hell.

"And I promise you he will. But not like this. Killing him now would be a mercy. One he doesn't deserve."

I glower at Mal in his semi-conscious state as Zadyn checks the pulse of the girl's father. My star buzzes out of the building, popping back into the locket before Zadyn can see.

He turns to me, panting, as I clutch my searing shoulder. With zero warning, he takes hold of my arm and yanks it into place. I scream before the pain dissipates.

"Where else are you hurt?" he rasps.

"My ribs." I wince, dragging his hand to the tender spot just beneath my breast. He holds me close, warmth emanating through my thin nightgown as he repairs my bones. "And I probably have ten concussions."

"He's going to pay for this," Zadyn promises, his voice quiet. Our eyes link. "But I'm going to make him suffer before he does. And I want to take my sweet time."

His thumb skims up and down my ribs, barely brushing the under-side of my breast.

"Better?"

I nod as we continue to stare at each other. A loud gasp snags our attention as the male beside us springs upright, gasping.

"She's here!"

Our heads whip toward the cluster of golden soldiers spilling around the corner. Furi lets out a battle cry somewhere behind us. I don't see where she is before Zadyn grabs my hand, and we sprint into the tall brush.

All I can hear is the sound of rustling reeds and my own pounding heart. Something whizzes past my head. I turn to Zadyn in time to see the arrow rip through his sleeve, taking a slice of flesh with it.

"Fuck," he curses.

"Are you—" I don't get to finish my sentence before another arrow lodges itself in my lower back. My knees buckle as I cry out.

"Hold onto me." Without even pausing, Zadyn scoops me into his arms and rips the arrow out in one smooth motion. He curls himself around me as he runs, shielding me from the onslaught of arrows the best he can.

The pain in my back is intense. I'm not healing.

Furi? I ask in a panic. But her answer doesn't come.

Blood ore arrows.

A flash of blue fire illuminates the sky, reassuring me that she's okay.

Zadyn barrels on until we take our final step through the grass and plummet over the cliff's surprise edge. I cling to him for dear life, burying my face in his neck. He doesn't let me go as we fall toward the rocky surf below.

If this is how we die, at least it will be to—

Freezing black water sucks us under, and the world bleeds into slow motion. For a moment, it's utter calm. Until we break the surface and are hit with a wall of angry waves. I struggle to stay afloat, blinking up at the massive ship looming beside us, its name sprawled in bold, curving letters between wooden carvings of merfolk and sea creatures.

The Maid of Mercy.

Zadyn grabs me and swims us toward the rope ladder slung over its side. He climbs the worn out fibers with my body wrapped around his until someone reaches out to haul us onto the deck. We fall to the floorboards, panting.

As soon as my head lifts toward our savior, a blunt object connects with my skull, and I hit the deck face first.

47

SERENA

I wake with a dry mouth and the worst headache of my life.

That last concussion must have really done me in.

Something itchy pokes at the backs of my bare arms. I glance down at myself. I'm still in my nightgown, sprawled out on a bed of hay…

Where the hell am I? And why am I covered in blue powder?

I jolt forward, realizing my hands are bound. For a moment, I'm sucked back into that cold, dark cell in Vod, blood ore cuffs encircling my wrists. Panic seizes me as I yank against the matted rope.

Rope, I remind myself. Not metal.

The faintest pinpricks of magic in my veins confirm it. I'm alright. I made it out of that place. I made it out alive.

Blackblood. Relief sweeps through me at the sound of Furi's silky voice. *What is going on?*

I'm asking myself the same thing, girl. I squint across the dank space.

Are you harmed?

I don't think so.

Are your limbs intact?

All four. Yours?

I am over two thousand years old, and I am very fast. Certainly, you can answer that question yourself.

Why do you sound all muffled? And why does it smell like shit *in here?*

Movement stirs in the corner of my eye. I'm in a barred pigpen. With *actual* pigs.

"Serena."

I whirl, finding Zadyn's eyes in the darkness and scurrying toward him. He's in a pen beside mine, with a bunch of...*chickens?*

I reach for his hands through the bars. "Zadyn, thank god. Where are we?"

"I think we're still on the ship."

"What happened?"

"The last thing I remember is getting us on board. They must have knocked us out. Are you alright?"

My back, where the arrow struck me, feels like it's healing, but at a slower rate than normal.

"I'm fine. Where are the others?"

"Over here, savior."

Across from me is another pen filled with fugly little goats. Inside is Kai, lazing on a bale of hay like he's at a Sunday picnic in the park.

"We're all here," Mar responds from down the way.

"You're all okay?"

"We're all fine," Eaton answers.

"Except my head is pounding," Mar mutters. "I think we've been drugged. My magic feels dulled."

"Same."

It will wear off, and there will be hell to pay, Furi threatens.

You are in a very murderous mood lately, if I do say so myself.

I'm growing tired of people trying to end you. It's slightly stressful.

Huh. You don't say.

"What in hell happened to you two last night?" I can barely make out Dover's pale blue eyes shifting between me and Zadyn—the only light coming from the two hanging lanterns framing the pitch black stairwell. "One second you were right behind us, and then—"

"Mal showed up," I answer. "Again."

"Yes, after you ran back into a burning building. Which we *will* be having words about once we get out of here." Zadyn's stern threat sets off a flutter in my belly.

Shrugging it off, I ask, "Do you think Kylian is behind this?"

Zadyn shakes his head. "If it was Kylian, he'd have us all in blood ore chains by now."

Tell me who I must flay, Furi demands.

I'll let you know when we get to the bottom of it, Buffalo Bill.

I do not understand your reference, she mutters, her tone making it clear that nor does she want to.

The sound of stomping boots draws our gazes upward, dust coming loose from the boards overhead. Heavy footfalls trample down the creaking stairs as three looming shadows appear, stopping outside our pens.

A tall, brawny fae with tattoos and a multitude of gold piercings steps into view looking like Khal Drogo.

"Bring them," he commands his lackeys.

Something about them feels so familiar. Their rugged builds, the dark kohl lining their light eyes, their worn leather vests, the smell of spices and salt water. Strapped across each of their broad chests is a bandolier filled with knives—as if their fists alone aren't weapon enough.

They burst into Kai's cell first, hauling him to his feet with a blade pressed to his throat.

"Careful, this hair takes hours to perfect."

"Shut your mouth," barks the male now deliberately holding him by said hair. He shoves Kai into the chest of the hulking one giving the orders.

A snarling grin twists up his pierced lip. "We meet again, princeling."

"I'm sorry, do I—" Recognition takes over Kai's face as he squints up at the giant. "Oh, it's you! How are you, old friend?"

Meaty hands grip the collar of Kai's jacket, forcing him onto his tiptoes. "Save it for the Pirate King."

Pirtate King.

Pirates!

That's why they look so familiar! Zadyn and I lock eyes, piecing it together.

This is the same group we brawled with at that tavern in Iaspus. The ones Kai cheated at cards. On multiple occasions, apparently.

The pirates drag each of us from our pens with curved blades pressed to our throats.

I'm weak, I tell Zadyn. *I'm not sure I can fight like this.*

Allow me to assist, Furi purrs.

Furi wants to know if she should attack, I relay.

Not yet. His response is muffled, like hers. *You win more bees with honey, and right now we could use more allies than enemies. Let's try the diplomatic route first.*

Spoken like a true emissary.

Going to charm the Pirate King? I tease, allowing a bit of a smile to color my words.

If that's what it takes. He winks at me.

It seems we have now graduated to mind flirting, even in the face of imminent danger. Not that I'm mad about it.

We're dragged up the decrepit wooden steps, onto a massive deck. It's dusk, the sky an eerie, sleepy blue, casting the bodies around us in navy shadows. A heavy layer of fog clings to the air, obscuring the sea beneath us and keeping our whereabouts a mystery.

There are pirates everywhere, swinging from ropes and pulling at sails, shouting commands back and forth in some coded language as we're ushered toward a cabin with thick stained-glass windows.

"The Pirate King will see you now. Try anything and you're dead."

We glance at each other warily before the cabin door opens, and we're flung inside.

The Pirate King of Bleakwater Bay rises from his seat, removing his wide-brimmed black hat and placing it atop the old wooden desk. Platinum-colored waves tumble out, and eyes of ice blue rimmed with gold peer out from between the curtain of long hair. Our mouths drop open.

The Pirate King is a *she.*

"You're a girl?" Kai sputters, his jaw slack.

"And you're the little prince that's been causing my crew so much trouble lately. Cheating them at cards, burning their cargo, swindling them out of their purses." She walks around the front of her desk, her heeled boots clacking against the hollow floorboards. "You've been somewhat of a thorn in my side."

"Well, if I had known whose side I was pricking, I would've let them take me a lot sooner." Kai's eyes sparkle as he drinks in the stunning female before us.

"Crossing a pirate is punishable with the plank."

"My blood belongs to the sea. Rest assured, I am an excellent swimmer, my lady."

"*Your Grace,*" she corrects, her voice velvet-smooth. "You will refer to me as your Grace."

"And how will you refer to me?"

"Kai, shut it," Dover hisses, but Kai delights in the challenge. He stares at her like she's an anomaly, and truth be told, she kind of is.

She offers up a canary-like smirk, leaning in to grab his face. "Astonishing. You second sons truly have nothing but dicks for brains. Dismantling you is going to be *such* a pleasure."

"Forgive me, but I think there's been some kind of misunderstanding." She pins Zadyn with a slow glare. "Your Grace," he adds, an edge to his civil tone.

Releasing Kai with a shove, she spins toward the desk and lifts up a stack of flyers with our names and faces.

"I beg to differ. I've been seeing you lot around. There's quite a price on your heads. Happy accident that the little prince happened to be with you. I've been searching for him for some time now."

"Darling, the feeling is mutual."

A nip of fear climbs up my legs. "You're going to sell us out to Vod?"

She shrugs. "Or auction you off to the highest bidder. If Vod wants you, you must be valuable."

Fan-fucking-tastic.

"Either way, I suppose I should be thanking you. You're going to make me very, very rich."

No. Absolutely not.

"Kylian is going down," I warn, my fingers curling into fists. "You hand us over to him, and I will have a debt to repay you."

Easy, Zadyn warns.

"You? You're nothing," she scoffs.

"I am the last Blackblood witch," I declare, my words coming out stronger and steadier than I feel. "If I were you, I wouldn't want to get on my bad side."

She eyes me doubtfully, an amused expression on her face.

"It's the truth," Zadyn says, earning her gaze. Her head angles back to me.

"Where's your dragon then?"

"Oh, she's here, circling overhead. Waiting for the perfect moment to torch this piece of shit boat. I hear termite-infested wood is highly flammable. Hope you have insurance."

"I have all the insurance I need in this room." She laughs, crossing her arms. "But now I'm intrigued."

"As am I. Hey, what's with the petting zoo downstairs?" Kai asks. "Got a kink for farm animals? Don't worry, I don't judge."

"I'm in the business of stealing and selling. Goods are goods. And your flyer didn't specify dead or alive, so I'd mind my tongue, little prince."

"Oh, there's nothing little about me. Would you like me to prove it? More than happy to."

"Bronyn's right, you really don't shut up, do you? Bronyn, please shut the princeling up."

Jason Mamoa steps forward and stuffs a handkerchief in Kai's mouth.

"Careful. He's kind of into that sort of thing," Dover warns.

"We have gold, you know," Zadyn swoops in, steering us back on track. "And more diamonds than you could ever dream of."

Eaton takes a slight step forward. "I'll double whatever Vod is offering. I'm a prince of Hyrax."

The Pirate King groans, sinking back against the lip of her desk. "Good gods, not another one. Look. I don't give a flying fuck about gold, and I already own enough diamonds to suffocate me. I want something…bigger. Better. Even more rare. If King Kylian wants you that badly, he may have to up the ante."

Kai manages to spit the rag from his mouth. "Trust me, I know my brother. He doesn't take kindly to extortion."

"I've been bartering since I could walk. I'll get more than you lot are worth."

"He'll kill you," Kai rushes to explain, momentarily sober.

She laughs, tossing her head back. "Sweet of you to be concerned, but I'm untouchable. Your big brother relies on me too much. As do the rest of the royals."

We exchange a confused look.

"What are you talking about?" Zadyn asks.

"Do you know what the largest trading port in all of Solterre is?" she muses.

"Bleakwater Bay," he answers.

"Correct. A point for the good-looking one. And who do you think runs that trading port?"

"Let me guess. You."

"Two points. Care to make it three?" Her eyes glint as she circles us. "What do you think it takes to keep commerce here thriving? Little hint—it isn't farm animals."

"All out of answers, I'm afraid," Zadyn retorts.

"Favors," she whispers, a little too close to his mouth for my liking. "Pirates get a bad reputation—thieves, brutes, rogues. When really, we're just independent contractors for those whose hands need to remain clean."

My gaze narrows on her. "You're mercenaries? For who?"

"Royals mostly. Or anyone with deep enough pockets. We don't discriminate."

"You're employed by the kingdoms?"

"Who do you think reports on the borders? When someone needs to disappear, who do you think makes it happen? They want something? We get it for them—by any means necessary. My job is to keep the royals happy. And in turn, they make me rich and allow me to run my little market without consequence."

"Your market?"

"Bleakwater Bay. You should have seen it before my father came along. Total shit-hole. And now look at it. Thriving," she purrs. "As long as I comply with orders, I get free rein over the seas and the Bay. So unless you can provide me with a startlingly good reason to shatter the fragile alliance I have with the kingdoms, then *The Maid of Mercy* sails west in the morning."

I can't actually believe that Derek would have employed the pirates to do his dirty work. That would require him having dirty work to be done. Although maybe that's a naive thought—he *was* a king. And no crown was ever kept with kindness and virtue.

"Look, whatever you want, we'll get it to you. Just do not steer this ship to Vod," Zadyn entreats, tugging against his restraints.

"And what if I want the world? Are you going to get it for me, handsome?"

The Pirate Queen—King—trails a finger down Zadyn's chest, and the fury that attacks me has me snarling, fangs bared.

Zadyn's eyes flash to me, surprised, but the pretty female slowly turns my way, a brilliant smile on her face.

"Possessive over this one are we?" She stops before me. "Tell me, do you breathe fire like your dragon?"

"Untie me and find out."

She chuckles, appraising me from head to toe, before speaking.

"Leave us. I think it's time for a little girl talk."

IT FEELS like a full minute that we sit there staring at each other from across the desk, each tick of the carved antique clock on the wall dragging by with ironic leisure.

She purses her lips, eyes curiously tracing my face.

"Are you truly the last Blackblood?"

"Yes."

Her hand unfurls, extending a pretty little switchblade to me. It springs open, boasting its silver brilliance. "I require proof."

Glowering at her, I rest my elbows on the desk and accept the knife. The rope digs into my wrists as I angle the tip across my palm and flash the onyx slash to her with a phony smirk.

"Satisfied?"

She leans back, bemused, crossing her buckled boots over the corner of her desk. I flip the blade down and toss it to her. She catches it midair, watching as I make a show of wiping my blackened palm on the papers scattered over her desk.

"Oops. Hope those weren't important."

She chuckles, pointing the blade at me. "I like you."

"I would say the same, but you're about to sell me out to evil incarnate."

"I'm running a business. You understand."

"I understand that anyone in business with Kylian is not only untrustworthy but also guilty by association. I meant what I said. He's going down whether he gets his hands on me or not. And everyone who sided with him is going to burn with him."

She doesn't look fazed. Just steeples her hands, elbows resting on her chair. I notice a faint line of blue caked beneath her fingernails. "If only there were another alternative."

"Just cut the shit, and tell me what it is you want."

She picks up a coin and sets it spinning on the desk. "Right now, I want to know why you're wanted by the King of Vod."

Mentally exhausted, I give her the abridged version, outlining how Kylian orchestrated this whole elaborate plan to marry me and use me to help him conquer the other kingdoms. How we narrowly escaped and why we were hiding in Bleakwater Bay to begin with.

"So you stabbed yourself to avoid going through with your own wedding?" She snorts when I finish. "To *Kylian Triori*?"

That's her whole takeaway from this?

"Yes," I grit.

"You do know that most females would stab themselves for a chance *to* marry him, don't you?"

"Well, luckily for them, he has a brother who's a lot less cruel."

She shakes her head. "Either you're reckless or insane."

"Probably both."

"Actually," she says after a beat, "I believe there is a way for us to help each other."

She plants her knee-high boots on the ground. "Something of mine was taken a while ago. I want it back. I think you and I would make quite a persuasive pair, don't you?"

"That's it? You want me to help you get back something you lost?"

"That—and I'll also take what Muscles was offering. Double the price on your heads."

"Fine. Then we'll also be needing safe transport back to Hyrax. *Alive,*" I clarify. "You can collect your pay then."

"Perfect, we're heading in that direction anyway." She reaches out a hand and quirks a perfectly manicured brow. "Do we have a deal?"

I nod, grasping her palm in mine. "We do."

She flashes me a blinding grin.

"Bronyn?" The hulking pirate appears in the doorway. "Change of plans. Tell the crew we sail north. To Skull Valley."

48
SERENA

My stomach dips as the ship lurches to the side again. The sea crashes, cradling us between eager waves, slamming against the mermaids and monsters carved into the sides of the salt-worn ship.

Blue above us, blue below. Blue everywhere, like the world begins and ends with it.

The good news is that if Mal plans on gracing us with his sparkling company again, he'll have to wait until we're on dry land or risk being harpooned in the middle of an ocean.

Or suffering a brutal shark attack. A sight I would pay good money to see.

The bad news is—we're on a ship. I have half a fear I'm going to develop scurvy or scarlet fever—some old-timey disease that probably ravaged the Mayflower.

I turn from the railing, using my hand as a visor to block the sun's glare. "So what exactly do you need me to retrieve?"

The Pirate King stands at the helm, fingers wrapped around the spokes of the wheel while the breeze toys with her platinum hair. The ship obeys her every command without hesitation, reminding me of

the way Furi and I are together—how I barely have to think to have her respond.

Speak of the devil. I peer up to see her soaring overhead, bobbing between the clouds like a dolphin.

Thought I told you to lie low.

This is *lying low.*

No, my dear, this is what we call a humblebrag.

"It's a compass," the Pirate King says, stealing back my focus.

"You want me to go to Skull Valley for a compass?" I quirk a brow, glancing at Zadyn. The sun dances off his golden skin, the wind tunneling through the loose white tunic tucked into his navy pants.

"It's not just any old compass, girl. This one is special."

"Why?"

"Not that I owe you an explanation, but it has magical properties. It's said to be one of the oldest objects in the history of the world."

"Sounds valuable. What do you need it for?" I answer her scowl with a sweet smile. "I just want to know what I'm getting myself into."

"Let's just say it has sentimental value."

"Really? You don't strike me as the sentimental type."

She pushes a sigh through her dainty nose. "If you must know, it was my father's. And now it's mine."

"Now who would be fool enough to steal from the ghastly Pirate King of Bleakwater Bay?"

She turns over her shoulder and hits Kai with a look sharp enough to draw blood.

"Aside from spoilt siren twats seeking certain death? The Valley Dwellers. Nasty little beasts."

She pushes up the sleeve of her peasant blouse to reveal a long patch of creamy skin with swirling black tattoos. Running up her forearm parallel to the ebony ink is a large pearlescent bite mark.

"It's from their teeth."

"That is gruesome." Kai pops between us, marveling at the double crescent moons. She tugs her sleeve down and faces forward, the blunt edges of her hair smacking him in the face.

Shuddering, I ask, "What exactly are the Valley Dwellers?"

She tosses her head back, the sound of her laughter annoyingly attractive. "For a Blackblood, you are startlingly clueless."

I look to Zadyn, frowning.

"Treasure-hoarding cave creatures. Touch their gold and they will shred you to bits," he explains, stands of brown, red, and gold skating across his forehead.

"I've read they'll eat anything that moves. Including each other," Eaton warns.

"And then they'll eat you for dessert." The Pirate King snaps her jaw at me and snickers. "Why do you think they call it the Valley of Death?"

"You want me to risk my life? For a *compass*."

"I'm risking mine harboring you fugitives," she retorts, thrusting her thumb over her shoulder.

Someone retches behind me, and I turn to see Dover curled over the ship's railing, Mar holding back his shoulder-length brown hair and smoothing his head. Poor guy has been sick for almost a full day.

"We're not fugitives—"

"You're wanted by the King of Vod. If he found out I was defying him by abetting your escape, I'd be ash in a split second. *Despite* how good I am at my job. I'm doing you a favor. I'd better get mine in return."

I sigh. "So these valley creature things have your father's compass. How are we supposed to get it back?"

"Well, I know one thing." She cracks a wicked smile. "They don't like fire."

I lift a shoulder, slumping back against the carved oak railing. "I can work with that."

She whistles for a crew member to take over and plops down on a nearby bench, fishing a gleaming red apple and switchblade from her pocket.

"So what's the story with your name?" Kai scuffs up to her, hands in his pockets.

"Elaborate your thought," she drones, sinking the blade into the skin of the apple.

"Why go by Pirate *King* when you are the very portrait of femininity? Or you hiding a little something between those pretty legs?" Kai smirks, nodding toward her lithe form.

"Female I may be, but make no mistake, what I lack in manhood I make up for in other ways. I am every bit my father's daughter, and I would delight in cutting off that famous cock of yours and wearing your balls as a necklace"—her eyes flicker up from the apple—"prince."

"So you've heard of my cock? My lady, I can now die happily." Kai gives her his most rakish grin.

Ignoring his attempt at flirtation, she sighs and says, "My father was the Dread Pirate King of Bleakwater Bay. I was born on this very ship. He taught me everything I know. When he died, I had a reputation to uphold, and Pirate Queen doesn't instill the kind of fear I needed it to. So I took up my father's title to continue his legacy and remind all five kingdoms who owns the seas."

Kai measures her with impish curiosity. "What's your real name?"

"None of your gods-damned business, prince."

"Shall I guess?" He takes hold of a rope suspended from above and drapes himself over it.

"I'd rather you didn't."

"Sabella."

She scoffs.

"Carina? Angel?"

"Do I look like an Angel to you?" Her eyes score him with complete detestation.

Kai cocks his head, beaming at her. "You walked right into that one. I'll find out. One way or another."

"Please do. Try and try until you're blue in the face. Until the curiosity just—" She finishes her last rotation on the apple, waiting for the skin to drop in a perfect coil at her feet. "Kills you."

"Ah, but then you'd miss me too much."

She stands and walks up to him, drawing out each step. Positioning her blade beneath his chin, she tilts her head and murmurs, "You think you're so charming, don't you?"

A flutter of dark lashes. "I don't just *think* it."

I watch them go back and forth, enthralled, neither missing a volley. Her knife drifts up to his cheek, and I can see in her face just how badly she wants to add to that scar below his left eye. The one Kylian gave him.

"What happened here?"

"What's more impressive? Rabid wolf or female scorned?"

"The truth."

"The King of Vod is what happened here." Kai's fingers shoot up to wrap around her wrist. Something guarded slips into his tone, darkening some of that flirtatious levity. "Let's put down the sharp objects, shall we, darling? Wouldn't want you to slip and hurt yourself."

His palm closes over her hip, one finger at a time.

"Get. Your hands. Off of me."

"You first, sweetheart."

Another pregnant beat passes before the Pirate King wrenches herself free and struts away, hips swishing in time with her hair.

I giggle into my hand. "Kai, you are so barking up the wrong tree."

He stares after her, transfixed. "You forget how persistent I can be. She'll come around."

The loud slam of her cabin door punctuates his sentence.

"Don't count on it," Dover groans, turning back to the sea. "Mother of Zed, not again."

I cringe as he hurls again. "I'm going to see if she has something to help with that."

Thank you, Mar mouths to me.

I slip into the Pirate King's cabin, finding her office empty.

I do a quick scan of the room—my gaze sweeping across the floor-to ceiling wooden shelves filled with leather-bound ledgers, and glass cases displaying strange oddities and exotic artifacts. Skulls of unfamiliar animals, a collection of golden vases painted with ebony whorls, a row of vials with labels too small to read.

Trophy cases, I realize.

"See anything you like, Blackblood?"

I turn to find her feline form behind me.

"You've got quite the collection."

"Live as long as I have, and it's easy." She stares me down, waiting for an explanation.

"Dover can't stop retching. Got anything to help with that?"

She inverts her lips. "Depends. What are you willing to give me for it?"

"Boy, nothing comes for free, does it?"

"You of all people should understand. You're the one being hunted like someone's lost possession." She breezes past me.

"Touche. But there is such a thing as kindness. Ever heard of it?"

"Kindness, you will learn, is only a crutch for those too meek and cowardly to act according to their mind's truest impulses."

There's a wariness to her voice as she wrenches open the glass cabinet, snatches up a thin vial of clear liquid, and tosses it to me. I scramble to catch it.

"Have him take it with rum. Kills the taste."

"Not poisoned, is it?"

"No, I keep all my poisons here." She twists her delicate wrist, gesturing to an array of vials resting inside the locked case to the left. My eyes go wide.

Oh, she wasn't kidding.

"I consider myself an expert. Some of these I even crafted myself."

I read the labels in wonder.

Water Nymph Tears-weakens psychic connection

Poppy Flower-impairs judgement and makes one more susceptible to influence

Mandrake root-causes dangerous hallucinations

Calder Essence- causes temporary paralysis and in extreme cases causes the blood to boil

"You know, they say poison is the coward's way."

"It's not. Take it from someone who's tried every manner of murder—the best weapon is the one they don't see coming. Nothing works better than being underestimated. Kills faster than any blade in this world."

She keys open the compartment and starts digging around, passing me a glittering orange vial to hold.

"Careful with that—it will grow you horns."

I shoot her a look, catching a glimpse of a familiar blue powder in a glass jar.

"That blue stuff—what is it?"

"Blue moon? Oh, just a sedative. This one might be my favorite. Comes from the venom of the rarest reptile in the world." She proudly holds up a beautiful iridescent vial, like crushed diamonds in liquid form. "Hunted the bastard for years in the jungles. Nearly killed half my crew before I severed its head and took its tail as a keepsake."

Okaaaay.

"What do I owe you for this?" I hold up Dover's cure.

She walks over to a small broom closet, pulling out a bucket and a long, rough-bristled brush.

Shoving it at my chest, she says, "Tell your little prince friend that the deck needs scrubbing."

AFTER A WEEK OF ROUGH SAILING—THE six of us crammed into one claustrophobic cabin—the ship rolls to a stop in a shallow, rocky harbor. I stand on the deck, listening to the crew shout orders as they lower the creaking ramp to the pebbled shore.

Heeled boots echo across the floorboards, and Kai glances up from his scrubbing as the Pirate King appears from the upper deck, a jeweled belt of weapons slung low on her hip. I take it as no coincidence that Kai chooses that moment to shuck off his shirt and wipe the sweat from his brow.

He's been on cleaning duty for days as punishment for his crimes. The scutwork doesn't look fun, but it beats the plank.

He sinks back on his heels, the wet floor around him glistening as the Pirate King approaches.

"Missed a spot," she says, breezing right past him to stop before

Zadyn and me. Kai's gaze climbs her legs as she adjusts her wide-brimmed hat over one eye. "Showtime, witch."

Our feet have barely touched down on the ramp before she wheels around, pressing a hand to Zadyn's chest. "Where do you think you're going, handsome?"

His eyes shift between us. "With the two of you."

"I don't think so, lover boy. The more the merrier does not apply here. But don't worry, I'll take good care of her." She flashes him a flirty smile as she wraps her long fingers over my shoulder. "Let's go."

Zadyn catches my hand.

You call me the second you feel something is wrong, he says, a stern expression on his face.

I will.

His hold tightens a fraction before he releases me.

The Pirate King leads me through a patch of wild trees until the forest thins and we step onto ashen ground.

Skull Valley yawns before us—cold, barren, and brittle. As we wind the grim-looking gap between gray, snow-dusted mountains, I see where it got its nickname.

Piles of skulls line our path through the towering ranges. The sun-bleached skeletons of people and horses are littered all around in a macabre fashion. There are so many, it's hard to avoid stepping on them. I try to focus my attention ahead, but every so often my gaze wanders, and my stomach twists. I squint up at the bright sun as a dull ache begins to form between my brows. I rub my temples, trying to ease some of the tension.

"Still breathing, Blackblood?" the Pirate King calls over her shoulder.

"I'm fine," I grouse, picking up my pace to match hers. "So if this compass was so precious, how did you manage to lose it to the Valley Dwellers?"

A dark expression crosses her face.

"A few decades ago, we were sent on an errand. We had no choice but to take this pass. Some things were lost in the crossfire."

She stops short at the mouth of a dim cavern. I nearly bump into her back. "What I'm looking for is in this cave."

Without hesitation, she plunges into the darkness.

It's quiet here. Quiet enough to hear the thin ribbons of water trickling down the walls, the crawling of insects on the uneven floor beneath us. The cave narrows into a jagged tunnel that we have to duck to fit through. The outside world grows smaller and smaller until it is no more than a tiny pinhole of light behind us.

When we come out the other side, my jaw drops.

We're standing in a cavernous dome of glittering gold. Piles and piles of jewels and trunks brimming with treasure. It looks like King Midas' palace.

"Don't touch a thing," she warns me.

"I'm not." Although I can't say that I'm not tempted. "The compass is in here? It will take days to search this place."

"No, it won't."

"Why is that?"

She shushes me. "I know exactly where I left it."

I lower my voice to match hers. "How do you know it's still there?"

"I just know."

I stagger, a strange wave of dizziness hitting me. "Woah. Hang on a second."

The Pirate King threads her arm through mine and hauls me forward. Every step becomes harder until I'm depending mostly on her to keep us moving. That sickly feeling intensifies, pooling in my stomach and making my head foggy.

"Something's wrong. I need to sit down."

"Quiet," she hisses, glancing around the cave.

She pulls her arm from mine, and I sway on my feet, catching myself against the rocky wall. She stoops beside a humanoid skeleton leaned up against the cave. Disintegrated scraps of clothing hang from its tall frame.

"Hello, Father."

The Pirate King reaches out a gloved hand, carefully running it down the milky cheekbone. Hollowed-out eye sockets stare back at her like two dark voids as her fingers close around the circular pendant dangling from her father's neck. With a hard tug, she yanks the chain free. The skull topples off, knocking against her boot. She skitters back, falling on her ass. Then she's scrambling to her feet, towing me toward the sliver of daylight at the mouth of the cave.

"Let's go."

I'm all but delirious at this point.

My boot catches on something. I see a flash of gold, and then I'm on the ground. Pebbles bite into my palms as I try to push myself up. The Pirate King freezes, watching the gleaming chalice that tripped me roll away. It rattles across the floor until it disappears into a dark corner. My ears zero in on the sound.

Then the rattling stops altogether.

It doesn't take a rocket scientist to figure out that silence is not a good thing.

"Get. The Fuck. *Up*," she demands.

Through my delirium, I swing my head in the direction of her gaze.

Out of the shadows steps a giant clawed foot. Skin like albino leather is stretched over its tall, gangly frame. It stands easily over seven feet, red, beady eyes peering out with eerie vacancy. Yellow hair like straw sprouts from its head, forming a thin line down its thick neck and horned back. It licks its lips, the rancid saliva leaking from its gaping jaw adding to my nausea.

I stop breathing.

It sniffs the air, its nostrils flaring. Then it falls forward onto its taloned hands and roars.

"Run," the Pirate King says before sprinting headlong toward the exit.

I try to dash after her, but everything feels heavy. Lethargic. The cave walls seem to be closing in on me as I trip through the tunnel. It takes a moment for the beast to cram itself through the narrow space. That is my only saving grace as I army crawl toward my escape.

"Wait! I need help!" I call out. Her hand closes around my wrist, and she groans, hauling me out of the tunnel and to my feet.

"Gods damn it, you're heavy."

I don't have time to snap a witty retort as the creature springs for us.

"Sorry about this," she whispers before shoving me into the beast's waiting claws.

Grizzly teeth sink into my arm. Blood spurts everywhere as I howl, trying to wrangle free.

I'm rummaging through the pain, searching for my magic in my state of disorientation, but before I find it, the creature's jaw unlatches from my skin. I stumble backward.

Just in time for it to projectile vomit all over me. Black, sticky, tar-like goop drips from my head to my toes.

The creature makes a mewling sound, clawing at its throat. My fingers start to spark, and I shoot out whatever I can muster to torch it. My flames are pathetically weak, but at this point anything is better than nothing. I spin, scanning for the Pirate King.

"HEY!" My shout echoes off the cave walls as her silhouette darts out into the light.

That bitch left me!

More creatures appear from the shadows, cramming into the tunnel, shoving against each other, bloodlust lighting up their crimson eyes. I stumble outside, teetering on my feet. The Pirate King is now a small dot bobbing in the distance.

That backstabbing little—

The beasts tumble after me, lured by my blood—charging at me on all fours like a pack of hyenas with the speed of a Stygian horse. I'm no match. My muscles lock, and suddenly I can't move at all.

I'm going to die. It's been real, world.

That's when I hear the snarl. Feel it in my bones.

A flash of white appears in the distance, growing closer and clearer through my fuzzy vision.

Zadyn bounds toward me in *OrCat* form, his thundering steps kicking up mountain dust as he gallops at the speed of light. He leaps over me as I collapse, latching onto the neck of the beast hot on my heels.

I flatten out on a bed of broken skulls. And I don't even care. It feels so nice to rest.

Don't you dare go to sleep, Zadyn commands. I hum in response. *Serena, answer me, damn it!*

Mkayyy, I'm just resting.

STAY. AWAKE.

Another growl rattles the ground. It's louder. Loud enough to shake a few rocks loose from the surrounding mountains. I lift my face from the dirt to glance at the shadow blotting out the sun.

Powerful arms shift beneath me as I'm lifted into the air. My head lolls against Zadyn's shoulder, bouncing violently as he runs me out of range just in time for Furi's blue fire to incinerate the horde of Valley Dwellers. Her rage is palpable as she breezes overhead, scorching the earth and doling out death. She finally settles on the ground, and I watch as she bares her teeth and chomps down on them one by one.

That's my girl. I smile to myself.

"Serena?" Zadyn slows as we reach the trees, his voice thick with concern.

"Hmm."

A slow clap sounds from up ahead. I manage to pry my head off Zadyn long enough to glimpse the Pirate King leaning against an evergreen tree, a smug smirk on her face.

"Bra-fucking-vo. I really didn't think you were going to make it."

My stomach gurgles.

"Puhmedown," I slur, struggling against Zadyn's chest.

"What?" He glances down at me, still breathless.

"Down!"

He lowers me to the ground, and I squirm away just in time to puke my guts up.

"Hey. Hey, you're okay." He holds my hair back as I retch on the forest floor. My vision almost instantly sharpens, and my senses return. I glare up at the feline pirate towering above me.

"What the fuck did you do to me?"

"The Dwellers have a taste for powerful blood. So I poisoned yours."

She shrugs as if she just told me it was Tuesday.

"What the fuck?!" I screech, fighting back another wave of nausea.

"Oh, relax, I didn't give you enough to kill you. Honestly, that was mild compared to the cocktail I slipped you and your friends to dampen your magic."

"You poisoned me and fucking left me to die!" I seethe, black tar still dripping from my face and clothes.

"Self-preservation," she explains with an unnerving level of nonchalance. "Oh, don't pout. You'd do the same."

"No. I would not."

Rolling her azure eyes, she says, "You'll get over it. You're alive, aren't you? Lover boy over there is quite the hero." I want to smack her when she tosses him a wink. "Besides, you should be thanking me."

"Really. Why is that?"

"I just provided you with a very valuable lesson. Never trust a pirate."

She spins and sashays away. I glare at the back of her head as Zadyn helps me back to the ship.

Kai straightens when he sees me clomping up the ramp still covered in black-tar, Valley Dweller vomit. "What in hell happened to you?"

"Don't ask."

The Pirate King's poison takes an hour to exit my system. An hour in which I can barely lift my head from the bucket. Zadyn coaches me through it despite my futile efforts begging him to look away, and let me suffer my hideous fate alone.

Once there is nothing left in me but my soul, he guides me into the bath, then back into bed where I sleep like the dead.

49

SERENA

I'm pulled from a thick, groggy sleep by a clash of boisterous voices singing shanties from above deck. My muscles feel wrung out as I stretch through my fingertips, pushing back the thin blanket and scanning the empty cabin.

The last of the sun slips away as I pad onto the deck to find my friends lodged smack dab in the middle of a private revelry. Clanking pewter mugs, burly bodies joined at the shoulders swaying back and forth, happy shouts ringing through the open air.

My eyes find Zadyn almost immediately on one of the small upper-decks. He turns as if sensing my presence, leaping over the low rail to cut through the raucous sailors.

"You're awake." He breaks into a wide smile as he reaches me, brushing the damp hair off my neck. It's a casual move, but my skin warms when his fingers graze my collarbone. "How do you feel?"

"Like I just vomited up a fuck-ton of poison," I admit on a laugh.

"Sit." He pats the top of a wooden barrel. "I'll get you some water."

Zadyn returns a moment later with a waterskin. I catch his hand in mine. "Thank you."

"For what?" he asks, brows knitting together.

"For saving my ass earlier. And for taking care of me." He reaches

274

out to tuck my hair behind my ear, waking the butterflies in my stomach.

"I always will," he promises. "It's my job."

His statement leaves me with a twinge of disappointment, though I'm not really sure why. I push it out of my mind as I drink, directing my attention to the drunken karaoke unfolding before me.

"What's going on here?"

"While you were braving Skull Valley, the crew was on a job. Raided the home of some wealthy merchant and brought back ten barrels of gold. Hence, the celebration."

I glance around at the pirates—their golden-brown chests and tattooed arms on display in their skin-tight vests—noticing the multitude of gold jewelry dripping from their necks, wrists, and ears. I even spot one in a tiara, rolling a set of dice and pumping his fist in the air.

Toward the edge of the fray, the Pirate King lounges on a throne of stacked trunks, her inked fingers toying with the compass. Her stare is fixed on the antique brass, but it's clear her mind is far away.

Bronyn claps his tattooed hands, and one of the pirates hops off a crate, passing him an instrument that resembles a guitar with six strings and a hollowed body.

"Who's next?" he booms in his thick accent.

"I've a song to sing." Kai stands, dusting off his jacket as he makes his way down to the quarterdeck. "It's very old and very sad. One of my favorites. A love song."

He steals a look at the Pirate King lazing on her throne, pointer finger pressed to her forehead, giving him full-on deadpan.

Kai turns to whisper something to Zadyn, who takes the guitar from Bronyn and slides onto the empty crate.

He plays guitar too?

Great. Just what my ovaries need.

Zadyn starts to pick at the strings, but when Kai opens his mouth, mine hits the deck.

His voice is otherworldly. He sings proudly, his tone rich and husky and full of passion. Mar and I exchange a look of astonishment. The song is sad and sweet—a story about a maiden whose love abandoned her, so she cut out her heart and cast it into the sea after him.

Bleak, but you know, kind of sweet.

The Pirate King inspects her nails as Kai pours his heart out, his sights set on her and her alone. But she can't ignore it when he kneels before her, and on the final note of the song, takes her hand and kisses it.

I don't know how *anyone* could remain indifferent to being serenaded like that. Voices like his are typically rewarded with fainting spells and flying bras.

But the Pirate King rips her hand away and plants her feet on the ground. "Bravo, little prince. At least that smug mouth is good for something besides talking people to death."

He takes this as a compliment, his lips parting into a blinding smile. "Give me a chance, and I'll show you just how good this mouth can be."

She slowly reaches out a hand, then leverages his head to push out of her seat. I can't contain my laughter as she stalks away.

It's hilarious. The more Kai tries, the more she loathes him. And the more she loathes him, the harder he tries.

Kai is not used to being told no by the opposite sex. The only one who's likely resisted his charm is me. But I suspect that's because despite his harmless flirtations, Kai and I care for each other in a different way. It's never been like that between us.

I turn back to find Zadyn still leaned over the guitar, his fingers moving deftly over the strings, drawing out beautiful music.

God, he looks gorgeous. Slightly disheveled, sleeves rolled up to his elbows, hair falling over his eyes, and nose pink from our days of sailing. As if all that weren't enough to have me drooling, he has to whip out a secret musical talent? It's like a double Cupid shot right to the ass.

We lock eyes as he starts to play a familiar riff. I tilt my head.*

No.

---

* Cue: *Mamma Mia* by ABBA

Yes, he flashes me a grin, and then starts singing. Terribly.

"I was cheated by you, and I think you know when…"

He stumbles through the first verse, laughing through every word as I clutch my gaping mouth, dually endeared and impressed by his commitment.

Don't leave me hanging, he begs halfway through the chorus.

Fuck it.

I jump out of my seat and shout back, "*Yes, I've been brokenhearted, blue since the day we parted. Why, why did I ever let you go!*"

He joins in again, "*Mamma Mia, now I really kno-ow, my, my, I could never let you go!*"

The deck bursts into wild applause. His smile warms my entire body, starting at my toes and traveling upward. It's contagious, that smile. I don't recall moving my feet, but suddenly I'm standing right in front of him.

"You remembered."

He scoffs. "Of course I did. Spring Break. Panama City."

"Never forget."

"RIP Annie." He kisses his hand and lifts it toward the sky.

"I miss her," I admit, barely above a whisper.

"She's right here." He rubs the spot over his heart. I clear my throat, pushing away the melancholy thought.

"How come you never told me you played guitar?"

He shrugs. "It never came up."

"Color me impressed."

He reaches up to scratch the stubble on his jaw. "Well, I learned that one for you."

Warmth flares in my chest. "You did?"

Before he can answer, someone bumps into me, sloshing ale down the front of my top.

"Apologies, lady—" the pirate stops short, gaping at me. "Oye. It's you."

"Me?" I point to myself, glancing between him and Zadyn as if he's going to have some explanation.

"Yes, *you*. Chair girl!"

"I'm sorry—*what?*"

"The tavern in Iaspus—you broke a chair over my back. You were there too." He jabs a finger at Zadyn. "All of you."

He turns around, lifts up his shirt, and points over his shoulder to the faint scar between the faded black ink. "Never healed proper. Wood splinter I waited too long to get out."

"Oh, uh, sorry about that."

"No need. Pirates wear scars like badges of honor. Maps and tales of survival. That arm of yours is really something." He pinches my bicep, his pierced mouth curving into a lazy smirk. Zadyn takes a step closer to me.

"You didn't seem all too impressed that night as you were trying to kill us," I shoot back, crossing my arms over my soaked shirt.

"Ahh, if we had wanted you dead, you'd already be six feet under. Brawling is—uh—how we show affection. Ask your prince friend. He'll tell you. Name's Coyle."

"Serena."

"Charmed." Coyle steals my hand from beneath my arm and kisses it. My gaze shifts to Zadyn, who looks about ready to snap this dude in half.

"This is Zadyn." I lay a cautionary hand on his shoulder.

Down boy. He's just being friendly.

A little too *friendly.*

I roll my eyes. Coyle nods to Zadyn, then turns to snatch his friend from another conversation.

"Oye. Look who I found."

His friend's pale green eyes pop when they land on me. "Chair girl!"

Before I can react, he's swept me up into his tawny arms and pulled me into a lively, wild dance. Another sailor tugs Mar out of her seat and whisks her across the boards.

Then the entire ship is dancing, twining arms and switching partners in time to the music. One second I'm spinning, and the next, Zadyn grabs me around the waist and pulls me to a dizzying stop. My laughter fades, and in the middle of the ship, he's suddenly the only one I see.

He hasn't tried to make a move since that night at the inn, even though we've been sharing a bed since we got on board. And we still haven't spoken about that kiss. Or how he told me he wanted to get to know every square inch of my body.

Swoon.

"Chair girl." He teases a smile. "Has a nice ring to it."

"Are you kidding? It's legendary."

Through the crowd, I notice the Pirate King slipping off toward her cabin. A little twinge of guilt nips at me. I place a hand on Zadyn's arm.

"Hey, I'll be right back," I tell him.

Weaving between bodies, I overhear someone slur, "Don't get me wrong—you cross a pirate, you die. BUT if you cross a pirate and manage to live, you've made yourself a friend for life."

I turn to see Bronyn tuck Kai beneath his hulking bicep and give him a hearty shake. More pirates join in, reaching out to ruffle his hair. Kai's transgressions seem to be forgiven as they clap him on the back and commend him for being the only one on board capable of carrying a tune.

I smile to myself, stopping outside the Pirate King's door. Sniffles sound from inside. I give a tentative knock. The sniffling immediately stops.

"What is it, Bronyn?" the cold voice snaps.

"It's not Bronyn, it's Serena."

Silence.

"Can I come in?"

"No."

Rolling my eyes, I twist the handle and step inside.

"I said—"

"I know what you said."

Her eyes are glassy and red around the rims. So is the tip of her button nose. She glares at me from behind her desk.

"What do you want, witch?"

"I came to check on you."

"And why in gods' names would you do that?"

"Because," I sigh, slinking further into the room. "That was your father. In the cave."

She steels herself. "And?"

"I can't imagine having to do that. To see that."

Her icy gaze falls to the jug of clear liquor sitting on her desk. She pours some into a crystal glass and tosses it back.

"I've done worse. And I'll do more before my time here is up."

I help myself to the empty seat across from her. "I lost my father too."

Her smart blue eyes land on mine. "Do you think that makes us the same? That we're now bonded by the sisterhood of dead fathers? Shall we braid each other's hair and exchange dark secrets?"

I prop my chin on my hand. "You really are a bitch, aren't you?"

She snorts a laugh, twirling the empty glass in her hand. "Suppose I am."

"You're not made of steel. You don't have to pretend you are. Feeling doesn't diminish your strength."

"Doesn't it though?" She gives me a sober look, then twists around to grab a second glass from the bar cart. I watch as she fills both and slides one across the desk to me.

"Here." I eye the drink, then her. "Don't worry, I used up all my poison earlier."

I accept the glass, lifting it into the air. "Cheers. You fucking owe me."

"Fine, Blackblood. I owe you."

Our glasses clink.

"Look." I plop my forearm on the desk. Two pink crescent moons peer back at us. "Twin scars. It's kind of badass."

A reluctant smile spreads on her lips. Shaking her head, she kicks her feet up on her desk and reclines back in her chair.

"Yes. I suppose it kind of is."

5 0

SERENA

The Pirate King's heeled boot collides with the door, forcing it open with a loud crash. We spill into the foyer, herded by pirates holding cutlasses to our throats.

It's all an act, of course. We know each of them by name. Have gotten drunk with them for the last week on our trip north. And now we're performing with them.

"What a dump." The Pirate King scans the hall, dusting off her hands and the remnants of blue powder she used to knock out the behemoth soldiers standing guard. "Knock, knock, anybody home?"

"*ALIX!*" Eaton's shout echoes down the spacious torchlit hall.

The princess peels around the corner, her face shifting from confusion to ire. The two guards at her back draw their swords as she pops a dagger from her belt.

"How did you get past the guards?"

The Pirate King shrugs, drifting toward a concrete sculpture and trailing a finger along the surface. "They looked a bit tired, so we offered them a nap."

"Get. Your hands. Off of that." Alix glowers at her.

The Pirate King stops, cocking one hip and resting her elbows on the hilt of her sword. "I'll be brief. Your little brother and his side

281

squad ran into some trouble on the road. I ensured his safe passage back here."

"Great. You want a medal?"

"I want compensation."

Alix barks a laugh. "You've got some balls, barging in here, ransoming a prince of Hyrax and making demands in my home."

"It's only fair. Hand over the gold, and we can all walk away happy."

"Alix, just do it," Eaton says. "I promised her."

"You promised to pay your kidnapper? Where is your backbone, Eaton?"

"I had to, Alix. Just do it, we had a deal."

"Look at that. Your brother is a man of honor after all."

If looks could kill, Eaton would be a pile of ash.

"Well. How much?" Alix bites.

Bronyn reaches into his pocket and hands her the wrinkled wanted flyer.

The Pirate King inspects her nails with indifference. "Triple that sum should do it."

"Triple? We agreed on double!" Eaton bursts.

She shrugs a lean shoulder. "I'm running a business here."

"Wait here," Alix growls, before disappearing around the corner.

The Pirate King scuffs her heels as she meanders through the foyer. "This place is hideous," she says appreciatively.

Alix returns with another guard holding two large sacks. He dumps them at the pirates' feet, a few coins spilling out onto the cold stone floor.

"There's your ransom. Take it and get out before I change my mind."

"Gladly." The Pirate King removes her hat, crosses it over her chest, and bends to her outstretched leg in a low, graceful bow. "Pleasure working with you. Let's do it again sometime."

With a snap of her fingers, we're released. She's almost to the door when Kai slides in front of her.

"Princeling. You're in my way."

"I'll see you again."

"Not if I can help it."

Kai breaks into an elusive smile, lifting her hand to his lips. She takes a step closer.

"Move."

"Oh, yes." He nods, a glint in his ocean eyes. "I'll most definitely see you again."

"Steal from me again or show your face in Bleakwater Bay and I won't be so forgiving."

"Is that a threat or a promise?"

"A warning." She closes the gap between them, trailing her finger down his torso to snag on his belt. "And here's a little something to remember me by."

Kai doubles over as she thrusts her fist into his groin.

"Hah. And they said you were big. Disappointing." She sucks in a breath through her teeth, shaking her head. "Let's go."

Kai watches her leave, his face a mask of wild surprise.

"Pirates, Eaton? Really? Do you have any idea how much I had to pay her?"

"Oh, relax, it's not like we can't afford it."

"That isn't the point. I am sick of always having to bail you out of your little shit traps. What is going on?"

"It's been a long week, Alix, maybe you can save the shrill tones for breakfast and give me a night to rest."

"That's it? That's all you have to say?!" She tosses a beseeching look at Zadyn, but he drops his gaze to the floor. A bitter laugh leaves her as Eaton leads us away.

"Thank you," I say as I pass, earning her razor-sharp glare. "For bailing us out. We owe you."

Not deigning to answer, she gives me a harsh once-over and spins on her heel to stomp away.

THE GRIMOIRE SITS in my lap, buzzing with energy as I thumb through pages of age-old charms, enchantments, and potions, wondering who wrote them. Some entries appear in a coded language, but others adapt to my eyes, translating themselves for me to better understand.

"Good read?"

Zadyn strides into our room, unbuckling the belt of weapons at his hip. My eyes track him as he carelessly tosses it onto the daybed and peels off his jacket. He catches me watching, and I quickly look back to the book.

"Best nonfiction I ever had."

He chuckles, leaning against the bedpost as he rolls up his sleeves. Which shouldn't be as hot as it is.

"There's so much in here. Half of it I don't even understand, but it makes me feel connected to my ancestors in a weird way." I close the book, setting it on the bed beside me.

Zadyn's brow creases. "You said the book and the mirrors spoke to you. What did they say?"

I sigh. "Nothing, it's dumb."

"Come on," he says, sinking down beside me. I shake my head. "Fine. A question for a question."

"You want to play the question game?"

"Why not? I'll let you ask me anything."

"Really? Anything at all?" I give him a wicked look.

"Anything within *reason*." He rolls his eyes. "Now spill."

"They called me—" Zadyn slides closer. "Queen. They called me queen."

He goes still.

"It's stupid, I know."

"No, it's not."

"What are you thinking?"

"I'm thinking you need to take this a little more seriously. You've got magical objects calling you queen—Arden herself said the same thing. These things have weight."

"Zadyn, I'm no queen."

"You really don't see it, do you?"

"What?"

"The kind of power you hold—the things you represent." His thumb brushes over my cheek, light as a whisper. "The effect you have on people."

I laugh even though I don't find the notion of me being the rightful queen of Solterre funny. At all. I can just file that along with the list of absurdities that have recently been proven true and call it a day.

"My turn," I announce. "Why did you stop me from killing Mal when I had the chance?"

Zadyn sighs. "Trust me, his days are numbered."

"Then why stop me? He would have been one less thing to worry about."

"We didn't have much time, and I needed to heal you. And honestly, I didn't want you to have to feel everything that comes with taking a life. I know you. The guilt would have eaten you alive."

"I've killed before, Zadyn."

"The Stryga don't count. They're undead. Taking a person's life is different."

"You've done it."

He shifts on the bed, his hand falling from my face. "Do you hear yourself right now? Yes, I have done it. When I was left with no other choice. Which is why I intend to protect you from doing the same."

"Do you hear *yourself*? You sound so self-righteous. I don't need you to protect me from anything. He needs to be dealt with one way or another."

"And I intend to deal with him," Zadyn claims. "Thoroughly."

"No, *I* want to deal with him. He's mine. That traitor almost killed Kai."

He would have killed me if Kylian hadn't stopped him. I still remember the murderous glint in his eye after I tried to peel Ilspeth's face from her skull.

There's a light tease in Zadyn's voice as he says, "So I should just lie back and let you loose on the world?"

"Maybe then we could get some things accomplished."

"You're not a killer."

"I will be before this is all over." I run my fingers over the fur throw. "War is coming. I'll do whatever it takes to protect the people I love."

"That's *my* job. And I don't care if you want my protection or not, Serena. Because you have it. And I am going to do my best to ensure you don't ever have to do anything you'll regret."

"Worried I won't make it to heaven?"

"Not really." He shrugs. "Heaven or hell, wherever you go, I'm going too."

His words pluck one of my heartstrings. I can feel it vibrating throughout my entire body.

"You can't stop me, you know," I whisper.

"You don't think so?" He gives me an arch look before launching forward, attacking my sides with jabbing pokes. "Huh, *Chair Girl?*"

"No!" I squeal, attempting to shove his hands away. I finally get a hold of his wrists and force him to look at me. He shakes his head, one dimple popping as he gives me that boyish smirk.

"I'm not afraid of you."

"You should be." My words hang in the air like a smoke ring. I drop my voice. "I wanted him dead. I wanted to watch the life leave his eyes as I choked it out of him. Maybe I'm more like Kylian than I originally thought."

He reaches out to pinch my chin between his thumb and forefinger.

"You are *nothing* like him. Don't ever say that."

I can hear my heart pounding inside my chest as his eyes burn into mine. His hand drifts down my neck. I'm practically panting when he slides his finger beneath my locket.

"Where did you get this?"

"From him."

"Kylian?"

I nod, my entire body tensing and eager with him this close.

"And you kept it?" A dip appears between his brows. The air cools as he drops the necklace and pushes back from me a bit.

"I thought it might be useful somehow." I open my mouth to explain, but with no words to justify my actions, I seal it shut again.

He nods, quietly contemplating something, but he doesn't ask me to extrapolate. Sometimes I find myself dying to know what's going on in his head beyond the unspoken words he occasionally shares with me.

The wind howls outside the window, breaking the moment's spell.

"It's getting late. I'm gonna get ready for bed." The air is still thick as I slide off the bed and head toward the bathroom to change.

51

ZADYN

This is getting out of hand.

First the kiss in the street, then the *almost* kiss at the inn. Sharing a bed for weeks on the ship, waking up accidentally tangled around each other. The constant teasing and flirting. These moments when we're face to face, nearly nose to nose, testing each other—pushing the boundaries of our friendship to its absolute breaking point.

Any moment it could shatter.

And the idea of that partially thrills me.

I used to think this attraction was entirely one-sided. But now? I'm not so sure. Not when she looks at me with that glint in her eye—that little spark of mischief.

It's utterly irresistible.

I pull the shirt over my head and toss it down on the daybed as the door behind me clicks open. My jaw goes slack.

Seven fucking hells.

Serena steps out of the bathroom wearing this slinky black slip with barely enough material to cover her perky little ass. Heat slashes up my neck at the sight of her bare legs—the smooth, tan flesh peeking out from beneath the lace panels on either side.

288

As if it weren't enough that her voice haunts me everywhere I go. That she distracts me from being fully present in every conversation I have. That I can read every shift in her scent, that I know what it means when she bites her lip, when she arches her back slightly more than usual, the way her thoughts scream at me even when I try to shut them out.

No. As if all of that weren't enough, she has to go and wear *that.*

She has to know what she's doing to me.

"What?" She blinks, the portrait of cruel innocence.

"Nothing." I scratch the back of my neck, wiping the shock from my face. "That just seems like an impractical outfit with temperatures like these."

I nod toward the blizzard starting up outside the window.

"You try sleeping under a thousand pounds of animal pelts."

Leaning over the bed, I strip off one of the heavy furs. "They *are* removable, you know."

She snatches the throw from my hands and flings it back into place. "I like to be cozy when I sleep." I roll my eyes as she brushes past me, her naked arm grazing mine. "You sleep shirtless. I don't see how it's any different," she tosses over her shoulder, climbing into the massive bed.

"I sleep shirtless when you're around. When I'm alone, I don't wear anything."

Her eyes snap to mine before trickling lower over my bare chest and abs. So I allow mine to do the same, letting them run down the length of her sinful body.

All the blood drains from my head.

That fucking slip.

I clear my throat, sinking back onto the daybed. She settles into the sheets behind me and leans over to blow out the candle, shrouding us in darkness.

"Night, Zadyn," she murmurs.

"Goodnight."

I lie on my back, staring up at the ceiling for what feels like hours.

Starlight dances in through the narrow gap between curtains, slicing across the room like a giant spotlight on Serena.

I listen to the sound of her ragged breaths, each one a new torture. I'm so on edge lately, even the slightest breeze against my skin has me ready to burst. It's only made worse when the sheets begin to rustle, and I hear her turn over, a little sound like a whimper falling from her lips.

My ears perk up. She's not usually a sleep talker. Then the whimpers turn into sighs, coming faster and harder.

Dear gods.

She's having a sex dream.[*]

Fuck *me.*

I drag my hands down my face. At the sound of her moan, the blood rushes to my cock so fast I get lightheaded.

This is going to be the death of me.

I'm dying to look back, but—no, that would be so wrong.

But maybe just for one second…

Nope, no. Still wrong.

"Please," she whispers.

My head whips around, ending the debate. I stare helplessly as her back arches and her dark hair spills across the pillow. The satin strap of her slip falls down her shoulder.

I should wake her.

She wouldn't want me to hear this, to see this. She would be mortified.

But wouldn't it be worse not to let her finish?

I blow out a long sigh, burying my head in my arm.

Breathe, Zadyn.

But it's hard to think beyond the insistent throbbing in my pants. I'm fucking aching.

"Please," she calls again, louder this time. I gape, watching her hand roam over her breast and up into her hair. What I wouldn't give to be that hand.

---

[*] Cue: *So Sweet I Could Die* by Lucia & The Best Boys

She writhes again, like a cat in the sun. I have to literally bite my knuckle to keep from groaning.

I can't take anymore. Surging from the bed, I dart out of the room.

Heavy breaths rock my chest as I press my palms to the door. I can still feel her from the other side. I can feel her pleasure as if it were my own. It sings in my veins, rolls through my blood, through my body.

Pushing off the door, I stalk through the torchlit halls, up the winding staircase leading to one of the spiked towers. I burst through the darkness toward the glassless window. It isn't until my fingers wrap around the cold brick sill that I realize I'm not alone.

"Needed a little space from your bond?"

Alix's low, raspy voice has me turning. Bitter blue eyes roam over me, peering out through the shadows.

"I didn't realize anyone was in here."

"No shit." Rising from the rocking chair in the corner, she steps into the sliver of moonlight. Her head tilts as she sinks her hip into the wall beside me. "Did you forget this was my favorite place to go and think?"

"It's also the most haunted place here."

"Why do you think I like it so much?"

How could I forget? Alix has a bit of a kink for the paranormal.

Alix, Eaton, and I used to come up here all the time during the witching hour, hoping to catch something supernatural happening. Supposedly, this was once a nursery for a queen whose child was stolen in the night and never found. She locked herself inside this tower and died in that rocking chair, waiting for her baby to return.

Alix studies me for a moment, then reaches out to wrench my jaw to the side. "I was worried I'd permanently damaged your pretty face. Females everywhere would have rioted."

She releases me.

"Alix. I'm sorry for the way I left—"

"I don't want your apology, Zadyn." Her tone is clipped. "I shouldn't have expected things you weren't capable of. I was only ever Eaton's little sister to you."

"That's not true. You were my friend."

"I thought so. But friends don't do the things we did together. And they certainly don't leave the way you did."

"I had to. I didn't really have a choice."

"You could have said goodbye. I would have understood."

"You're right. I'm sorry."

"Are you?" She snorts, crossing her toned arms over her chest. "You haven't changed a bit."

"Why do you say that?"

"You show up here after thirty years like it's your gods-given right, and my brothers welcome you back, no questions asked. Then you and Eaton immediately take off on some mysterious quest, and once again, I'm left behind. You were always doing that. Running off to be boys, to go find adventure. I was never a part of your little brotherhood. Much as I wanted to be."

"Alix—"

"Why did you come back here?"

"It's a long story."

She tosses out a jaded laugh. "Of course it is. Did it ever occur to you that I might be able to help with whatever big secret you're keeping? I'm smarter and sharper than my brothers. Always have been. I can best any of them in a match. But that was never enough, was it?" I give her a look of regret. "Even after all this time, I'm still just a second thought to you all."

"I didn't ask you because I didn't think you'd want anything to do with me."

"Could you blame me? Zadyn, I know my worth. But you and my brothers…you've never treated me as an equal. I'm just another female to you. And after we got together, it felt like my value just dropped in your eyes. You could barely look at me."

Guilt churns in my gut. "I never realized we were doing that, leaving you behind…or that it hurt you."

"Why would you? You only really paid attention when I spread my legs." She gives me a sad, stinging smile, and a wave of shame washes over me.

"I'm not proud of the way I acted back then."

"Don't worry, it's not keeping me up at night. Not anymore." She sighs, staring out at the falling snow. "She seems…interesting."

I laugh, pushing my hair back. "You want to talk about her?" She shrugs, indifferent. "Interesting?"

"What?"

"I know what that means."

"It means she seems interesting." Alix shifts her weight, meeting my gaze again. "I just find it ironic."

"What?"

"You clearly have a type. Headstrong women who could probably kick your ass. Definitely, in my case."

I chuckle, glancing down at the floor. "Definitely in your case."

"Does she know how you feel?"

I shake my head. Alix looks sympathetic for a moment—a rare break from the fierce, slightly pinched expression she often wears. She reaches out to brace my shoulder as she says, "Don't make the same mistakes over and over, Zadyn. Use your words. And speak the hell up."

WHEN MORNING COMES, I place a hand on Serena's shoulder, giving her a gentle nudge. Her skin is hot to the touch. She stretches, her chest straining against the smooth silk slip, sending a flood of desire through me.

"Hi." She yawns, looking at me with those starry eyes. "Did you sleep last night? You have bags under your eyes."

"No, not really," I admit with a rueful smile.

"Oh, no." Her face falls. "Was I sleep talking? I'm sorry, usually I don't—"

"You weren't…talking, per se." I press my lips together.

She tilts her head. "What are you not saying right now?"

"Well"—I push my hair back and try to stumble forward—"you were dreaming…and you started to…"

She waits for me to spit it out.

"You were…having a sex dream. I think."

She jolts upright, clapping a hand over her mouth.

"Oh my god!" A blush creeps over her cheeks and chest. She gets to her knees, shaking her hands with splayed fingers. "*Oh my god!* What did I do?! What did I say?"

"You didn't really say anything, you were just…making noise."

"Stop, I don't want to know!"

I reach out to pry her hands from her face. "It's okay, it happens!"

"Why didn't you wake me?!" Snatching a pillow off the bed, she whacks me on the arm. I laugh, unable to help myself.

"I thought it would be rude to interrupt."

"How considerate."

"I know it's been a while for you."

She scoffs, pushing off her heels to smack me again. I yank the pillow from her so fast, she falls back on her ass squealing. Then it's war.

She reaches for another, swinging at me with brutal force. I climb onto the bed, kneeling above her as our pillows collide. This time, a little too hard.

They explode, raining white feathers down on us in slow motion. Her laughter fills the room with the sweetest music I've ever heard.

I collapse over her, my arms bracketing her head as she stares up at me, a giggle dying on her lips.

"Was it good at least?"

"I don't remember," she breathes, her lavender eyes sucking me in.

One of those long stretches of silence yawns before us where time stands still, and all that exists is her.

Then her mind forces out an image I have no choice but to face.

An image of my hands sliding over her waist. Of my lips crushing hers. Of a stone wall digging into her back. Of the look on my face when she accidentally bit my lip.

"*That's* what you were dreaming about?"

She gives me a sheepish nod. "Well, that's how it started."

Fuck me, I almost groan.

No, I actually do groan. Out loud.

Serena's brows knit together. *Maybe I shouldn't have shared that with you.*

My eyes flash. *No, no. I'm glad that you did. It's just...*

What?

If I had known that's what you were dreaming about—

Then what?

This girl.

I would have stayed to make sure you finished.

A naughty smile pulls at her lips. I can't believe I'm allowing myself to say these things. To think them and *share* them with her. I'm setting myself up for disaster.

What happens when we go home to Aegar and Jace is back in the picture? It would be foolish to think that a little time away from him has cured her of her feelings. That things have changed, that suddenly her eyes are open to what this is—what we are.

I won't be the one to say it.

Cursing myself, I slide off the bed.

"Zadyn," she calls.

Halfway to the door, I turn back to see her flipped on her stomach, clicking her ankles—a shameless grin on her face and feathers still poking out of her dark waves.

"You have serious game. Who knew?"

Shaking my head, I allow myself a smile, reaching for the doorknob.

"Put some clothes on. Before you catch a cold."

52

SERENA

Still mortified from Zadyn witnessing my sex dream, I skip breakfast.

I can't believe I showed him.

Yes, that was rather brazen. Furi's voice makes me jump.

Woah. You should really knock if you're going to pop in unannounced and eavesdrop on my inner dialogue like that.

He didn't seem to mind, though, she muses. *Quite the opposite, in fact.*

We are not. Discussing this.

Why not? He's rather handsome. For a measly fae, of course.

That is really not the point.

And you're well—you—

Thanks? I think.

You both clearly enjoyed yourselves up against that building in Aeix. Such urges are only natural.

What circle of hell is this?

Please excuse me.

Where are you going?

To drink bleach.

I find the library empty. Plopping down in front of the fireplace, I begin to sift through the grimoire's ancient pages, basking in the warmth and solitude until my neck is stiff from reading. I stretch my arms above my head, flexing through my fingertips and toes. The book slides from my lap before I can catch it.

"Shit," I mutter, bending to pick it up.

A folded piece of paper slips from the back cover. I pause to read it.

> My dearest love,
> I am so sorry. If you are reading this, then I am dead. Our star still burns bright. Two halves of a whole will always find each other. You know what you must do. Guard it with your heart and with your life. Together, you hold the key.
> Find me in the After. I will be here waiting.
> Yours forever,
> Arden

A love letter. From Arden.

To who?

I comb through the records section, eventually coming across what I'm looking for. The witches and their lineage.

I locate Arden's name on the parchment and follow the dash across the page to her mate's name.

Garron…Garron Barlowe *Triori*.

Arden, the High Queen…was mated to a Triori?

I stare at the page, unblinking.

"It's been in my family for generations," Kylian had said as he presented me with the locket. *"Keep it on you at all times, and you will never be lost. It will always guide you home."*

Oh my god.

I have one half of the key. I've been wearing it around my neck this entire time. My fingers close over the smooth metal at my throat.

Why would he give this to me?

The answer sits in the darkest corner of the room, staring at me from the shadows like a watchful demon.

One I'm not yet ready to face.

"WHAT DO you know about Garron Barlowe Triori?"

"He was Arden's mate," Eaton answers.

"Is there any information in here about him?"

"Maybe in this one." He slides a heavy, dark red tome from its place on the shelf and spreads it out on the polished table. I follow his eyes down the page, trailing his pointer finger.

"Garron Triori, son of Melanthe Barlowe and Vance Triori I. He was Arden's king consort. When she died and the kingdoms broke off, he relinquished his crown to his older brother, who then became the first king of Vod. He was a starsmith."

"What the hell is a starsmith?" I cock my head.

"Starsmiths were extremely rare and powerful. They could essentially capture stars and fashion them into magical objects."

"Objects like a key?" I glance around, locking eyes with Zadyn.

Eaton gives me a half-assed shrug. "It's definitely possible."

I unclasp my locket and place it down on the table. Zadyn leans over, watching intently as I take a breath and flip it open. The star bounds from its shell, trailing light across the library as it dashes in all directions.

"What is that?" Eaton breathes.

"A star fragment."

Kai swings his legs off the table and stands. "Where did you get it?"

"Kylian gave it to me. Right before I walked down the aisle."

Zadyn gives me a long, wary look, his lean-muscled arms crossed over his chest.

"Did he ever say anything about a star passed down from your ancestors?"

Kai shakes his head. "No, he never mentioned it. But then again, we are not particularly close."

"What makes you think this is a key?" Eaton draws my focus.

"This letter." I pull the parchment from my pocket and smooth it out, allowing them to read it for themselves. "I found it tucked inside the grimoire. This book belonged to Arden."

My friends stare at me, brows slashed together. I toss open the grimoire to the page with the Aurea Dei constellation.

"Eaton, you said this page is a bunch of notes on this constellation? I think Arden was trying to figure out how to harness one of its stars, and I think Garron was helping her."

"You think Garron fashioned the star into a key for Arden?"

I nod. "Kylian said this was in his family for generations. Probably starting with Garron."

"Hold on. A key for what?" Zadyn asks.

"The portal, if I had to guess," I conclude. "Look. This line says it right here. 'Together, you hold the key. Two halves of a whole will always find each other. You know what you must do'. When I asked the grimoire to show me something that could help us, it chose this page. There has to be some connection. I think we have to find the other half of the star and join them."

Eaton hums. "A star key. I've never crossed anything like that in my research."

"Would you want anyone to know about a magical key that can lock and unlock the only gate known to Solterre? Think about if it fell into the wrong hands."

"I think it already has," Kai says under his breath.

Mar shakes her head. "But what would they need a key for if they had already installed the Guardians?"

"To keep something out, maybe. Something more powerful than a Guardian," Zadyn mutters.

I snap the locket closed. "When I saw Arden in that tree, I asked her if a key existed, and she just stared at this. She *knew* what it was. She warned me not to let it fall into the wrong hands. Maybe this is why."

"If the other half is out there, we have to find it," Marideth says.

"Wouldn't be surprised if Kylian was already in possession of it." Kai's voice is grim.

"Two halves of a whole will always find each other," Zadyn repeats. "I know how to find the other half."

He moves around to the grimoire and begins thumbing through it. "We need a tracking spell."

"I saw one earlier—I think it's here." I move to his side, finding the page for him. Eaton fetches a large map of Solterre and spreads it before us. I settle into the chair, taking a deep breath.

"I've never done this before," I say, glancing up at Mar.

She offers me an encouraging smile. "Time to spread those wings."

"Right." I nod. "Somebody knife me."

Zadyn draws a dagger, his eyes secured to mine as he takes my hand and pricks my finger. A drop of black rushes to the surface.

Clutching the locket, I recite the words from Arden's spell and squeeze three drops of blood onto the map. Then we wait. I feel the cool metal heat against my palm, vibrating as the blood on the scroll begins to travel. I flip it open, freeing the star, and the blood moves faster, forming a single black dot across the Praxian Sea.

"It's in Vod." I leap to my feet. "We got a lead!"

Finally, *something*, no matter how small. I turn to Zadyn, high on the rush of the spell, ready to launch myself at him. His smile sparkles with pride, but I stop myself at the last second, holding up my hand to give him the most emphatic high five in the history of the world.

A high five? *What is the* matter *with me?*

"Well, the good news is, it's in Vod," Eaton announces. "And the bad news is, it's in Vod."

Our smiles falter.

"Alright, so all we have to do is find a way to obtain it," Dover says brightly.

We shoot him an incredulous look. Easier said than done, I fear.

"I think we're on the right track," Zadyn says, "but if this is the answer to the portal problem, why would Kylian put that kind of power in your hands? It's risky."

"I believe it's what they call hubris," Kai interjects, flipping his onyx waves out of his eyes. "Not that I would know."

"You? Of course not," Mar retorts.

Zadyn and I are the last to make our way to dinner. I slip the locket over my head, cursing when the chain snags on my hair.

"Here." He pauses in the doorway to help untangle me.

"Nice job with the spell," he murmurs, his voice low. He keeps his eyes on the knot as he patiently works to unravel it. "You're a natural."

Heat races to my cheeks at the compliment. He frees me and glances up, his hands still in my hair. I clutch the grimoire against my chest, leaning back against the door frame, biting my lip like a fucking schoolgirl with a crush. The way he drags his eyes over me makes my breath hitch. Then he gives my hair a tug and walks off, chuckling after our friends.

I sag against the door, all the air exiting my body.

I am so fucked.

53

ZADYN

It's been nearly a week since we arrived back in Hyrax, and I'm still trying to wrap my head around the fact that Kylian Triori gave Serena a priceless heirloom that's been in his family since Garron Barlowe Triori.

And that heirloom is a fucking *star*.

And that fucking star could be the key to closing the portal.

He's either an idiot or severely underestimates Serena's intelligence.

We've been strategizing and tearing apart the library for any information to back our suspicions. Eaton even wrote to his scholar friends with private libraries dedicated to ancient texts. But so far we've had no luck. Knowing where the star is definitely helps, but apprehending it seems like an impossible task.

It's twilight when Serena and I head out to the forest to hunt for Furi. The final echoes of sunlight bear down on her hair, glinting off the stream of her braid through the gaps between trees. I stand a few feet back, absentmindedly admiring the way those leather pants turn her curves decadent.

"You know, it's really hard to concentrate with you staring at me like that," Serena murmurs, pulling her elbow back. She lets the arrow

302

fly, and it sticks in a nearby tree, missing the rabbit crouched in the distance. She heaves a loud groan.

I chuckle, taking a step toward her.

"Oh, I'm sorry"—I place a hand to my heart—"am I making you nervous?"

"No," she lies, loading another arrow. She lifts the bow and angles it toward the rabbit again.

"What about now?" I stop behind her, my chest brushing her back. I can feel her breathing—feel the uptick in her heartbeat.

"No."

I slide one hand over her glove and place the other on her elbow, lifting it higher so that her thumb is level with her lips.

"There," I murmur, my cheek skimming her hair. "Now let go."

The rabbit is dead before it has time to squeak.

"Very good." We stand there for a moment, barely touching, before I drag myself away.

"Didn't you know you were an archer too."

"I'm not. I've just got what some would call animal instincts." I flash her a wide grin as I plop down on a tree stump.

"Sexy," she teases, coaxing a laugh from me.

"It comes with being a shifter."

"Right, you've got those super special senses."

"They're definitely heightened. And they come in handy whenever you decide to wander off and find trouble."

Her mouth pops open. "That has only ever happened like three— five times. Five times tops."

I smirk. "Whatever you say."

"Can you pick up my scent? Like a dog?"

"Some might find that offensive, but yes. I would know your scent anywhere."

"And how do I smell?"

Fucking delicious.

I walk up to her, inclining my head toward her neck. "You smell like…vanilla."

She holds still as a statue, barely breathing as her chin lifts a fraction higher, granting me silent access to her throat.

"Lavender." I lean in to inhale her other side, watching the vein in her neck pulse erratically. "And trouble."

A new scent springs to the forefront, but I don't mention it. The one that tells me that on a cellular level, she wants me. Musk with a hint of spice. Like cinnamon and freshly watered soil fusing together. It's intoxicating. The thought makes me smile to myself, makes me dizzy with need.

So I force myself to draw back.

"That is disturbingly specific," she rasps.

"I've been around you for thirty years. I could find you with my eyes closed."

"Let's see it then."

I quirk a brow. "Are you challenging me?"

"Sounds like it."

"Alright, well. Hope you like losing."

Her eyes twinkle, then narrow to slits. "Count to twenty, then come find me."

"Oh, this is going to be too easy." I throw my head back, ambling closer. "Give me a challenge, at least."

"Oh, I plan to."

In an instant, her shadows have gobbled her up, leaving a blank space where she stood just moments ago.

I count to twenty out loud, certain that wherever she's hiding, she can hear. Then I follow her scent. I follow it until it leads me in circles. I retrace my steps, coming up empty.

"Serena?" I call.

She doesn't respond.

54

SERENA

My shadows drop me near the edge of the forest. The trees blur together as I dart between them, pushing myself to the absolute limit.

Everything about being fae is a rush. The speed, the strength, the adrenaline, the magic. I've barely had time to adjust to it, let alone appreciate it.

A flood of endorphins hits me as I slow to a stop at the mouth of a cave. Catching my breath, I press my palms into the stone and rock back on my heels, bowing into a stretch.

The hair on the back of my neck stands up. Zadyn must be close.

It's exhilarating—the thought of him chasing me. Catching me.

I slip behind a groove in the rock, smirking at the sound of his footfalls. A shadow darts into my vision, and I open my mouth to greet him with a witty remark. That anticipation morphs into dread as something hard slams me back into the mountain and a hand shoots out to silence me.

"Don't scream. Don't make a sound."

I meet Kylian's gaze with a bitter intensity. He waits until I stop struggling to slowly lower his hand from my mouth.

"I could kill you right here and now," I bite. He rattles off a laugh.

305

"Give me one good reason not to burn you alive before you can even blink."

"You've been dreaming about me."

I'm taken aback. "I've been having *nightmares* about you," I hiss, shaking off my surprise. "There's a difference."

"Come home."

"How did you find me?"

"I told you I would. Come home."

It's my turn to laugh. "You'll have to drag me by my hair."

"That can be arranged."

"You touch me and I will fry your ass."

He suppresses a smile. "You're awfully confident in your power."

"Rightfully so."

"Come. *Home.*" He leans in, lowering his eyes to mine. When I make no move to answer, he continues, "I will go to war if I have to."

"I have a dragon. You don't stand a chance."

"You think I don't know how to handle a dragon? Darling, I've been preparing for this for longer than you've been alive."

I shove against his bare chest. "I will *destroy* you."

"I welcome you to try." That arrogant smirk boils my blood. My magic gathers, coiling within me like a snake preparing to strike. "I've missed this mouth. This neck—"

Fitting his hand over the side of my jaw, he tips my head back and presses his lips to my throat. I push him back and move to slap him across the face. Long fingers shoot out to stop me, wrapping around my wrist in a vice-like hold. "And your spirit."

I focus, sending out a wave of heat to scorch his palm. His eyes shift to my searing arm. Steam rises from where we're connected.

I stare in awe.

He just put out my fire.

"I'd like to propose something." He scans my body, head to toe. "Two weeks."

"What?"

"I will give you two weeks to bid farewell to your life in Aegar— say goodbye to your friends, your so-called home. Then you join me."

"How is that a fair deal? You plan to kill them all anyway for your ceaseless ambition."

He hangs his head and sighs like he's dealing with a petulant toddler. "Fine. I solemnly swear to leave your friends unharmed."

Real convincing, bucko.

"Are you still hell-bent on world domination?"

"If that's how you choose to view it."

"Hmm, well in that case, let me think. *No.* What makes you think I'd go anywhere with you? After all you've done?"

"After all I've—" His voice rises, a rare look of surprise skipping across his face. That scent of his breezes toward me as he takes a step closer and says in a lethal whisper, "I'm not the one who drove a dagger through her heart moments before her nuptials."

"You didn't leave me much choice," I snarl. "How do I know you won't just chain me up like last time?"

He smiles, his eyes giving nothing away. "We have to be able to trust each other, darling."

"That is the single most hilarious thing you've ever said to me."

"I'm being serious."

"I know you are. That's why it's so absurd."

"The bargain seems more than fair." His hard body grazes mine as he palms the rock behind my head. "Two weeks, then you're mine. It's simple. I won't even punish you for running from me."

Oh, gee, thanks.

"All I need in exchange is for your friends to bend the knee to me, and they can keep their little lives."

"No one is going to bend the knee to you, you sadistic *fuck!*" I shout, shoving against him. Kylian catches my face in his hands.

"You want to avoid a war?" His eyes gleam. "This is your chance. No one has to die. Your friends...your kingdom. Think of the lives you'll spare."

I bite my lip. A victorious smile spreads over his face as he releases me and slips a hand into his pocket. "Two weeks."

He begins backing away.

"I haven't agreed to anything."

"You agreed to marry me, darling. A deal is a deal. Don't you know about faerie bargains? They are ever-binding. So you *will* be my wife. Or you will pay *very* dearly. I'm offering you a chance to make good on your word. I'll see you in a fortnight."

"No—"

"And if you try anything, the bargain is forfeit, and your little friends are fair game."

"Kylian—"

But he is gone. Vanished into thin air.

How the hell...

"Serena?" Zadyn calls. I smooth my jacket and step out to meet him. "I've been looking everywhere for you. Your scent just kept leading me in circles. What happened?"

"I just had a little run in…with Kylian."

Zadyn's pupils flare. "*What?*" Gripping my shoulders, he looks around, snarling. "Where is he?"

"He's gone."

Zadyn stares at me. "He *left?*"

I nod.

"Well, are you alright? What happened?"

"He offered me a deal."

"What deal?"

"He's giving me two weeks. To say goodbye to everyone. And in exchange, he's promised not to harm any of you. If you all agree to bend the knee to him."

Zadyn laughs, releasing my shoulders. "That's ridiculous."

"Is it?"

He scoffs. "Yes. It is. I don't think I have to explain to you how fundamentally preposterous that is."

I stare at the ground.

"Hold on. You're not actually considering this, are you?"

"I'm not ruling it out."

"Serena."

"The other half of the star is in Vod. This could be our shot to get it and shut that portal down."

"You are not fucking going with him."

"Zadyn, if I don't go willingly, he will use force, and he will kill you all." I reach for his hand, but he rips it back.

"I don't care! Don't you get that? I'm not giving you up, I'm not letting you go. He will have to pry you from my *cold dead hands*," he fumes, pacing in circles.

My shoulders slump. "And what about me? Don't I get a say?"

"Not when your say is sacrificing yourself. *Again.*"

"No one wants a war. What if—what if it can be avoided? I can save you, I can save all of us. No one has to die."

"I will never bend the knee to that bastard! Do you think Jace will? Do you think after everything that's happened—after taking you, after Derek—he'll just fling his sword away and fall at Kylian's feet? You're out of your mind."

"So what's your plan, Zadyn? Because right now we don't have one."

"We have you. We have a dragon."

"Kylian said he has ways of dealing with Furi."

"He's bluffing."

"What if he isn't? Am I to risk her too? When we don't know what he's bringing through this portal? He is *powerful*. I just watched him extinguish my fire like it was nothing more than a candle in the wind and then vanish into thin air, Zadyn. And I'm—I'm worried, okay?"

"There is no way in which this doesn't end horribly. So what? We're safe, but what about everyone else? Kylian is not the gentle giant type. He will burn through the kingdoms like a wildfire, no matter what he promises you."

"I made a deal with him, Zadyn. It's done."

"You *what?*"

"Before you came for me in Vod, we struck a deal. That I would marry him if he promised not to hurt you all."

"Serena, what have you done? Faerie deals are binding."

"I know that," I snap. "I was doing what I thought was necessary. If I honor it, I keep you safe. That's all I want—do you understand that?"

I slide my hand over his cheek, but he refuses to look at me.

"He will be back for me in two weeks. So we have until then to figure this out. Two weeks to figure out how to destroy him and end this."

"And what if we can't figure it out? What then?"

"Then in two weeks, I marry him," I decide. "I find the star. And then I kill him in his sleep."

55

JACE

My boots stomp over tall grass and overgrown weeds as I reach the wave of crimson flowers swaying in the breeze. Angelfyre. My mother's favorite.

In the quiet of the afternoon, with not a sound around save the song of the birds and the trickling waterfall nearby, my mind finally empties.

I haven't had a moment's peace since Derek died. Not a single one to breathe—to think long enough to ask myself what the hell I'm doing.

You are no king. King of fools, that old crone in Vod had said.

She was right. I *am* no king. I never wanted a crown. I just wanted to fight and die a soldier's death. But Derek always had bigger plans for me.*

Fresh pain rips through me at the thought of him.

I'm furious. So furious at him for having to be the hero. For throwing his life away for mine.

He should be here. If he were, maybe we could find a way out of

---

* Cue: *Funeral* by Phoebe Bridgers

311

this mess. He knew what he was doing, and I just—don't. Hand of the King was one thing. King regent is another entirely.

My days are filled with endless meetings. Endless questions and planning. What little time I have to myself is dedicated to worrying about Serena.

Where she is. What she's doing. How am I supposed to run Derek's kingdom when she is all I think about?

I know I'm obsessing. If I'm being honest, I've been obsessed since that day I found her in the Bone Forest. The day I tortured her, stabbed her in the leg, and she *laughed* in my face.

She was an enigma. Wild, tenacious, scathing—yet somehow warm and inviting. Addicting.

Haunting.

She's somewhere across the seas, but she is the ghost in my head, the one I reach for but can never grasp. I keep chasing, and the farther I wander, the faster she evades.

I can't let her go. No matter how hard I try.

I gather the biggest flowers I can find, making my way toward the two headstones beneath the willow tree.

Jon Fallyn and Sabel Fallyn.

Derek placed these headstones here in their memory, along with two Everblooms. The white petals hold strong no matter the season, their flame visible night and day, rain or shine, never to extinguish. That was the kind of male Derek was.

He loved me before he even knew me.

He saved me from certain death and made me his son.

He brought me up in this world, then left me his only daughter and his crown.

And here I am. Ungrateful and wallowing.

How could I go against his wishes? After everything he's done, everything he sacrificed.

I lay the bouquet down at my mother's grave, and pick a few weeds off my father's. Then I head past the towering wrought-iron gate and stone pillars lining the path to Derek's shrine.

The door to the crypt groans behind me, sinking closed. Sealing me in as if to say, *it should have been you.*

I drift past the tall painted vases of fading flowers, past the gifts and offerings left in his honor, stopping before the freshly laid marble tomb that houses Derek's heart.

My hands smooth over the surface, cold and unflinching as death itself.

Derek's body was burned on a funeral pyre and set loose on the river, according to our customs. But like all other kings before him, his heart—a representation of his valor, courage, and selflessness—will remain here, encased in stone, to beat eternally among his people.

"You were right." I sigh, the echo of my broken voice shattering the silence.

"I love her. And I'm lost. I'm so lost. I don't know what you would say. I know you would want me to make sure Sorscha was protected and looked after, and I promise you she always will be...but I don't love her the way I should. The way she deserves."

I swallow, my throat thick.

"I've never wavered in my loyalty to you. I've never faltered. But this is a bridge I don't know how to cross. Just send me some kind of sign. Please."

I tip my forehead against the tomb, locking down the swell of pain, the guilt, the sinking fear clawing at my mind, demanding to be let free. Then I push away, squaring my shoulders, and start back toward the castle.

My heart skips a beat as I step into the hall to find her waiting.

56

SERENA

14 DAYS

My stomach is a bundle of nerves as we touch down in Aegar. My shadows rescind, folding into me as I release my hold on Zadyn. We decided to shadow walk for the sake of time, Mar volunteering to get the others back on her own. The clock is ticking, and every second counts.

But as we make our way through the brilliant diamond cave leading into the keep, I'm hit with a flood of poignant memories. We walk beneath crystals shaped like icicles, past the sparkling throne where I first saw Derek.

I think that was the moment I decided I would do whatever it took to know him. Be his servant, his errand girl, his Dragon Rider. It was never even a choice. I did it all to be close to my father in some perverse way. And it wasn't enough.

Because somehow he managed to slip right through my fingers. Again.

I follow Zadyn through the halls, lost in a time loop, seeing things that aren't there, fighting the bitter taste in my mouth.

Derek is dead. I have no choice but to face that now. I'm also terrified to see Jace and tell him what I've decided.

I meant what I said. I do plan on killing Kylian and finding that

314

star, whether I do it before or after we're married. But if this back-fires, if I die trying, then I want every minute of these two weeks to be spent in Aegar, surrounded by the people I love. With Zadyn and Jace.

I want to spend them at home.

I know he'll fight me on this, but unless he can offer me another option, this is the best defense we've got. And I refuse to back down.

But when he pushes through the towering doors of the hall—when his golden eyes lift to mine—it's like a punch to the gut.

A giant *fuck you* from the universe.

He strides toward me as time slows. My heart beats out of my chest, only for him.

Get it together.

"You look…different." I fight the urge to smack myself in the fore-head at that lame greeting.

Before me is a version of Jace I've never seen. He's dressed impec-cably in a fitted black jacquard doublet and leather pants tucked into tall black boots. His hair is pushed off his face in a way that makes him look a bit older, his stubble slightly grown in. He's so handsome in that severe way of his.

His mouth twists into a grimace. "It's the clothes. I'm not used to all this." He messes with the collar of his jacket.

I step forward to smooth it. "No, you look good."

Good? He doesn't look good.

He looks gorgeous. Stunning. Delicious. Drop-dead sexy in a way that should be a felony.

I force myself to step back before I can say anything else damning. His eyes bounce from me to Zadyn.

"I'm not sure if it's a good sign or a bad sign that you're standing here right now."

"We should talk," I tell him.

He nods, leading us away. With a deep breath, I brace myself for the shitstorm that's about to follow.

57

JACE

14 DAYS

"**Y**ou did *what?*" I slam my hands down on the table separating me from Serena.

"My reaction exactly." Zadyn leans by the council room door—arms crossed, a scowl on his face.

"Is this some kind of fucking joke?"

"Yes. My sense of humor's gotten much darker since the last time you saw me." Her eyes roll. "This is called *compromise.*"

"You are not going with him! It's out of the gods-damned question."

"You and Zadyn seem to forget that this is my decision. Not yours."

"Masochism doesn't suit you, witch." I shove off the table, raking a hand through my hair and staring up at the ceiling.

Gods, give me strength.

"Look, I've thought about this long and hard, and this is the best solution. We avoid a war if I go with him. All you have to do is bend the knee."

"Oh, is that all?!" I fight the urge to pound my fist through the wall. "If you think I will *ever* call that black-hearted mongrel king—if you think I will surrender Derek's kingdom, go against my honor, my

blood-oath to *my* king to grovel at that bastard's feet…you don't know me. At all."

Serena stands there, a crease between her brows. "I won't see Derek's kingdom destroyed because of me either, Jace. But sometimes self-preservation is worth the price of your honor. Honor doesn't keep you alive. It's usually the thing that gets you killed fastest."

A long silence hangs in the air.

"Swearing my allegiance is out of the question," I say through gritted teeth.

"Then we figure out a way to end him before it comes to that."

"I'm assuming that look in your eye means you have some sort of plan?"

Her shoulder lifts. "I'm going to kill him."

I laugh. "That's cute. Real fucking cute."

"I'm serious. If I marry him, I'll be close enough for him to let his guard down. I can find the star and cut off his access to the portal."

"What makes you think he won't lock you up in blood ore chains the second he gets you alone?"

"Because I won't allow it to happen. As long as I'm giving him what he wants, he won't lock me up."

"And what's that? World's best pussy?"

I wince as soon as the words leave my mouth. My skin heats to the point of discomfort. I can't even peel my eyes off the floor to meet hers. "I didn't mean that. I'm sorry, I'm so—"

"No need to apologize to the *whore* trying to save the kingdom." A bitter smirk plays on her lips. Zadyn lets out a long breath, shaking his head as he stares at the ground.

"Serena," I say, moving to her.

Her hand shoots up, stopping me. "I don't have the time to be offended by your crude comments. So just save it."

You managed to do it again, asshole. Managed to widen that gap that you so beautifully installed between you in the first place.

I drop the hand reaching for her as she starts again, "And as a matter of fact, I do have a few ideas."

"What ideas?" Zadyn crosses to us, perching on the table.

"We need all the power we can muster. Which means you have to do something you might not like." She glances at me.

"I'll do anything."

"You need to marry Sorscha and perform the Bloodfast with her."

It's like being doused in ice water. I take a step back, my heart sinking.

"Before you say no, hear me out. If you do this, both you and Sorscha will inherit Derek's gifts."

It's bad enough that Serena never answered my proposal before she left. Now, apparently, it's just getting swept under the rug like it never happened.

"She's right," Zadyn admits.

Of course, you'd like that, wouldn't you, I refrain from snapping.

"That gives us two more major weapons. Then we write to the other kingdoms and try to gather whatever aid we can. Once Kylian is done with Aegar, he will reach for them as well. I'm guessing they'll be more than willing since this affects them too."

"Hyrax is already in. Eaton guaranteed his father's aid," Zadyn provides.

"And what if all that isn't enough? What if this goes wrong? Be realistic for a moment. Two weeks is not much time. Not at all." My words are a plea, a plea for her to see reason—to see how losing her again would be the end of me.

"I'll tell you the same thing I told Zadyn. I will end him with my bare hands if I have to. And I will do it before he can take this kingdom and the others. But I will not sit by and watch my home, watch my family burn."

The fire in her lavender eyes is staggering. So is her unwavering resolve.

Forcing a swallow down my throat, I nod.

Because what choice do I have but to follow her lead?

This is not the girl I plucked out of the Bone Forest. The girl I spent months sharpening into a weapon. This is not even the girl who kissed me under the stars at solstice.

The person before me is a warrior. A queen.

Resolute and determined.

How can I refuse her? How can I do anything but worship at her feet?

58

JACE

13 DAYS

'm up at dawn.

Dressing quickly, I head down the hallway, and before I can even register where I'm going, I've stopped outside Serena's door.

I stand there staring at the smooth oak finish and give it a tentative knock. My fingers curl into fists at my side, squeezing before slowly flexing open—a tactic we were taught in training to help calm the nervous system.

And nervous is an understatement of what I feel right now.

What am I doing? Hoping reason abandons her and she decides to forgive all the shitty things I've said and done?

Yesterday's reunion was a disaster. As if she needed more reasons to resent me after the way I acted in Vod. I apologized for calling her a whore, only to do it again.

My jealousy is getting the better of me. It's not just Kylian. It's Zadyn too. It's every male she looks at who isn't me. My insecurities are being transferred to her, and I know it isn't fair or right.

All I wanted to do yesterday was fall at her feet. Tell her how excruciating these last few weeks without her were. How I never want

320

to go that long without seeing her face again. I don't want to go a day, an hour, a gods-damned *minute* without her.

She'll probably tell me to go fuck myself, and she has every right to. But I have to try, I have to—

The door opens, bringing my inner monologue to a screeching halt.

Zadyn stands in her doorway, barefoot and shirtless.

I don't like that. Not one bit. In fact, I fucking hate that.

A torrent of envy sweeps through me, and it takes every ounce of control I have not to throttle him and beat his face in.

"Are you okay?" Zadyn squints at me, running a hand through his mussed hair.

Am I okay? Hah. No, I'm going to end you.

I set my jaw, tightening my fists again. "I was just looking for Serena."

Zadyn pushes the door a bit wider, and her scent hits me like bricks. She pops into view beneath his arm, clothed in a nightdress and robe, thank gods.

"Hey," she says, rubbing her eyes, her voice raspy and sleepy and utterly tempting. She scans my face with concern. "Is everything okay?"

I stare between the two of them, their messy hair, Serena's rumpled clothes—my mind going to some dark places. The one thing that keeps me from losing it is the fact that their scents haven't mingled. Which means nothing intimate happened.

Not that it matters. I'm getting married, and Serena has the right to do whatever she wants with whomever she wants.

Doesn't mean I have to like it, though.

Usually it takes a little more than the sight of them together to rile me this much, but being pent up behind a desk all day with these newfound royal duties has me on edge. My magic has become this incessant itch—one that can only be scratched by letting it out.

While I've been contemplating cutting off Zadyn's air supply to dispel some of that excess energy, the two of them have been waiting for my answer.

"Yes," I blurt. "I thought you might want to get back to training."

"I probably should." Her eyes skirt toward Zadyn as if seeking his permission. Or approval. He nods, and she looks back at me. "Okay. Just let me get dressed."

I pace the hall until the door swings open to the two of them fully dressed—Serena in those leathers that hug her legs and chest in a way that simply isn't fair.

"You're coming too?" I spit, unable to bite my tongue. Zadyn flashes me a smug little smirk.

"She asked me to."

"She ask you to be shirtless in her room, too, or was that just a fashion choice?"

He takes a menacing step my way.

"Alright, hold on." Serena stops short, wedging herself between us. "We are going to make a pact to be adults and put a pin in this little pissing contest, got it? Right now, we are a team with one common enemy. You're on the same side."

Tell that to the cocky motherfucker behind you.

"If you can't ditch the guy PMS at the door, then I'm more than happy to train myself. Understood?"

The two of us grumble yes's before falling in line behind her.

59
SERENA

13 DAYS

"No."

Jace's deadpan eyes land on mine from across the ring. I toss up my arms. "What did I do this time?"

"Have you forgotten everything I taught you?"

It's barely been two days since I got back, and already he's back to being a hard-ass.

Fun, fun, fun.

"Fine. Maybe I'm a little rusty. I haven't had much time to practice my footwork between being stolen by a sadist and freezing my tits off trying to solve our portal issue."

"You're sorely mistaken if you think that gets you a free pass. You're a warrior. Start presenting like one."

Wowwwww. Please dislodge stick from ass.

"And you." He tosses a nod at Zadyn, who's been sparring with me for the last half hour. "You're not doing her any favors by letting her win."

"I'm not going to hit her," he spits.

"Then someone else will. Kylian most likely."

"Is that how you trained her?" Zadyn bellies up to him. "By showing her how to take a punch?"

"She doesn't need you to fight her battles, Rhodes. She's more than capable." He sends a pointed look my way. "When she *wants* to be. Now are you going to be a worthy opponent for her or would you like me to step in and get the job done?"

Zadyn bites his tongue and paces back to me, his brown eyes finding mine.

"It's okay," I tell him. "You don't have to be gentle with me."

His hands curl around the hem of his sweat-drenched shirt, pulling it over his head and tossing it aside.*

Well now, that is just unfair.

A lump forms in my throat at the sight of his glistening torso, tiny beads of sweat sliding between the contours of his abs, rolling over the deep V-cut that disappears beneath his waistband. I try to focus on tucking my eyes back into my head. And fail. Miserably.

He pushes his hair back and crouches into a fighting stance.

You ready?

Before I can nod, he springs forward. He's quick and agile, his movements more lupine than fae. I block a punch, landing a hit to his stomach with my free hand. He absorbs it like it's nothing, latching on to twist himself beneath my arm. Pain lances up my wrist as I'm forced into a bow. I grunt, shifting my weight to kick back into his thigh.

"Never put your back to your opponent, witch." Jace stalks around the perimeter of the ring with scrutinizing eyes. "How are you going to get out of this one?"

I reach for my fire, casting it toward my arms. Not enough to do any serious damage. Just a quick sting. Zadyn sucks in a breath through his teeth, releasing me.

"No magic. Reset," Jace says.

"Why no magic? If this was a real fight, I would be using my magic —I'd use whatever was at my disposal," I protest, rolling my wrist.

"If this was a real fight, your magic could be easily depleted, and

---

* Cue: *Bike Dream* by Rostam

you would need to rely on your physical faculties alone. So like I said. Reset."

Muttering a few colorful nicknames for him beneath my breath, I take a lap around the ring before meeting Zadyn in the center.

"You got this. Just imagine I'm Kylian. You hate me. You want me dead. Now let me have it." He offers me a smirk that, combined with his half-naked body, is completely mind-boggling. I soften my knees and bounce on my toes a few times, winding up for a punch.

"Stop." Jace's voice shatters my focus. I turn to see him walking up behind me.

"Why—"

He takes my hips with a firm grip, and I lose my train of thought. His foot knocks against mine, forcing me to widen my stance. "Legs further apart."

I do as he says without question.

"You're not twisting when you punch. Engage your core, and twist from here, like I taught you." His fingers curl into my sides, angling me toward Zadyn—steering me with his hands.

Zadyn holds up both palms, creating a target for me.

Jace guides my hips again as I throw another punch, this one with more power and better control. He nods in encouragement.

"Again, witch. Jab and cross."

I'm far too aware of his hands on me, of his breath hot on my ear, of his dark, looming presence demanding attention. Demanding respect. Part of me is desperate to sink back into him, just for one second.

With him at my back, breathing down my neck, and Zadyn in front of me, it's hard to focus on anything other than keeping the drool safely secured inside my mouth. The heat of their eyes, of their bodies, so close to mine—my senses are in overdrive, my mind wandering to thoughts that are so not appropriate for the training ring. Not appropriate period exclamation point the end.

Head out of the gutter, you animal.

As if reading my thoughts, Jace chuckles, his hand sliding across my low back as he shoves me in Zadyn's direction.

I continue the combination—jab cross, jab cross—as Zadyn starts to move around. I pursue him, falling into a rhythm as we track our footprints across the dirt ring.

"Now give her something to work with," Jace calls, sounding slightly less annoyed.

Zadyn attacks at full speed. I would be impressed if I weren't so focused on dodging his blows. I barely duck in time to avoid his shin whacking me in the head. Gasping, I slip around him, my hand forming a blade to strike him in the back. His chiseled arm swings around like a scythe. I duck again—popping up in front of him this time to grip his broad shoulders and sink my knee into his ribs. He grunts, hunching over, but then his arms form a vice around my back and waist.

What is he doing?

A scream rips through me as he flips me upside down, throwing my feet over my head. I land on wobbly legs, without a stitch of grace or balance. Before I can fall, he catches my shirt and rips me backward. I slam into him.

His heart pounds against my back—a loud, steady drumbeat. I'm plastered to his chest, one hand restraining my wrists, the other locked around my throat. I crane my neck to look up at him, watching as his eyes dilate, focused on my mouth. He wets his lips, and I feel an ache swelling deep in my core. Our faces are so close I can feel his ragged breaths skittering across my mouth—

Jace claps his hands, and Zadyn unlocks his grip on me.

"That's enough for today."

"Are you okay?" Zadyn asks, his voice rough. "I didn't hurt you, did I?

I shake my head, still too breathless to speak and afraid of what might fall out if I even attempt to.

6 0

JACE

13 DAYS

The air is thick as she gazes up at him, her chest heaving. I want to break every finger he has wrapped around her neck. But she doesn't seem to mind. The shift in her scent tells me she's actually enjoying this.

It's a sickening realization.

My clap bounds off the walls of the ring, and they break apart as if just remembering my presence.

"That's enough for today."

Zadyn guides her toward the wooden bench, his hand on the small of her back.

He better watch that placement…

"We need to come up with an actual plan for Kylian," I bark as they take a seat and chug down some water.

"Stabbing sounds like fun," Serena breathes, wiping her mouth on her sleeve.

"He's bigger and stronger than you."

"So are you, and I handle you just fine."

"Only on your best day, witch. Don't overestimate your abilities."

She fires a mild glare at me, cheeks beet red, dark strands of hair clinging to her neck.

327

"We need to figure out his weakness and exploit it."

"He doesn't have a weakness. I mean he lost it anytime someone hit me or touched my face…"

Zadyn and I both tense. She stares at the ground, turning over a thought. "Actually, there is something. But it definitely doesn't play to our advantage. It seemed like Kylian was able to read my thoughts."

"Fucking sirens," I curse under my breath.

"I need the element of surprise on my side if I'm going to kill him. There has to be a way to keep him out of my head long enough for me to do what I need to do."

"It's not going to come to that," Zadyn assures her.

Placating is still his first line of defense when it comes to her. What he should be doing is trying to talk sense into her. Scaring her. Because apparently she lacks the sense to be scared on her own.

"What if it does? I'm the only one who's going to get close enough to him to do this."

The thought of her going anywhere near Kylian again is enough to boil my blood.

"Kylian's power is strong—strong enough to shred the minds of the Guardians. Strong enough to put out my fire. And he has shadows. They looked like mine, only he didn't use them to walk. I could feel them. They were more solid."

Great. Another problem to solve. I decide to stick with the one thing we might be able to manage.

"You need to work on shielding your mind," I tell her.

"How do I do that?"

"Well, first you need to fix your face. It's a dead giveaway of every thought passing through your head."

She frowns, further proving my point.

"You've done it before," Zadyn says.

"What do you mean?"

"You shut me out all the time."

"I do?"

He laughs. "Without meaning to, but there are times when your mind is wide open and others when you've got it sealed like a vault."

They can mind-speak?

"I didn't realize I was doing that," she admits.

Shaking off my surprise, I settle on the ground, waving a hand for them to proceed. "Practice makes perfect."

"You want me to try it right now?" She arches a brow.

"Do you have some prior engagement?"

"Yes, I'm due to punch you in the face in about three seconds."

Gods, she's infuriating. That smart little mouth never fails to turn me on. But hell if I'm going to show it.

"Just do it, witch."

She tosses me a dirty look before angling herself toward Zadyn on the bench. "Okay, try to guess what I'm thinking."

I watch them stare at each other wordlessly.

"I was *not* thinking that!" she bursts. He breaks into a giggle.

"I heard it *very* clearly."

"You know what? I don't like this game." She springs to her feet, but I grab her wrist, yanking her down beside me. Her mouth pops open.

"It's not a game," I say, ignoring her seething. "It's an exercise. And we're not leaving here until you've figured out how to shield."

Wrenching her arm away, she scoots in front of me to face Zadyn, deliberately giving me a view of the back of her head.

"Could you be more of a child?"

"I can do anything I put my mind to." She sneers at me over her shoulder.

"Then maybe you should put your mind to shutting up and getting to work."

"You know, you really don't have to be here for this."

My eyes snap to Zadyn. "Are you dismissing me, dog?"

"*Don't* call him that," Serena bites.

Gods, they make me want to spear myself on my own sword.

"You two are in*sufferable*."

"You can either sit there and pick useless fights with her or you can let me deal with this. I think you'll find the second option will prove to be more effective." He flashes me a smug smile.

Who does he think he is, her handler?

My palms twitch with the desire to pummel the ever-living fuck out of him. But I loose a tight sigh, clenching my fists until the simmering rage has settled.

Serena closes her eyes, making an effort to concentrate. After a moment, she tenses, her dark lashes twitching every so often as they carry on their wordless conversation.

"Imagine you're stacking bricks one at a time, building up a literal wall in your mind," Zadyn murmurs, watching her. "Good. That's much better."

The strain on her face grows more pronounced, her jaw grinding, her breath coming in short, rapid bursts.

"That's it. You're doing it," he encourages.

A small whimper escapes her lips. I jolt forward, moving in front of her. Serena's fingers are curled around her knees like talons, her nails threatening to puncture the leather and her perfect skin beneath.

"That's enough," I mutter. But Zadyn's eyes are fastened to hers in an unbreakable hold. I grip Serena's shoulders. "That's *enough*."

Her eyes fly open with a loud gasp. She blinks a few times, disoriented.

"Are you alright?" I demand.

"I'm fine." She winces and clutches her temples. "Fuck, my head hurts."

"It takes a lot of concentration to continually block someone out. That was great for your first real try," Zadyn says, reaching out to brush her hair off her neck. I zero in on that move, scowling as he stands and offers her a hand. "Come on, let's get cleaned up. We can try again later."

She allows him to hoist her up, and we make our way back toward the hall.

"Zadyn?" Serena asks. "Why are *you* able to read my mind?"

He hesitates, as if debating how to answer. "I'm your familiar."

"Oh." That single word carries a slight air of disappointment. Serena stares at her feet as we enter the keep. "But Kylian's not."

"If he could get into the minds of the Guardians, I'm guessing it would be nothing for him to waltz right into yours," I supply.

"Damn."

"What?"

"Nothing. It's just—I was hoping maybe I would be able to crack into his mind the way he can with mine or that I could hear him like I do Zadyn. I could be one step ahead of him and he'd never even know."

"Yeah, that would have been nice." I steal a quick glance at her. I'm going to regret asking this, but, "Have you ever tried to hear someone other than Zadyn?"

She peers up at me. "No. It's not like I actively try to hear him, it's just like this…channel between us that's always been there. I never had to work for it."

They share a look, and suddenly my presence feels so redundant. I could self-combust beside them, and I don't think either of them would notice.

And that makes my gut twist.

She's moving on. And all I can do is watch.

61

SERENA

13 DAYS

"I can't feel my legs."

Mar glances up when I slip through her door. "That good, huh?"

Hah. "I wish. I was training with Jace. *And* Zadyn."

"My question still stands."

I shoot her a warning look. She chuckles, parting the dresses hanging in her wardrobe.

"It's like babysitting two toddlers. They're constantly bickering. I thought I was going to have to banish them to opposite corners of the ring."

Although to be fair, Jace and I would also benefit from separate corners.

"They don't get along? Hmm. I wonder why."

Scowling at her less than subtle implications, I flop down on the bed, face first.

"Serena..." She turns to me, suddenly serious, and says, "Are you sure you know what you're getting yourself into with this plan? Or lack thereof?"

The velvet comforter muffles my morose response. "I never know

what I'm doing until I'm doing it." I force myself to sit up. "This is my mess. All this shit with Kylian is happening because of me."

"No, it's because Kylian is a monster who happens to be obsessed with you. None of this is your fault. Not to mention he would have marched on Aegar with or without you just to acquire more power."

"Yes, but now he's unhinged."

"Wasn't he always?"

"But even more so now. Running from him was a bruise to his ego."

"Males are so fearful. They see a female with power to rival their own and seek to either contain it or crush it when they cannot."

She's right, but it doesn't change anything.

"Either way, I'm the one he wants, which means I need to be the one to do this. I just wish the guys would back me up on this."

"Why would they? They're petrified of losing you."

"I don't want to leave them, I don't want to leave any of you, but Mar, you see what I'm seeing, right? That right now I am our only bargaining chip."

Dropping her stormy eyes, she gives me a reluctant nod.

"We can keep searching for ways around this. Two weeks isn't nothing," she says quietly, resting a hand on my shoulder.

"Less than two weeks. And instead of spending it beating our brains out trying to dodge what's pretty much inevitable, I would much rather just enjoy my time with all of you."

Mar purses her lips, then yanks me up by the wrists. "Get up. Come on."

"What are you doing?" She fishes a hand into the wardrobe and pulls out two cloaks, tossing one to me.

"We're going out. We need to clear our heads. Maybe an idea will come to us if we stop thinking so hard."

Sliding off the bed, I ask, "Where do you suggest we go?"

She shrugs her slender shoulders. "Shopping, of course."

"*THIS IS* what ladies do in times of crisis?" Zadyn mutters under his breath as we make our way through the sunny streets of Iaspus. Diamond City is a madhouse, bustling with vibrance and life.

"Did you know that procrastination is one of the most useful tools for brainstorming? Proven fact," Mar tosses back, her arm linked through mine.

"I'm sure." He shakes his head, keeping close behind us.

The smell of chocolate hits me as we pass by a sweets shop. With a dubious look, Mar tugs me through the door. We emerge minutes later with bags of chocolates and candies and macaroons.

"You want one?" I offer Zadyn a caramel, chewing through the gooey texture. He declines, a grimace on his face.

"No thanks. I like my teeth where they are."

"Of course, that's why you look the way you do." I roll my eyes and catch the smug smirk that teases up the corners of his mouth.

We drop into a few shops, sifting through clothes and hats and jewelry, taking any diversion we can get. Our escapades actually seem to be easing some of the tightness from my chest.

That is, until we come across a bridal shop, and in the window I see a silk ivory gown similar to the one I wore the day I was to be married. My whole body turns to ice as I slip out of Mar's grasp, suddenly rooted to the ground.

"Serena, are you…" Mar gazes from me to the source of my horror. I force a swallow. That's when something else catches my eye in the reflection.

In my rearview is a cloaked figure, a hood drawn over her head. A long, loose braid the color of thick honey spills out over her chest. She stands watching me for a moment that stretches on too long to feel casual.

I turn, locking eyes with her as she nods for me to follow.

I've found that when my intuition tugs at me, it's best not to ignore it. So I duck into the crowd after her.

"Serena, where are you going? What did you see?"

"That female."

"What about her? Why are you following her?"

"Because she wants me to."

I don't give them the option to argue, trailing the figure through the Markade, inside of an old ale house and up the rickety stairs. I push open the door she's left slightly ajar, Zadyn and Mar piling in behind me.

The figure drops her hood. I gasp as it falls, revealing what I already suspected deep in my bones the moment I spotted her.

"Hello, Serena."

I stare, unable to talk or think or breathe.

Taking a tentative step forward, I say, "You know me."

She sinks into a seat at the round table, picking up a stack of painted cards and beginning to shuffle.

"You don't think I would recognize my own daughter? Have a seat."

62

ZADYN

13 DAYS

A shark smile spreads over her face.

Gods, she looks just like Serena. I can see Sorscha's features there too, in the color of her hair and the wide set of her amber eyes.

"We finally meet in this lifetime."

Serena takes a slow step forward. "You *know* me, know me? How?"

Without breaking their stare, she purrs, "Marideth. Always a pleasure."

My head whips toward Mar, who's gone pale as if she'd seen a ghost.

"Queen Margot," she gasps, dropping into a deep curtsy.

Queen Margot?

"I'm sorry—*queen?*" Serena's gaze collides with mine, wrought with shock and confusion.

Did you know who she was?

No, I swear I've never seen her before.

"Former queen," the female corrects, waving a dismissive hand.

"But you—you're dead. I watched your pyre burn." Mar staggers forward, a slight tremble in her voice.

336

"What you saw, Marideth, was what I wanted you to see. Sometimes our minds play tricks on us. Tell me, what do you recall from that day? Was it summer or winter? Was it raining, or was the sun beaming down on your face?"

Her mouth opens as she grasps at straws and comes up empty. "But everyone thinks you're dead...why did you..."

"Being queen was never in my cards. But my past is not the reason you are here now. I would appreciate if our little run-in remained between us. The last thing I need is Derek attempting to track me down."

"Derek is dead," Serena snaps.

The stranger looks surprised for the first time since we arrived, her throat bobbing as she swallows.

"I see."

"What are you doing here?" Serena asks.

"Please, sit." Margot's bejeweled fingers reach across the table, spreading the cards out in a half moon as Serena cautiously slips into the open seat. I keep close, lingering by her shoulder and eyeing her mother's doppelgänger with suspicion.

"You seem to have found yourself in quite the predicament." She begins to pluck a few cards from the spread, placing them down strategically before Serena.

"Well, I almost got married. So I took a page out of your book and ran."

A melodic laugh spills out of her. "I'm not responsible for what the version of me you know did in another lifeline. That was a different person entirely."

"You faked your own death and left your family bereft and broken. You're no better than my mother. You're exactly the same in every lifeline. So again. How do you know me."

"I've had the gift of sight for as long as I can remember. I am able to see all versions of my line, in other worlds, other dimensions."

"Is there another one of me running around somewhere?"

"No. There is only one of you. Ever and anywhere. And you—"

Margot points a manicured finger at me. "I knew your parents. Heard what happened. Such a shame. Nice people." Her voice lacks any sort of empathy despite her condolences.

I clutch the back of Serena's chair with an iron grip.

"He is loyal to you, isn't he? But then again, aren't they all?" She pauses, glancing over Serena with a mix of curiosity and wonder. "You are not what I expected."

Serena snorts. "Did you think I'd show up here with flowers and a Mother's Day card?"

"You're sharper than the visions I've seen of you. You were weak. Soft. And now you're…a warrior. You're a leader."

"I'm no leader."

She gives Serena a sardonic smile. "You've got an army of friends you've won with love. That is the most dangerous kind of leader there is. The kind who inspires action in others. They would die for you. Some of them will before this is over."

"If you know something, I suggest you spit it out," Serena growls. "Why am I here?"

With a loud sigh, she says, "You have been resisting your path."

"Did you get that from the cards? Maybe they can clarify some things for me. Like how to close the portal in Hyrax."

"Do not waste your time on what does not concern you."

"Oh, but this does concern me. It concerns all of us." Serena palms the table. "Kylian Triori has control of the portal. He wants to conquer the kingdoms. He will do whatever it takes to get his way. Even if it means destroying this world in the process."

"Ah, but you"—Margot leans in—"will prevent that."

"I intend to kill him before it comes to that."

"No. You will not. You will try, but when the moment comes, you will falter."

The color leeches from Serena's face. She shoves back, her chair screeching against the floorboards.

"You are wasting my time."

"So blind," Margot tuts, shaking her head.

"What are you talking about?"

Her gaze lands on me. "Your friends should go. You may not want them to hear what I'm about to tell you. It's quite...personal." She torques a perfectly arched brow.

My fists clench. I have no intention of leaving. I know what a trigger Serena's mother is for her. And it's obvious this female is just as cold and calculated. So I don't feel bad for scowling at the face that has caused her insurmountable suffering.

"It's okay." Serena pinches the bridge of her nose. "I'll meet you downstairs."

"I'm not leaving you," I bite.

"Run along, shifter." Margot lifts a hand to *shoo* me, then breaks into a laugh. "What—you really think I'd harm my own *daughter?*"

Serena twists in her seat, peering up at me with pleading eyes. "Zadyn, please. Let me hear what she has to say."

Fine. But I'm not going far.

Fine.

I turn sharply, towing a shell-shocked Marideth from the room with me.

MY FOOT TAPS a steady beat against the wood panels in the hall. "She's been in there a while."

Mar slides her gray eyes to me.

"I'm going to check on her—"

Long, slender fingers wrap around my arm. "Don't. She needs to do this alone."

I know Mar is right, but I'm concerned.

Since Margot wasn't exactly shy about spilling Serena's secrets, I had to explain everything to Marideth while we waited. I told her all about Serena's past and the people here that resemble the ones she knew—Sorscha, Jace, Derek, and now her mother, I guess. She was shocked, to say the least, but she swore to keep it between us. Knowing how much Serena trusts her, I'm not worried.

"And don't you dare eavesdrop," she hisses.

I hold up two hands in surrender. "I'm not."

I'm actively doing my best not to listen through the walls. But it's not easy. I finally breathe again when the door opens, and Serena steps into the hall.

"Hey." Her eyes look glazed when she looks at me. "Are you alright?"

She nods absently, staring at me with a strange expression on her face. As if she's seeing me for the first time. "I'm good. Let's go."

"What's wrong? What did she say?"

"Nothing. She was just fucking with me in typical Dianna Avery fashion. Were you listening?"

"No. I wanted to give you some privacy."

Without further explanation, she stalks down the stairs.

"So that was your mother…" Mar finally says.

"Unfortunately. Some alternate version," she mutters. Mar shakes her head, her brows knit together.

"Do you think we should tell Sorscha about this?"

"No. I don't. She faked her own death to abandon her daughter and husband. Sorscha is better off without her. Trust me."

"She would want to know—"

"Then tell her, Mar." Serena cuts her off, perturbed by whatever was said in that room. "I'm sorry, I don't mean to snap at you. She just gets under my skin like you wouldn't believe."

"Trust me, I feel the same way about my mother."

The rest of the trip back is quiet and tense. I keep one eye on Serena at all times, wary of the drastic shift in her mood. She refuses to look at me. I keep pleading with her in my head, *look at me, let me in.*

But she doesn't. She sets her jaw and seals herself up, leaving no opening for me.

"You guys go ahead. I'm going to take Furi out for a ride," she says as we reach the grounds.

"Are you sure you're alright?"

You can tell me.

I need to be alone right now. Please just give me an hour.

"Of course," I breathe.

Furi lands a moment later, kicking up a brutal wind. Serena mounts her with fluid ease. I stand there staring long after she disappears, a black dot skating past the moon.

63

SERENA

13 DAYS

The wind snaps at my face as we cut across the stars.

But it feels good. It reminds me I'm alive when I feel dead inside. Furi doesn't press me to open up, which I'm grateful for. She lets me breathe, nudging against my mind every so often to remind me I'm not alone.

As we make our descent, Zadyn is making his way out of the castle toward us. I slide down, keeping my back to him.

"How was your ride?"

"Fine. Good." I nod, smoothing Furi's scales as he comes up beside me. His eyes burn into me like a brand.

"What?" I don't mean to sound as nasty as I do.

"You've barely spoken a word since we left the city, Serena. What's going on?"

"Nothing," I mutter.

"What did Margot say to you?"

"Nothing."

"Serena."

"It's personal, okay? What she said is…personal."

"Personal?" He scoffs. "You used to pee with the door open when we were in college. I think we're past personal."

342

"Yeah, you could have warned me about that, by the way," I spit.

"Don't do this." The wind rustles his hair as he shakes his head. "Don't shut me out."

I sigh, swallowing the tightness in my throat. "I'm allowed to keep things to myself. I'm allowed to have secrets. You don't need to know what I'm thinking one hundred percent of the time."

He laughs, exasperated. "Serena, I never know what you're thinking. And it drives me insane."

My eyes find his, and he holds my gaze for a moment. Thunder crackles overhead, drawing our faces skyward. Then it starts to rain.

With one last pat, I send Furi off to her mountain and march toward the thicket of dense forest.

"What is *wrong*?" He races to catch up with me.

"Maybe I'm just in a pissy mood. It happens."

"Where are you going?"

"I don't know! For a walk."

"It's pouring. Just come inside."

But I can't. *

Another roar of thunder rattles the ground, and I break into a sprint.

The trees are nothing but tall, black masses, blurring together as I race through the forest. Freezing rain soaks through my clothes, my hair. But I keep going. I run until I'm breathless and panting. Until my lungs are screaming, begging for a break. I run until I'm lost, until finally the tears I have been holding back since this afternoon—since Vod—burst to the surface, mixing with the fat raindrops stinging my face.

I stumble to a stop, bracing myself against the trunk of a giant oak. My knees sink into softened soil.

Everything I have been holding back, holding in, slams into me with unrelenting force.

It's staggering.

Like those dreams where you're speeding down a highway and

---

* Cue: *circle the drain* by Soccer Mommy

you've lost control of the wheel. And suddenly a truck comes out of nowhere, coming at you head-on. Nowhere to run, nowhere to hide as the headlights grow closer and closer. All you can do is wait to wake up.

Except I can't. Because the nightmare is real.

It's everything, all at once.

It's Derek dying. Having to lose my father twice. It's the rift between me and Jace. It's Kai's abuse. It's Kylian's hands on my body. It's my mother...my *mother*.

It's who and what I need to become.

It's the weight of the world resting on my shoulders.

I open my mouth to scream, but nothing comes out.

"Serena!" Zadyn shouts as he jogs toward me. I can't answer. I'm paralyzed.

"Hey." He reaches me, gripping my shoulders as the rain streamlines down his face.

He tries to get me to breathe, but I can't. The pain is not done with me. Not yet. It sinks its talons in and pulls and pulls and pulls until I am fully unraveled.

When I don't respond, he scoops me into his arms and carries me back. I let him. I don't fight as he takes me to my room, sits down in front of the fire with me on his lap, and goes silent—allowing me to cry until there is nothing left.

I don't know how long we sit like that. He holds me until I still, until the thoughts plaguing me recede, replaced by a peaceful silence. His hand smooths over my back, each sweep softening the shards of glass threatening to poke through my chest. I relax into him, letting the soft steady beat of his heart ground me.

When I pull back, our cheeks brush. Both of us are soaked to the skin, but his body is warm. He's so solid, so safe. I know I should move away.

But I can't. Our noses touch, and his cool scent hits me as I inhale, heady.

Something in the air shifts.

"Tell me what you want," he whispers. My stomach goes taut at the sound of his ragged breaths.

"I want you."

His eyes fall to my mouth. "Be more specific."

"Kiss me." *

With excruciating slowness, he leans in and brushes his lips against mine. It's tentative and sweet. Heartbreakingly careful.

He pulls back for a moment.

It's not enough.

I surge forward as Zadyn's hand knots in my hair, fisting it until a small gasp slips out. He seizes my open mouth, molding his lips around mine until no space exists between us.

No more pretense, no more dancing around it. He claims me, and every thought eddies from my mind.

Cradling the back of my head, he lowers me to the carpet beside the crackling fire. My hands weave through his wet hair, the strands like silk between my fingers. His palm traces up the curve of my waist, curling around my neck and sending my pulse into a sprint.

Our tongues tangle as I open deeper for him. His breathy moan spears through me, sending a shock of heat down between my legs. My body becomes a live wire, every hair standing on end, every part of me clenching, tightening, thirsting for him. It's only when I break away from his mouth, gasping, that I remember I need to breathe.

He doesn't falter, sweeping soft, languid kisses down my neck and chest. His fingers hook around my shirt, tugging it down until his lips brush over my heart. There's reverence in it—a silent vow that it will always be safe with him. That he will always protect it.

Gripping his hair, I pull his mouth back up to mine. A tiny whimper slips out as I bow off the floor, curling my leg against his hip, needing more. My lips and cheeks burn, as if the blood inside me is just as desperate for him as I am.

I yank his shirt up and press my palm against the taut, fevered skin of his chest, skimming over toned muscle and contoured abs. He

---

* Cue: *So Hot You're Hurting My Feelings* by Squirrel Flower

shivers when I latch onto his waistband, his hand going to my breast, his teeth tugging at my bottom lip as he groans into my mouth.

It's *Zadyn*.

Zadyn's hands are roaming my body in the most tender, intimate way. I would giggle if my mouth wasn't already happily occupied.

"I want you so bad." It doesn't even occur to me that I've said it out loud until he pulls back abruptly. "Zadyn?"

"I can't do this."

Embarrassment burns through me, stinging my cheeks.

"Did I do something wrong?"

"No." He sits up, turning his back to me, and runs his hands through his tawny hair. "I can't do this when I know you still love him."

Jace? I shake my head.

"He's engaged."

"What does it matter?"

"He's getting married. I've let go of the idea of us. It's over."

"You've let go of the *idea* but not *him*. I don't know if you ever will."

"I will. I have," I correct. I have no choice. He shakes his head, staring into the fire. "Zadyn, please. I want this. I want you."

"Yes, but I don't *want* you." He whirls to me, his face twisted in anguish. "I *love* you."

My jaw drops, and I stare at him blankly.

"I love you. *I love. You.* I always have. I've watched you fall in love and get your heart broken by people that couldn't even come close to being worthy of you if they had a hundred lifetimes to get it right, and even though that hurt, I could endure it. But what I can't endure is being a substitute for the person you really want. The person you really love."

"Zadyn." I shake my head, swallowing pins, tears brimming in my eyes. "You know I love you."

"That's not the kind of love I'm talking about, and you know it."

"I didn't know you felt that strongly."

"Yes, you did, Serena. You just didn't want to face it so you didn't have to feel the guilt of not returning my feelings," he says coldly.

"That is not true! I never thought you were *in love* with me. If I had known—"

"If you had known then what? It wouldn't have changed anything. You would have done everything the same. And come on. You never thought that my reaction to you at solstice or to you and Jace had anything to do with how I felt about you?"

"But you were with Cece. And then Ilayna."

"I asked you to give me a reason *not* to be with Cece! I practically begged you like a fool. I would have sat like a dog at your side if you'd asked me to. I would have waited until you came around, until you—they were nothing to me. All they did was ease the pain that was always there, just bubbling beneath the surface."

Every part of me feels cold without the heat of his body over mine.

Maybe he's right. Maybe a part of me always knew how he felt. And I was either too afraid or too swept up in the hope that Jace and I might somehow work out to notice. I'm such an idiot.

"Zadyn," I whisper.

I get to my knees and slowly pull my dripping shirt over my head. Sitting before him, exposed, I take his face in my hands. "Zadyn, look at me. Look. At me."

Tears line his beautiful brown eyes as he pries my hands from his face.

"Please don't torture me like this. Don't offer me your body when I can't have your heart."

He gets up and leaves without another word.

6 4

ZADYN

13 DAYS

This is a bad decision.

A very bad decision.

These thoughts have to stop. These *fantasies* have to stop.

But I'm not imagining it when she pulls back, her mouth dangerously close to mine. Her thick lashes cast shadows down her tear-streaked face, and—

Gods damn it. She's staring at my lips.

I freeze, worried that the slightest movement will frighten her off, like a deer in headlights. But that's all it would take. One tiny, minuscule shift in our positions to have my lips against hers.

It would be easy.

It would also be incredibly stupid.

I promised myself that if I was ever going to do this, the timing would be right. That she would be ready for this—for me.

The timing of *this* could not be worse. She is grieving Derek, healing from Kylian—she is shattered.

But the shift in the air, in her scent, the sudden tension so palpable I can almost taste it in the small space between us, is undeniable. Our foreheads touch, and my eyes drift closed, drunk on her mere proximity.

348

"Tell me what you want." The lazy words fall from my mouth without any real thought as to the damning consequences.

She bites down on her lower lip, sucking it between her teeth.

Seven hells.

"I want you."

I rein in a shudder, feeling her voice breeze over me. But I need more. I need her to say it.

"Be more specific."

Those hypnotic eyes flicker up to mine as she annihilates my resolve with just two simple words.

"Kiss me."

There will be no coming back from this if I do. Because there is no world in which kissing her now does not change everything.

My mind shouts in warning. I should deny her momentary lapse in judgment. Chalk it up to being bereft and in need of distraction. But despite my better judgment, despite reason and sanity and honor, I find myself leaning in like a slow-motion car wreck and placing a ghost of a kiss over her waiting lips.

It's a test. Barely even scratching the surface. I pull back, almost afraid to meet her eyes. But when I do, all I see is hunger. Rare, raw, and desperate.

I wait one more second and then—

Oh, fuck it.

I braid my hands through that thick head of hair and tilt it back. The sweetest sound of surprise leaves her mouth as it parts for me, and I cover it with my own.

The first taste of her has me groaning. I take control of the kiss, no longer able to hold back, feeling her body melt into my touch— forming to me like we were made for each other.

Because we were.

I lay her down, tucking her beneath me as my fantasies burst to life. She kisses me back, her fingers clutching my collar, curling in my hair, tugging me closer like she needs this as badly as I do. I let my mouth wander lower, over her neck and chest, tracing each perfect curve with my hands.

This is all I ever want to do. Make sure no part of her goes untouched, unloved.

Her hold grows rough as she cranes her neck off the ground, her lips working around mine as if to consume me. Every little noise she makes sends a surge of blood straight down my body until I'm straining against my waistband, begging to be buried inside her.

Her scent teases me, invades every part of me, making it impossible to breathe around her—like she's all that exists.

She becomes the air itself.

"I want you so bad," she murmurs against my skin.

You have no fucking idea, I want to say.

But then I remember.

I remember that she isn't mine. That her heart is still broken from Jace. And what I'm doing, how I'm taking advantage of that break, is detestable.

The guilt rips my focus from her warmth, from her sweet little hands slipping beneath my shirt. I try, but I can't ignore it—the funnel of anger and frustration overshadowing my desire.

It takes all my willpower to tear my lips away and push off of her. But I do.

"Zadyn?"

"I can't do this."

She sits up beside me, laying a hand on my shoulder. "Did I do something wrong?" Her voice nearly trembles, and my heart clenches.

She thinks it's her. *Oh, Serena.*

"No." I swallow. "I can't do this when I know you still love him."

"No. I've let go of the idea of us. It's over." She tries to smooth my hair, but I drag my head away, worried that one touch from her and my resolve will crumble. Hurt skids across her beautiful face.

"You've let go of the *idea*—but not him. I don't know if you ever will."

"I will. I have," she says more forcefully. "Zadyn, please. I want this. I want you."

"Yes, but I don't *want* you. I *love* you."

Her jaw goes slack, and I watch the shock register on her face. But I can't stop the words from spilling out.

"I love you. *I love you.* I always have. I've watched you fall in love and get your heart broken by people that couldn't even come close to being worthy of you if they had a hundred lifetimes to get it right. And even though that hurt, I could endure it. But what I can't endure is being a substitute for the person you really want. The person you really love."

Silence falls as we stare at each other, chests rising and falling out of sync. I watch her finally face the truth she already knew deep down.

"Zadyn," she whispers, a dip appearing between her brows. "You know I love you."

"That's not the kind of love I'm talking about and you know it."

"I didn't know you felt that strongly."

"Yes, you did, Serena. You just didn't want to face it so you didn't have to feel the guilt of not returning my feelings." I can't keep the ice from my tone, the disgust at my own foolish hope, at my desperate actions, my inability to resist her.

"That is not true!" she protests, her voice rising. "I never thought you were *in love* with me. If I had known—"

"If you had known then what?" I meet her intense gaze.

Even in her confusion and frustration she looks like a goddess. Lips swollen, cheeks flushed, a halo of fire coming from the flames behind her. I close my eyes and pinch the bridge of my nose, just to stop her angelic image from distracting me.

"It wouldn't have changed anything. You would have done everything the same. And come on. You never thought that my reaction to you at solstice or to you and Jace had anything to do with how I felt about you?"

Her voice is so fragile. "But you were with Cece. And then Ilayna."

Cece? She has no idea, does she? No idea that the only reason I was with Cece was to try to escape the constant thoughts of her. To distract myself so I wouldn't do anything stupid. Anything like this.

I fight back a cruel laugh. "I asked you to give me a reason not to be with her. I practically begged you like a fool. I would have sat like a dog at your side if you'd asked me to. I would have waited until you came around, until you—"

Until you decided to take pity on me or release me from this torment once and for all.

"They were nothing to me. All they did was ease the pain that was always there, just bubbling beneath the surface."

"Zadyn," she says, her voice soft as night.

I watch as she slides onto her knees and peels her sopping shirt over her head.

I turn away, but she pulls at my face until there is nowhere else to look but at those eyes.

"Zadyn, look at me. *Look* at me."

I can't help it. I look. Tears blur my vision as I pry her hands from my face.

"Please don't torture me like this. Don't offer me your body when I can't have your heart."

Unable to stand another second, I get to my feet and leave the room.*

SPRING BREAK, PANAMA CITY 2016

A lamppost flickers overhead, twitching on and off in the quiet night.

I'm standing on a dock, leaning over the railing as the gentle waves of the inlet ebb and flow. A light, salt-kissed breeze skates over my bare arms and legs. I'm wearing clothes that don't belonged to me. I'm wearing skin that doesn't belong to me either.

Serena brushes past like a whirling dervish, cross-faded off three-month-old weed and frozen margaritas.

"Doesn't this look like *Mamma Mia* to you?" she sings, arms outstretched as she drunkenly twirls around.

---

* Cue: *back to friends* by sombr

"Yeah, if *Mamma Mia* were set on a dive-y boardwalk in north Florida instead of Greece."

"You don't think this looks like that scene when they're on the dock? Wait, there's a bunch of scenes when they're on the dock, but still—this definitely looks like it."

She teeters on her feet as we near the end of the dock, and starts belting out the chorus of her favorite song, triggering a string of dog barks and slamming windows.

"Okay, Meryl." I steady her. "Watch your step there. I'm not calling 911 if you fall in."

"But I want to go in! The water looks like glass." Her voice is filled with wonder, and I can't help but smile. She turns to me, her expression intensely serious. "We have one item left on our list. And that is skinny dipping."

Ah yes, the list we compiled on the never-ending bus ride from Manhattan to Panama City to make our spring break unforgettable. It was packed with silly, idiotic tasks like bull-riding and shotgunning beers and…skinny-dipping.

Serena thinks I'm wild. Free. The life of every party.

The truth is, I was never wild by nature.

She makes me wild. It's the combination of us—fire and gasoline— that makes sparks. That could burn down cities if left unattended.

I watch her from a few feet back, staring out at the water, the moonlight turning her skin pearlescent. She turns to me, and I hope I have enough time to wipe that look off my face. The look of hopeless desire. The gaze of a man in hapless, stupid love.

But Serena doesn't see a man when she looks at me. She sees a woman.

She has no idea that behind the exterior of her friend, Annie, a vivacious female with dirty blonde hair and a reckless smile, a woman I curated, there lies a stranger.

"This was your big idea." She fixes me with a sharp stare, her hands glued to her hips. "You first."

I laugh, shaking my head, and start to strip. I have nothing to be shy about. It's not like she can see the real me—not with this glamour.

Stark naked under the moonlight, I run and leap off the abandoned dock, howling at the moon before landing inside the chilly water. As I come up for air, Serena lands with a loud splash. She bursts through the surface panting, an invigorated smile on her face.

"Holy shit, why is it so cold?!" Her laugh echoes down the dock.

"Coming from the girl who likes her baths boiling," I tease, splashing her. She splashes me back.

I try not to stare. Try not to make it obvious the effort it takes not to let my gaze linger on her naked shoulders, the strip of skin above her breasts as she bobs up and down in the gentle waves. I try to forget that she's only a foot away from me in nothing but her own skin.

But, fuck, it's impossible.

I don't know when it started or when it got this bad, but it's become a cavity inside of me. A dull pain stretching into my gums, my blood, my roots. Constantly hurting. A need throughout my entire body not only to protect her and keep her safe, but to touch her. To hold her. To constantly be near her.

She swims closer, parting the water as she paddles up to me.

Please don't come any closer. I'm already struggling to keep my hands to myself.

"I can't believe those guys earlier," she says.

"So rude," I agree, thankful for the distraction.

They tried to pick her up at the bar. She thought it was me they wanted, but it was glaringly obvious. She doesn't see herself as others do. She's heartbreaking.

Serena drifts even closer, her pink lips dipping beneath the water like a silent invitation. And every part of me is screaming, *Do it. Kiss her.*

That nagging voice is so loud, I worry she can hear it. I shove it down, smothering it with finality.

Then the realization hits.

I can't keep this up. I can't keep pretending to be her friend. I've gotten too close.

Two weeks ago at this abhorrent college party full of frat boys and bottle-blonde sorority girls, we lost a game of flip cup and had to kiss. It was brief. And to her, it was just a harmless kiss between two friends being egged on by a bunch of jocks. But her lips had scalded mine in a way I'll never forget.

She branded me with her name that night. And she never even knew it. And when I pulled back, careful not to seem too eager, there was this look in her eyes that was impossible to interpret. I had wondered if she felt something more in that moment. I didn't want to confuse her any further.

But this? This is too much. It's wrong. She has no idea, but I do.

I have to pull back. I've seen too much, shared too much, and now—

I shouldn't be feeling this way. I *can't* be feeling this way.

Annie has to go. It will hurt her, I know, but this can't continue. It's not good for either of us.

After graduation, I'm drawing the line. I'll make some excuse, and she and Annie will drift apart like friends often do. Eventually she'll move on and forget about me, and everything will be the way it should be.

I can keep watch from a safe distance until it's time to bring her home.

Or maybe I'll stay just a little longer—just until I'm sure she doesn't need me.

It's for the best. At least, that's the lie I sell myself.

6 5

SERENA

12 DAYS

I sleep like shit and wake the next morning with puffy eyes and a guilty conscience. I don't know how I'm going to face Zadyn after last night.

After he told me loved me and I…didn't say it back. I simply took off my top. As if that would make it better.

Hey, sorry, my feelings for you are complicated. I might love you, but for now, here are my tits.

Stupid.

The conversation with Margot flashes through my mind. Her words had felt like an anchor dragging me down to the bottom of the ocean. But can I really trust the person who faked her own death to escape her role as queen? Who abandoned Sorscha and Derek? This could all just be some attempt to manipulate me.

She says she's on nobody's side, but who knows if that's true. My mother has only ever looked out for herself. Why should her double be any different?

I find Mar, Dover, Kai, Cece, and Eaton in the dining room having breakfast.

"No Sorscha?" I ask, sinking into an upholstered chair. Mar shakes

her head. I hadn't expected Zadyn, but I was hoping to at least see the princess.

"She hasn't really been eating lately." Cece's jade eyes link with mine as she sips her tea.

My heart sinks. I've been an awful friend to her. With everything going on, I haven't even been to see her yet. To ask how she's doing. My friends make idle chit-chat as I peer out the window, too anxious to eat a bite. I eventually drag myself upstairs to the council meeting.

Jace looks up as I pass through the door, his gaze tracking me all the way to my seat. My heart stutters, but I force myself not to meet his stare.

Gronwen, Conwell, and the High Priest are already seated. Sir Max, the new Captain of the Guard, stands stoically behind Jace. Without his bright, lopsided smile and the mischievous quirk of his brow, he looks more like Mal than usual. I shift uncomfortably in my seat.

I hear footsteps as Zadyn and Sorscha enter the room, closing the door behind them. I stand, wanting to run to her and wrap her in a hug, but she looks right past me, drifting around the table to take a seat next to Jace. Her face is vacant and grim, no remnants of the bouncing, bubbly party princess I met when I first arrived in Aegar. Death has ravaged yet another friend, stripped them of their vitality and vibrance, leaving only their lifeblood behind.

I open my mouth, but what is there to even say?

Zadyn sinks into his usual seat beside me, leaning as far away from me as he can manage. As if my very presence insults him.

"Thank you for gathering on such short notice," Jace says, his intense eyes scanning the round table. He stands in Derek's place, his palms braced on the table.

But he doesn't sit in Derek's seat.

"There are some...pressing matters we need to discuss." He straightens, adjusting the lapel of his perfectly cut jacket. "Kylian has offered us a deal. In two weeks' time, he will strike again unless Serena goes with him."

The lords and the High Priest slide wary glances my way.

"Provided she agrees, he promises to refrain from waging war. If we relinquish the crown to him."

Gronwen shoots to his feet. "Absolutely not."

"Just hear him out," I groan.

"If we don't agree to his terms, he will march on our land," Jace finishes.

"Surely, my King, you can see how surrendering the crown will do more harm than good in the long run."

"Will it?" I ask, earning a glare from Gronwen. I lean back, folding my hands over the table. "We could save countless lives by avoiding a war."

"What do you think will happen, girl, when you've joined him? He will weaponize you like he's intended all along, and we will all be at his mercy, regardless."

"No, you won't." I don't flinch from his stare. "Because I intend to kill him. One way or another."

Gronwen snickers. "I warned Derek about you. That you would be harder to control than a raging forest fire."

"I'm willing to give myself up to make sure no one else has to die. A thank you would be nice."

"You are damning us all if you do this."

"How so? Kylian has promised that you would be protected."

He throws his head back and scoffs, "You are new to this world and to faerie deals. I'm certain *Kylian* chose his words carefully. There was a reason for that."

"So you think war is a more suitable option then?" I argue.

"I think with a dragon it won't be much of a war. Maybe instead of making back alley deals with devils, you should be learning how to wield your dragon's power."

I seethe at him.

"Enough." Jace's voice cuts through our spat. "Kylian made mention of knowing how to deal with a dragon. We need to find out if he was bluffing."

"I'll have my spies look into it." Max nods dutifully.

Jace tosses him a grateful look.

"In the meantime, we have less than two weeks to come up with a solution. I want everyone focused on this." Jace's gaze shifts to Sorscha, sitting silently at his side. He clears his throat.

"The princess and I have discussed it at length, and we intend to move forward with our wedding by week's end."

"The Bloodfast will certainly play to our favor once completed," the High Priest encourages. "I'll have the preparations made."

Jace nods, and I swallow tightly.

Good. This is a good thing, I remind myself.

"Conwell, you've written to the other kingdoms?"

"Yes, Sire."

"Any responses?"

"Only from Hyrax, your Grace. Berringer will send twenty thousand men. They set sail in two days' time. The other kingdoms may prove more reluctant to provide aid."

"I could see Aeix remaining neutral," Gronwen mutters.

"I'm sure they'll be singing a different tune when Vod starts banging on their doors," I point out.

"Max, what is the latest on Vod's numbers?"

"My sources at the border reported seeing golden fleets on the Praxian Sea sailing east."

"How many?"

"Five—"

"Five is manageable," Gronwen interrupts.

"*Hundred*," Max finishes. "Five hundred."

Jace closes his eyes, pinching the bridge of his nose. "That's at least 100,000 men."

I'm no mathematician, but from the looks on everyone's faces, I can tell Aegar's armies don't come close to totaling that.

A grim silence settles over the room.

"If we can't gather more men, then I'm going with Kylian. And I'll find a way to stop him before he can cause too much damage." My eyes skip over everyone at the table. Zadyn still refuses to meet my gaze, his mouth propped against his fist.

Jace hangs his head.

Knowing there is nothing more to be said, I rise and walk out the door.

66

ZADYN

12 DAYS

I storm back to my room after the council meeting, only to find that Serena has beaten me there. My muscles lock, freezing me in place.

Great.

This is the last thing I want to deal with right now. I can barely look at her after last night. I debate walking right back out the door and avoiding her for as long as possible, but I can't outrun her forever.

I'm bound to her. There is no escaping. I can only turn and face my torturous fate.

"Zadyn, I hate this." She moves toward me, her shoulders sinking as she hits me with a pleading look. "What can I do? What can I say to make things right?"

I brush past her to the armoire and snatch my jacket from inside. "There's nothing you need to do or say, Serena. You did nothing wrong."

"Well, it really feels like I fucked up somehow."

"You know, contrary to your belief, not everything is about you." I punch my arm through my sleeve.

"Oh, so your piss-poor mood right now has nothing to do with last night? With me? Great. Cool."

361

"It's my problem to deal with. Not yours."

"Zadyn—where are you going?"

"I'm still the king's emissary. I have business to tend to."

I refrain from telling her that the business Jace has "tasked" me with involves me finding out whatever I possibly can in order to break her bargain with Kylian. Which I was planning to do, anyway.

Am I being purposefully vague and elusive about it? Maybe a little. Sue me.

"Oh, so now we're being secretive?"

"I thought we were allowed to have secrets."

"Zadyn, please. Don't treat me like this."

Sighing, I turn back to her. "I just—I need time, Serena. I think we both do."

Disappointment creeps over her perfect face, and I feel a stab of pain knowing I'm the one causing it. Shoving it down, I start to exit the room, but her voice stops me in the doorway.

"I meant what I said last night," she says. "I do want you. And I do love you. I'm just really confused right now. I'm trying to figure it out. I'm sorry."

Rare words from her.

"I'm sorry," she repeats, no louder than a whisper.

And instead of showing her compassion, instead of saying, *I appreciate you telling me that,* I nod once, wrenching open the door and say, "Got it."

I STARE at the odd-looking bird in Gnorr's study. It peers back with eyes too aware for a small winged creature, its snow-white feathers ruffling as Gnorr's wrinkled hands tuck it back inside the cage.

"I found her with a broken wing. Nursed her back to health. I tried setting her free after she had healed, but she seemed quite content to stay." Settling into the chair behind her desk, she waits for me to speak.

"Madame Gnorr, I need to ask you something."

"What is it, child?"

"It's about a bargain. Serena made a deal to leave here with Kylian. To marry him." I pause. "Is there any way for it to be undone?"

"Aside from both parties agreeing to dissolve the bargain? No. It cannot be broken. Not short of death."

Acid eats through my stomach. "But Kylian will never agree to that."

Reaching across the desk, she pats my hand. "It is her path to walk. Have faith in her."

"I have all the faith in the world in her. And still I wouldn't risk her like this."

"To love someone is to risk everything. But I think you already know that." She appraises me with cool blue eyes. I shift forward in my seat, desperation creeping into my voice.

"What can I do? There has to be something. If she goes with him…"

"You fear you'll be parted from her forever."

Sick at the very thought, I nod.

"I've not known the girl long, but I do know that she will not balk at a challenge. No matter how much you beg and plead, it is not in her nature to bend. Not with blood like hers."

I sit there for a moment, at a loss, the lump in my throat growing sharper with each breath.

Gnorr may not think it's possible, but I'm not giving up. I'll do whatever it takes. Sell my soul if I have to.

Thanking her for her time, I stand and move to the door.

"She will not choose." Gnorr's voice stills my hand on the knob. "So *you* must make the choice. Either accept who and what she is, and all the unwanted things that come with that, or walk away. Before you no longer can."

Glancing back over my shoulder, I say, "There is no part of her I don't want."

"It isn't her I'm referring to." She gives me a knowing look before turning back to her dove.

Serena bursts into the library a few hours later carrying a linen-wrapped bundle, our friends in tow. Clearly, she has no idea what space means.

I'm almost grateful. Because as much as we both need it, it's the last thing on earth I want.

"We brought snacks." She offers me a timid smile, and I try not to gawk at her as she dumps the contents of her arms out onto the table. "You skipped breakfast."

Eaton plops down beside me as she flips open the cloth. Inside are buttered biscuits, grapes, some wedges of cheese, and a few tiny quiches.

"I didn't know what you'd want, so I brought options."

She's trying to atone. As if she has a reason to be sorry when I'm the one who made the foolish mistake of kissing her. I feel like a dick for the cold shoulder I've thrown her way. But she's not giving up.

"So thoughtful, isn't she, Zadyn?" Eaton gives me a deviant smile, each word loaded with irony.

Bastard.

"That's—thank you." I finally allow my eyes to link with Serena's. And then I'm thinking about leaning over the table to thank her with a kiss. I'm thinking about drinking from her mouth, sucking at her skin, sinking my teeth into her—fuck.

I'm almost certain everyone in the room is aware of the shift in the air. My cheeks heat, and it's only made worse when I catch the look Mar gives me as she slides into a chair. I shoot her a quick scowl before forcing the lustful images from my mind.

"How's the research going?" Dover slips into the seat beside his mate, taking in the spread of books before me.

"Slow. I could use another set of eyes."

"You've got five." Mar gestures to the group. "Well, four. Kai is certainly illiterate."

"That's because my education was better spent on learning how to be the finest lover in all the kingdoms." He puckers his lips and makes a kissy sound at Mar as he slumps onto the couch behind us.

"Actually, make that three sets of eyes," Serena says. "Jace wants to take me out to train with Furi for a few hours. To try wielding."

"Oh." I try to sound casual about it, but do I think it's a horrible idea for her to be alone with Jace? Absolutely.

Do I think he's a dog for being engaged and still undoubtedly trying to have his cake and eat it too? Absolutely.

Though I thought he was a dog long before he and Sorscha were ever engaged.

I clear my throat. "I think that's a good idea."

Or it would be if anyone but Jace was teaching her. She'll be too busy making eyes at him to even absorb a word he says.

And he'll be licking it right up.

"I'll leave you to it, then. Kai, get off the ladder with that leg," Serena warns as he whizzes past, dangling from a rung despite the injury that still sometimes bothers him.

"She's right. Don't come crying to me to heal you when you're sore tonight," Mar pipes, sliding one of the thick tomes toward her.

Their bickering fades to background noise as Serena reaches the doorway, pausing to take one last look at me before disappearing into the hall.

67

SERENA

12 DAYS

"**L**esson number one," Jace muses, his voice militaristic. "Do not attempt to wield dragon fire without a set intention. Nothing must be left to chance. You have to be very clear in your mind about what it is you want. And you cannot waver."

Ah, decisiveness. My one true enemy.

"The point of this is to convert her fire into pure energy, which you then get to shape into a weapon of your choice." He meanders through the clearing, pausing to glance at Furi—propped on her hind legs, nibbling the nearby treetops. "Maybe you can get her to pay attention. This is training, not snack time."

Her massive head swings in his direction. *Maybe I'll feast on your entrails and bathe in your blood.*

I can't help but laugh.

"Keep it up, and they'll be no forest left," he digs.

"If I were you, I'd be trying a little harder to get on her good side."

"Yeah, well, she's not my favorite either."

I roll my eyes. "Okay. Clear intent. Got it. What's lesson number two?"

"Oh, we're not moving on until you've mastered the first one. Mount her."

366

"So bossy," I mutter under my breath. "Okay Furi, let's give this a shot." She nudges me with her nose before I climb up onto her back.

"Are you comfortable?" Jace calls up to me.

"Yes."

"Good. Now let your mind empty. Focus on the link between the two of you. You need to be on the exact same frequency for this to work."

I try doing what he says. Try to focus. Clear my mind of tyrants and mental shielding and night terrors and near-wedding experiences and—aww, fuck.

"No," he drones. "You're not connected. You have to be in complete synchronization."

I groan. "We're trying."

"Try harder."

"Dick."

"Brat."

"Shut *up*. I'm trying to focus."

Concentrate, Blackblood.

I am.

You're distracted. By him.

Am not.

We share a bond. I can hear your thoughts.

Then you know that right now you are *the only thing distracting me.*

"Let's try something else. Come down. Put your hand on her chest. On my count, inhale for four, hold for two, and exhale for five."

"That's confusing," I say, slipping onto the ground.

"Only if you can't count to ten."

"Can we just keep it simple? Four, four, and four?"

"Fine. Whatever. Three, two, one, inhale."

Jace counts, anchoring my thoughts as Furi and I breathe together, my hand resting against her smooth scales. Her breaths rise and fall beneath me, and I become acutely aware of her heartbeat aligning with mine. "When you're perfectly in sync, you'll feel it lock into place. Hold onto it. Don't let go."

A moment later, I sense the shift. It's like a rope tightening around the very fibers of my soul.

"I feel it."

"Good. Now slowly call her fire."

Sweat breaks through my skin as her fire begins to flow through me like a river of lava, streaming into my veins. Hot and thick, it mingles with my blood, twines with my magic and races through me at an alarming speed.

The heat intensifies, vibrating within me so fiercely that my entire body trembles.

"That's it. Keep going," Jace coaches. But his voice is far away.

Furi is silent, focused on funneling her fire into me. The sound of my gnashing teeth grates against my ears, but I don't feel it. All I feel is endless heat, mere seconds from devouring me.

A loud, choked cry cuts through me.

"That's it! You're almost there—"

"I can't take anymore! It's killing me—"

"Now! Push it out now!"

I break away from Furi, my hands turned up toward the sky. My roar bounds off the trees, shaking every branch and leaf for miles around. I become a live wire, electricity coursing through me as my eyes fly open.

The blast feels nuclear.

A line of blue fire explodes from my palms, sending two twin beams of light up into the sky. My shout is lost to the rushing flames. It's a purging. A cleansing, burning away every impurity, every thought drifting around my head as I become a hollow vessel for Furi's magic.

Jace catches me as I collapse, easing me down to the ground.

"That was it. That was fucking amazing. You're—"

His words drift off, lost to the wind as his golden eyes roam over me. We stay like that for a moment, my head leaning against his shoulder, tension coiling around us like a brewing storm. I'm so engrossed in him that I don't even notice Furi ducking to lick my face.

With the size of her ridged tongue, it's really more of a full upper-body lick with Jace in the crossfire.

"Lovely," he mutters, wiping his cheek clean.

The tension breaks as I crawl out of his arms and haul myself onto a tree stump. He follows, sinking back on his heels.

"What is it?"

I'm all too aware of his touch. His thumb sweeping over my thigh—the same one he stuck a dagger in the day we first met. And damn if that touch doesn't feel so perfectly normal. So perfectly perfect.

"I've never felt anything like that. I thought it was going to consume me."

"What did it feel like?"

I hold his gaze. "Power. It felt like power."

"Well, you better get used to it, witch." He nods toward Furi, a hidden smile threatening to peek through. "Time to go again."

6 8

JACE

12 DAYS

"That fucking *hurts!*"

"You're channeling an obscene amount of dragon fire and converting into pure magic. Of course it fucking hurts."

I sit on a large rock, sharpening my blade. After this morning's awkward as hell council meeting, and a grueling two-hour strategy meeting with Max and his lieutenants afterward, I desperately needed to get away.

"Shouldn't this be getting easier?" Serena glances down at me from Furi's back.

"It will if you keep practicing."

"We've been at it for hours. Can I take a break now?"

"No."

Blatantly ignoring my answer, she slides off Furi's wing and hops onto the ground. "Still a hard-ass, I see."

"Still a *pain* in the ass, I see."

She laughs, strutting toward me and scooping up the waterskin. "How many times do I have to do this?"

"Until you can do it in your sleep. What you're doing requires intense discipline," I explain, glancing up at her leather-clad body.

370

Big mistake.

Seeing her in beautiful gowns and courtly finery was one thing, but the way she looks in her training clothes, disheveled and flushed, is my weakness. "Once you're able to harness Furi's fire, you can funnel it into any kind of power you want. Hence, wielding."

I focus on my blade, running a small stone along its edges until tiny sparks pop off. Serena plops down on the ground, staring up at me with those wide purple eyes.

"So I should be able to convert it to whatever I want?"

"In theory."

"Well, what if I wanted it to rain unicorns?"

I pause what I'm doing to shoot her a stern look. "This is not a joke. You need to take this seriously."

"And I'm seriously asking what would happen if I wanted it to rain unicorns."

"They're an endangered species," I mutter.

"Unicorns are real?" She gapes, her voice jumping an octave.

"Yes. If you really wanted to, you could make it rain unicorns. But you can do a lot more than that. Say you wanted to incapacitate, but not kill. You could freeze an entire army in place, render them immobile. You could use compulsion, you could do anything. It's all about control. Without it, you'll kill everyone within a fifty-mile radius."

Satisfied with my sword, I slide it back into its sheath.

"That's not a terrifying thought."

"That's why we're here, learning how to do it safely. It's going to hurt the first few times, but you'll get used to it."

She nods, getting to her feet. I have to admit, this is a welcome distraction. Being at the palace right now is stifling.

For decades, I watched Derek handle being king with grace and charisma. He was the perfect balance of stern and gentle. I am nowhere near as polished. I'm all rough edges. Raw and crass. I was never a courtier. I don't know how to sit where he sat and rule in his name. I already feel like a failure.

"Do you want to talk about it?" Her question startles me.

"About what?"

"Anything. Everything. Your wedding is coming up."

"Forgive me for not wanting to discuss the floral arrangements with you."

"Jace." She purses her lips, then glances at the ground. "How—how is Sorscha doing with everything? I'm a little worried about her." Concern crosses her beautiful face, drawing her brows together.

"I don't know." I sigh, pushing my hair back. "I try. She won't talk to me. She says she's fine, but it seems like she's pulling away from everyone. I don't want to push her."

I should make more of an effort. But I've barely had time to eat or sleep since becoming regent. Aside from a few public appearances with her, there's hardly enough time to get in a *how are you.*

"I've thought about going to see her."

"What's stopping you?" I ask.

She sighs. "I'm not sure she wants to see me. Lately I feel like a walking disaster, pulling everything into my wake. Every bad thing that's happened these past few months, I've been right there front and center. Derek, Ilsa…you. I wouldn't blame her if she never wanted to see me again."

"I don't think she blames you for any of that."

"I don't know, she just seems so…different."

"Her father was murdered by the same monsters that killed her best friend. If she weren't different after something like that…then I'd be concerned."

Serena shakes her head, staring out into the clearing. "We never really talked. About Derek."

She gazes down at me, her expression sympathetic. I still can barely look her in the eye, ashamed of my behavior since Vod. And still, instead of falling at her feet and begging her forgiveness, I just pushed her away. I insulted her. I hurt her, like I always do.

But rather than letting the crippling remorse hit me full force, I shove it down under layers of cultivated hardness I've spent years building up.

"How are *you* doing? Really."

I set my jaw and shake my head. "I'd rather not talk about any of it."

Her hands slide to her hips. "Well, if you don't want to talk, then I will."

"Serena—"

"You're going through with this wedding in a few days, and I'm happy for you. I really am. But I think you and I need some clear boundaries."

"Do you now?" I lean on my knees and peer up at her, really only thinking about how cute she looks when she's trying to be serious.

"I do. I'll continue training with you if we can both agree that from here on out, you and I are strictly platonic. As crazy as you drive me, I can't lose you as a friend. Not at a time like this, probably not ever. So, I need you to agree to be my friend. And I will be one to you."

Her openness and vulnerability have always stunned me. How can a person be so willing to share, so willing to give? I envy her and admire her at the same time for it.

I stand, walking closer until her pointed finger meets my chest. "And don't tell me you're too big for all of us small folk now that you're king."

"Never." I allow the tiniest hint of a smile to show. "Let's switch gears. I want to work on your hand-to-hand."

She cocks her hip. "You're just looking for an excuse to spar."

"Do you blame me? I've been stuck behind desks all day, signing documents and striking deals with nobles. I need to get some of this pent-up energy out."

"Well. Let's see what you've got then, King." She quirks a brow, getting into the fighting stance I taught her.

And because I taught her, I know she'll strike first—which she does, throwing out a punch that would shatter a male's jaw. She whirls as I slip out of the way, rolling her neck and crouching again. I advance this time, taking advantage of her open gait. My fist finds her stomach as her elbow slams into my face. The tang of blood coats my mouth as I laugh, staggering back a step.

"There's that vicious streak I've been missing."

She shrugs, a smug little smirk on her lips. "Learned from the best."

I lunge for her again, and we fall into a dance of flying fists and swinging kicks. It's lighthearted. Playful. And even though each of her hits hurt like hell, they feel tender. Like a kiss.

And I meet her move for move. Every punch I land, I imagine I'm kissing her back.

Hit. I want you

Hit. I need you.

Hit. I love you.

Breathless, I lock onto her shoulder, dragging her into my punch. She takes it in the ribs, the air whooshing out of her before she knees me in the groin.

"*Fuck.*" I taught her well.

Grabbing my hand, she twists beneath me and flips me flat on my back. I heave a half-groan, half-laugh as she plants her boot on my chest and peers down at me.

"Say I won."

"Who said we're done?"

I yank on her ankle, cackling as her ass hits the ground. Then I drag her closer until our thighs touch, and sit up on my knees to lean over her.

"Look at you. Always falling for me."

Her lavender eyes flash. She gets to her knees, mirroring my posture, grabs a fistful of my hair, and leans in.

And I'm helpless.

Utterly helpless. Boundaries be damned.

She's close enough to taste, and I'm suddenly starving. I open my mouth as she replaces her hold on my neck with a dagger to my throat.

My eyes peel open. "Dirty move."

She nods. "Like you said. Vicious. Now say I won."

"You won," I pant. "You won this round."

A feline smile cracks her lips as she releases my hair, twirls the blade in her hand, and slides it back into its sheath. She pats my cheek and sashays away, high on her victory, leaving me there on the forest floor staring after her.

Friends?

Yeah. Right.

I'm totally screwed.

69

SERENA

12 DAYS

*O*h, just spit it out.

Furi blinks at me oh-so-innocently, her scales irides-cent beneath the crystal refractions of the cave.

Spit what out?

I can smell your judgment from here.

She settles into her nest of diamonds. *The Blackblood knows my thoughts.*

You judgy little dragon! I set the boundaries, and I stuck to them. We're going to be friends.

Not that we have much of a choice.

Sure.

Uh, excuse me, miss. Can we tone down the sarcasm?

Sarcasm is your native language. I'm being considerate.

I snort.

Does the Blackblood disagree?

No, no she does not.

She nudges me with her snout. *What weighs on you?*

Between this deal with Kylian, the mess I've made of my relationship with Zadyn, and seeing my mother's doppelgänger, it's pretty much a toss up at this point.

376

Was it seeing her or hearing what she had to say?

My eyes snap toward her. *How do you know about that?*

There are things I just know.

Hold on. I straighten, dropping the game bag filled with bloodied forest critters. *What things?*

Furi is silent.

I said, what things? Did you know about this? She gives me a noncommittal shrug. *All of it?*

Some of it, perhaps.

And you didn't tell me?! Furi!

I whack her with a dead squirrel before flinging it up in the air. She catches it in her snapping jaws.

How could you not say anything?

Little traitor.

Not my information to share.

I scoff, tossing my arms up. *It's vital information! Whose side are you on?*

She gives me some fierce side-eye. *I would think the answer to that is relatively clear.*

Furi, if you know something else, you better spit it out.

A loud sigh blasts from her nostrils, blowing my hair back.

What the seer said is true.

My heart plummets. *How can you be certain?*

I rely on my senses. And when he is around, there is cold like I've never known.

But...how? It just doesn't make sense.

Some things do not make sense. But they are as they are.

And the others?

You must come to that on your own.

Fuck that, we all might all be dead in two weeks.

We will not die. I will prevent it.

Furi, unless you've been hiding the ability to see the future, then you don't know that for certain.

You already know, Blackblood, you've just yet to face it.

I shake my head, trying to clear away the warring emotions.

No. *No.* It's just too absurd to be true. But Margot's words seem inescapable. And the thought of that feels like a poison in my mind.

I groan, leaning against her and sliding onto the cave floor. The jagged spikes along the ceiling angle toward me like a sky of daggers.

How is it possible to have all this power and still feel so out of control?

Power is not synonymous with control. To believe otherwise is foolish.

I have to believe I have it for a reason, though. And that I'm meant to use it to do some good in the world. AKA stop the psychotic king obsessed with world domination.

Heed your ancestor, Blackblood.

Who, Arden? How can I when her advice seems ass-backwards? She and Margot both basically said the same thing...but I can't be queen.

I can't be his *queen.*

Do you doubt her? Do you doubt that you are meant to lead?

Yes. Who would follow me?

This earth would fall to its knees before you if you were willing to claim it.

I'm not a conqueror. I'm not Kylian.

No, you were born to this and for this. The thing you are most afraid of—Arden said you must face it.

I have many fears.

You have one.

Well, please—clue me in.

Her tail curls around me. *You don't fear the young king. You don't fear war. What you fear is yourself.*

I stare into her glowing green eyes. *That's ridiculous.*

Is it? There is darkness and light in us all. The only way to see to the bottom is to look. You fear the darkness. You fear the shadows. But you are the shadows. And you are the light.

Maybe I do need it. Maybe I need the darkness in order to see the light.

If I look...if I stare into that darkness, I'm afraid of what I'll find.

I've always hated that part of myself. That well of feminine rage, that secret desire for chaos. I've kept it locked tight. But now...

Now is the time to look. You cannot do what is required of you without first facing the beast that looks back.

70

JACE

12 DAYS

erek's study is as he left it. His scent still lingers in the air, clinging to the scrolls of parchment neatly stacked on his desk. On the last book he read, splayed facedown on the smooth wooden surface. My finger trails along the edge, where already a light layer of dust has begun to congregate.

I couldn't bring myself to move anything. To touch anything. I've ordered the maids not to enter, either. As if keeping everything as it is would negate the truth of the way things are. That this room no longer belongs to him. It belongs to me. And I'm expected to do all he did. Be all that he was.

An impossible task.

A knock on the door shatters my reverie.

"Come," I command.

A steward pushes into the room and bows, a small stack of cream envelopes in his hand—each sealed with a crimson press. "Letters, Sire, from Vod."

I stalk around the desk, snatching them from his shaky grasp.

They're addressed to the *Queen of Vod*.

She's been back two days and already the bastard has written her a pile of letters?

380

Snarling, I rip open the first, and my eyes land on curling black ink.

> *My dearest wife,*
> *News of our impending nuptials has spread throughout the land. Our people are eager. Too long have they been without a queen. I trust your affairs are in order. I patiently await your return.*
> *Adoringly yours,*
> *Kylian*

I toss the letter aside in lieu of the second.

> *My love,*
> *The days are long without you, the nights, infinite. The halls are dull. I grow tired of the views. Without you in the frame, the cliffs have lost their majesty. The sea no longer dazzles beneath the sun. The sand is cool, and the palms wither and sag. Even the wine is more bitter.*
> *A fortnight has never before felt like an eternity.*
> *Your betrothed,*
> *Kylian*

> *My Queen,*
> *This bed offers little comfort without you here to warm it. I'm haunted with yearning. Sleep continues to evade me. I've abandoned any hope of apprehending it until you return. I toss and turn, cruel dreams plaguing me, reminding me of your scent, your taste...*

This bed is yours now. As is every part belonging to me.

Kylian

My wife,

Why do you not return my letters?

What can I do to atone for that which I know not what I am atoning for?

Will it be jewels? I will shower you with them until the sight makes you ill.

Silks? Gowns? You shall have entire wings dedicated to your wardrobe.

Will it be servitude? Every male, female, and child in the kingdom shall kiss the ground beneath you.

Is it adoration? I vow to worship your body, day and night, on my knees at your altar, until you are sick of my hands, my fingers, my mouth, my—

Unable to read another nauseating word, I gobble up the letters in my fist, crumpling them into a tight ball before tossing them into the fire.

"Send for Lord Gronwen and Sir Max," I bark, seething at the surging flames.

❧

"My King." Gronwen enters the study, Max at his side. "You sent for us?"

I nod, gesturing for them to sit as I lean against the desk.

"There's something I've been considering. I didn't want to involve the entire council."

"Of course," Max nods, his face solemn.

Shifting my eyes between them, I say, "I want to launch an attack. Before the two weeks are up, before Vod can strike first. I want to obliterate them."

They remain quiet, weighing my proposition. Gronwen crosses one spindly leg over the other, his chalky fingers curling over the carved wooden armrests. "Should we not wait for Berringer's armies to arrive?"

"We don't have time to wait. By the time they arrive, Vod's forces will be here, and it will be too late."

"I understand your desire to act, Sire, but doing so could backfire."

"Captain?" I turn to Max.

My friend. One of my *only* friends at this point.

"Vod has already reached our shores. Their forces are marching as we speak," he answers regretfully.

"Exactly. And here we are, waiting with our thumbs up our asses. We cannot just do nothing," I fume, looking back to Gronwen. "You expect me to wait until he shows up here with his fleets and armies and Serena hands herself over? No. I will end this before it comes to that. I refuse to put her at risk."

Gronwen peers at me from beneath dark brows, a grave warning in his eyes. "Sire, forgive my saying so, but it is the Dragon Rider's choice."

"Because for some gods-damned reason, she feels it's her responsibility to fix this! She is hell-bent on sacrificing herself, and I will *not* allow it."

Gronwen clears his throat, exchanging a glance with Max. He continues in a measured voice, "While I agree that things should not be left to chance, I feel that we must proceed with caution."

I grip the armrests of his chair, a cold, calm rage creeping over me.

"You misunderstand me. I called you here as a courtesy. But make no mistake, I am not asking. I am telling." I lean in, letting my voice sink in volume. "This ends tonight. I will destroy him with my bare hands if I must."

An image of my fingers wrapping around Kylian's throat and

squeezing until he turns blue swirls around my mind. It's a beautiful thought.

Max rises from his seat. "Say the word, and we'll dispatch."

I hold his gaze for a long moment. Straightening to my full height, I give him a curt nod.

"Do it."

71

SERENA

11 DAYS

"Y ou may now kiss your bride!"

The High Priest lifts his palms in exultation. Jace and Sorscha exchange an uncomfortable look.

"And then you will descend back down the aisle, and your ladies will follow behind alongside the males. Any questions?"

The seven of us hold our tongues as the Priest claps his hands together. "Excellent. Let us practice."

"Is this really necessary?" Jace turns to him, a grimace on his face.

"It is choreography. It needs be rehearsed. One weak link will drag down the rest, so if you please, Highness."

Jace rolls his eyes, threading Sorscha's arm through his and leading her back down the stretch of white carpet already rolled out for the wedding in two days. I take Kai's arm, and we fall into line behind them, making our way past the servants on ladders, stringing up flower garlands around the perimeter of the ornate chapel.

Cece and Sorscha continue out into the hall while the rest of us linger in the doorway.

"What time is this dinner? I'm starving," Mar grouses.

"You're always starving," Dover mutters.

385

"What can I say? Being this attractive burns energy like you wouldn't believe."

I chuckle. "I'm going to check on Zadyn. He's been in that library for days."

He claims to be searching for a way to break this deal without horrific consequences. But I think he's using it as an excuse to avoid me.

"If anyone can tempt him out, it's you, savior." Kai's brows wag as he gives my hand a squeeze. I rip it away.

"That's not funny."

"It's a little funny. Been meaning to ask—were we interrupting something when we burst into your room the night of the fire? You two seemed so…alarmed." He slinks back against the marble pillar, a smirk twisting up the corners of his mouth.

"We were sleeping," I lie.

He tosses his head back and laughs. "Sweetheart, those didn't look like the faces of two people who'd been asleep—"

"Who's been asleep?"

I jump at the low rumble of Jace's voice behind me.

"No one," I say too quickly. His gaze skirts between me and Kai.

"Right." Kai clears his throat.

Subtle.

"Well, better get changed for tonight's festivities." He salutes us before following our friends out the door.

I lock eyes with Jace.

Furi was right. Getting up close and personal in our training sessions does not aid in our quest for wholesome, G-rated friendship. So this morning was a lot of me trying to limit physical contact, which isn't very conducive to a productive session. And I'm sure he noticed.

"I should go too."

"Are you avoiding me?" His question stops me before I reach the hall.

I turn back, offering him a humorless smile. "I can't really avoid you when we train together every glorious morning."

"You barely said a word to me this morning. I don't think it's fair of you to punish me for going along with an idea you insisted upon."

"I'm not punishing you. And your marriage wasn't my idea."

"To have it in two days was."

I limit my voice to a hissed whisper. "I'm sorry to impose on your busy schedule, my dear King Regent. We're only trying to prevent war from breaking out."

"Forgive me, maybe I'm still a little bitter."

"You?"

"Yes, witch, me." He leans a shoulder against the pillar, every inch of him packed with lethal grace. "I never did catch your answer."

"Answer to what?"

He glances up, muttering a cruel laugh. "Was my proposal that forgettable?"

My mouth parts. "That was…hardly a proposal."

"What else would you call me asking you to marry me? Please enlighten me."

"First of all, you can't ask someone to marry you when you're already engaged—"

"I did, guess I'm a rule breaker."

"And second—I was giving you an out."

"An out?" His eyes narrow.

"Derek had just died. You were in shock, and you were saying things you didn't really mean. I couldn't take advantage of that."

His face hardens. "Don't you dare tell me I didn't mean what I said. I knew what I was doing, and you brushed it aside."

"I'm sorry if you felt that way. But what did you expect?"

"Like a fool, I expected you to take the offer."

"I couldn't run away with you. Aren't you the one who told me we can't escape our fate?"

"Maybe I changed my mind. Maybe you changed it."

"You're getting married. You're going to be king. Talking about this is pointless." I don't mean for my words to sound as harsh as they do.

"It is, isn't it?" He gives me a cold glare and tears past me. It feels like a punch to the gut.

I MAKE my way into the Grand Hall, pausing at the steps to take in the splendor waiting on the other side.

If this is the precursor to the wedding, I shudder to think how decadent the real deal will be. The entire room has been transformed into a woodland dream. Every inch of wall and ceiling is covered in moss and tangling vines with tiny fae lights sprinkled throughout.

The beauty of this world is never lost on me—even when that beauty is wrapped in thorns sharp enough to draw blood.

I step into the sea of ballgowns, feeling strange without Zadyn by my side. He was with me the first time I danced in this room, when I met the people I would claim as my family. He's been with me every step of the way, easing my transition into this world.

And I may have ruined everything between us.

Spotting Mar's mass of auburn hair on the terrace, I cut through the party to find my friends huddled by the open doors. Every head is angled toward the sprawling lawns below, where two lines of archers are assembled. Their flaming arrows release at the same moment, shooting up into the night sky and criss-crossing before exploding like dying stars. The crowd of onlookers "ooh" and "ah" in response.

"I'm going to get a better look." Eaton excuses himself to join the horde of nobility gathered along the balcony, stopping beside Sorscha.

"Anyone care to dance? I have skills that need to be shown off," Kai drawls, dusting off his shoulder.

"Don't look at me." Mar snickers.

Kai turns to me and inverts his lips into a pout that would be ridiculous on most males. He somehow manages to make it look pornographic.

"Fine," I cede. "I will be the sacrificial lamb."

He smiles and snakes his arm around my waist, steering me to the dance floor.

"How are you feeling?" he asks. I place my hand on his shoulder, and we begin to waltz.

"Fine. Why?"

"Well, it's just that the last wedding you attended got a little"—he makes a face—"bloody."

I have to laugh.

"As long as you're not planning any repeats."

"Nope. I'm praying this wedding will be absolutely uneventful. Boring, even. No surprises."

"Haven't you learned by now, *Lady Accostia*? Court life is chock-full of surprises. Not always the good kind. Couldn't tempt our little Zadyn from the library?"

"He is not little—"

"Wait, how do you know that?" Kai gives me a dubious grin.

"You know what I mean." My cheeks flush. "He's probably getting dressed now."

"He didn't come the moment you beckoned? The scandal."

"Oh, shut up." We fall silent as Kai's ballroom expertise carries us across the floor. "We haven't really had much time to talk. Alone."

"If it's a rendezvous you want, you need only ask."

I press my lips into a flat line. "I want to know how you're doing. Really."

"I'm fantastic."

"Are you? Because I know how good you are at pretending everything is perfectly fine and life is one big riot." I search his face, but he avoids me, adopting an air of cool indifference. "You went through hell. And you made it out."

"We both did."

"Your situation was worse than mine."

"It's not a competition."

"I just want to make sure you're alright."

"What answer are you looking for? The truth or the one that makes it easier for you to sleep?" Kai's ocean eyes finally snap to mine, void of all humor. "Are *you* alright? Do *you* get through the nights without waking?"

I blink. "I…manage."

He barks a cold laugh. "We both know that isn't true. I can't give you the answer you want. And if I asked, you'd be unable to do the same. So if you're wondering why I haven't brought it up since we escaped, there it is."

I nod, swallowing. He's right. He's not okay. Neither of us is.

"This is the last thing I'll say about it. I know my brother, Serena." Kai twirls me, never missing a beat as I finish the rotation and fall back into step with him. "When he thinks something belongs to him, there is nothing he won't do to keep it that way. He's not the sharing type."

"I'm aware."

"Do not underestimate him. I know you think you're invincible, but you're not. Nobody is."

I sigh. "Kai, please, not you too."

"I'll be the first to admit that Jace and Zadyn are a bit too worrisome for my taste, but in this case, they have a point," he says, hoisting me into the air.

"This is my mess. I need to be the one to fix it."

His voice is soft when he speaks. "You may be the savior, but you don't corner the market on sacrifice."

"Kai, when the time comes, I plan to kill him. I know he's done unspeakable things…and I also know that he's your brother."

"Are you asking my permission or my forgiveness?"

"Both, I guess."

His gaze locks with mine. "My loyalty is to you. Do what you must."

I nod.

"May I cut in?"*

Jace is suddenly beside us, the fae lights glinting off his golden eyes and the silver crown nestled into his dark hair. I lose all train of thought. I barely even notice Kai transferring my hand to Jace's and backing away.

____

* Cue: *another woman* by Coral Moons

His sturdy arm slides around my waist, pulling me against him with aching gentleness. I shudder. "I'm not really sure this is a good look."

"What's not?"

"You and me dancing." I swallow, forcing myself to stare past his shoulder. "At your rehearsal party."

"How else was I supposed to get you alone?"

"We're alone all the time. We're alone too much." He quirks a dark brow, spinning me beneath my own arm. "What do you want? You have until the end of this song."

"Nothing in particular. I guess I just wanted to do this because—"

"Because what?"

"It's the only chance I'll ever get."

Jace becomes the current, pushing me out and pulling me in. Crashing into me with relentless force. Each spin is a claim.

Mine. Mine. Mine.

"Besides, I should be allowed to dance with my…friend."

"I don't think I've ever heard you use that word before. The 'f' word."

He ignores my statement, his gilded eyes drinking me in from the crown of my head to the lace trim of my violet gown. "You look beautiful. But then again, you always do."

"I'm not sure friends are supposed to say that."

"I'm past the point of caring." Going off my surprised expression, he asks, "What?"

"Your compliments are usually more backhanded."

"I may not say it often—or ever—" He glances at the floor. "But every time I look at you, I find something else to fall in love with."

"And what is it this time?"

"I could never choose just one."

My stomach flutters.

"It's everything. Your spirit. Your touch. Your voice." His hands press against my back, holding me a little tighter. "I think you're the best and worst thing to ever happen to me."

"I'm not sure that's a compliment."

"Not a compliment." I blink up at him. "Fact," he reminds me, earning him a laugh.

"But for posterity's sake, just this once, with no one able to hear—" He leans down, brushing his whisper over my ear. "I will tell you how unfairly beautiful you are. How I wish this entire world were the color of your eyes. How this tiny freckle has become the center of my universe, and it's no bigger than a pin prick." He reaches out to tap the tiny beauty mark below my lip.

My mouth opens, but he shakes his head.

"Don't say anything. I just want to enjoy this."

"Jace—"

"Without your yapping ruining the moment," he teases, lifting me above his head and making my stomach dip. "Just until the end of the dance—don't say anything. Let's just pretend this isn't ending."

"I don't know if I can do that." My voice is a flimsy leaf trembling in the wind.

"Like I said," he murmurs. "Pretend."

So I try. I let our eyes do the talking. I let my body succumb to him, moving to his lead as the music swallows the silence between us.

This moment is ours. Just him and me. Our first dance. And our last.

I spin out, and time moves slower. At the last moment, he finds my hand and reels me in, catching me over his knee mere inches from the ground. And for that one second, he lets me read in his face all he's never said.

All he will never say.

I lose my breath as he sets me on my feet. But his mask is already back on. The hard-shelled mask I've come to know so well. He doesn't spare me another glance as he walks away, ignoring my parted mouth and the words that just died on my tongue.

72
JACE

11 DAYS

I am not a person of faith.

Trusting in something greater than you, believing that everything happens for a reason—that all the terrible things in life are somehow justified, and that in the end our pain and suffering is rewarded…

That requires hope.

Which is something I simply do not have.

I never did.

I take that back—I did have it. For a little while.

I didn't even realize how empty my life was until she burst into the frame like a dying star, lighting up a dark void. I saw that light, and I held on as tight as I could for as long as I could.

But it wasn't enough. You can't contain a fire. You can't hold it in your hands without getting burned.

And that's exactly what I tried to do.

Now that light will burn for someone else. And that will haunt me until my dying day.

Every possibility of us is dashed because I couldn't speak up sooner. Because I couldn't stand up for what I wanted. Because I simply was not strong enough.

A warrior and a coward.

A death machine and a scared little boy.

It's time to grow up. I just wish I knew what that meant.[*]

The sound of soft footsteps interrupts my train of thought. I turn toward the back of the empty chapel, all decorated for the wedding. Sorscha stands in the doorway, framed by golden candlelight. Her startled gaze lands on me, and she hesitates—as if deciding whether or not to run in the opposite direction.

But she moves closer, looking at me with the sweet amber eyes of a doe, and slips into the pew beside me.

A twinge of guilt nips at me. I open my mouth and then close it.

What can I say to her?

What can I say to somehow bridge the divide? To reach around the person who stands between us, whose presence is felt even when she's not in the room. For all of Sorscha's innocence—her naivete and optimism—she isn't stupid.

She knows. Everyone knows, I'm beginning to realize.

"Pink."

"I'm sorry?"

"Pink. It's my favorite color." She stares straight ahead, toward the rows of lit candles on the altar. Warm colors dance across her face, mingling with the blue-gray moonlight seeping through the glass dome overhead.

"Hydrangeas are my favorite flower. I hate the rain, but love the snow. I prefer sleeping late and staying up until morning. I find tournaments awfully dull. I love silk. Silk dresses, silk sheets, silk everything. And warm sun on my face. And I think ale is the most detestable thing I've ever tasted."

She turns to face me.

"We don't know each other, Jace. I mean, we do, we have for ages, and yet...I only know you from arm's length. I know your respect, your manners, your chivalry. But I do not know *you*. What you like...

---

[*] Cue: *Glimpse of Us* by Joji

what makes you truly laugh or smile…what you hate. And I've never known how you felt."

"Sorscha, I'm sorry."

"What do you have to be sorry for? We're merely two people who have found themselves in the middle of a political predicament."

"I'm sorry because I want to be a better male. For you, for our future."

It's the truth. The only truth I can give her that isn't wrapped in thorns. I want to give this perfect person everything she deserves. I want to be a good and faithful husband and a strong king.

But I'm not a better male. I'm not good, and I can't be what she deserves. Not when my heart is wrecked for another.

Her brows knit together as she studies me. "Please don't pretend for my sake."

"I'm not pretending." I take her hands, staring at the smooth skin, and the absurd diamond on her finger. "I do want you to be happy. I want you to get everything you deserve."

"But you can't give it to me. And we both know it."

I shake my head, frustrated with the way my words are coming out. "Listen, I've never been…good at expressing myself. What I'm trying to say is—I'm trying."

She gives me a sad, sympathetic smile. "If someone has to try that hard to want me, then maybe it isn't worth trying at all."

She withdraws her hands. "This doesn't have to be misery for us. It's possible for us both to be happy as long as we fulfill our duties and keep up appearances. We can lead separate lives."

"That isn't what I want. I just wish—"

"What? That you didn't love her? Would that make it easier to be married to someone you don't want?"

"It isn't like that. You are—you're perfect."

"But I'm not perfect for *you*." Her gaze falls to the floor. "It's my fault for reading into something that was never there."

"It was there, believe me it was—"

"Until Serena came," she finishes, shaking her head at me like I'm a fool.

I am. I hang my head guiltily, at a loss for words. "I didn't mean for this to happen. Please understand that."

"I do, Jace. At least, I'm trying to." A sad expression mars her beautiful face. "Who wouldn't take one look at her and fall in love?"

We stare at each other for a prolonged moment. I don't know what I can say or do to make this any better. Before I can answer my own question, the princess stands and ducks out of the pew.

"Sorscha—" My voice halts her stride. "In two days, I'll be yours. And I won't look back. I won't betray you. I won't hurt you. I'm sorry if I already did, but I will do my best every single day. I will put in the work, I—"

I will put her out of my mind forever. Even if it consumes me. For you and for Derek.

"I will do better."

She leans in and plants a kiss on my cheek. When she pulls back, her lip trembles almost imperceptibly, and she offers me a sad excuse for a smile.

"I know you'll try."

<h1 style="text-align:center">73
ZADYN</h1>

11 DAYS

Barely over a week left.

And instead of savoring every moment I have with Serena before the shit inevitably hits the fan, here I am, hiding out in the library. Using any excuse I can to avoid confronting the complicated mess I've made of our relationship.

I knew it was a bad idea. And yet, I was completely helpless against her. Defenseless.

I can't run from it any longer. I can't quell the desperation to be with her. The constant craving.

At times, it's hard for me to even understand the complexity of my feelings for her. How when I focus, I can feel exactly what she's feeling. I can feel her joy and sorrow as if they were my own. I can feel her laughter in my bones. I can taste the salt of her tears when she cries.

My heart is divided in two, and she wears the other half like a badge, completely unaware of the power she holds.

She's there on the other side of this door, and I *miss* her. It's pathetic.

If there were a way I could love someone else—if it were possible for me to carve these feelings out of my heart—I would.

Because it is agony.

It is agony to want her the way I do—to have every cell in my body screaming at me to touch her, hold her, please her—and to know that some small part of her will always belong to someone else.

"Should we have a bed moved in here for you?" Eaton saunters in, plopping down in the seat across from me.

"Har har."

"I'm serious. Do you intend to cloister yourself behind these walls forever, or will you at least come out to bid Serena farewell when Kylian comes calling?"

"Why do you think I'm in here?" I snap, shoving the book I've been combing through aside. "I'm trying to figure out how to end this for her."

"And that's the *only* reason?" He quirks a brow, drumming his fingers on the table. "It has nothing to do with your constant pining?"

"You're way off base," I scoff.

"Want my advice?"

"Not particularly."

"Too bad. Here it is. Stop wallowing. Grow some balls. Get the fuck out there and get your girl."

"Eaton, you have no idea—"

"I know what I'm talking about, Zadyn. Nobody likes a downer. You can either sit here like a bump on a log, hoping she can see how perfect you would be together, or you can get out there and show her. Win her over the old-fashioned way."

"Which way is that?"

"Woo her. Sweep her off her feet. Make it impossible for her to resist you. It's not as though you lack experience. You've never had a problem landing other females. "

"She's not other females. She's special."

"Oh, listen to you. Wrapped around her witchy little finger." He makes a whipping sound and mimes snapping it at me.

I'm not in the mood for this. "Eaton, either make yourself useful or get out."

"Stop trying to deflect."

"Stop acting like you know everything! You don't know how this feels because you have never experienced it. You go through people like tissue with barely any time to come up for air. I don't know if you're even capable of having a real relationship. So should I really be taking the advice of someone who would fuck anything that moves?"

Eaton looks stung.

"I'm sorry. I didn't mean that, I'm—"

"Contrary to your beliefs, Zadyn, I do know how this feels." His eyes fall to his feet as he stands. "And I also know that if you don't make a move, someone else will. And you will be forced to watch as they ride off into the sunset."

74

SERENA

10 DAYS

"**S**hit," I squeak, dropping the silk gown and the pushpin that just accosted me.

Igrid's cerulean eyes flash up to mine as a black bead forms on my fingertip.

"Oh, no, did I get you, missy?"

She pauses sticking tiny pins along the bottom of my bridesmaid dress for tomorrow.

I shake my head. "It was all me. I wasn't paying attention."

Mar glances up from the book in her lap. Dover is snoozing beside her, his cheek propped on his hand.

"I'm almost through here," Igrid promises.

"Still too long in my humble opinion."

I turn toward Kai—who is, of course, making himself at home on my bed. "You think so? It has to at least come to the top of my shoes."

He sighs, sliding off the bed and sauntering over. "You don't want to be tripping over yourself all evening. We're all well acquainted with your level of coordination."

"Wow, nice."

"I think it has to be at least—" He reaches down, hoisting the dress up to my thigh. "There. That's perfect."

400

"You little shit." I give him a playful shove, turning when I hear a light knock on my door.

Jace steps through, drinking in the sight of me in the silver floor-length gown.

"You're going to catch flies if you don't close your mouth, Captain," Mar mutters, flipping a page. "Forgive me, I mean, *King*," she says, not an ounce of apology in her voice.

Jace's face turns red as he blinks away from me. "Kai said we were meeting here."

Right on cue, Kai ambles toward him, rubbing his hands together in a diabolical manner.

"Jace, you devil! Last night of freedom," he sings, kicking Dover awake. "You don't expect we'll let you live it peacefully, do you?"

Jace looks mortified.

"Don't give me that look. I've taken great care in planning tonight's festivities!" Kai grips the back of his neck and gives him a shake, mischief oozing from his every pore.

"Any excuse for debauchery." Dover sits up, stretching his arms toward the painted ceiling. He leans in to plant a quick kiss on Mar's cheek as Kai hauls Jace toward the door.

"Do *not* do anything stupid." Mar closes her book. "Kai, I'm serious. He has to walk down an aisle tomorrow!"

"He'll be good as new by morning. Cross my heart." He winks. "Don't wait up."

"Didn't plan on it."

Igrid stands, sticking a spare pin back into its velvet cushion. "All done. I'll have it ready by morning."

"Thank you, Igrid." I offer her as much of a smile as I can, slipping out of the dress and into the silk robe she holds out.

"How are you?" Mar asks once we're alone.

"I wish everyone would stop asking me that. It's a wedding, not a funeral."

She angles her head, giving me a doubtful look. "It's not just any old wedding."

"Still. I'm fine."

"I never liked weddings." Mar gets to her feet. "But if the boys get to have their fun, then so do we."

A few minutes later, we're knocking on Sorscha's door. She and Cece are already inside, relatively drunk, surrounded by towers of colorful miniature cakes and pastries.

"My friends!" Sorscha throws her arms around Mar's neck and then mine. I'm glad to see her spirits a bit higher, but there is no warmth behind her energy. It's surface-level. Almost manic.

Cece's suspicious gaze shifts toward me as I slide into a seat at the table across from her.

"Wonder what the boys are getting up to this evening," she muses, shuffling a deck of playing cards.

"If I know Kai—booze, drugs, and females. Not necessarily in that order," Sorscha says, moving toward the bar cart.

Mar snorts. "You left out thievery and arson."

My brows shoot up. "*Arson?*"

Waving a hand, she says, "He claims it was an accident. No one got hurt. Let's just say his 'acquaintance' with the pirates goes *way* back."

"I'm sure Zadyn will keep them in line tonight," Sorscha mutters offhandedly, pouring herself a glass of bubbles.

"Zadyn didn't go." Sorscha cocks her head at me. "At least I don't think he did."

Then again, who knows? He continues to avoid me after the tragic makeout debacle.

"He had something better to do?" Cece asks.

"I'm not sure. He's probably with the Prince of Hyrax."

A loud clank sounds from the other side of the room.

Our heads snap toward Sorscha, bracing the bottle she nearly toppled over on the bar cart. Pink flashes across her cheeks. She's not usually clumsy.

"Huh. Thought you two were attached at the hip." Cece sifts the cards through her nimble fingers, sizing me up with that cat-like stare designed to cut through to the bone.

I flash her a smile. "We are."

"What's all this?" Mar asks, moving toward a large chest full of white garments.

"Wedding gifts," Cece boasts, "from your mate's fiancé's family."

"Wyneth's family sent these?"

"Along with an entire trove of rare jewels."

"How generous," Mar deadpans, fishing out some lacy lingerie and holding it up to her chest. "For the honeymoon tour?"

Sorscha glances over. "If there even is one. Given the current state of things, our travels may have to wait. Who knows if there will even be a wedding night."

I try to force the dark flashes of Jace and Sorscha tangling together from my head, but they keep sprouting up like stubborn weeds.

"Wear that, and there will be." Cece nods toward the stringy thing in Mar's hands.

"Where does this even go?" she marvels, turning the contraption—for lack of a better word—upside down.

"This is a marriage of convenience," Sorscha says to Cece. "Besides, I can't imagine Jace being ensnared by such things. He doesn't strike me as a male who cares for frills and lace."

"He's male," Cece drones. "Of course he does. And if that fails, simply throw yourself into peril. I hear he has a weakness for damsels in distress."

She sends a pointed look my way. I don't deign to respond, although that statement was clearly for my benefit. Mar squeals, drawing our attention as she pulls something with ostrich feathers out of the trunk.

"This. Is. Hideous. You have to try it on."

Sorscha grimaces. "It's a monstrosity."

"Which is why I need to see it on you," Mar begs. "It's a matter of life and death. Please. It will prove my theory that you can make even the most hideous fashions look court-worthy."

Sorscha begrudgingly snatches up the garment and slips behind the changing panel. Cece picks up right where she left off.

"It was awfully heroic of him to aid in your rescue. Although surely Zadyn had the situation under control."

Another shot fired.

"I owe both of them my life." I'm not letting her rile me. Not tonight. "Mar too."

"And Dover and Kai. It must have been thrilling for you."

"What?"

"Having every male in the kingdom clambering to save you."

"I assure you it was anything but glamorous."

"That doesn't mean you didn't enjoy it."

"Cece," Mar warns.

I lower my voice, leaning across the table so the bitch can hear every word crystal clear.

"Yes, I thoroughly enjoyed watching Kai get the shit kicked out of him while I was wasting away inside of a prison cell wondering if everyone I loved was already dead. It was a real riot."

A hollow laugh slips past her painted lips.

"Perhaps I was wrong before." Cece presses closer, emerald eyes prowling. "Maybe Jace holds no interest in frills and lace. Perhaps he prefers calloused hands and fighting leathers. Maybe he's a fan of fire."

"I wouldn't know," I grit, seconds from losing my cool.

"No?"

"What exactly are you implying?"

"Nothing everyone hasn't already considered."

"Enough," Mar hisses as Sorscha appears in the ugliest outfit I have ever seen. She does a twirl and holds up her hands.

"Are you pleased?"

"Oh, they should paint your portrait in that!" Mar cackles, clapping her hands. Even Cece and I pause our little standoff to laugh.

We continue to drink as Mar forces Sorscha to try on the rest of the trunk's contents. She finally emerges dressed in one of her signature pink gowns and tosses the last of the garments back into the trunk with a sigh.

"All this for a wedding."

"It's going to be beautiful," Mar assures her.

"I suppose." She sounds utterly unconvinced, her voice vacant.

"Let's make a toast."

Phew, Mar to the rescue.

She pours some champagne and passes it around to us. "To our darling Sorscha and Jace. Long may you reign."

"To the unexpected." Sorscha clinks her coupe against Mar's. "And to the death of freedom."

She doesn't wait for a response before tossing back the drink in one go. Without a beat in between, she pours herself another. An awkward silence settles.

And just like that, this is back to being the most uncomfortable bachelorette party in the history of the world.

"You might want to ease up on that, Sorsch. Tomorrow is going to be an early day."

"I'm perfectly fine, thank you," she says to Mar, moving to lean against the windowsill.

She's lost weight since we got back to Aegar. She's still beautiful in the extreme, only now it's a haunted sort of beauty.

"What's the matter, Sorscha? Getting cold feet?" Cece sips her drink.

"I'm not certain they were ever warm."

"You could do worse." Cece twists a lock of golden hair around her finger. "He's a far cry from unattractive. A bit rough around the edges, but that's nothing that can't be fixed."

"That is not the issue."

"Then what is?"

"This is wrong." Sorscha turns to us, deadly serious. "This is a mistake…"

"It shouldn't feel like that." For once, Cece actually sounds sincere.

"Don't you think I know that?" Sorscha comes as close to snapping as she physically can, then resumes staring off into the night.

I'm almost afraid to move closer. "Sorscha? You alright?"

Her head slowly swivels back to us. "Let's go out. I need some air."

The night is void of stars as we make our way to the stables in silence, the moon looking full and fat as if she gobbled them up and absorbed all of their eerie light. We dress a few horses and head toward the flowered path that winds the gardens.

A loud bray sounds from behind me. I twist around in the saddle as Sorscha snaps her reins and speeds off into the dark woods.

"Sorscha!"

"What is she doing?" Mar hisses, turning her horse. "She knows these woods aren't safe at night."

"Come on."

We race after her, splitting off to search. Sorscha's name echoes through the tangled trees, but no response comes. I will my pounding heart to quiet, straining to hear or see her through the shadows.

This was a terrible idea—she'd had so much to drink and—

A flash of pink snags my attention. I yank my horse to a stop.

She stands at the bottom of a hill, before a glassy black pool streaked with silver moonlight. Despite the cold, she drops her cloak, slips out of her shoes, and walks out into the lake.

"Sorscha!"

She doesn't turn. She keeps drifting forward, the skirt of her gown dragging behind her, fanning out over the surface like a lace film. The water creeps higher, nearing her waist.

I hop off the horse and scamper down the hill.

But not before Sorscha goes under, disappearing into the black stillness. I hold my breath for her to emerge, but she doesn't. Panic pricks at my skin.

"Sorscha?" I shout again. "Fuck."

She's going to drown in that damned dress.

I throw myself into the water after her. The icy temperature is a shock to my muscles, but I keep pushing, scanning the dark lake until I spot her dress pluming around her like the petals of a twisted flower.

I kick forward past the painful cold, grabbing her around the waist and dragging her up to the surface. She takes a wild gasp as we hit the air.

"Let go of me!" she screeches. I relent, and she scrambles away, dragging herself up the pebbled beach.

"What the hell are you doing?! Are you trying to get yourself killed?"

"Just seeking a moment's peace," she snaps.

"Sorscha! Wait. Talk to me. Please."

"I'm not in the mood."

God, she sounds like me when I'm pissed.

"What were you doing? That water was freezing!"

"I am aware. That's why I went in."

"Because it's cold?"

She whirls to me, sopping wet, eyes hostile. "No. Because I wanted to feel something! Anything! Not that you or anyone else would understand."

"Sorscha, look. I don't know how else to say this, so I'll just come right out with it." My shoulders sink. "I'm sorry."

"You're...sorry?" Her amber eyes narrow to slits.

"I know your life was perfect before I arrived. And since then, your world has been turned upside down. It's been chaos. And it's all because of me. Kylian coming here—bringing those creatures with him, attacking the castle. If it weren't for me, Ilsa and Derek might still be alive. I know that. So if you hate me, I understand. I would hate me too."

Her pale pink gown clings to her body, looking heavy as she regards me with a lightless expression.

"Hate you," she mocks under breath. "I do not hate you. And you're wrong, by the way. My life was not perfect. Neither was my relationship with my father."

"Either way, he's gone because of me."

"He is gone because he bit off more than he could chew and because he was far too selfless for his own good," she declares in a voice that tells me she's had lots of practice giving commands. "He died defending his *son*. And I'm sure he regrets nothing."

And boy, I must be a glutton for punishment because I keep pushing. "Jace is more torn up about it than you can imagine."

"I don't want to talk about him."

"Well, maybe I do." I'm really asking for it at this point, but I want the air cleared. "Before you got engaged—"

"We do not need to rehash this." She latches onto her horse's reins and hikes up the hill. I trudge after her, snatching up our cloaks.

"We tried to fight it. For so long. And once I knew you cared for him, it stopped. I didn't want him to come to Vod for me, and he shouldn't have done that, and I'm sorry—"

I grab her arm and pull her to face me.

"I've already said you've no need to apologize. For any of it. What is it you'd like me to say?" she hisses.

"The truth! You have every reason to despise me! And I deserve it. You, of all people, should never have gotten hurt in this mess. And I am so, *so* sorry, Sorscha. Because I know what you're feeling right now. I have lived it. And I know that you hide it well beneath that smile, but you don't have to go through this loss alone. Jace says you've been pulling away from people, from your friends—"

"My friends abandoned me," she spits. "They abandoned me. *You* abandoned me when I needed you all."

There it is. The slap to the face I've been waiting for. The one I deserve.

"I know," I whisper, watching the ice settle over her features. "I know, and I'm sorry."

"But the kingdom needed you more than I did. So I can't fault you for that."

"It's no excuse, but I didn't know what else to do. I just wanted this place—wanted you—to be safe. I didn't want Derek's death to be for nothing."

"It's not that you left, it's that you didn't take me with you!" she shouts, bursting through the royal mold that keeps her voice, her actions, her manners in check. For the first time, I see her for what she truly is.

A scared, hurt female with this undeniable rage bubbling inside her.

Looks eerily familiar.

"I was alone. Wondering why, wondering if I'd ever see any of you again." She scoffs. "You think I'm *upset* that you went to Hyrax? That you tried to stop Kylian before he could do his worst? You think I'm upset that Jace came to rescue you? I would have never forgiven him if he hadn't!"

Her words hang in the air as we stare each other down. I drop the cloaks and throw my arms around her. She stiffens but doesn't fight. I keep holding.

One more second.

There.

Sorscha cracks, arms threading around me as her tears mingle with the water droplets clinging to my neck.

"I'm sorry," I murmur against her hair.

"I was alone," she sobs, her words barely audible. "Why does everyone shut me out? I'm not some delicate piece of glass in danger of shattering. I'm tired of being protected. I'm tired of being cloistered and babied and *left*."

I pull back to cup her cheeks. "I promise you, it will never happen again. I will do whatever I can to make this right. You're my sis—my friend. And I care about you more than you could possibly imagine."

"I believe you, cousin."

"You do know we're not actually cousins, right?" I laugh through the tears. She smiles, and for a second, she's herself again.

"You may not be my actual cousin, but I do not believe that blood chooses family for us."

I JOLT awake to the sound of a loud crash.

My heart thunders as a dark figure barrels through my door and slams straight into the back of the leather chair.

"*Shit.*"

I leap out of bed, sparking the candles on my nightstand with a flick of my fingers.

"*Jace?*"

"Hello, little witch." He straightens, and I get an eyeful of his disheveled hair, glazed, hooded eyes, and vacant expression. He's practically swaying on his feet.

Drunk off his ass.

"What are you doing here?"

"No Zadyn tonight?" He slumps down on the window seat as I pour him a glass of water.

"Not tonight." I refrain from saying, *he's giving me space so I can sort out my feelings for the both of you.*

"I hate to admit this, but he's not a bad male."

"You're just now realizing this?" I hand him the water, and he glances up at me.

"I still don't like him, but if I have to lose you to anybody, at least it's to someone I know would die for you too."

"Losing me to him? I don't know what you're talking about. You're the one getting married tomorrow."

"Let's just get it all—let's just lay it all out, shall we?" he slurs.

"Let's. I'll start. You're wasted."

"That I may be, but I know what I'm talking about. We're all big pretenders. We can all stop pretending now, it's just you and me here."

"I'm not pretending."

"You're pretending you don't see the way your little guard dog looks at you. And that you don't feel more for him."

"Our relationship is…complicated."

"Hah. Okay."

"What do you want, Jace? You're getting married in twelve hours. You know you shouldn't be here."

"You're wrong." He wags his finger at me. "I should be here. With you. This is the only thing that makes sense in this entire world."

I groan and sink into a chair. He watches me rub my tired eyelids.

"I don't know if I'll ever be able to forgive you," he says softly.

I glance up. "Forgive me for what?"

"For making me love you. For making me love you and then pushing me away." His golden eyes clear, locking me in a stare that makes breathing a chore. [*]

My voice is little more than a whisper as I say, "What choice did I have?"

---

[*] Cue: *loml* by Taylor Swift

He stands and walks over to me, stopping when his legs touch mine. "I love you. And it's ruined me beyond repair."

"And you're so innocent? You've pushed me away too. We both made choices that were necessary."

"Fuck necessary. What about what you want—what I want? What we both deserve? I'm tired of fighting off what seems inevitable. What has *always* seemed inevitable. I'm tired of my only happiness in this world feeling like a sin."

Jace falls at my feet, bracing the backs of my legs as he stares up at me—a broken man, pleading and repentant.

"Stop," I breathe.

"No, just let me say this. I've done terrible things in my lifetime, but not saying this would be by far the worst."

He takes his time, a deep inhale filling his chest.

"My entire life has been a fight. A battle to be good, be worthy, be better. But this? You and me? This was choiceless. I have tried—*so* hard—not to feel what I do. And now, it's tearing me apart.

"Because it is impossible. It is impossible not to love you more with every beat of your heart. Every laugh, every smile, every scathing look. Every insult you throw at me. And I know I'll never be worthy of you, but I can't make myself stop. No matter what I do, you're here inside me. You're in my chest, my head—you're in every gods-damned breath I take. Because you, little witch, were made for me. And I was made for you. I hate myself for realizing it too late, hate the Fates for keeping you from me until our time had passed us by. Serena." His voice cracks on my name.

"I'm so sorry. I know I've done nothing but hurt you from the moment we met. But all of me, body and soul, my heart, my life, my fate is entirely yours. I will do whatever you say. If you want to run away tonight, I will. I'm tired of pretending I can live without you. I can't." He shakes his head. "I can't."

My heart cleaves in two. His words—words I didn't even know how starved I'd been to hear—wrap around me like a blanket in a crashing storm.

But it's all just a fantasy. We can never belong to each other. Not in this lifetime.

"Jace, get up."

But he doesn't. He yanks me down so that I crash into him. Tears well in both our eyes as he smooths my face.

"If we had met anywhere but here, I would have courted you. I would have won you over—taken you for garden strolls, scaled a trellis to sneak into your room after dark."

I laugh through a sob, and he holds me tighter.

"I would have worked every day to be worthy of someone like you. And not a single one of them would have passed, where you didn't know exactly what you meant to me."

"Jace, please, *please* stop."

He has no idea. No idea how he is gutting me.

I try to turn away, to hide the onslaught of tears now choking me, pooling behind my closed eyes. It's foolish to think avoiding his stare will save me when I'm already completely wrecked.

He doesn't let me get away with it anyway. He pulls my face back to his. My head and heart war, half of me wanting to give in and half of me knowing we'll damn ourselves and everyone else if we do.

"Let me stay. Please. Give me one night to stay and hold you. We won't do anything, but we deserve this. One night."

His tearful gaze, his hands, are relentless, refusing to let me shy away from what we both know I want.

But I made a promise. To my friend. My sister.

And to myself.

"I'm sorry." I get to my feet. "But you need to go."

He stares at me, stunned, as if his entire world just stopped spinning. Then he gets to his feet and, without a word, walks out.

My dreams are haunted by him. Of his arms around me, of the heat of his skin on mine, of the love that burns right through his eyes whenever we're alone.

But that's just it.

I don't want to be loved behind closed doors.

Because a love like that is lonelier than no love at all.

75

SERENA

9 DAYS

"Come in."

I'm surprised when Zadyn slips through my door, looking dazzling in a dark blue jacket with silver embroidery. A crisp white shirt peeks out from beneath, making his tan skin pop.

"You're not dressed." He comes to lean against my vanity as I slide on a pair of silver earrings.

I shrug. "It won't take me long."

"How are you feeling?"

"Great."

"I mean about the wedding," he says.

"*Great.* I'm happy for them." I paste a smile on my face and peer up into his big brown eyes.

"You are not." He reaches out to flick my nose. I flinch, scoffing in surprise.

Is he flirting?

"Excuse me. I'm just…stressed. Can't imagine why." I lift the diamond necklace on the vanity to my throat, struggling with the clasp.

Zadyn steps in, moving my hair to the side, his fingers sweeping

413

the back of my neck as he hooks it closed. Our eyes lock in the mirror.

"We're going to figure something out."

"How do you know that, Zadyn? War doesn't wait. And neither will Kylian."

His hands move to my shoulders, massaging them through my silk robe. I fight the urge to groan.

"I don't want to hear his name today. Let's just set it aside for one night. We deserve it. To drink and dance and pretend things are normal for a few hours."

"But—"

"Just one night," he whispers, leaning closer, a secret smile tilting up one corner of his mouth. I can't help grinning back, thrilled to have things somewhat lighthearted between us again.

"You're not still mad at me?"

He drops his hands.

"I was never mad at you. I was just trying to give you space to decide what you want. You know I just want you to be happy, right?" He sinks back into the vanity, his caramel hair swooping down over his eyes. I stand and brush it back, holding the top of his head as I give him an affectionate little shake.

"That's better. I can actually see who I'm talking to."

He smiles fully, flexing one dimple, and something clenches in my stomach. Like a single butterfly flapping away.

"I haven't had time for a haircut. You know, with coming to your rescue. Repeatedly."

"My hero," I lilt.

When our laughter dies and our chests still, I become very aware of how I'm pressed between his parted legs—how I'm still fisting his hair. I notice how hard he's gripping the edge of the wood beneath him, like he's clinging to his restraint for dear life.

The last time we were this close, I was a hot mess, crying and slobbering all over him until I asked him to kiss me, and everything subsequently swirled right down the drain. His hand grazes my hip, lingering for a moment before he presses away from the vanity and stands to his full height.

He opens his mouth to say something, but then he changes his mind, stepping around me.

"You should get dressed. I'll wait for you outside."

I slip into the silver gown and matching shoes, adjusting the thin straps before opening the door. Zadyn straightens off the wall and does a double take, blinking in a way that's so adorably him. His eyes heat as they travel up and down my body, setting off little sparks in my belly.

He shakes his head. *You're perfect.*

I smile, reaching for his outstretched hand. The moment I take it, Mar stumbles around the corner, breathless, clutching her gown.

"What's wrong?"

She skids to a halt. "It's Sorscha."

MY HEART POUNDS as we fly down the hall. Mar flings open Sorscha's door to reveal Jace kneeling on the floor, a piece of parchment clutched in one hand and a white gown in the other. He glances up at me, his face blank.

"She's gone."

76
SERENA

9 DAYS

"What? What do you mean?"
"She left a note. She's gone."
"Let me see."
Jace passes it to me in a daze.

Dear Jace,

I am so sorry. But we both deserve more than this. I am releasing you from your word and your obligation to me. I know this may not be what my father hoped for. I have to believe that he valued our individual happiness as much as his legacy. Please forgive me.
With love and regret,
Sorscha

"Oh my god."
"I don't understand. She just disappeared? No one saw her leave?"
Zadyn asks.

Jace runs a hand through his hair, looking spent. "Max checked with every guard on watch."

"We need to send out a search party."

"My men are already searching," Max assures me.

Jace sinks onto the edge of the bed, his shoulders curling inward. "What's the use? To drag her back? Force her down the aisle? I'm not Kylian." I try not to flinch at that statement. "This is all my fault."

"It is not, Jace."

The door cracks open, and Kai's mess of raven hair pops through. "I'm a firm believer in being fashionably late, but the wedding guests *are* about to whip out the pitchforks—"

He stops when he sees the matching looks of dismay on our faces.

Dover pushes in behind him, glancing around. "Woah—what's the matter?"

"Sorscha is missing," Mar says.

"She ran away," I clarify.

Kai bursts into laughter.

"Why are you laughing?! This is not funny, Kai."

"It's just that I've known Sorscha for a long time." He plops down in the center of the bed, popping open the button of his jacket to reveal a sleek black collared shirt beneath. "Suffice it to say, I am not surprised by this sudden turn of events. Not in the least."

"Well, if you know her so well, then maybe you could shed some light on where she's run off to." I lean against the bedpost, crossing my arms.

Kai shrugs. "Wish I could, savior, but she's predictable in that she's *un*predictable."

"He's right," Dover agrees.

I toss my hands up. "Wonderful."

"You should stop infantilizing her. She's a big girl. She can take care of herself."

Mar gapes at Kai. "She is the future Queen of Aegar! She should not be out there unprotected—especially when we are on the brink of war!"

"Our men are already scouring the city for her." Max steps

forward, his calm jade eyes locking with each of ours. "We will find her."

"We can't just sit around and wait." I gather up my dress, heading for the door.

Jace lifts his head. "Where are you going?"

"To find her. Are you guys coming or what?"

Kai rolls his eyes and drags himself off the bed.

"You're the boss."

THE SEARCH IS A BUST. After hours of combing through the nearby valleys and villages on horseback, we return to the castle empty-handed to wait in Sorscha's room. Jace stands across from me, peering out the bay window at the stars now dusting the faded blue sky.

"If something happens to her because she was running from me," he trails off, a bitter expression crossing his face.

I reach out to clasp his arm. "We will find her. Trust me."

He nods.

"I don't understand. Where could she have gone?" Cece inverts her red lips into a pout, hovering near Zadyn on the chaise. "I'm worried sick."

Leave it to Cece to make Sorscha's disappearance about her. I fix my gaze on her.

"She never said anything to you about leaving? About wanting to run away?"

"No. Not really." She lifts a slender shoulder.

"What do you mean, *not really*?"

"It's no secret that she wasn't thrilled with the idea of marrying. I don't blame her. Especially after everything that's happened." Cece's green eyes flash between me and Jace, barreling right through discretion. "But she made no mention of running away."

The door swings open, and in steps Sorscha, hair windblown and button nose tinged pink from the slight bite in the air.

Everyone leaps to their feet. I'm surprised to see Eaton step through the door behind her.

"Thank gods," Mar breathes, clutching her chest.

"Sorscha, what the hell!" I throw my arms around her neck, nearly knocking her over. "Are you alright? Where have you been?"

"I'm fine." She pats me, pulling back. Her eyes look brighter, her cheeks a little rosier. She's been a ghost around the castle since Derek, but she looks alive again. Like herself.

I glance from her to Eaton, sensing something different about the two of them.

Jace steps closer, his voice tight. "What's going on here?"

Sorscha's honeyed eyes slide toward him. "I can't marry you, Jace."

Her fingers slip into Eaton's.

My mouth *drops*.

"Because we're already married."

Before I can register a thing, Jace's fist slams into Eaton's face, ramming him back into the door.

"Jace!" I shout.

Sorscha cries out, whirling toward Eaton, but he's already on his feet, lunging toward Jace. Dover and Zadyn rush to break them up.

"Aerill's tits!" Kai doubles over behind us, roaring.

"Let's just take a breather, shall we? We're all friends here," Dover says to the room, now so clouded with testosterone it's hard to breathe.

"What is wrong with you?" I hiss at Jace.

"Me?!" he shouts, flinging an accusatory finger in Eaton's face. "Do you have *any* idea what you've just done?!"

Zadyn grasps Eaton's collar, shoving him backward.

"Are you kidding me, Eaton?!" he bursts. "I didn't bring you here so you could hijack this wedding!"

"Don't you think I *know* that?" He tosses Zadyn off so that Sorscha can fuss over him. Some of his hostility eases as he peers down at her with intense adoration. "This wasn't planned."

"Can someone please explain what in hell is going on?" Mar barks, tossing up her hands.

"We're mates," Eaton replies, rubbing his jaw where Jace hit him.

"Oh my god," I sputter, taking a step back.

Jace's chest heaves as he coughs a bitter laugh and turns away. I'd be lying if I said I wasn't slightly relieved in this moment.

"It all happened so fast," Sorscha rushes to explain. "Eaton and I got to talking at the rehearsal party. I honestly thought nothing of it. But then last night as I was heading to bed, we bumped into each other in the hall, and I knew right then and there. We didn't mean to worry you all. Jace, I'm so sorry—" She moves toward him. "I didn't mean to run off like that. But I couldn't marry you."

Jace is quiet for a long time, bracing his hand on the window frame.

"Sorscha, I'm glad you found your mate, I really am. But we had a plan." He finally lifts his gaze to her.

"I know." Sorscha's eyes fall to the carpet, a twinge of regret turning her pink lips down. "I know my father wanted it to be you, but you know this was the right thing. For both of us."

She takes Jace's hand, and slowly he begins to thaw. No one can withstand the warmth of Sorscha's touch. There is nothing—not even an ice storm—that would not melt before her.

"Gronwen is going to take a fit when he hears," he murmurs.

"This doesn't really change anything," Kai pipes. "You're both royals. You perform the Bloodfast and we gain two more weapons. Big ones. Win-win." He gestures between Sorscha and Eaton.

He's right. Still, an awkward silence falls over the room.

"Well, are we going to just stand here staring at each other, or head downstairs?" Kai looks around expectantly.

"What?" Jace hisses, annoyed.

"We've got a thousand caskets of wine and enough cake to feed a kingdom. Why waste a perfectly good celebration?" He waggles his brows, his lips parting into a mischievous smile.

Dover's mouth twists as he surveys us. "He kind of has a point."

"Kai is right," Sorscha says, turning from Jace. "Today may have been unexpected, but there's been so much gloom lately, so much sorrow...I want tonight to be different. I want to celebrate with my friends, like old times." She reaches for Mar's hands. "I'm sorry I've been distant. But I'm starting to feel like myself again." She slides a grateful look toward Eaton. "So please, for this one night, can we all just *pretend* to be happy?"

"Sorscha, we *are* happy for you." Mar's face softens. "Of course we are."

"Then let's go downstairs and party like only we can." She tugs Mar's hands, making her shimmy.

"Last one downstairs has to break the news to Gronwen!" Kai yells, swinging around the bedpost and sprinting for the door. Dover dashes after him, shoving him into the frame and barreling past.

Zadyn looks at me, shaking his head. I shrug, giving him a half-smile. But the weight of Jace's eyes has me turning to find him watching the two of us intently.

The room has emptied, leaving only the three of us behind. The silence screams in my ears.

"Shall we?" I force my feet to move toward the door.

I don't have to look back to know that they've followed behind me.

77

SERENA

9 DAYS

Ding, ding, ding.

A hush settles over the diamond-encrusted hall as Eaton stands, champagne flute in hand. Sorscha beams up at him, sunlight pouring from her eyes.

"I'm not one for speeches—especially long, sappy ones—so I'll keep this brief. I know this wasn't in the cards. Quite frankly, I'm just as surprised as all of you." Eaton's blue-eyed gaze bounces around the room, earning him a few light chuckles.

"But I have waited a long time to feel something real. And now that I've found it, there's no way I'm letting it go. Sorscha, I vow to be the kind of male you deserve. To be a husband and partner you are proud of, and to be a king worthy of a land such as this one. Everyone, raise a glass to the angel seated beside me. You are proof that perfection exists and that the gods are good. Cheers."

Tears well in Sorscha's eyes, her smile quivering as Eaton takes her hand and sweeps her up into a deep kiss. Thunderous applause shakes the chandeliers and crystal glasses dressing the tables.

I watch them, heads pressed together, Sorscha grinning for the first time in months. They're beautiful. Their bond is beautiful. So simple and easy.

I'm happy for them. So why does seeing their smiles, their joy, make me sad?

I swirl my glass, the bubbles inside popping and fizzing before I toss them back. Something grazes my arm from elbow to wrist, whisking away my empty glass and replacing it with a warm hand.

"That isn't allowed," Zadyn says, dropping my flute onto a silver tray and leading me to the dance floor.

"I'm sorry?"

"You standing there alone, looking that pretty. Not dancing," he explains, pulling me into his arms. I suppress a smirk.

"I'm going to look a lot less pretty when I'm tripping over your feet."

"Lucky for you, I'm an excellent dancer." He sends me spinning to prove his point. "And I promise I'll catch you every time."

He holds me close, and we dance, cheek to cheek. Over his shoulder, I see Eaton and Sorscha, locked inside their own little bubble. She tips her head back and laughs at something he said, the sound like twinkling bells.

"They make perfect sense."

Zadyn pulls back, following my gaze. "Don't they? I mean, I wanted to kill him at first, but look at them. They're two sides of the same coin."

Twin flames. Two matching rays of sunshine—pure warmth cut with a surprising degree of ferocity.

There's a soft smile on Zadyn's face as he watches his friend. "You're in a good mood tonight."

"What can I say? I love weddings. Especially when you're not being forced into them."

I chuckle. "Sucker for a happy ending?"

"Does that surprise you?" he scoffs.

"I just didn't realize you were such a romantic."

"Then you haven't been paying attention."

I laugh, shaking my head. "Hey, can I ask you something? About...mates?"

The levity in his eyes evaporates as they snap to mine. His swallow looks strained. "What about them?"

"How does it work? Sorscha said she just knew. Is it like love at first sight?"

"It can be, but not always. Sometimes there's a moment when it all clicks. Other times, it's more of a slow burn."

A slow burn. Like Zadyn.

"I know it's annoying, that *'when you know, you know'* saying. But in this case it's true. It's a visceral reaction. When you find your mate, they just feel like home. Everything about them—their scent, the way their touch feels."

His thumb skims over my spine, leaving behind a trail of goosebumps.

"Is it—like a pull of sorts?"

"It can feel like that. But it's more than just attraction. It's an instant recognition and this excruciating, desperate need for that person. You know immediately you would do anything to see them smile, to make them happy—even if you're not the answer. There is nothing you would deny them."

It's my turn to swallow, the weight of his words wrapping around me and drawing me closer.

"You mean it can be one-sided? That seems so unfair."

"There are few things in life that are ever truly equal or fair." He smiles, his voice melancholy. "It isn't always reciprocal. Just like accepting the bond isn't mandatory."

"So there *is* a choice," I confirm. His brows draw together. "If someone really didn't want it, they could choose differently?"

"Why are you asking me all this?"

We've stopped dancing. We stand perfectly still, attached to each other while ballgowns swirl around us like a tornado of tulle and glitter.

"I don't know, just curious, I guess."

"Do you think you—"

"No." My answer is too quick. Probably see-through. "I mean—I would know. Like you said. Right?"

It's a test. I wait for his response, holding my breath, holding his stare. Another tight swallow.

"Right. Of course."

Disappointment settles over me. "You seem to know a lot about the subject."

"I've heard from people who've experienced it."

"But not from *firsthand* experience?"

He looks at me, saying nothing. I decide to come right out and say it.

"Do you have a mate, Zadyn?"

His jaw clenches. But he doesn't answer.

Tension sizzles in the sliver of air between us. The dance comes to a close, but we're frozen in time, his fingers grazing the skin of my lower back, his eyes on my mouth, stirring a string of dirty thoughts in my mind.

"It's time!"

The room explodes with joyful shouts. We break apart, like two dogs zapped by a shock collar.

Confetti rains down on us as Eaton and Sorscha are hoisted into the air on a set of gilded chairs and towed into the hall. I lose Zadyn in the rush of bodies and find Kai sunken into one of the velvet alcoves, a crown of laurel leaves adorning his head.

I plop down beside him as a female he'd been dancing with earlier saunters over and flings herself onto his lap. She's clearly had a couple of drinks—her lids heavy, limbs loose. Kai tenses, then gently shifts her off, depositing her at his side. Bristling at his blatant rejection, she stands and stomps away.

I gape at him. "What was that all about?"

"What?" he asks, dusting off his lap as if she'd left behind a string of cooties.

"I've never seen you turn down a pretty girl. Especially one so... readily available."

He shrugs, indifferent. "Eh. Not my type."

"Your type is anything that breathes."

"Maybe I'm reformed." He smiles faintly, tipping his glass to his lips.

"You can have anyone at this party."

"Are you offering?" he teases, eyes dazzling.

"Correction. Anyone but me. I'm off limits."

"Don't we all know it," he mumbles. "Honestly, I've already had half the females in this room. Not looking to stroll down memory lane tonight."

"Poor little siren boy." I take the crown from his head and plop it on my own. "So far above the masses."

"Don't mock me, *Little Miss Can't-Make-Up-Her-Mind*."

"*Excuse* me?"

"Don't kid a kidder, sweets." He tips my chin up. "I've seen that look before."

He nods toward Zadyn, standing near the dance floor, wrapped up in conversation with Cece.

"You don't know anything." He purses his lips, unconvinced. "Let's circle back to you. Your favorite subject," I say.

"Always happy to divulge my deepest, darkest secrets."

"Of course you are. Would this newfound celibacy have anything to do with a certain Pirate King?"

"Now that"—he steals back his crown—"is a subject I refuse to broach tonight."

"Kai." I clasp my heart. "I think she's changing you."

"Not that deep, savior. She's simply a puzzle I am intent on solving. And by solving, I mean getting very naked in my bed." He gives me a double brow wag and polishes off his drink.

I sneak another peek at Zadyn, monitoring his reaction to Cece in a silver gown similar to mine, except with a plunging neckline accentuating her absurd cleavage. Jealously bubbles up inside of me as she tugs him toward the dance floor.

I stand. "I'm gonna go get some fresh air."

Kai tips his empty glass to me. "You do that."

My fingers curl into fists as Cece slinks closer to Zadyn with her damned long legs and perfect bust-to-waist ratio.

Freaking fae barbie.

I bite back my frustration and force myself to keep walking.

They make no sense together. Cece is vapid and vain. Not Zadyn's type at all. Not that I really know his type. But I guess if he's in love with me like he said, then it gives me somewhat of a baseline.

The party fades away as I make my way onto the crowded terrace and down the stone steps leading to the gardens. To my relief, I find them empty. That is until I stumble upon a familiar shape beneath a weeping willow.

Jace is seated on a swing beneath the drooping vines, idly pushing himself back and forth. I draw closer, undetected, until a twig snaps beneath my heel and his head flies up. *

"I didn't think anyone would be out here."

"I had the same thought."

I drop the hem of my shimmery gown and sink into the empty swing beside him. "How are you doing?"

For the first time tonight, I get to appreciate how handsome he looks—the way his lush, velvet onyx jacket molds to his shoulders and arms, his polished war medals pinned beneath the silver king's collar draped around his neck. His dark hair is slicked back for a change, making his proud facial features stand out. He looks like a brooding warrior prince.

"I'm fantastic. My betrothed finds her mate the night before our wedding and runs off to elope. This is one of the pinnacle moments of my life."

"Jace."

"What."

"Stop feeling sorry for yourself." He blinks up at me. "You didn't want this. Any of it. This isn't a problem. This is a solution. You're free now."

"It's not that. I'm happy for them—I'm relieved. But am *I* happy? No." He stares at the moss-covered ground. "I might be if I thought it would change anything."

———————————

* Cue: *End of the World* by Searows

"You don't have to be king—this changes everything."

"Does it? Does it change things between us?" His golden eyes meet mine, glowing in the darkness.

I say nothing.

"You're right. I'm free now, Serena. There is nothing standing in the way of us being together." He angles himself toward me. "But somehow, I don't feel hopeful. Because I know that wasn't the only thing stopping you. I came to you last night. I begged you to run away with me. When I asked you to marry me—you just stood there, pretending like I hadn't said a word. And now you're about to run straight into the arms of our enemy. So do I feel hopeful for the future? No. I don't."

My throat tightens as I push to my feet. "You know I couldn't go with you. Running from our problems won't solve them."

"Even if it weren't for all that, I still don't think you would be with me."

He's right, but still I ask, "Why do you say that?"

"Because for all that bravery, all that reckless wildfire in you— you're afraid."

I scoff, leaning against the tree. "Afraid of what?"

"I don't know. Afraid to let yourself fall."

"Well, the ground isn't the most comfortable place to be," I admit, nudging the moss with my foot. He stands, walking over to me.

"I'm not going to try to convince you. But everything I said last night—look at me." He reaches out to tilt my chin up. My heart skips half a beat. "Everything I said, I meant. I was afraid of you. Of this. I'm not anymore. I'm done being anything but yours. Whether you want it or not."

I meet his gaze, a mixture of devotion and desire. "I don't know what I want anymore. I'm just trying to get by—day by day."

"Then maybe you need a little reminder."

"A reminder?"

With one more shift, his hand slides beneath my hair to cup the back of my neck.

"A reminder of how you make me feel. Every second"—his hips

push into mine, cool breath coasting over my neck—"of every day. It gnaws at me. It's so sweet, but so....painful. To want someone this much and not be able to touch them." His pointer finger glides over my throat, eyes devouring every detail of my face.

"You touch me all the time." I swallow hard. "In training."

He lets out a quiet laugh. "That isn't what I meant."

Then his mouth is at my throat, and I can't think, I can't breathe, I can't see reason if it were a high beam in the middle of the night.

"I want to touch you so deep you feel it in your soul."

Shit. I just lost feeling in my legs.

"What about being friends?" I rasp. He pulls back, giving me a soul-melting look.

"Serena. I could never be your friend." He leans in, close enough to taste. "If I got down on my knees and begged you to stay, to give up this insane plan, would you?"

"Jace," I caution, clutching his jacket.

His hands trace a scorching line from my neck to my waist as he lowers himself to the ground. And the look he's giving me—his eyes blazing up at me with a near-religious reverence—

"Here it is, little witch. I'm begging. I am begging you not to go. Stay and let me fight for you. Stay and fight *with* me. Stay and break me if that's what you desire. But I am begging you. Stay."

"You're not playing fair." His callouses glide down my leg as he lifts my heel onto his shoulder. My dress parts over my thigh, revealing a flash of moon-kissed flesh.

"I will play as dirty as I have to in order to keep you." He presses his lips to my calf. "Tell me you ache for me the same way I ache for you."

Oh god.

"I—" I'm confused. Why does his touch feel so *good*? I struggle to maintain focus with his lips on my skin, with the sight of him, a mighty warrior on his knees, begging me. Wanting me.

His hands wander higher up my exposed leg, hooking around my upper thigh. My heart thunders loud enough to shake the tree behind me. I should stop this. I really need to stop this.

"Show me," he whispers, nipping at my thigh with his teeth. His breath against the sensitive flesh there has my stomach curling. "I'll give you everything. Just take what you want from me. Take what's yours."

What's mine? That word triggers the faintest glimmer of reason in the back of my mind. My hands dart out to hold his face, stopping him from going further.

The sound of musical laughter shatters the moment. Our heads whirl toward the curtain of vines as it parts to reveal our friends drunkenly stumbling toward us. Their mirth dies when they see Jace on his knees before me. A bottle of wine slips from Zadyn's hand as he goes completely rigid. His fists clench, knuckles bleaching white.

"Well, you two certainly wasted no time," Cece remarks, breaking the heavy silence.

I can only imagine how this looks. Jace drops my leg, rising to his feet as I smooth my gown.

Golden curls fly over Cece's shoulder as she turns and slides her palm up Zadyn's chest. "See, *I told you.*"

I see red.

"Get your hands off him."

Instead, she snakes that stupid hand up his neck. Her liquor-glazed eyes widen as I march over and rip it away myself.

"How dare you—"

"What did you tell him? Please share it with the class."

"Serena—" Zadyn starts, but I hold up a hand.

"I told him the truth."

"What truth is that?"

"That you're fickle as the wind and that the two of you will never stop salivating over one another." She sneers, tossing a glance over my shoulder at Jace. "And that he shouldn't waste his time on things that are beneath him."

"Beneath him?" I laugh. "The only thing that's beneath him is you."

"I *have* been beneath him. More than once. And let me tell you"— she leans in so that her lips are pressed to my ear—"you're missing out. Little tip? He has a sensitive spot two inches below his ear. He absolutely lost it when I—"

My hand shoots out to grab a fistful of her hair. Her shriek is like music to my ears.

"Let go, you fucking animal!"

"Gladly." I yank hard, and she falls back on her ass in the mushy sod.

The shock on her face is priceless. She's on her feet in an instant, launching herself at me with bared fangs.

"I will flatten you," I threaten as we grapple.

Cece is scrappy, using her long nails to latch onto me and gouge red lines into my arms. I can feel my power rising to the surface— begging to be unleashed. Its call is seductive.

Kai stands off to the side with Mar and Dover, his whoops and whistles echoing through the midnight expanse.

I manage to land a satisfying punch to Cece's face before Zadyn and Jace pull us apart.

"Okay, that's enough of that." Jace hooks an arm around my waist and throws me over his shoulder. Cece wails upon seeing the blood pouring from her broken nose. Zadyn and Mar crouch beside her, attempting to settle her down. "My nose! She ruined my nose!"

"Get off of me!" I kick and squirm as Jace drags me from the scene of the crime.

"Not a chance."

"Damn it, Jace, let me go!"

"I enjoy a girl fight as much as the next guy, but I know you. You'll kill the poor girl. You need to control your temper."

"Like she didn't have it coming?"

His stride doesn't let up. "She was trying to rile you."

"Well then, mission accomplished. Put me down."

"Are you calm?"

"No, I'm not fucking calm, I want to claw her stupid face off," I say as we reach the steps of the terrace and he lets me drop to the ground.

"So possessive. You're worse than your guard dog." He leans against the stone railing, sounding slightly amused.

"I am not," I huff, dusting myself off and smoothing my hair.

"If you're going to lie to my face, then at least be honest with your-self, little witch."

"*What* are you *talking* about?"

"You're attracted to him," he mutters, lifting a shoulder. The others appear in the distance, ushering a sniffling, blood-drenched Cece toward the castle. "Or you wouldn't have tried to rip Cece apart."

I glance away, wondering if I should even bother denying it.

My feelings clash. I want Jace, but I—we can't go there. And it's tough to keep pretending that there is nothing between Zadyn and me. Something that's getting harder and harder to suppress.

I don't know when it changed. Maybe that kiss in the alleyway, maybe the night I met Margot. But somewhere along the line, I started seeing him as more than my familiar. More than my friend. Seeing him with Cece after the few moments we've shared—I couldn't bear it. Couldn't bear to think that, like me, he might have conflicting feelings or that I said the wrong thing and basically drove him into someone else's arms.

"It's alright." Jace pushes off the railing and walks up to me, tilting my chin up. "I want you to explore it."

"You want me to explore things with Zadyn?" My brows shoot toward my hairline.

He shrugs. "Do what you have to. Fuck him if you want. Get it out of your system. So when you choose me, I'll know it's because there's no one out there who can love you better than I can."

Without another word, he walks up the steps. I stare after him, baffled, my feelings a tangled-up knot in my chest.

"How's her face?" I ask as Zadyn walks me to my room.

"I think it will make a full recovery." He strokes the stubble along his jaw. "You didn't have to break her nose."

No, you really did not, Furi chuckles. *Why* did *you feel the need to maim the girl?*

I toss her a mental scowl.

"I know, I know. I just lost it, okay?" I slide my eyes toward him and take a deep breath. "I saw you two dancing, and it got me upset."

He glances down at me. "Serena, we were only dancing. It didn't mean anything."

"It did to me. You guys have history."

He rolls his eyes. "You're in no position to talk."

Furi snorts.

"Excuse me?"

"The way we found the two of you—" A muscle in his jaw flutters. "Not exactly the portrait of innocence."

He's not wrong. Furi agrees.

You. Bed. Now, I order.

She grumbles something that sounds like, *fine,* and then gives us some privacy.

"He was just trying to get me to stay. To give up this plan with Kylian."

"Yeah, and he needed your leg hooked over his shoulder for that?" He scoffs, shaking his head. My cheeks heat. I glance from the disgusted smirk on his mouth down to his clenched fists.

"I don't—I don't know what to say. Everybody thinks I'm this big whore, guess I just keep rising to the occasion—"

Zadyn pivots toward me, tugging me to a stop.

"Don't say that. You're not a whore. You know that. I know that. I don't give a fuck what anyone else thinks." My breath hitches. "And neither should you."

Regrettably, he releases me and forces himself to step back. I hadn't realized we'd stopped outside my room. I'm not quite ready to say goodnight.

"You want a nightcap?"

His eyes are on my door as he responds. Like he's forcing himself not to look at me. "I don't think so. Not tonight."

Leaning against the wall, I say, "Does Cece need a night nurse?"

I'm only *half* kidding.

He, however, is not when he moves closer and braces his arms on either side of my head so that I'm sandwiched between him and the wall. His head dips down.

"I've made my feelings for you very clear. And you should know that everything that came before is inconsequential. There will be no going backward for me. And no going forward. I'm here. I'm here until you make your decision or order me away."

My heart stutters. He sighs, dropping his voice. "Jace isn't engaged anymore."

"And your point is?"

"This doesn't change things?"

"You think because he's not engaged I'm just going to run straight back?"

"I don't know, are you? Based on what I saw under that tree? Can you honestly say you aren't relieved Sorscha married Eaton? That it doesn't matter? I know it does. I know exactly how you're feeling."

My body strains toward him, hyperaware of his presence looming over me. I bite down on my lip to keep from driving them into his. But I allow myself to stare at them.

Like a dog looking at a bag of bones.

"You don't know what I'm thinking," I whisper.

"Yes, I do. Your shield is down."

"Then what am I thinking now? Because I can promise you it has nothing to do with him."

He smirks, shaking his head as his eyes gloss over me. His thumb smooths over my lips, tugging my bottom one down with taunting slowness.

"Then hold that thought." He leans down and brushes the softest kiss against my cheek. My stomach does a double back handspring. "Hold it until you're ready for me."

7 8
ZADYN

8 DAYS

The doors of the dining room swing open with a loud shove.

Eaton and Sorscha breeze in, hand in hand, quite literally glowing. Their collective beauty is blinding, making the sunlight beaming in through the floor-to-ceiling windows look dull.

Sorscha has color in her cheeks again, her eyes no longer sunken and hollow as they've been since we returned. Even Eaton carries a more regal air about him. I can feel their power in spades—generations of Accostia magic now flowing through the couple I see before me.

"Well, well, well, look what the dust blew in." Kai places his tea down on the saucer, winding up to deliver his hourly innuendo. "You're half an hour late. What could have kept you, I wonder."

Eaton pulls out a chair for his wife, chuckling to himself.

"Couldn't decide what to wear," Sorscha sighs, sliding Eaton a knowing glance.

"Hah." Kai sinks his teeth into a piece of bread, ripping a chunk free with animalistic vigor. "I'm sure."

"So. How was the Bloodfast?" Dover hops on the bandwagon, wagging his brows.

"Dover!" Marideth grabs a roll off the platter and pelts him with it. "You can't just ask that. It's personal."

Then, turning toward Sorscha, she drops her voice and murmurs, "But really, how was it?"

Sorscha laughs, shaking her head.

"You look wonderful. You're glowing. Actually glowing." Serena reaches for her hand, smiling ear-to-ear.

It makes me so happy to see her like this, with the sister she always wanted and never really had until now.

Cece stalks into the room a moment later, scoring Serena with a look sharp enough to kill. She makes a show of ripping out a seat and sinking down. Her jade eyes land on my arm draped around the back of Serena's chair.

"Cece, what happened to your face?" Sorscha gasps, a hand flying to her chest. Cece's gaze snaps to her.

Her nose is back in place, but with last night's booze slowing down the healing process, it's still red and bruised, purple shadows fading beneath her eyes.

"Ask your *cousin*." Snatching up a pair of tongs, she plops a few pieces of fruit on her plate. "It seems for all your *courtier lessons*, Zadyn, she's still got the manners of a wild beast."

Serena's eyes roll as she takes a bite out of a pastry. "I said I was sorry."

"No. You did not."

"Hmm." Serena drops the pastry and dusts the sugar off her hands. "You know what? You are absolutely right. I guess I'm not sorry after all."

The look on Cece's face has me choking on my juice. Serena turns to me, clapping me on the back.

"You alright there, buddy?"

I nod, pounding my chest, tears leaking down my face as I try to keep my laughter at bay. Serena snorts, watching me turn red. Then the two of us are cackling, rocking back and forth, soundless laughter racking our bodies. She clutches my arm, trying to regain control over herself. Which only makes Cece angrier.

"You two hyenas deserve each other," she snarls.

Dover chooses that moment to reach for the jam—and instead knocks over the glass set before her. Orange juice gushes out, spilling onto her lap and splattering her face. Cece goes rigid.

Dover freezes mid-reach. "Oops."

Wood screeches against tile as she springs out of her seat. "Please excuse me."

"Cece, wait!" Sorscha tries—and fails—to suppress a giggle.

Cece cuts her off with a swish of her hand. "I'm no longer hungry!"

The second she's gone, the room explodes.

"You shouldn't provoke her," Kai clucks at Serena, slathering some jam on his bread. "That kitty's got claws."

"Yeah, I learned that last night."

"It seems we missed out on the excitement," Sorscha says.

"Oh, you sure did." Kai chuckles. "You should have seen them going at it. They managed to fill my fantasy quota for the year."

"I may have overreacted to something she said." Serena clears her throat.

"What did she say?"

Serena's face flushes, her eyes linking with mine for a quick moment.

Yes, what did *she say?* I ask, watching her squirm in her seat.

"I think it had something to do with our dear Zadyn." Kai flashes me a congratulatory smile. "Who knew you were capable of inciting an all-girl smack fest? My hero."

I huff a laugh.

"Speaking of. Anyone seen Jace this morning? Savior?"

"No, why would I have seen him?"

"Last time I checked, you train together every morning."

"Oh." She shrugs. "Not this one."

A steward pops through the door a moment later with a letter for Eaton. I can tell from the sheen of the parchment that it's been enchanted.

"For me? Who in hell is writing to me here?" He reaches for the missive, still chewing.

"Your mother, Sire."

Eaton nearly chokes on a grape.

"Everything okay?" I ask.

"Well, I've managed to piss my entire family off once again," he mutters, tossing the letter onto the table.

"Really? I'd think your father would be pleased with this little plot twist."

Two sons inheriting thrones? That's Berringer's wet dream.

"It's not that. They're livid that they missed the wedding. Mother especially."

"This literally happened last night," Serena says. "How did word travel so fast?"

"It didn't." Eaton sighs. "My mother has the unfortunate gift of seeing through the eyes of those in her bloodline when she feels so inclined."

"Let me get this straight—your mother can just pop in unexpectedly and get a front-row seat to whatever it is you're doing?" Kai gapes.

"She always knew when Eaton and I were up to no good," I toss out.

"Oh, I couldn't get away with anything as a child. Imagine trying to lose your virginity with your mother watching. Mortifying." He shudders. "Anyway, I've warned her about keeping her eyes to herself unless it's an emergency. She must have been concerned when she and father arrived back and we were gone."

"We left word with your brothers."

"Zadyn. They've little to no brain cells. You really think they retained that information?"

"Tell me about your mother." Sorscha bounces in her seat. "Do you think she'll like me?"

"She'd have to be made of stone not to," he says, nuzzling her neck.

It's odd seeing Eaton so smitten. For as long as I've known him, he's been the very definition of a bachelor. Between his looks and the whole flirty prince bit, attention has always followed him freely— from males and females. He'd indulged in pleasure houses and harems, and I thought he was content to do that for the rest of his life while his older brother sat his father's throne.

But watching him with Sorscha, staring at her like she's the most precious piece of treasure this world has to offer—he's never looked happier.

"I cannot wait to meet her!"

"She probably got an eyeful of you last night," Kai snorts.

"The Queen of Hyrax is one of the kindest females I know. She pretty much adopted me when I lived at court with Eaton," I tell Sorscha.

"She will love you. So will my brothers, who will no doubt try to steal you from me, which will then result in their slow, painful deaths."

Sorscha giggles. "And your sister?"

"Well, Alix doesn't like anyone. Except for Zadyn. Once or twice." He flashes me an innocent look. "How many times was it exactly?"

I shoot him a glare, feeling Serena tense beside me.

"Good morning, Majesties. I trust you slept well." Gronwen bursts into the dining room, a scroll in his hand.

"If they slept at all." Kai jabs an elbow into Dover's ribs.

"I was hoping to secure a meeting this afternoon to go over the… logistics of this unexpected arrangement."

Clearly, he doesn't approve of the slight change of plans. Shocker.

"Or we could do it right now." Eaton gestures around the table. "No time like the present."

"Your Grace, these matters are reserved for the ears of the small council. Perhaps we should keep to formalities in this particular instance."

"This afternoon is booked, I'm afraid." Eaton drapes his arm over the back of Sorscha's chair.

"With what, pray tell?" Gronwen can barely bite back the acid in his tone, and it's hilarious to watch him try.

"Worshipping my wife, taking her out to the stables for a ride, worshipping my wife again, staring into her eyes uninterrupted for immeasurable amounts of time, and then again, worshiping my wife once more before bed."

Eaton flashes him a blinding, toothy grin.

"While I understand that the...*bliss* of marital union is demanding, I would suggest we not wait. With the current climate, the threat of war hanging overhead, the people crave stability. And they will not have it when their leaders are in flux. Details of your coronation must be finalized—"

Eaton cuts him off with a swish of his hand. "Alright. But just so you'll stop talking. Gather your little council and we'll meet you in five."

"Your Grace." Gronwen bows and exits the room. Eaton turns back to Sorscha.

"Fun's going to have to wait, I'm afraid."

"Regret marrying me yet?"

"Never. But just so we're clear, I married you. Not your crown. This is your kingdom. I want to see you rule it." He presses a kiss to Sorscha's hand, gazing at her with intense adoration.

"Together," she corrects.

We make our way to the council room not five, but fifteen minutes later—because Eaton agrees with Kai about his fashionably late theory.

Gronwen, Conwell, the High Priest, Jace, and Max are already inside, shocked to see our entire group file into the room.

Gronwen turns to his comrades, dropping his voice to a low hiss. "The entire point of the small council is that it is small. Not open to all heathens living amongst this court." When Sorscha steps into the room, he straightens. "Princess, I was not expecting your attendance today," he notes, if not a bit pointedly.

"Oh, you can expect the both of us at every meeting moving forward, seeing as this is *her* kingdom now," Eaton retorts.

Once he pushes in Sorscha's chair, he sits and claps his hands. "So. What is so important you have to rip me from the bliss of my marital union?"

"First order of business." Gronwen pulls a few documents from a pile. "These licenses must be signed, since the two of you were not married before the eyes of the gods and the people. Without these, your marriage is as good as a sham."

"It's far from a sham, let me tell you." Eaton snickers.

"I mean no offense, Highness. But the marriage needs be legitimized. Sign here and choose a witness to sign below."

Eaton whistles and snaps his fingers at me. "Rhodesie."

I come around the table, taking the fountain pen and sprawling my name on the line.

"Sweet of you to give me away, darling." He ruffles my hair, and I shake him off to take my seat by Serena. Jace watches us from beside Gronwen, looking moderately uncomfortable.

"I trust you performed the Bloodfast as agreed upon last night."

"Yes, we did."

"And the results?"

"As you'd expect, though, if you're looking for a demonstration, it might have to wait until after the meeting."

"Noted. Onto other matters," Gronwen drones. "The coronation."

"We should do it as soon as possible. Before Kylian arrives." All eyes shift to Sorscha. It was rare for her to attend meetings when Derek was alive, let alone for her to speak up. "I think it would be best to present a unified front."

Eaton smiles at her with pride.

"I'll make the arrangements for next week and have the announcement sent. That should give the nobles in the south time to travel from their estates," Lord Conwell says.

"The public will also need to be informed of the changes made to the late king's succession," the High Priest adds. "Although word has likely spread after last night's *celebration*."

He says it like it's a dirty word.

"We tell the public the truth. That Sorscha and I discovered we were mates, and the rest is history," Eaton declares.

"I understand that you are mates. Forgive my saying so, but the late king was very clear in his choice for a successor." Gronwen's gaze shifts to Jace. "We have been left with little choice but to accept this union, lest we upset the entire line of succession to carry out his wishes and in doing so, turn our own people against us. I want to make sure you understand the implications that come with this alliance. Are you prepared for this? The people will look to you as they would to him, and as a second son, I'm not sure that you're suited to the role."

"More suited than he is." Eaton nods toward Jace. "Never got to compliment you on your right hook, by the way."

He tips his head in thanks, eyes murderous as he drums his fingers on the table.

"That may be. However, as Derek was a close personal friend, the responsibility falls on me to make sure his kingdom and his only daughter are protected."

"Lord Gronwen, I appreciate the concern, and while I understand this may not have been my father's wish, I do believe he would have been pleased with my mate and my choice to put him on the throne beside me. Eaton is a prince in his own right, and with the help of the council, of course, he and I intend to rule with the grace, wisdom, and integrity that my father was so well known for."

Everyone stares as she lifts her chin a degree higher. Gronwen draws up his spine.

"Couldn't have said it better myself." Eaton beams. "And to answer your previous question—I am up for the challenge. We both are." His fingers thread through Sorscha's—a united front. "While we're on the topic of choices, Sorscha and I have been discussing the kind of leaders we want to be. We plan to do things differently. None of this court posturing and stiff council bullshit."

"The council is a fixture. We were Derek's most trusted advisors."

"We don't intend to dissolve it. But it is important to both of us that we have people *we* trust, people who would go into hell for us. Right, angel? And the people in this room have all proved themselves. The ones I know, at least."

I hang my head.

Eaton, this is not the place for rash decisions.

"That being said, Sorscha and I would like to appoint some new positions to the council. Starting with Zadyn. Hand of the King. And Queen."

My eyes bulge. "Jace is Hand. Really, I don't want—"

"Too bad, it's done. Serena—Dragon Rider—enough said. Meredith…Temperance Advisor? Mistress of Witch Operations? We'll think of something. Kai, Master of Persuasion. Dover—Assistant to the Master of Persuasion."

"I think we might need to finesse these titles later," Dover mutters to Mar.

"None of those are actual positions." Gronwen seethes, red splotches creeping over every inch of his ivory skin.

"They are now!" Eaton holds out his arms.

"A council must retain a High Priest, a Head of Records and Coin," the High Priest says in his paper-frail voice.

Sorscha nudges her husband.

"Fine. The two of you can stay," Eaton decides. "But this one's becoming a real sourpuss and, quite frankly, dragging the whole mood down." He points at Gronwen.

"This is an outrage!" Gronwen slams his fist against the table.

I leap to my feet. "As your *unwilling* Hand, my first piece of advice is to keep Gronwen on. He's been a fixture at court and on this council for a long time. He's experienced. Derek trusted him."

"Fine. He can stay. If he promises not to be a stick in the mud."

I toss Gronwen a pleading look for the sake of peacekeeping. Beside me, Serena is fucking convulsing, her hand over her mouth, trying to keep her laughter at bay.

You're not helping, I snap.

Oh, this is all you, she responds through her fit.

"Fine. I agree not to be…a stick in the mud," Gronwen grits, each word begrudging.

"Fantastic, then welcome to Queen Sorscha's small council."

"Lord Gronwen, I must apologize for my husband's *enthusiasm*." Sorscha sends Eaton a pointed look.

He melts into a smile. "Is this our first fight?"

Sorscha ignores him, redirecting her attention to Gronwen. "What other matters did you plan to discuss today?"

"Well, I had hoped for some progress on the deal with the King of Vod." He glances at Serena, who's finally starting to sober.

She clears her throat. "None worth mentioning."

"As far as we know, their deal is binding," I announce. "I'm still searching for a way out of it."

"The best we can do is prepare for the worst."

"We *will* figure something out," Sorscha vows, nodding at Serena.

"Here's something you'll enjoy, Gronwich," Eaton says. "My father has agreed to send another ten thousand men to defend your walls."

"He has?" Sorscha gasps.

"Not yet, but he will."

I drag my hand down my face.

"Well. Are we done here?" Eaton asks after a moment. "Good. Successful first meeting. You're all dismissed."

Before he's even finished, his mouth is on Sorscha's with an indecent display of tongue. Everyone promptly makes for the exit before clothes start flying off.

I stop Jace on his way out the door.

"Listen. He's just power-tripping right now. I'll talk to him. I don't want to be Hand of the King."

"Neither do I. He's your friend. You deal with him." He makes to leave, but I hold him in place.

"I'm not going to displace you from the council."

"My place is not seated at that table, and we all know it. I'm happy to stick to battles and bloodshed." He gives me a bitter look, rips his arm away, and stalks off.

I glance back as Eaton ushers Sorscha into the hall to join up with Serena and Mar. I step in front of him.

"You cannot just walk in here and flip everything on its head. This is serious, Eaton. Your father did not train you to be king. And you need to rely on those around you who have experience to guide you."

He claps me on the shoulder. "This. This is exactly why I need you as Hand."

I hang my head. "I will be emissary, just like I was before."

"Fine. If that's what you really want, we can save your true title for behind closed doors." He gives me a dubious look and slaps me on the ass.

This is going to be a long fucking reign.

"Now if you'll excuse me, it's about a quarter past fuck-my-wife o'clock."

We start to walk, and I can't help but laugh at the little hearts in his eyes as he stares after his mate.

"I have never seen my friend so pathetically whipped before." I pull him into a headlock, groaning when he punches me in the gut.

"Sad I won't be pining for you forever, Rhodesie? I have a feeling you'll find someone to keep you company. Someone with lavender eyes and kissable lips." He makes a smooching sound in my face.

"Shut up." I shove him off. "When you said you knew how it felt, you were referring to Sorscha."

"Why do you think I was pushing you so hard? You've always made yourself responsible for other people's happiness." He gives my chest a gentle smack. "It's time you went after what you want. I've seen the way she looks at you."

For my own selfish sake, I hope to gods he's right.

7 9

JACE

8 DAYS

"Damn. We demolished this." Max rattles the near-empty bottle of wine. "One sip left." He raises his brow at me in question.

I shake my head, declining. Lifting the bottle into the air, he toasts, "To jilted grooms."

I slide him a slow glare. "Too soon."

"Yep, I got that." The clouds hanging overhead shift, giving way to a pearlescent moon as Max drains the dregs of the wine.

I'm grateful for his company. The truth is, I don't know what to do with myself now. I know what I'd *like* to do. I'd like to knock on Serena's door, sneak into her room, and just…talk.

Talk? What the hell has happened to me? When did I become such a sucker?

I fall into a trance, staring off my balcony into the endless night sky, images of her drifting through my head like background music. Her face has become my mind's default. I see her without any conscious effort. Even when I don't want to.

"That meeting was…" Max trails off, at a loss for words.

"A flaming fucking disaster? Yeah, I was there."

"As long as the old council stays on, I'm sure they'll keep the prince in check. Zadyn too. He seems to have a pretty level head on him."

I grunt in assent.

"Do you miss it?" Max asks after a moment.

"Miss what?"

"Being Captain."

I look at him, my buzz already beginning to fade.

Of course, I do. Without that title and the duties that come with it…I'm lost. I have no idea who I am lately. But instead of the honest answer, I just shrug.

"Some days."

"So what's your plan? Zadyn seemed adamant that he didn't want Hand. You think Eaton will let you stay on?"

"Depends," I say, slouching back in the wicker chair. "I've spoken less than ten words to him and then fucking decked him when I found out he and Sorscha eloped. So it doesn't look promising."

"I'm sure the princess has some sway. She'll vouch for you."

"I'm not even sure I want her to."

Max's green eyes appraise me. "Are you alright?"

"Fantastic."

"You seem—"

"How do I seem, Max? Please tell me. Dying to know."

"I don't know if I've ever seen you so…down."

My laugh is a bitter sound.

"If Eaton lets you go as Hand, I would gladly relinquish Captain to you."

"I don't want your pity, Max."

"It's not pity, Jace, it's what's right. You're still Captain in my eyes. People don't respect me the same way they do you."

"Because you're too nice." I wag my pointer finger at him. "And you smile too much. Try being a dick, it goes a long way."

He, of course, smiles in response, casting his gaze out over the distant mountain peaks.

"Look, we both know if things had been different, it would have been Mal you chose to succeed you."

He's not wrong. Max is an exceptional fighter. He and Mal have that in common. But a captain needs to be ruthless. Needs to be able to turn his heart off when the time comes to get the job done. And Max's heart is too big for that.

"I wonder what he's doing right now."

"Traitor things, I'm sure," I mutter without thinking. Max's jaw tightens, and I instantly regret the words. "I'm sorry, man."

Max hangs his head. "It's fine. You're right. I just don't know where I went wrong. How I missed the signs. He's my brother. I came into this world with him. I know him better than anyone. I just can't fathom how he could turn like this."

"That's the power one female can hold over you."

I think about if the situation were reversed. If Serena were capable of the evils Ilspeth was, if she used her power and position to create suffering, would I do what Mal did?

And the answer is yes. I would burn villages to the ground if she asked me to. I would do terrible, depraved things for her love. And that's a terrifying thought.

"I tried to warn him about her." Max runs a hand through his long copper hair. "He kept telling me it was nothing. It was his job. That bitch got her claws so deep in him."

"Max." I lean forward. "You know what will happen if he shows his face back here. If we get our hands on him."

Max swallows hard. I clap my hand over his shoulder as he studies the callouses on his hands.

"The brother you knew is already gone."

He nods. I'm sorry. I truly am. But I can't suffer him to live. He is part of the reason I lost Serena in the first place. He is the reason she gave Kylian everything. The reason for the rift between us.

I will take his head with a smile.

A knock at my door draws our attention inside.

"Come," I call.

"Captain," the steward says, stepping onto the balcony.

"Yes," our voices overlap, and we exchange a look.

"Old habits." I shake my head, slightly embarrassed.

The steward looks torn, but I nod to Max. He accepts the note, eyes scanning the parchment with furious speed.

"When did you get this?"

"It arrived an hour ago, sire. You weren't in your room."

Max glances up at me, his face leeched of color.

"What is it?" I bound out of the chair, ripping the letter from his hands. I scan the words once. Twice.

Fuck.

"It's happening. Gather as many people as you can, and get to the tunnels. Now."

8 0
ZADYN

7 DAYS

There's a knock on my door sometime after midnight. Blinking away the sleep, I toss back the covers and open the door to a worse for wear Jace.

The flickering candlelight in the hall deepens the dark hollows beneath his eyes, making him look haunted.

"What is it?"

"May I?" His eyes skip to my room.

"Last time I checked, you were still king." I hold the door open. As soon as it closes behind me, he turns and says, "We need to talk. About Serena."

"What about her?"

"We can't let her do this."

He knows as well as anyone that there's no deterring her when she wants something. "Her mind is made."

"I don't care. I'll do whatever it takes to stop this." He steps forward. "But I need your help."

I give him a long look.

"What do you have in mind?"

8 1

SERENA

7 DAYS

The sound of shouts outside my room jar me from a restless sleep. I sit up, squinting through the dark as I hobble out of bed. Jace is waiting on the other side of the door, hand poised for the knob, his expression grave.

"He's here."

My stomach plummets.

"No."

Behind him, the hall is madness. People running from their rooms down the candlelit corridor, guards in sleek black armor rounding them up and herding them toward the stairs.

I duck past Jace toward the window across the hall. Through the starlit night, I can see the unmistakable gleam of golden soldiers drifting closer over the hill, the Vod banners proudly shivering in the wind above them.

"He's early." Shaking my head, I back up a step and bump into Jace's chest. "No, this isn't right, this wasn't part of the bargain. It hasn't been two weeks yet! Why would he send his armies?"

His arms steady me, but it feels like the earth is sinking and I am going down with it. Our plan, my plan—it's over. Kylian lied. He broke his word.

451

But then again, did I really expect anything different?

It shouldn't surprise me. But something in me, some part buried deep inside, was hoping he was better than that. Was hoping that he… that he what?

I scoff at my own naivete. Kylian is no fixer-upper. He is not redeemable. He deserves to burn in hell for everything he has done and intends to do. And yet somehow, I know exactly what he would say to that.

Burn with me.

"Come on," Jace urges.

"I have to change."

"Serena—"

"I can't fight in a nightgown." I dash into my room to stuff my legs through the first pair of pants and boots I can find and snatch the dagger from beneath my pillow. I'm still tucking the short slip into my waistband when Jace hauls me through the door. "I need to find Zadyn."

"He's already out there."

"What?" I half scream. "We need to get down there, Jace. I'm not letting him fight alone!"

"He's not alone, he's with our armies."

"You know what I fucking mean."

"I already spoke to him. We have a plan."

"Great. Mind clueing me in?" He says nothing. "Wait, when did you speak to him? Jace. Did you know they were going to attack?"

"Max's men reported it an hour ago." He shakes his head in disgust. "I should have known he would retaliate like this."

"Retaliate? Against what?"

Jace forces a breath through his nose, his jaw clenching.

"What are you hiding from me?" I demand.

"I launched an attack on Vod two days before the wedding."

"You did what?!" My heels dig into the ground, but he holds on tighter, dragging me alongside him. "Jace, why would you do that? We had a plan!"

"I had to do something," he growls, sliding his molten eyes toward me. "Did you really think I would just sit back and wait for him to come whisk you away?"

"You have no idea what you just set in motion. He is going to come at us ten times as hard now. This was my mess, and it was contained—"

"Wake up, Serena. It wasn't contained! It never was! It was an avalanche waiting to happen. There was never going to be any containing it or stopping it."

"If you had trusted me and stuck with the plan—"

"You know, if I didn't know any better, I would think you actually wanted him to take you."

"You're a bastard," I spit, struggling against him. His grip doesn't relent as we weave through the chaotic passageway. "I can't believe you did this."

"You'll get over it."

"You sure? You sure I'll get over the blood that will be spilled here today? The people that will die because of your ridiculous pride? No one else needed to be involved."

"When are you going to get it through your thick head? This mess is all of ours. It's yours, mine, your familiar's. It's Kai's and Marideth's too. This is bigger than you. This is about protecting what is ours. Our land, our home, our people. And you are one of them. So stop acting like a fucking martyr."

We reach a part castle I'm not familiar with. The halls are dark, leading up to a narrow spiral staircase.

"Where are you taking me?"

"Just trust me, Serena. For once."

"Forgive me if I have a bit of trouble with that at the moment."

He doesn't answer. He just stares straight ahead, his face set in a hard mask of determination as I follow him up the steps.

Where are you? I call out to Zadyn in my mind.

I'm fine. Stay with Jace.

Zadyn, tell me where you are right now, or so help me.

Worried about me? he teases.

This is not the time for jokes.

I'm fine, Serena. Promise me you'll stay with him.

No, I'm coming for you.

Serena. The sudden command packed into my name takes me aback. *I said, promise me. We have a plan.*

That seems to be the company line.

I can't do what I need to if I'm worried about you.

Okay. I'll stay with him. Zadyn—

Yes?

I—nothing. I'll tell you later. Just don't be the hero, okay? Come back to me.

Always.

"Jace, whatever this is can wait. Zadyn is out there, we need to— "

I reach the landing as he swings open a door and holds it open for me. Casting him a concerned glance, I step inside and look around. It's empty except for a cot and a blanket that look about a thousand years old.

"Jace, what—"

The door slams shut behind me. My blood goes cold as the lock turns.

"No," I breathe. "NO!"

I fall on the door, pounding against it with all my might.

"I'm sorry, Serena. It's for your own good."

"Let me out of here, Jace! Right now!"

"I can't let you do this."

"Let me out! If you don't open this door, I will *never forgive you!*"

"It's spelled, Serena. Stop trying to fight it. I'll come back for you. I promise."

"JACE, DON'T YOU DARE DO THIS TO ME! *JACE!*"

"Forgive me."

His footsteps fade as I rail against the barrier. My screams chase him all the way out.

8 2

SERENA

7 DAYS

Hours.

That is how long I've been locked in this fucking tower. I've tried it all. Blasted the door with fire. Rammed it until I thought my shoulder might dislocate. Screamed until my voice went raw. There are splinters in my nail beds from where I clawed at the door. But I gave as good as I got. The gouges in the wood are proof of that.

And now I'm sitting here. Waiting. Stewing. Boiling.

Either Jace has forgotten about me or he's dead. Maybe they all are.

The lock clicks. I'm on my feet within seconds.

I'm not expecting it when the door swings open and Kylian appears, his shoulders sinking as his eyes find mine.

"There you are," he breathes, stepping into the tower. His arms open as he reaches me.

I don't hesitate before I plunge my dagger into his chest.

But when I stagger backward, pulling the knife from his heart, it isn't Kylian who crumples to the ground.

It's Zadyn.

455

83

SERENA

7 DAYS

Time slows.

The entire world quiets until the only sound I hear is the roar of my own heart in my ears.

I blink.

No. No, no, no. This isn't real. It can't be.

But it is.

It's Zadyn, not Kylian, lying there on the floor in a pool of his own blood.

Oh god, no.

Cold dread slams into me, taking me to my knees. Everything blurs. I'm suddenly fighting through a fog so thick and endless—dulling my senses, slowing my movements, slowing down the world itself. I'm moving in quicksand, and he's bleeding out far too quickly.

I clamp my hands over the wound, trying to seal the blood inside his body. But it's spilling out in droves.

A throbbing pain spears through my chest, as real and as raw as the time I pierced my own heart.

"Zadyn? Zadyn, stay with me."

His hand fumbles for mine as a cluster of bodies cram through the door.

456

"Good gods," Jace breathes.

My head reels, refusing to make sense of the nightmare unfolding before me.

"What did I do? What did I *do?!*"

"They're retreating!" someone shouts from the hall. My eyes snap toward the door, then back to Zadyn, the realization clicking into place.

"I—called off the armies. For now." A drop of blood leaks from his mouth. I brush it away through bleary eyes. "Serena."

"Just—don't talk. Just hold on, okay?" My voice betrays me, bordering on hysterical. "I'm going to fix it."

I try to breathe around the stabbing pain, around the insurmountable fear clamping down on me. My eyes snap shut, a few tears escaping as I narrow all my energy into one single thought.

Heal him. Just heal him.

Adrenaline pumps through me as that piercing pain intensifies, tightening around my heart like a vice, winding tighter and tighter until I can barely breathe.

"Why aren't you healing? What am I doing wrong? Zadyn? Zadyn! *Help!*" I screech over my shoulder at my horror-stricken friends.

No one moves.

"Why is there so much blood? Why can't I—*somebody help me!*"

Zadyn's eyes begin to roll back. A hand lands on my arm, but I brush it off it, shaking Zadyn's shoulders. His head drops to the side, caramel hair spilling into his eyes like it always does. I clear it away, clutching his face, as if my iron grip is enough to keep him here, tethered to this earth with me.

"No, no, no. Stay awake, Zadyn. Zadyn? *Zadyn!*"

There is a roaring in my head. Or maybe I'm screaming. I'm not really sure.

His eyes go still on the ceiling as the last of his life drains out of him.

Silence echoes down the corridor linking our minds. I'm suddenly the only one standing there. I'm standing there alone in the darkness.

An empty stillness settles over the room, and I'm certain I've stopped breathing too.

"No. Wake up. Wake *up*," I demand, shoving the stinging tears off my face with blood-soaked hands. I stifle my burgeoning anguish, sucking back the sobs lodged in my throat.

"Wake up. Wake up."

The words become an incantation, falling from my tear-soaked lips. I give his face a few brisk pats. When that does nothing, I climb on top of him and start chest compressions.

One, two, three.

Breathe.

One, two, three.

Breathe.

Somewhere in my mind I know that CPR doesn't work on fatal stab wounds to the heart. But I do it anyway.

Silly me.

"You're not going," I grit, bearing down on his open chest. "You're not leaving me. *Come. On. Zadyn.*"

All logic, all sanity leaves me as I work like a woman possessed over his pale body, pumping his lifeless heart. My lips slam into his, pushing air down into lungs that refuse to fill.

Those lips that once kissed me soft enough to crack me open, those lips that once tasted like him…Now they taste like blood and tears.

"Serena." Jace murmurs my name with unnerving gentleness. As if I'm in danger of shattering. His hands wrap around my arms. I whirl, heaving a violent shove to his chest, fire brimming in my eyes and heating my fingers.

The distraught faces of my friends stare at me, at us, with sympathetic eyes. "Why are you all looking at me like that? He's fine. He's gonna be fine."

My hair falls into my eyes as I lift my fists and begin pounding his heart to no avail. But as I stare down into lifeless eyes, warm even in death, there is no denying that I'm sitting on top of a corpse.

I take in the blood now pooled around his outline—the blood

dripping down my fingers. The cloying scent of salt and iron. The dull pallor of his skin. His colorless mouth.

And I fracture.

A banshee howl bursts from my throat as something in my chest tears. I rock back and forth, keening, every single cell inside of me aching with overwhelming grief.

Somewhere behind me, stone is crumbling, trees are bending. Furi is howling like a wounded wolf. Inside me, it's like something pivotal has been severed. Something has burst. Something I cannot live without. I collapse on top of him, sobbing into his neck and clutching his hair.

He's still warm.

"Please!" I scream, my chest heaving. "Please, no!"

I feel the absence of his arms around me like a gaping hole in my heart.

"Serena, he's gone. I'm so sorry." Jace tries to pry me away, and I resist, clinging to Zadyn with desperate need. "We didn't know—this wasn't supposed to happen."

Slowly, I peel my face from Zadyn's shoulder to peer up at Jace. "What wasn't supposed to happen."

"We only wanted to keep you safe here." His eyes are filled with regret. With guilt.

"You...the two of you planned this?"

"I'm so—I'm so sorry—"

Jace's words are cut off as I slam him into the wall, my fingers wrapping around his throat.

"HOW COULD YOU DO THIS? YOU FUCKING RUINED *EVERYTHING!*"

Utter rage devours me. Shadows spill out around me, serpentine tendrils lashing out to fill the tower. Fire bubbles beneath my skin, piercing through the barrier as my grip on Jace's neck constricts. Before I can think to stop it, the room is on fire. Someone curses, and in my periphery, Kai douses the flames with his water. But my focus is on Jace.

"Serena, stop! You're going to kill him." Kai rushes toward us, latching onto my arm. I burn him without even meaning to. He breaks away gasping, but it's Mar's voice that edges me back to reason.

"Stop it. You don't want to do this, and you know that."

Jace, for all his strength and power, all his prowess as a warrior, is no match for the boiling rage inside of me. The rage and adrenaline fueling my magic. His hands grasp at mine, and I see in his eyes that he is afraid.

For the first time, he is afraid of me.

He fucking should be.

I rip my hands away as the shadows clear, slinking back toward me. Jace falls to the floor gasping, clutching at his neck. He reaches for my legs, but I step back, crashing to my knees beside Zadyn.

Even in death he is heartbreakingly beautiful. I don't know how anyone could ignore it. How *I* could have ignored it for so long.

I look down at myself. At my clothes, at my hands wet with his blood. The hands of a monster herself.

I did this. I killed him. I *killed* my familiar. My Zadyn.

Monster.

The room begins to spin. I can't breathe. And what's worse—I don't want to.

Then Jace's hands are pushing back my hair as he forces air down into my lungs. I try to resist, but he wins. Choiceless, I let his eyes ground me as he fills me with his gift.

Why couldn't he just let me go? Let me suffocate? Without Zadyn, I'm dead anyway.

Then something occurs to me. Something Zadyn said to me a long time ago, when I first arrived in this world.

"I can bring him back," I croak, pulling away from Jace. "He told me that some Blackbloods were necromancers. I can bring him back."

I push the tears and snot from my face as my vision clears and my mind empties, focused solely on this one sliver of hope.

Mar sinks down beside me, laying a gentle hand on my shoulder.

"Serena," she says softly, like she's approaching a cornered animal. And I feel like one, ready to attack—to claw and fight and *end*. "Life and death magic is not easy. One mistake and he could come back... wrong."

"I have to try. I can't lose him. I *won't*."

"You cannot do this."

A nasty hiss works its way up my throat as I pin her to the ground, snarling in her face. Dover is there in an instant, but Jace appears in front of him, pressing a cautionary hand to his chest.

"You will bring back something unnatural that you will have to kill all over again if you do this," Mar says calmly, despite my assault.

"I have no choice. I can't lose him."

"You cannot do this alone," she pleads.

"Then *help* me." A loud sob severs my words. I try again, whispering, "Help me."

"I don't know how." She hesitates for a moment. "But I know who might be able to."

I fall back onto my heels, releasing her.

"Who?"

She sits up. "My coven."

84
JACE

7 DAYS

"Let's go."

Serena shoves to her feet, the tears drying on her blood-streaked face as an eerie calm befalls her.

"Jace, get his other side," she orders. I give her a wary look.

"Serena—"

"GET HIS OTHER SIDE!"

Her shout rebounds off the tower walls. She glowers at me, fangs bared, her fingers sparking tiny flames. She doesn't seem to notice. She is possessed. There is desperation in her like I've never seen. Reasoning with her in this state will be impossible.

This is my fault. Mine and Zadyn's. We thought we were protecting her by locking her up. Zadyn succeeded in getting the armies to retreat. But once they find out it wasn't Kylian who gave the order, they will be back.

It was a temporary solution with catastrophic consequences.

Dover takes the blanket off the cot in the corner to shroud Zadyn's body. Even though I think this is a terrible idea, I help lift him.

Serena stops at her room to change and grab Arden's grimoire, then meets us on the lawns where Furi waits, sending blaring howls

462

up into the cresting sunrise. My eyes snag on the two bodies bounding toward us.

"Who is that?" Sorscha asks, noting the covered body. Eaton stands beside her in silver armor, breathing hard, his hair windblown.

I turn to him, shaking my head. The realization settles in his eyes. "I'm sorry."

He sheathes his sword and takes a step toward his friend's body, his face twisting in confusion and rage. Sorscha claps a hand over her mouth.

"What happened," Eaton grits.

"I did," Serena says without looking back. "And I'm going to make it right."

Eaton watches Dover and Kai load Zadyn onto Furi's back, his face a mask of shock.

"You have to stay here," Mar says to me.

"How can I let her go like this? This is our fault, it's my fault—"

"She cannot be around you right now. We will take care of her. But right now she needs space, and you're needed here. This war is far from over. In fact, after today, I think it's only just begun."

"Kylian will find her, and I won't be there."

"He won't find her. Not where we're going."

I give her a desolate look.

"What she's about to do…" I shake my head, my eyes caught on the dark banner of her hair waving in the wind as she takes her place on the dragon's back. "Don't let her lose herself."

"Never."

As I watch them disappear into the bleak sky, I try to think of anything but Serena's haunting cries. I try to un-feel her hands around my neck, her nails digging into my throat, determined to end my life right then and there.

The way her fingers trembled afterward, wet with crimson blood as she sank onto Zadyn's chest, wailing—it broke me.

If I had been a second earlier in getting to her, I could have stopped it. But I was too late.

I pray to the gods he lives.

But either way, she may never forgive me.

And I may never forgive myself for ruining us.

PART III: FALLEN STARS

85

SERENA

7 DAYS

Lightning slashes across the midnight skies, followed by another crack of thunder. We slice through weeping storm clouds, rain pelting us as we soar over the agitated onyx waves of the Sunken Sea.

"This is it!" Mar shouts over the deafening winds. "Steer her straight down when I say."

"It's all ocean beneath us!" I call back.

"I know. Trust me."

Mar begins to chant behind me in Ancient Fae. I glance at her over my shoulder. A line of blue blood trickles from her nose as she continues louder.

"Now!"

Furi obeys without hesitation, diving toward the water with unrelenting speed. I suck in a breath, bracing to go under as we spear through the surface and are swallowed up by the sea.

My ears start to ache as we plunge deeper and deeper into the depths of the abyss. My lungs burn, desperate to expand as the pressure builds in my head. Panic sets in. The moment my vision begins to blink out, we break through the barrier.

We're still plunging downward, only now we are plunging toward

466

a twilight sky. Gasping, I glance below us toward the water we just emerged from. The world has turned upside down.

"Head toward the shore," Mar calls.

The night grows eerily quiet as we land inside a dense forest—the only sound the patter of rain falling against the dusty ground.

"We have to go on foot from here," Mar says, nodding toward the camp in the distance. I glance back at Zadyn's body, secured to Furi's saddle, and another wave of nausea rocks me.

I can't believe this is real.

I will watch over him until you are ready. Go, Blackblood.

I nod, words evading me.

I keep expecting him to pop up beside me. I keep waiting for that moment when he shows up like he always does and offers me that smile that tells me that no matter what, everything is going to be okay.

But it doesn't come. Zadyn isn't coming. And it's all my fault.

We make our way toward the edge of the trees, where the forest gives way to a village of rustic cabins. Mar holds up a hand to stop us.

"Let me go first." She hesitates before stepping out onto the dirt path.

The hair on my arms stands up.

Something is wrong.

The second my mouth opens, a handful of figures step out of the shadows, forcing Mar to the ground. A silver blade glints against her throat. We lunge forward, but before we can reach her, we hit an invisible wall and bounce backward.

A shield.

"Marideth!" Dover pounds against the translucent dome.

The figures haul her to her feet, twisting her arms behind her back to knot a thick rope around her wrists.

I do the only thing I can think of. I hurl out a wave of fire. It hits the wall and blossoms out, sliding along the undetectable surface. But it doesn't penetrate. The figures freeze, turning back toward us. Two of them approach, leaving Mar in the hands of a third. Their angular faces come into view. Sharp and beautiful, they stare at us with snarling mouths.

"Let her go!" Dover bellows.

"I will burn this forest to the ground if you don't lower this shield," I threaten.

"Do it, and you seal your own grave," one of them hisses.

"You wanna bet on it?" I send another stream of fire flying at the dome, and it quivers. They jerk backward, exchanging a glance. "I can do this all night."

Recovering, the smaller one snaps, "You wish to be tried with the traitor?"

"Drop the shield. Now."

"One wrong move and she burns without trial."

"And you'll join her," the other adds. With a wave of her hand, she lowers the shield. "Bind them."

"It's alright," Mar croaks, eyes pleading with me.

With the knife pressed to her throat, we comply, holding out our hands to be bound. We're dragged through the Blueblood camps, past the rows of identical cottages, each of which looks dark and empty. When we're thrust into a large hut packed with bodies, I realize it's because everyone is here.

Waiting for us.

A hush falls over the crowd of females as we're shoved forward, earning hateful stares on the way. We're tossed at the foot of a dais housing five thrones made of twigs and wild brush, four of which are occupied by witches in crowns of thorns. They're beautiful, with eyes different shades of gray and silver and ice-blue. Beautiful and terrifying.

The blades remain pressed to our throats as one of the crowned Bluebloods stands, her voice slicing through the hushed murmurs of the gathered covens.

"You dare show your face back here? With a pack of outsiders, no less?" Her ice-blonde hair falls like a silk sheet to her hips, her black nails filed to dagger-like points.

"Please, Esther," Mar entreats. "I know I've broken the covenant. You can tie me up and burn me on the pyre, but first I need to speak with her."

"Silence! You do not come here and make demands of the elders. You made your choice when you defected."

"Just let me speak with her—"

"The law is the law," another Blueblood with rich dark skin and smooth ebony hair says from her throne. Her irises are so pale they nearly blend with the whites of her eyes. "And you have broken several—including our most sacred one."

Though her words are firm, her face lacks the same contempt as the scary blonde with the claws.

"Once the Matron arrives, you will be tried for your crimes, and when you and the intruders are found guilty, you will answer with your lives."

"Threaten my friends again, and it's you who will answer with your lives."

Four heads snap toward me as my rage comes to a boil.

"What did you just say?" Esther takes a menacing step toward me, her claws curling.

A darkness creeps over me, and though it frightens me, I don't have the strength to fend it off. It's heavy. My power just itching to be let free. Itching to destroy something.

"Enough."

This voice is different—chilling and ancient—coming from behind us.

She walks toward us at an unhurried pace, the horde of Bluebloods parting for her with bowed heads. Her hair is braided down her back, the auburn strands streaked with silver ones. Her face is soft and ethereal, showing a bit of age through the gentle lines and creases. She wears no crown, but something tells me she doesn't need to. The female mounts the dais and comes to a stop in front of Mar.

"Grandmother."

Grandmother?

"What have you done, Marideth?" She shakes her head, regret lining her silver eyes. I catch a tear streaming down Mar's face as she bows at the witch's feet. I've never seen her cry before.

"Save your tears, child," her grandmother says, her voice gentle.

Then her cool gaze lands on me. Reaching out a wrinkled hand, she cups my face and studies my irises. I try to control the scowl on my face.

"You fools do realize who you hold captive, do you not?" Releasing me, she turns back to the bloodthirsty witches enthroned before us. "Are you that blind?"

The elders study me. One by one, their faces change, their jaws dropping as they take in the constricted amethyst eyes peering back at them.

"It can't be," the small one on the end whispers, a hand pressed to her chest.

"Oh, but it is." I sneer, melting the rope from my wrists. Two flames burst from my palms. A gasp ripples through the crowd, and the dagger threatening me clanks to the ground. "And unless you want your homes to be razed, you'd better release my friends. Now."

"Imposter!" Esther snarls, drawing a long curved blade and surging toward me with crazed eyes.

Without any conscious effort, my shadows lash out, wrapping around her wrists and throat, forcing her to her knees. The rest of the room gasps as the elders leap to their feet. My shadows preen at the taste of their fear.

"Serena," Mar breathes, her face ashen.

"No harm will come to you here. Any of you." Marideth's grandmother assures me. "Release her."

"Tell your witches to stand down first," I bite, nodding toward the ones still holding knives to my friends' necks. Mar's grandmother delivers a terse nod, and they back away into the crowd. I seethe for another minute, my chest heaving.

"Serena." Kai nudges my leg with his shoulder, snapping me out of it. My shadows retract, and Esther crashes forward, coughing and clutching her throat.

"It's her," the petite elder whispers in awe. "The last Blackblood."

She takes a cautious step away from her sisters and sinks to her knees. The rustling of clothes has me turning toward the crowd. Around me, the gathered Bluebloods are dropping to the ground.

"What are they doing?"

"Bowing. To you." Mar's grandmother's voice sends chills down my spine. Then she too dips at the waist. The other two witches on the dais follow suit, dropping down to one knee. I don't count Esther, who's still on all fours, all but foaming at the mouth as she glares at me.

"Get up, just—get up," I mutter in exasperation.

The first elder to bow rises. "The Blackblood is welcome here. However, the traitor must be dealt with as our clan's tradition demands."

"I'm the one who begged Marideth to bring me here. Practically forced her."

"Grandmother, we wouldn't have come if it weren't absolutely necessary."

Esther's shrill voice interrupts. "Laws have been broken by one of our own. This defector has returned to our camp and brought *outsiders*." She calls to the crowd like she's trying to incite an angry mob. "I demand a trial."

Mar's grandmother takes a seat on the empty throne centered between the other four and waves a hand. "Name her."

"Marideth Whitlocke, you stand hereby accused of treason," Esther says with predatory joy. "How do you plead?"

"I plead guilty."

Shouts erupt from the crowd. The only elder not to speak slams her staff into the ground, enforcing a tense silence.

"Marideth, come forward," her grandmother beckons. Mar gets to her feet and steps up onto the dais, hands still bound in her lap. Dover growls on his knees beside us, jerking against his restraints.

"Tell me true, why have you returned?"

"Our friend is dead." She glances back toward me.

"Someone I can't lose," I interject, earning her grandmother's gaze. "If you want to punish someone, punish me. She was just trying to help. I promise we will leave here and never return if you just help me. Please." My voice fractures. "I love him."

The witch's face softens as she appraises me.

"Why she returned is irrelevant," Esther caws. "Did you or did you not choose to defect from the clan, to relinquish any and all abilities passed to you by your bloodline, through your mother and grandmother?"

"I did."

"And did you not return with a slew of outsiders? Did you not keep your power, thus endangering us all?"

"I only used it when it was necessary. To defend our queen."

My eyes snap to Marideth, my blood going cold at the mention of that word in reference to me.

"The law is absolute," Esther retorts.

"It was my duty to help her! She is the last of her kind—the true leader. I would deny her nothing. Or have you forgotten that the Blackbloods once ruled you? Has time eroded your sense of loyalty? Your respect?"

The witches behind her are silent. Mar's grandmother bestows a proud look on her. "This witch speaks the truth. The Blackblood came to her for help. I see no reason for punishment to be doled out."

"This is blasphemy! Will justice not be served?" Esther rushes forward, desperate. I take a step in front of Mar, staring the bitch down.

"It has been. No blood shall be spilt this night."

"The outsiders have seen too much." Esther's gaze shifts toward Kai and Dover. "They are a danger, and I will not suffer them to live."

"Don't you dare touch them!" Marideth snarls.

"They bear no ill intent." The elder with the black hair and strange, striking eyes gives them a knowing look.

"And what of her magic? She defected! That magic no longer belongs to her." Esther flings an accusatory finger at Mar. A few shouts echo through the room, backing her claim.

"Quiet," her grandmother commands. With a sigh, she says, "Put it to a vote."

"All in favor of stripping the traitor of her power?" Esther turns toward the thrones, her hand flying up before her sentence is complete. Four hands lift into the air.

"Very well. It has been decided."

"You cannot just decide this!" I shout. "I am Serena Avery, the last Blackblood witch, and I *demand* you stop this right now."

"Tradition demands a price," Esther taunts. I feel my shadows curling around my wrists, poised to lash out and force them all to their knees if I have to.

"Serena, don't—don't hurt them. Please." I've never heard Mar's voice shake, but it does as she begs me to stand down.

Her grandmother steps forward, placing her hands on Mar's shoulders and muttering a quiet incantation. Mar goes pale, her eyes closing. Her body starts to twitch as if submerged in a nightmare. Then her grandmother slips the ring off her finger, and she crashes to the ground, gasping. Dover falls down beside her, reaching for her face with bound hands.

I walk up to Esther. "You will pay for this."

Her only answer is the ugliest grin I have ever seen.

"Come. All of you." Mar's grandmother waves a hand, and the ropes binding my friends fall to the ground. We follow her outside—Dover a few feet behind, supporting Mar as I sidle up to her grandmother.

"Why did you do that?"

"To prevent mutiny. They would never have relented without some form of retribution. They cling to the old ways."

"Mar didn't do anything. She only used her magic to help me. This entire time, she has been helping me. She shouldn't lose her power over that."

The Blueblood stops, turning to me. And though she is several inches shorter, it's as though she's looking down at me.

"She is my granddaughter, and she always will be. But she did break the law. Do not question my choice to protect her and your friends the only way I know how."

We follow her inside a nearby cabin. The multiroom space is large, fully furnished, and decorated with cottage-like warmth. Closing the door behind us, she moves toward Mar.

"Come here, child, let me have a look at you." She tilts her chin up to the little fae lights dancing around above us. "You look different."

"I was fifteen when you last saw me."

Her lips invert into a frown as she regards the rest of us, windblown and steely. "You always did know how to find trouble. Just like your aunt."

Mar's mouth opens like she needs to say something, but the elder points at the plush-looking couch. "Sit."

"I'm fine, Grandmother."

"I won't ask twice."

She sinks onto the couch without further protest. The witch walks around and stops in front of me. "Now what is it you need, child?"

"My familiar is dead." I swallow, the words tasting like charcoal on my tongue. "I need you to help me bring him back."

She retreats a step, her mouth flattening into a thin line.

"I do not know what my granddaughter told you. But we do not deal in such magics."

"But you know about them. You know how to help me."

"It is dark magic, girl. Magic borrowed from the gods by your kind. You do not belong meddling in it."

My temper flares. The walls begin to tremble, and the fae lights flicker. It's only when I feel the flames dancing on the tips of my fingers, feel my eyes narrowing to slits, that I realize I'm the one causing it.

"His mother was one of us." The elder's eyes go wide as she stares at Marideth, unblinking. An unspoken conversation happens in the look they share.

She lets out a long sigh, glancing back to me. "I assume you brought the body."

I turn to Dover and Kai. They nod, heading out the door to retrieve it.

"Is it in one piece?"

I cringe, forcing myself to nod. When they return with him, Mar's grandmother waves us forward.

"Come."

We follow her through a doorway hung with beaded curtains. Wooden shelves line the walls, housing colorful vials, grimoires, spices.

"Lay him here," she commands as we duck beneath the bundles of dried flowers hanging from the ceiling.

Kai helps Dover lower Zadyn onto the wooden table. The witch moves closer, undoing the rope around his waist and pulling back the cloth draped over him.

I clutch my mouth at the sight.

He's already starting to decay, his body a bluish-white color, the dried blood around his chest nearly black. Horrible flashbacks play in my head. The sound of my blade cutting through flesh and bone to strike him in his most vulnerable place. The sensation of my hands doused in his hot blood. The vacant look on his face as he left me behind with a mountain of remorse.

As if noticing my horror, Mar's hand slips through mine. I turn to her.

"Marideth, I'm so sorry. Your magic—"

"I was working with borrowed time anyway."

I clutch her hand tighter. "I promise you, I will figure out a way to restore it."

I'm not sure if she believes me, but she nods, a somber expression on her face. We watch as the elder gathers a bowl of blue liquid and smears a series of runes over Zadyn's unmoving chest.

"What are you doing?" I ask.

"It's a spell to preserve the body while we work."

"Work?"

She lifts her argent eyes to mine. "If you go diving into the After without any training, you'll never come back. Just know before we embark on this journey that there is always a cost to these bargains. The price is to be paid with another life."

"I'll have to kill someone?"

"No. The Fates will decide who to take in his stead. It will be out of your hands. Are you still willing to proceed?"

I nod without hesitation. "Yes."

I don't care if that makes me a bad person. I don't even care that I'll be taking someone else's life, taking someone from their family or friends. I just want him back.

I never claimed to be a good person. And right now, I'm beyond desperate.

She proceeds with her ritual, plucking a sprig of dried lavender from overhead, crushing it between her palms, and sprinkling it over the runes.

"You can trust her," Mar says quietly. "She's the Matron of our entire clan. If anyone can help, it's her."

The Matron's eyes drift closed as she mutters something I can't make out. She beckons me with a bony finger.

"Come forward, Blackblood." Mar releases me so I can stand across from her on Zadyn's other side.

"I require a drop." Her hand unfurls toward me, a small knife glinting in the other. Without hesitation, I lay my hand in hers. More whispered words follow as she slits my palm and flips it over to squeeze a few drops onto Zadyn's chest.

"We will see if there is anything left to work with."

"What does that mean?"

"If your blood disappears into the runes, it means your connection is not fully severed. A modicum of life remains, though the body is expired. If the blood remains pooled and does not dissolve…I fear he is too deep into the After, and there is nothing to be done."

My breathing quickens at the notion.

"It will dissolve," I decide, glancing down at his face. I smooth back his hair as the Matron studies me.

"Your familiar, you say?"

I eye the tattoo on his chest, the ebony ink peeking through the gaps in blood and crushed lavender.

"I see the mark," she says in an obvious tone.

"What are you asking?"

She arches a brow, her eyes roaming over me.

"Simply making an observation." She moves toward the wooden

cupboards, dipping her hands into a basin of water and wiping them on a towel. "Come. The body must be left alone now."

"I'm not leaving him."

"If you want to have a shot at this working, then you will. The spell needs room to breathe. And that room does not belong to the living. We petition Death now. Give her a moment to consider."

She pulls back the curtains and waits with expectant eyes.

With one last look back at Zadyn, I follow my friends out.

86

SERENA

7 DAYS

He's just in the other room, I keep reminding myself while the Matron fixes us some tea. The warmth of the mug is surface-level, doing nothing to ease the ice inside my bones.

"Very clever—the ring." The Matron eyes Marideth, a thin layer of pride coating her tone.

"I thought so." Marideth gives her a wry smile.

"You are my blood, aren't you?" She chuckles. "Well, won't you introduce me to your young friends?"

"This is Serena Avery, Prince Kai Triori of Vod, and my mate— Dover Hallister."

"It's an honor to meet you, my lady," Dover says, on his best behavior.

If I wasn't still sick to my stomach over the events of the last few hours, I would laugh at his sudden propriety.

"Tell me, child," the Matron says, "was it worth it? Seeing the world in exchange for leaving this behind?"

"I would have never met any of them if I hadn't. I would have never found Dover. I was never meant to stay here, Grandmother."

A brief silence falls.

478

Then the Matron asks, "Did you ever find her?"

Mar's shoulders sag the slightest bit. "She was already gone by the time I arrived."

"Mother—" A pretty female with auburn hair pushes through the door.

The resemblance is uncanny. She stops short when she sees us. Mar gets to her feet and approaches her.

"Hello, mother."

A slap rings out, and Mar's head whips to the side.

"Calliope," the Matron hisses.

Dover is already there, pulling Mar into his arms to study her welted cheek. A beat passes where the two females stare each other down. Then Mar's mother reaches out and rips her from Dover, crushing her against her chest.

"You little fool," she whispers into her hair. "Why would you come back here? The elders could have done so much worse than demanding your magic."

"We needed help."

"People die all the time, Marideth. This is meant to be a safe place for us. A secret place. You cannot just bring your friends here on a whim." Her gaze sweeps over us, landing on me with a mix of shock and intimidation.

I stand a bit straighter. "Like I said before, this is not Marideth's fault. If anyone is to blame, it's me."

The witch steps back, adopting a cold and distant air.

"Calliope, set them up with sleeping arrangements," the Matron orders, rising from her seat. "The Blackblood and I have work to do."

"Mother, I don't think that's—"

"They are my guests now. Do not fuss with me, girl."

Calliope squares her shoulders and gives a brusque nod for Mar, Dover, and Kai to follow her.

"Let me stay. I can help," Mar entreats her grandmother.

"I don't want you anywhere near that kind of magic, Marideth," Calliope warns.

"She can stay," the Matron replies.

"Marideth—"

"I'm staying, Mother." Her voice carries a tone of finality.

Calliope bristles. "Fine. You two can follow me. Or sleep outside with the wolves for all I care."

Mar gives Dover a reassuring look, squeezing his hand one last time before he and Kai duck out the door.

"That was—" I shake my head, looking at Mar. She looses a hollow laugh.

"One of the reasons I left."

"Are you alright?"

She nods. "Let's just focus on getting Zadyn back."

I pull Arden's grimoire from my satchel and spread it on the table before us. "I figured we might need this."

"Go ahead." The Matron gestures to me. "It will open only for you."

I turn open the front cover.

Hello, my Queen.

Sigh. *Please stop calling me that.*

What shall I call you, Majesty?

Nothing. Don't call me anything.

Yes, your Grace.

The pages begin to flip at a furious pace before landing on one with incantations in Ancient Fae.

Is this what you seek?

"I—" I glance up at the Matron, who is watching with rapt fascination. "Is this what we're looking for?"

"It would appear so."

The Matron dives into the text on the page before giving me the crash course on the After—the place where souls go before they pass on fully. I don't know what time it is when we finally break, my entire body exhausted from crying and screaming and running on fumes for the last few hours. My head swims with new information. I pray it sticks for tomorrow.

Refusing to leave the cabin that houses Zadyn's body, the Matron sets me up with some pillows and blankets on the couch, giving me one last warning not to disturb him.

"Faith." She wags her finger at me, a stern look on her face, before disappearing down the darkened hall.

My eyes fly open at the first blush of dawn through the curtains. I fall off the couch, kicking myself free of the twisted blanket to clamber into the other room. My heart is thundering out of my chest as I race to Zadyn's side.

I sink to my knees beside the table. My blood has absorbed.

"Thank you, god," I breathe, snatching up Zadyn's icy hand and bringing it to my lips. The Matron appears behind me, parting the beaded curtains.

"It's time."

8 7

SERENA

6 DAYS

Death is no stranger to me.*
You can cling to a body all you want, but it's like clinging to air. It will never be yours. It will never fill the holes. It will always leave you grasping at nothing.

Zadyn lies on the wooden table, drenched in eerie stillness, his long legs dangling over the edge. The Matron lights candles and spreads them at eight points throughout the room. Taking a piece of white chalk, she scribbles a series of runes on the ground.

My Zadyn and the body that lies before me are two different people entirely. It sickens me to see him without color. To watch the gray set into his once vibrant skin. To see his beautiful mouth frozen in a tight line. To not feel the life and vitality rolling off of him.

No, this is not Zadyn.

And yet I cling to him, praying against all odds that I can make something out of nothing. That our bond is strong enough to rip him back from death's unrelenting grasp and return him to my side.

For Zadyn, I need to be a god.

So for Zadyn, I will.

---

* Cue: *Killer + The Sound* Phoebe Bridgers, Abby Gundersen, Noah Gundersen

"You are his anchor," the Matron says.

"What does that mean?"

"You are the only thing linking him to this world now," she murmurs, concentrating with her eyes sealed shut. "He remains on the other end of your bond. I can feel him there—eager to pass on, but reluctant to let go of you."

I squeeze his hand tighter, smoothing his brow with my fingers.

It isn't right. It's too rigid, too cold.

"You will need to speak to him. Remind him who he is. Remind him who you are."

I nod, drawing my hand over his hair.

"On my mark, you call to him."

A pit forms in my stomach, but I refuse to let doubt creep in. The Matron begins to murmur the incantation in Ancient Fae. I join in, just like we practiced, praying I don't mess up a single syllable. I can feel the room growing farther away. My vision zooms out, like a camera switching to a wide shot. Everything grows smaller, more distant, as I'm sucked backward—the color fading from the edges of my periphery.

"Now," the Matron says.

I plunge into darkness.

It is complete sensory deprivation. I know that I've left behind my body and entered into a place outside of time and space. There is nothing here but endless blackness.

Zadyn? Are you there?

He doesn't answer, but I feel him in the emptiness around me, in the absence of air. He's here somewhere.

Zadyn?

Nothing. I wander further in, my senses offering no help. Then I see it, like a tiny shivering candle in a sea of darkness. It's him, even though it's not.

Zadyn, it's me. Serena. You have to come back.

I can't see his form. But I feel him here stronger than ever. His soul is unmistakable.

Please, Zadyn. You've been with me my entire life. Even when I felt alone, when I couldn't see you, you were there. So I'm not leaving. I'm not leaving here without you.

This was not enough time. Not even close.

Unending silence answers me.

I'm so sorry. So fucking sorry for every time I took you for granted. Every fight we ever had. Every time I was so damn blind to what's always been right there.

I can't be without you. I just can't. So you need to come back.

I wait, counting seconds that don't exist here.

Come on, Zadyn, I plead, I beg, I bargain. *Come back to me. Come back to me. Please come back to me.*

He's there on the other side of my call, reluctant to answer, but I don't falter. I hold onto him for dear life—his essence, his heart, his soul. I cling to him, pulling him back from the divide that bars him from my sight.

Come back.

I strain against the bounds of my own mind. Tugging at him is like tugging at myself. Plucking one of my own heartstrings that belongs to him, has *always* belonged to him. It sings a song of woe, of howling pain, and the echoes of sadness.

I pluck again. And then I pluck harder.

Come. Back.

And he does.

My eyes fly open the moment his do. His chest rises beneath my outstretched palm as we both gasp for air.

"Did it work?" I breathe.

His wild eyes find mine, bewildered and confused. He stares at me as if I'm a stranger he's seeing for the first time. I watch him fight to concentrate, to sift through two hundred years of memories for one of me.

I don't know why that hurts, but it does.

Then I see the recognition flash over his face, and I burst into tears, throwing myself across his naked chest. My sobs shake the table as Zadyn settles back into his body.

Almost reflexively, his arms reach up to hold me. His skin starts to warm against mine, and I send up thank you's to whatever god is listening.

After an hour, he speaks.

I beg him never to stop again.

WE LIE ON OUR SIDES, facing each other. My hands are tucked beneath the pillow as I study the lines of Zadyn's face, my gaze hopping from freckle to freckle. I fight the urge to touch every single one—to commit them all to memory, their size and exact location on his perfect skin. His chest rises and falls with even breaths, each exhale tickling the tip of my nose. He looks so tranquil, so young.

"Are you asleep?" I whisper. His eyes remain closed, but one corner of his lips pulls up slightly.

"Yes."

"I'm not."

"I know," he replies, cracking an eye at me. His smirk spreads into a smile as I shimmy closer.

"I'm furious with you."

"For what?" he scoffs, his voice hushed.

"Why do you think? For dying."

He chuckles. "You can't be mad at me for dying. You're the one who stabbed me." His eyes fully open, and I can see the instant regret over his joke.

You're right. This is all my fault. I...I killed you.

You didn't know.

"I don't care. You should have told me. What you did—disguising yourself as Kylian—was reckless. And dangerous."

"It was necessary. It stopped the armies. It kept you safe. Alive."

"But you were dead. My life is worth no more than yours."

"You're wrong." He slides a bit closer, bringing his chest to touch my bent elbows. "This was what I was made for, Serena."

"You were not made to lay down your life for me—"

"I was, and I would do it again in an instant—"

I lay my fingers against his mouth, stopping the words from tumbling out.

"Don't," I whisper. "Don't ever say that to me. If you had stayed dead—if I hadn't been able to bring you back—I don't think I would have been able to go on."

"Serena," he says an inch from my lips.

"It's true, Zadyn. When you died"—I trace his face, pushing back his hair—"it felt like something died in me too. It was like a tether snapping. It hurt."

His fingers close over mine.

"It hurt *here*." I place our joined hands over my heart and lift my gaze to his. "It physically hurt to walk and talk and breathe."

Tears spring to my eyes, the memory too fresh.

"Now you know how it felt when I almost lost you."

Zadyn's thumb gently strokes up and down my palm. He closes the gap between us, tucking me against him. I breathe in that cool, familiar scent of his—black tea and cedar—alleviating some of that horrible ache still lingering in my chest. He traces lazy lines up and down my back, each sweep erasing the horrors of the last twenty-four hours.

"You were so pale." I shudder at the memory, wishing I could take a sponge and scrub it from my mind, sand it down to ash and scatter it to the wind.

"I'm right here," he murmurs, resting his chin on my head. I feel the rumble of his words through his chest as he repeats, "I'm right here. Try to sleep."

I snake my arm around his waist, holding him tighter. "I don't want to. I'm afraid you won't be here when I wake up."

"I'll never leave you. Not if I can help it." He plants a soft kiss on my forehead and smooths my hair until I lose my battle with sleep, and she overtakes me.

8 8
ZADYN

5 DAYS

It's an effort to move.

My muscles are so weak, I have to lean on Serena to help get me in and out of chairs—the numbness in my legs and feet bordering on painful.

"This will help the muscles recover more quickly." The Matron holds up a small glass jar of the darkest amber.

"Apply that to his lower extremities three times daily, and he should be walking without aid in a matter of days. And this—" She passes Serena a vial of blue-gray powder. "Sprinkle this in his bath."

The Matron presses her hand to my bare chest, inspecting me with clinical concentration.

"The heart is strong. How is the mind?" she asks, opening eyes strangely similar to Mar's.

"I remember everything." I look up at her. "Thank you for helping me get back."

"Who am I to deny our queen?" The Blueblood elder glances toward Serena, now perched on the corner of the wooden table across from me.

"What—"

"You must know by now." She gives her a meaningful look. "Tell

487

me, girl, do you hear voices in the presence of magical objects? Do they speak to you? Do you hear the whispers of the trees? Do you feel the forests bending to you? What do they say?"

Serena's face falls. She goes speechless.

"We've waited a long time for you."

"That…I think you're mistaken. I'm not a queen."

"Ask your dragon if you have trouble trusting this old crone."

"It's not like that—" Serena starts, but the Matron spares her, smiling knowingly.

"All in good time, Blackblood." With a hearty pat on Serena's shoulder, she takes her leave.

"Do you believe me now?" I ask, leaning my elbows against my knees. Serena glances at me, pushing back her thick mass of hair.

"I would prefer to remain in denial as long as possible. Blackblood—Dragon Rider—was one thing. Queen is another entirely." She blows out a long breath, sauntering toward the door with the vial the Matron left for me. "I'm gonna draw you a bath."

"You know, I don't need you fussing over me like this," I call out to her. "I'm not an invalid," I finish as she reappears around the corner.

"I didn't say you were. Besides, maybe I like fussing over you." She picks up the salve and eyes me.

"What are you doing?"

"Take off your pants."

I nearly choke.

"She said to apply this to the lower extremities."

"Yeah—I know what she said. I can do it."

"You can't even bend to lace your boots up right now. I can tell you're in pain. Just let me help you."

Bad idea. I exhale through my nose. "Serena."

"Zadyn."

She cocks her hip, her lavender eyes piercing a hole right through my chest. I know there's no winning this fight, so I sigh, tossing my hands up.

She slips her arms beneath me and hauls me up with a quiet grunt. I drape my arms over her shoulders, trying like hell not to breathe in the intoxicating fragrance lingering in her hair. Her fingers brush against my navel, and I suck in a sharp breath.

"Are you okay?"

"Your hands are fucking freezing."

Her giggle vibrates against my chest. "I'm almost done."

She hooks her fingers over my waistband and pushes my pants down. My face is buried in that hair, so close to the pulse crashing against the tide of her perfect skin.

"Okay, I'm going to sit you down."

We stumble back, slamming into the chair, her arms still tangled around me. Her mouth lingers so close to mine, but then she pulls back and sinks onto her knees.

She's on her *knees.*

In front of me. And I am sans pants. Of all the ways I've imagined this playing out, this one did *not* make the list.

Her fingers dip into the salve, and she begins to slather it over my legs, starting at my feet and working her way up to my calves. I clutch the wooden armrests hard enough to snap them clean off. The feel of her fingers kneading my numb muscles, slowly working life back into them…It takes everything in me to hold myself back.

Her hands glide up to my thighs, and I hiss.

"Sorry," she mumbles.

"Why are you sorry?"

"I feel like you're in pain. Am I hurting you?"

I tip my head back and laugh. "No, I'm not in pain. I'm trying to focus."

"On what?"

"On anything but your hands on me."

Her mouth forms a little "O" shape as her hands still.

"Do you—do you want me to stop?"

Does she not know what she's doing to me? The way she's teasing me? Tempting me?

"Not really. It's working."

And it is. I feel more sensation in my lower extremities than I care to right now.

"Oh. Good."

She resumes working the salve into my quads, and I have to channel all of my concentration elsewhere. I try to think of the most disgusting things I can, conjure the most grotesque images, but none of it can chase away the need building within me.

Her palms shift higher, disappearing beneath the hem of my undershorts. Her pinky nail grazes my hip, and my hand shoots out to grip her wrist.

"You don't have to go any higher." I swallow. "I have feeling from the hips up."

Her touch disappears, and I can breathe again. Then, using my knees for leverage, she pushes to her feet, her hands still gleaming with the salve.

"You have feeling here?" She presses them against my bare chest.

I nod. "Yes."

Her hands glide outward, smoothing the tight muscles until she reaches the top of my biceps. It feels so fucking good.

"Here?"

Gods, yes. I nod again.

Then she drags her nails down the insides of my arms, and my eyes nearly roll back in my head. She lifts my hand, her slick fingers slipping through mine.

"And here?" A wicked look shadows her eyes, stirring something primal in me.

I nod a third time, words evading me as she lays my hand at the base of her neck and slides her knee between my legs to rest on the edge of the seat. She leans in.

I'm dreaming. I have to be.

"And what about here?" Her thumb brushes over my mouth, pulling at my bottom lip.

And then I can't stop it.

I can't stop myself from touching her, from gripping her hips and bringing her closer. From taking her thumb in my mouth and tasting her skin. From sucking on it, letting my tongue swirl and my teeth nip as she watches me fucking crumble for her.

I release it with a pop and tug her forward, scooping her legs onto the seat to straddle me. That little smile finally blooms as she settles her weight down over the aching bulge beneath my shorts.

Fuck, that smile.

All I can think about is her on top of me. And I'm so tired of resisting.

My hands glide over the curve of her ass as I gaze up at her with hooded eyes. Her hips curl against me. The need within us both outweighs any sanity, any reason as she starts to move on me, as my palms guide her back and forth in a way that is completely maddening, in a way I want never to end. Her fingers thread through my hair. She brings her forehead to mine. Her cheeks are flushing deeper by the second, her breaths growing more and more uneven. She tugs on my hair now as she writhes against me faster and harder until we're both whimpering, about to speed right past the point of no return. Because in about three seconds, I'm ripping the clothes from her body and fucking her right here on this chair.

"You should really lock your door if you plan on getting down and dirty."

It's like a record screeching to a halt as Kai ambles in like he owns the place.

"Kai! What the fuck," I growl. Serena's head whips around, her hair smacking me in the face.

"Ever heard of knocking?" She scrambles off me, and I bite back a frustrated groan, attempting to cover my lap.

"I'm familiar with the practice, but I don't really believe in it. Mar sent me to see if you needed help getting Zadyn into the bath. But clearly my presence is completely superfluous. So I'll just be on my way. Carry on. Oh, and Zadyn—" He turns back, offering me a golf clap and says, "Well done, my friend."

I rip my shirt off the armrest and chuck it at him. He scurries away like the deviant little sprite he is.

Serena looks back at me and laughs, covering her mouth in the cutest way. She picks up the salve and screws the lid on. "What the hell is in this stuff?"

I stretch my legs. I definitely have more feeling than I did before. I'm sure I'll have more once the blood pooling in my dick decides to redistribute to the rest of my body.

"Would you hand me that?"

She passes me the walking stick the Matron dropped off. I push to my feet, taking a tentative step toward the bathroom.

"Zadyn, that's amazing!" she exclaims.

I take another step. The third step is a little tougher, so I pause to gather my strength. Serena steps in to help.

"I'm okay."

"I was just going to help you into the bath."

"That's probably not a good idea right now." My eyes helplessly trek over her body.

"That's on brand for us, isn't it?" she flirts.

I laugh, shaking my head, relishing the word "us" rolling off her tongue.

"I'm okay," I insist, nodding toward the door.

She looks torn. "I'm going to grab Kai or Dover. Just in case you need help."

I roll my eyes. "Fine."

"I—" She stares at me for a beat longer, nodding awkwardly. "Yeah. Okay."

Then she ducks out of the cabin, face still adorably flushed.

Yes. Bad idea is definitely our brand.

But fuck it.

I'm tired of caring.

8 9

SERENA

5 DAYS

What the fuck was that?

Once again, I have thrown myself at Zadyn like some hormone-crazed teenager. I have no idea what's gotten into me. I just couldn't stop myself from pushing him. From pressing those buttons and watching him give himself over to this thing between us.

It's addicting—driving him to the very brink and watching his restraint stretch to the point of snapping.

I press my back against the cabin door and squint up at the afternoon sun.

I can no longer outrun the fact that things are different. That *I* feel differently toward him.

Something changed ever since he opened his eyes. Since I followed that thread inside of me that binds us and saw that he and I are embedded in each other's souls. I saw our bond as clear as if it were a tangible thing. A braided chord of liquid starlight that was so painfully bright to behold. It glows inside us, the same exact shade, the same luminosity.

Which is why I can't lie to him. If what Margot said is true—it would change everything between us. And that would break my heart.

493

So I can't involve him. Not until I figure out this mess on my own.

"That was fast," Kai cracks, sidling up to me. I shoot him a glare.

"You're hilarious."

"I know."

"Will you go in there? Make sure he doesn't fall or anything?"

"Listen to you, like a fussy little mother."

"Kai."

"I'm going, I'm going."

I head toward the large hut in the center of the camp, where Mar and a few other witches are preparing dinner for the clan. They bow when they see me—which I immediately shut down. Their reverence sours, however, when they witness my tragic lack of domestic flair in the kitchen. I take their orders, grateful for the distraction from Zadyn.

He's already walking better by the time he and Kai step through the door. His color has improved so much, and he's barely giving his full weight to the cane. Our eyes link as he sits down at the long table across from me. I feel a little surge of nerves in my stomach.

His hair is still wet, turning the caramel strands a shade darker. He pushes it back, looking like a fucking Abercrombie & Fitch model. A single droplet slides down his neck, and I have to physically fight the urge to lick it up.

Holy shit, what is wrong with me?

He must notice my unabashed gawking because he gives me a funny look and asks, "Are you okay?"

To which I reply, not *yes*. Not *no*. But (drumroll)…

"Thank you."

Thank you? Fucking idiot.

That was embarrassing, Furi grumbles.

Hey. Get out of my head.

Zadyn chuckles, reaching for the glass in front of him. My eyes find his hand, and my mind flashes to earlier.

How those same strong hands pulled me onto his lap. How they dug into my skin. How they rocked my hips just the way he wanted them. I could feel how hard he was beneath me, and that spurred me on further, knowing how badly he wanted me. And from what I could tell, he was—packing.

God damn it, Serena.

What's got you blushing over there? Zadyn's words echo in my mind.

Oh. Nothing. I was definitely not thinking about your dick or anything.

I'm not blushing.

I'm looking at you right now, and I can assure you—you are.

Red as the blood of my enemies, Furi tacks on.

Stop eavesdropping, damn it, I shoot back, redirecting my focus to Zadyn.

Maybe stop looking at me then.

I allow myself a single peek at him. The corner of his mouth curls up into a reckless smirk, flashing that damn dimple.

It can't be helped, I'm afraid.

Un. Fair. He can't say things like that to me! Not when I'm trying to be on my best behavior.

His foot grazes mine under the table—an accident, probably. But that doesn't stop the spike of desire that rockets up my legs. I peer up at him through my lashes, devastated by his beauty.

I'm so torn between falling into this thing between us that is so clearly inevitable and fighting to keep my head above water. But he is wearing me down, and it's only a matter of time before I go under.

I slam the door to my mind shut, worried that given one more second, he'll be able to hear my thoughts as if I'd screamed them at him. For a moment, he looks hurt—confused.

This hot and cold act must be giving him whiplash, and if I could control it, I would. But it's hard to think clearly around him. Shutting him out is for his own good until I know how to navigate this.

I try to participate in conversation to distract myself. But I can feel Zadyn nudging from the other side of that door.

He wants me to let him in. He's assured me time and again that he knows me—the darkest parts and the lightest—and that he isn't afraid. And that nothing I could do—even shoving a dagger through his heart —would break the bond between us.

He will always love me. Which makes this all the more difficult.

I shove to my feet, earning curious looks from our friends.

"I'm full," I sputter. "I think I'll just head back to the cabin."

"Me too." I lock eyes with Zadyn, and my heart sinks. Grabbing the cane, he pushes himself to stand. "I'm kind of tired."

Kai blows on his soup, barely masking the evil smirk on his face as we exit the hut together. The silence as we make our way back is electric—full of hesitation and secret hope.

"Are you actually full? You had two bites," he finally says.

I turn to him. "No. Are you actually tired?"

"No." A small smile works its way over his mouth. "Why the excuse?"

"I just needed some air."

Honest enough.

"You're doing it again." I glance over at him. He taps his head. "Blocking me out. Are you acting weird because of what happened earlier?"

"I'm not acting weird."

"Yes, you are. You'll barely look at me." He pauses. "I didn't mean for things to take a turn like that."

"You didn't—I was the one who started it. Honestly, if Kai hadn't interrupted...I don't know that we would have stopped." He looks relieved, but I continue, "I just don't want anyone to get hurt."

"You mean me."

I say nothing.

Exhaling, he says, "Look, Serena, I don't care anymore. I want you. And I am so fucking tired of resisting you."

"Zadyn—"

He shakes his head and softens his voice. "Just let me finish. I'm tired of sweeping this under the rug for the sake of comfort. I don't know what you want, but you are all I think about. Even in my sleep, I am constantly searching for you. I can't escape you, and honestly, I don't want to. If you just want this to be physical, then fine. I will take whatever part of you I can get."

"I don't," I answer truthfully. "But right now that might be all I'm capable of giving you, and that isn't fair."

"Like I said—too tired to care."

"Trust me when I say I have my reasons for holding back."

"Then tell me."

I shake my head. "I—I can't."

Frustration flashes in his stare. "See, this is the shit I can't deal with —you constantly shutting me out."

"Zadyn, please—"

"Don't you understand that there is nothing you could tell me that would change the way I feel about you? Literally nothing. So why the secrets? Haven't I always been honest with you?"

My defenses shoot up. "You want to talk about honesty? Where was the honesty my entire life? Less than six months ago, I didn't even know your real name—didn't even know your real face!"

"That is completely different—"

"It is not. Lying is lying."

"Omitting."

"Semantics."

"I had a duty to protect you."

"And that meant you couldn't be *honest* with me?"

"You're trying to turn this around to avoid what's actually happening here."

"I'm curious, Zadyn," I steamroll over him, "where were you when I needed you? Where was Annie? After my dad died, after Jack—I needed my friend. And you just fucking ditched me without so much as a postcard."

He bolts forward, face twisted in rage, and drops his voice into a lethal whisper. "You have no idea how hard it was to walk away from you like that."

"Then why do it?"

"Because I crossed a line! I crossed a line with you. I was falling in love with you, Serena, and I was in over my head. I should never have gotten that close. I had to step back. And even when I did, I was always just out of sight. I never left you. Not really."

"Well, could have fooled me."

His eyes scrunch as he tries to dig past my tough act. "Why are you bringing this up now?"

"Maybe I don't want to get left again."

"So now this is a trust thing? You don't trust that I'll stick around? I would die for you, and you know it. I *did* die for you. And I'm still fucking here, so if you don't want this then fine, but don't insult me by lying to my face." He turns to leave.

"I know you would die for me, Zadyn! And this may come as a shock to you, but it doesn't make me grateful, it makes me pissed off and terrified." I groan, running my fingers through my hair. "Please. I don't want to fight with you."

He looks back in my direction. "Then stop pushing me away. What are you so afraid of?"

It's something in his eyes—so wide and vulnerable—that cracks my heart open. And my guts spill out.

"I'm afraid that I will love you so much it will consume me. I'm afraid that I will lose you again, and I won't be able to cope. I have been trying for so long to pretend I don't feel something more for you because I was worried I would ruin everything between us. I'm afraid of how connected we are, that sometimes I don't know where I end and you begin."

"Serena—" he starts, but I can't shut up.

"But mostly I'm afraid you'll never look at me the way you are now after I tell you what I need to tell you."

He pauses, concern drawing his brows together.

Unable to stop myself, I let the words that have been slowly eating away at my soul—Margot's words—pour out of me.

ZADYN STARES at me from the bed, wearing the world's best poker face.

He leans forward, propping his elbows on his knees, and drags his fingers through his hair. I chew on my nail from across the room, desperate to interpret his expression.

"You have to tell me what you're thinking," I say.

A long sigh empties from his chest. "I'd love to say I don't believe it, but…."

I swallow, nodding. "When you died—when I went in after you—I saw what we are as clear as if it were written on that wall. And I'm guessing you already knew."

His eyes find mine. "Yes, I did."

"That's why you can read my mind, isn't it?" I ask. "Why I can read yours."

"Yes."

I don't breathe. He waits, his stare locking me in place.

"Why did you lie to me before?" I whisper. "If you already knew, why not tell me?"

"I don't know, maybe because I didn't know if you felt a modicum of what I feel for you, and that is fucking terrifying." He pauses, dragging his hand down his face. "Because the last time something happened between us, it just seemed like you were looking for a distraction and I was the nearest option."

"Do you really think I would lead you on if I didn't feel the same? That I would hurt you like that?"

"You're the only one who can," he says, tossing me a desolate look. "It would be so easy. You could crush me."

"Your faith in me is truly inspiring." I rip my boots off and toss them aside.

He groans in frustration. "I'm just trying to keep up here. This is a lot to take in."

"Look, I'm sorry I didn't tell you what Margot said sooner. I just—I didn't know how. And I was so afraid that if I did…your feelings for me would change."

"That's what you were worried about? That I would change my mind once you told me?" He pushes to his feet.

"I wouldn't blame you if you did. You made it clear that you want me—all of me."

"Of course I do, Serena. But I would rather have some small part of you than nothing at all because that is how badly I *need* you."

I feel his words deep in my knees.

"Zadyn, you deserve so much more than—"

"Listen to me." He takes a few slow steps toward me, leaving the cane resting against the nightstand. "We deserve each other. We deserve to be happy."

"And what if I can't make you happy? What if I let you down?"

What if I find a way to ruin this?

"There is no world in which being with you doesn't make me the happiest I've ever been." His words are sincere and heartbreakingly honest, melting away my resistance. "Just answer me one question. Do you want me?"

I let my gaze drag over the map of his face—the bronzed skin, the hollow of his cheeks, the sharp curve of his jaw, the caramel hair shadowing those earthy, depthless eyes.

Want doesn't begin to cover it.

I give him a nearly imperceptible nod.

"Then the rest we can figure out in time."

"And what if there is no time? Two weeks is almost up. What if this is the worst idea in the world?"

His voice is so confident, so sure, that I almost believe it. "We will have time. Because I will make sure of it. And like you said—on brand."

I bite my lip, contemplating.

"You can't keep looking at me like that if your answer is no."

"I'm not looking at you like anything."

"Serena." He gives me a doubtful look, crossing his arms over his broad chest and sweeping dark promise into his voice. "You're looking at me like you want me to bend you over that chair and fuck you stupid."*

My jaw hits the ground.

Actually, that does sound pretty good.

---

* Cue: *River* by Bishop Briggs

He takes another slow step toward me.

"What's it going to be?" His hand slides into my hair, tipping my face up to his. "Because I can't go much longer without tasting you."

Heat slashes across my cheeks and pools in my belly. I pull him closer, the need for him growing painful.

"Neither can I—"

The words are barely out of my mouth before he slams me back into the wall, pinning me with his hips. He seems to have no trouble standing now with his body pressed against mine—his muscled arms caging me in, eyes drinking me in with ravenous thirst. His nearness chases away every thought, every worry, and my resistance withers away like leaves in a snowstorm. His eyes drift closed, and his mouth sinks into mine.

Holy shit.

Zadyn *knows* how to kiss. I mean really kiss. The kind of weak-kneed, jelly-legged, make you faint kind of kiss you only read about in books. If I wasn't sandwiched between him and the wall, I'd be a puddle at his feet. I don't know where he learned to do that—or how. And frankly, the thought of him practicing on anyone else makes me blind with jealousy.

But right now, he's mine.

He breaks off, his voice a low rumble against my lips. "Is this what you want?"

His words penetrate my skin, striking the very marrow of my bones. I nod, pressing myself against him.

"I need you to be certain. I need to hear you say it, Serena, because what I'm about to do to you—"

"Do it," I dare, my eyes burning into his. "Do it all, Zadyn."

His lips pull back.

I'm not expecting it when he surges forward and sinks his teeth into the side of my neck. A high-pitched sound leaves me. It pinches for no longer than a breath. Past the dull pain, there is a budding euphoria starting in my toes, slowly creeping higher, generating a wildfire within me.

Then all I feel is surrender. It's a marking of territory. A claim.

He lets out a muffled groan, tugging at the roots of my hair, angling my head the way he wants. I arch into him, feeling his fingers dig into my waist, and my only thought is of his handprints. How I want them on me, all over me.

I want everyone to see it. To know who I belong to.

He releases my neck and pulls back to look at me with blown-out pupils. I lean forward and flick my tongue out to clean the small drop of black off his lips.

And then it snaps.

I watch that precious restraint of his shatter like a crystallized wall of ice that I've just taken a steel bat to.

Animal hunger swallows his eyes as he plunges his mouth into mine with wild desperation. Years of pent-up longing. Years I didn't even know he was there—that he *existed*—or that his heart belonged to me, clueless as I was.

We're still mauling each other when he hoists me up and hooks my thighs around his waist. My ass meets the edge of the tall dresser as his arm snakes behind me, sweeping across the surface and sending the contents clattering to the floor.

It's ridiculously hot.

My legs part for him as I grapple with his shirt. "This needs to go."

Hauling it over his head, my fingers glide over the outline of his chest, the tattoo over his heart that signifies our bond. His scar. Even his *skin* feels good—fevered, smooth, and electric.

"So does this," he growls, twisting the hem of my shirt. I slowly tug at the laces down the front, testing his patience. In no mood for games, he gives me a scalding look before ripping it straight down the middle.

My jaw *detaches* from my skull and waddles out of the room.

"It was in my way," he says unapologetically. "Deal with it."

I gape at him for one more second before diving back into his lips.

"I wanted to murder Cece," I gasp between kisses. "I wanted to rip her hair out every time she laid a hand on you."

"I know the feeling," he hums, his teeth scraping across my bottom lip.

God.

I run my hand over the seam of his pants, over the prominent ridge straining against the material.

"Fuck," he rasps, pushing against my palm.

I swirl my tongue around his and with a low, feral noise, he tugs me toward the edge of the dresser. His mouth laves over the slope of my chest as I continue to stroke him. My breathing hitches as his teeth close over my breast, and I feel the echoes of his attention between my legs. I squeeze him through the fabric of his pants, making him hiss. Then he yanks me off the dresser and spins me around to face the mirror behind it. My heavy, lust-filled eyes peer back at me.

"Look at you," he whispers, dragging my hair behind my shoulders. Shaking his head, he marvels at my naked torso in the mirror like I'm some work of art. I watch his hand slide over my throat, his thumb skimming over the twin puncture wounds he left there. He leans in, grazing those sharp canines from my shoulder all the way up to my ear, sending a shiver through me. "You're un-fucking-believable."

I melt beneath his hands, his *mouth*, though his touch isn't tender like it was the first few times we kissed.

It is insistent. Demanding.

His fingers trail lower and lower at a taunting pace until I'm flustered and desperate and practically begging him to just touch me already. His dark chuckle nips at my ear as he finally has mercy on me, ripping free the laces of my pants and slipping inside to feel just how badly I want him.

"Serena." He lets out a soft moan. "Fuck, I knew you'd feel like this."

"How do I feel?"

He buries his face in my hair. "You feel like mine."

Mine.

My heart swells at the word.

His fingers begin to circle me, alternating between light teasing touches, and the perfect amount of pressure to have my hips writhing against him. He touches me like he's done it a million times, like he knows exactly what I want and what I need, coaxing sounds from me I didn't know I could make, awakening something dark and innately feminine and primal.

"Zadyn," I pant, my entire body pulsing in time to his touch.

My nails dig into the muscled arm wrapped around my waist as I urge him to give me more. He utters my name like a prayer, his eyes scouring me in the mirror, watching me unravel as he delivers wave after wave of perfectly balanced pleasure.

"That's it." He sighs. "Use my hand, baby, ride it how you like."

Fuck, Zadyn.

I clutch the back of his neck and tilt my hips backward, driving my ass into his lap as he mutters more deliciously filthy praises in my ear. I grind up and down his hard length, a sense of satisfaction blooming in me when he groans.

"Are you trying to drive me insane?"

I answer with another roll of my hips. "Just making sure you're still awake back there."

His fingers plunge into me in a punishing stroke. "Awake enough for you?"

"Oh my god, Zadyn," I choke.

"I'll let you in on a little secret," he continues, moving his fingers in and out. "You do make me insane. Absolutely feral. Every time I see you, I think about ripping your clothes off and driving into you so hard you scream. I think about you moaning my name. I'd die all over again just to hear it. I want you constantly. I *crave* you."

Those words combined with the way he's touching me nearly send me over the edge. I writhe against him harder, my hands gripping the tops of his thighs.

"But if you don't stop moving like that, I'm going to have to stop what I'm doing. And I really don't want to have to do that."

"Why? It's not fair for me to be having all the fun."

He snickers, his voice nothing more than gravel and ash. "Do you feel that?"

His hips brush against me, allowing me to feel the full extent of his attraction.

Yes.

"I still don't think you understand. I exist for you. You can't imagine the kind of pleasure it brings me to make you feel everything you deserve to feel. To be the one to touch you like this, to take care of you. It's better than fun for me. It's about to become my new addiction."

One hand reaches up, taking my breast and squeezing without restraint.

"You feel what you do to me? How desperate I am for you? Every day of my fucking life—Gods, why do you feel so *good?*"

His hips slam into mine. I bend forward, gripping the edge of the dresser for leverage as I press back against his lap. He lets out a guttural sound as his fist tightens in my hair, and he starts to grind on me, working me faster and deeper with his fingers until my mind starts to fracture. I close my eyes as all the feeling in my body begins to gather in my center, pooling there like it's the only part of me that exists.

Just as I'm about to shatter, he wrenches me upright by my hair.

"Eyes open," he commands, his breaths growing more shallow. "Right here. I want you to see how fucking beautiful you are when you're coming apart for me."

His words send another shot of fire straight to my core. So I watch as he gets me there, watch his wolfish eyes watching me in the mirror, my back arching, my mouth open, my head tipped back, my hand clasping the back of his neck. And at the very peak of that mountain, the blacks of my eyes sharpen into slits.

Holy. Shit.

My legs are shaking as I crane my neck to kiss him. Then we're migrating toward the bed, falling, wrapped around each other. I run my hands down the smooth plane of his chest and abs, smiling at the breathless noise that leaves him. I climb over him, marveling at how gorgeous he is—hair mussed and mouth swollen from my kisses.

He looks fucking edible.

I bend to sweep my tongue up the column of his neck, over his Adam's apple. His scent, stronger here than anywhere else on his body, hits me hard as his blood pools beneath the surface. The fangs in my mouth make themselves more pronounced, suddenly aching to sink into that perfect skin of his.

Are they getting longer?

"I want to taste you," I breathe, surprised at the sudden urge. His brown eyes light up. He sits up, cupping my head, and guides me toward him.

"I don't know how—"

"Just do what feels good," he encourages, running his thumb over my lips.

"What if I hurt you?"

"Hurt me?" He chuckles, dragging me further up his lap so that I'm positioned directly over the generous bulge in his pants.

Dear lord.

"Serena, if you stabbed me right now, I'd probably come."

"Not funny."

He answers by lifting his hips and driving into me through our clothes, which shuts me up *real* fast.

Instinct takes over as I suck his neck into my mouth, marking the spot with a kiss before sinking my fangs in two inches below his ear.

"Oh, fuck. *Serena,*" he cries, his whole body jerking in response. Pride spikes through me, feeling the shiver run down his immaculate body.

Hah. Thanks for the tip, Ceec.

His hands travel up my back with delicious, urgent need. He tastes as good as he smells, somehow sweeter than I expected, mixed with something elemental—like a cool breeze. I can feel his magic opening up to me, tangling with mine. Soon he is shooting through my veins, and I'm soaring. It's not only his magic—it's his innermost thoughts, his sight. I can see myself through his eyes, feel the way he feels about me, the myriad of beautiful emotions he's experiencing right now. I feel love, and I feel loved. It's bursting through me, starting up another tidal wave that I can't fight.

Yes. Fucking yes.

Now I get it. The reason my gums ached in response to Zadyn's bite. It's an intrinsic need to mark. To claim. To consume.

I rip my teeth free, high on the earthy taste of him, and attack his mouth, tackling him back onto the bed. He answers with equal fervor —growling into my mouth, his heart thudding beneath my palms.

I need him—skin to skin—all of him. But when I reach for his pants, he pulls back—one hand smoothing my cheek and the other stilling my wrist.

"Why are you stopping?" I pant. How dare he.

"If I don't stop now, I'm not going to be able to."

My gaze shifts back and forth. "Not seeing the issue there."

He pushes up and whispers in my ear, "The issue, Serena, is that I'm going to need my full strength for the things I want to do to you. So that when this finally happens"—he plants a kiss along my jaw— "when I finally fuck you"—another kiss—"you feel it every time you move. For days and days."

Well, shit. How very dare he indeed.

He brushes a kiss over my knuckles. "And because we've got time."

9 0

SERENA

4 DAYS

I wake up before Zadyn. Which is rare. But I take the time to relish the feeling of his arms around my waist, his breath dusting over my neck, his legs tangled with mine.*

Things between us are irrevocably different. Last night we forged something so unbreakable, so tangible, I feel it even now. Where before there was a string—a tether—there is now a shared heartbeat. Mine synced with his.

I bend to press a kiss to the scar on his chest, the one I gave him, right beneath the marking of our bond.

"Were you watching me sleep?" He blinks, sleep making his voice gravelly and ridiculously sexy.

"No," I lie.

"You little creep," he teases. He brings his mouth toward mine with enough slowness to send my heart into a sprint. But instead of kissing me, he attacks me with a round of tickles. I squeal, wriggling against him. It takes one second for him to restrain me, pinning my wrists above my head with one hand.

And that one second is all it takes for my mind to completely

---

* Cue: *Forward to the Kill* by Sydney Ross Mitchell

508

switch gears. I can sense the shift in his body too. It's amazing to me how he can go from my sweet, protective defender to a fucking animal in the blink of an eye. It's even more amazing that *I'm* the one who does that to him.

He swings his leg over my hips, laying one of those deep, branding kisses on me that erases my own name from my memory. Unable to move, I crane my neck toward him, desperate for more. It takes effort, but I break away, peering up at him with a vulnerability that leaves me painfully exposed.

"I know you said we have time but—" I shake my head, allowing him into my mind. *Anything could happen. We could both die tomorrow.*

That wouldn't stop me from finding you.

I don't want any regrets. I'm ready for this. I'm ready for you, I whisper without words, existing only for his answer.

He studies me for a moment, giving nothing away.

"Please, Zadyn."

He kisses me again. Hard and deep.

Then we're slipping out of our clothes and his warm hands are where I need them, nothing but skin between us. My heart is pounding loud enough for him to hear, but I've never felt more sure about anything.

My nails trace the dip in his back as he leans down, cradling the base of my skull and tipping his forehead to mine. I wrap my legs around him, guiding him toward me until he's filling me up, fitted to me so tightly I can barely breathe. He stretches me to the point of pain, but that sensation is second only to the perfection of our bodies joining together.

It's slow and intense, reaching into something dark in my heart and sparking a candle. I let his eyes anchor me, using them to keep me tethered to the bed, to the ground.

"Gods, you're so perfect. The way you fit in my hands," he marvels, watching himself push into me. "How you feel wrapped around me."

"Zadyn," I beg, lifting my hips for him. His mouth lowers to my jaw, my chest, peppering my skin with kisses. I pull him closer.

He doesn't fuck with his body. He fucks with his entire soul.

And I feel *all* of it.

His hand curls around the base of my neck as he gazes at me with heartbreaking adoration. His kisses turn fervent, hasty, needy—our tongues flicking and swirling, our teeth biting and pulling. And none of it is enough. Because for every piece of him I claim as mine, I want another. I only want more of him.

I flip him onto his back and climb on top, sinking down slow enough to adjust to all of him. His head rears against the pillow, eyes clamping shut as his length fully disappears into me. The groan he unleashes is like a spark, and next thing I know, I'm on fire. I reach for his hand—still poised over my throat.

Tighter, I urge. His eyes open, hesitation lingering there.

"Don't hold back. I want you out of control," I breathe, starting up a rhythm.

His eyes heat. He shoots up to a seated position, one arm wrapping around my waist. The shift has him pressing against my innermost sanctuary. A ragged breath leaves me as his grip on my throat tightens, intensifying every single thing he's making me feel. I struggle for air, but he denies me, wrenching me forward into a brutal kiss. I whimper against his mouth, unable to breathe, riding harder and faster, my nails digging into his shoulders and back, leaving tiny crescent moons behind on his skin. His hips meet mine, measure for measure, demanding I give him more, give him everything.

So I do.

I always believed that the power in any relationship lies with the person who cares the least. And two nights ago, that was me.

Now everything is different. Now I'm afraid. Because now I care so much, it's frightening. And I'm worried that leaves me absolutely powerless—something I promised myself I would never be again.

But it doesn't stop the confession from tumbling out as he drives into me over and over. As he delivers me to the edge of a cliff, and then shoves me over.

"Zadyn, I love you," I breathe through the free fall. "I love you."

91

ZADYN

4 DAYS

"Zadyn, I love you," she cries, her head rearing back. "I love you."

I come so hard I see stars. Literal, actual stars. Bleached spots dance across my vision, bursting like fireworks one after another.

My entire body—my entire soul—empties out to make room for her. I am completely hollowed out as I pulse with the aftershocks of her words, of her body still wrapped around me.

Finally, she knows what I know. What I have known for months. And she isn't afraid. She wants this the same way I do.

I tug her down and kiss her hard enough to bruise. She whimpers, threading her arms around my neck until our naked chests are pressed together, sweat trapped between them.

I've thought about this so many times. Dreamt of it. But nothing could compare to the real thing. Not even my wildest fantasies.

She is…everything.

"You have no idea how long I have waited to hear you say that."

Her answering smile decimates me and then pieces me back together.

511

She loves me. She fucking *loves* me.

Tucking herself beneath my arm, she asks, "When did this start?"

I twine our fingers together and kiss the top of her head. "My feelings for you?"

She nods.

"Honestly, I don't know. You were a baby when I was summoned. My only thought was to protect you and guard you for the longest time. When you got to college and I was posing as Annie, we started spending more time together, and I got to know you on another level—"

"I had wondered about that," she interrupts. "Our entire friendship. If any of it was real."

I pull back to look at her. "All of it was real. Every conversation we had was coming from a place of truth. We *were* friends. And in that time you became more to me than someone I was bound to protect. You became someone I would *choose*. Every single time. Even had my life not been tied to yours. The things we shared, the things you let me see as Annie just made me fall for you twice as hard."

My fingers dust over her cheek.

"You don't know how many times I came close to telling you everything. I didn't want any secrets between us. That's when I knew I was in real trouble. I hated that I had to take your friend away. I was just trying to do what I thought was best for you. You weren't ready at the time, and I knew that."

Her brows pinch together as she peers up at me. "You watched me fall for Jack. And you never said anything."

Yeah, that was rough. But it wasn't like I could go and throw my hat in the ring either. He was her first serious boyfriend, and she had it bad for him right away. I knew it would never work—her place was always here, on Solterre. Still, that didn't make it any easier to watch.

"Who was I to stand in the way of your happiness? I told you before, that's all I want. If that meant watching you fall head over heels for somebody else, as long as he was treating you right, I would have gladly stepped aside."

"I thought that was love," she says, reaching up to run her fingers through my hair. "But *this* is something else entirely. It's like love on steroids."

I laugh, brushing a kiss over her knuckles.

"When we got to Solterre, I watched you blossom. Completely. You coming into your power, owning who you are—I swear, I've never seen anything so beautiful. I hit the ground faster than I could blink," I say. "I am so sorry for lying to you…and for making you feel alone."

"I'm not alone anymore." She smiles this blinding, mind-altering smile that makes me melt, and I know I'm forgiven. "You can spend the next two hundred years making up for it."

"And how do you propose I do that?" I lean down, teasing my lips along her jaw.

Her lavender eyes twinkle. "I think you mentioned something last night. About bending me over a chair?"

I part her mouth with mine just as a loud knock shatters our perfect little bubble.

"Just dropping by to make sure the place is still standing!" Kai calls from outside the cabin. "We'll be at grandmother's house!"

I sigh as she gives me a peck and pulls herself out of my arms.

"We need to get back home soon," she says, sitting up. I can't help but watch, stiffening at the sight of her naked back all over again. I lean across the bed, planting slow kisses along her spine and smirking as she shivers.

"I know."

"Do you think you'll be good enough to travel by tomorrow?" She sighs, her eyes closing as she tips her head to the side, bearing her neck to me. My fingers trail over the rivets of my bite, which have now formed two pearlescent dots on her neck. I could heal them, but I don't. I'm sure as hell going to wear hers proudly.

"Probably. I've got ninety percent of feeling back. But I think the real trouble is going to be leaving this bed when you're sitting there looking like this."

I wrap her hair around my fist and tug her head back. She gasps, and I angle my mouth to hers, cutting off the sound. She kisses me back for one glorious moment before she turns and shoves me off, offering me a dazzling grin. I fall back and lie there for a minute, watching her dress.

Mine.

"Not to sound like the insecure boyfriend, but what's going to happen when we get back and you see Jace?"

"I'm going to strangle him is what's going to happen," she says, pulling a shirt over her head.

"I'm serious, Serena."

She snatches my clothes off the floor and tosses them to me.

"So am I. His idiotic plan is what landed us here in the first place."

"Don't forget, I was in on it too."

"Oh, trust me, I haven't."

I shake my head. "You're going to forgive him."

"I don't have to. Not if I don't want to." She crosses her arms, giving me an indignant look, which shouldn't be the turn-on that it is.

"Stop acting tough."

"What are you worried about? Jace changes nothing that happened here. Besides, it's best if we stay away from each other. For everyone's sake."

She moves around the bed to smooth a hand over my cheek. I catch it, pressing a kiss to the blue-black veins of her wrist. Her mouth twists into a devious smirk.

"So you're like my boyfriend now?"

I stand. "You can call me whatever you damn well want, and I will come running."

"I like the sound of that—you at my beck and call."

"I've always been at your beck and call, you little fiend," I growl, kissing her nose.

"Mmmm. Save the name-calling for later." She reaches around to pat me on the ass and turns toward the door. I catch her by the arm, tugging her back into a slow, lingering kiss. When I open my eyes, hers are still closed.

"Now you can go." I guide her forward, proud of the dazzled look I've left on her face.

"IF YOU'RE GOING to sit there gawking at each other, at least make good use of your hands," the Matron chides. Serena and I look away from each other, blushing.

You heard her, I say. *Stop eye-fucking me.*

A loud laugh bursts from her lips. She claps a hand over her mouth, and I chuckle, shaking my head.

"Sorry. Umm. What is all this?" she asks, sifting through the contents strewn across the floor of the Matron's cottage. Outside the window, the Blueblood witches are carrying woven baskets and bouquets of flowers toward the clearing.

"Preparations for the blood moon," Mar explains, weaving together a string of colorful garland.

"Tonight is a good night for magic. When the moon is eclipsed, magic is at its peak, and the veil between the living and the dead is at its thinnest. We give thanks to the gods tonight. We replenish our land, our magic. We light fires and dance—tell stories."

"It's my favorite tradition." Mar smiles at her grandmother.

"How can we help?" I ask.

"You fine young males can help with the firewood." She points toward the door.

Serena glances up. "I think Zadyn should be taking it easy."

"Nonsense," the Matron scoffs. "If he was good enough to do whatever it was the two of you were doing this morning, then he can sure as hell handle carrying a log or two. I'm certain it's far less rigorous."

Serena turns bright red. The same shade my face probably is right now. But I'm not embarrassed by it. I'm actually fighting a smirk. Dover and Kai snicker, exchanging a knowing look. I stand, laying a hand over my heart.

"I would be *thrilled* to help carry the firewood," I say, hitting the

Matron with as much innocent charm as I can muster. She gives me a sly look and nods toward the door as if to say, *beat it.*

"*I* know what they were doing," Kai mutters to Dover as they step outside. "It involves a beast and two backs."

"Kai!" Serena screeches. I toss her a wink before following after them.

9 2

SERENA

4 DAYS

"Does everyone in this damn camp know?" I hiss as Marideth and I carry our baskets down the path.

I've had at least five Bluebloods eye me up with that *I Know What You Did Last Summer* look—or in our case this morning—as we passed them on the trail.

"Do you want the truth?"

"God, no. I want the sugar-coated candy lie."

Mar slides me a look. "Your scents have mingled."

"That's the lie?"

"No, that's the truth. When two scents mingle, it usually means that some sort of bond was activated. *Consummated*," she adds, wiggling her brows.

"So everyone can *smell* that we've been together?"

She nods. Talk about a scarlett letter.

"Well, please. Don't spare me the gory details."

"I could never repeat such things. I'm a lady."

She lets out a cackle as we reach the clearing. A cluster of young Bluebloods is gathered behind the well, frozen in stillness, wide eyes fixed across the glade. We stop beside them.

"What is it?"

517

One of the girls lifts a trembling finger. We follow her gaze toward Kai, shirtless and sweat-slicked, swinging an axe through the air and bringing it down through the center of a log. The girls gasp as the wood cracks into two perfectly even halves and topples to the grass.

"Oh, that's just Kai," Mar assures them.

He looks up, giving them a polite wave. Another loud gasp and they skitter off in opposite directions, dispersing among the camp.

Mar and I burst into laughter.

"I think you've got some admirers," I call to him.

"What else is new?" Kai sticks the blade of the axe in the chopping block, shielding his eyes from the sun. Zadyn finishes setting down a pile of chopped wood. Dusting off his hands, he walks up to me.

"Hi."

"Hi." I know I'm smiling like an idiot, but I take comfort in the fact that he is too, so at least we look stupid together.

Mar's eyes openly dart between us. "Dear *gods*, you two." She makes a retching sound and spins on her heel to greet her mate.

"I learned something new today," I boast.

"Is that so?" Zadyn takes the basket from my hands and sets it down beside us.

"If I had known that when fae sleep together their scents are a dead giveaway, I would've sprayed some perfume or something."

"If you had done that, I would have made you bathe before you walked out the door and then scented you all over again."

My jaw hits the ground like a goddamn cartoon character.

"Oh, you would have *made* me?"

He nods, deadly serious. "See, there's a reason for everything in this world—in nature. The mingling of scents tells everyone when a female is taken. It's a warning for other males to stay away. And I want every living thing on this earth to know that you...are very much taken."

His fingers slide over my waist. And just like that, I'm fucking drenched. I fight to keep my face neutral as I nod.

"I'm okay with that."

A lopsided grin blooms on his face, turning him even more handsome, and I feel an actual tug on my heart.

I'm given a white dress with blue embroidery to match the other witches. Zadyn and I follow the rising smoke to the clearing where three giant fires light up the dark night. The soft breeze ruffles the vibrant garlands strung from the towering oaks, sending a dusting of colorful petals through the meadow. I smile up at the tiny fae lights suspended around us, twinkling like little fireflies. Overhead hangs the moon, the star of the show, shining so wickedly bright.

Zadyn drops his mouth to my ear, a smile in his voice. "Look at Furi."

I turn to find my dragon sitting on her hind legs toward the edge of the clearing, surrounded by a group of young witches. They toss up flowers, delighting as Furi catches them like grapes in her mouth. She purrs, reveling in the attention.

Mar stands waiting to greet us, a row of flower crowns slung over her arm.

"Welcome to the party." She smirks, plopping one on each of our heads. "This way."

Light music lingers in the air as we weave through the crowd of Bluebloods. A few witches join hands and dance around the fires, singing songs in Ancient Fae, wearing bright smiles and rosy cheeks.

I catch Esther across the clearing, scowling at us over her wine beside a few of the elders and Mar's mother. Calliope's expression shifts when she sees her. She looks like she might come over, but Esther's black nails wrap around her wrist in a warning to stay put. I feel a glimmer of anger as Calliope concedes, turning her back on her daughter.

As someone who's had her fair share of mommy issues, my heart aches for Mar. But I'm relieved to see her focused elsewhere.

We reach Dover and Kai, seated on a wooden bench beside a roaring fire, engrossed in a story being told by the Matron.

"Please don't scare them," Mar groans, slipping into the empty spot beside Dover.

The Matron looks offended. "I would never."

"Your stories are fascinating. I didn't know you were a thumb sucker, Mar." Dover snakes an arm around her waist, giving her an affectionate shake.

The Matron chuckles, patting his leg. "I had to concoct a special ointment to get her to stop."

Kai and Dover break into laughter, smacking each other on the arm.

"If I didn't know any better, I'd think the two of *you* were mates." Marideth crosses her arms, and Kai pulls Dover into a headlock, threatening him with a kissy face.

The same group of Bluebloods from earlier are once again huddled a few feet away, gawking and whispering amongst themselves. Kai twists around as if sensing their eyes on him and flashes them one of those million-dollar smiles.

"Ladies," he regards.

Their jaws spring open, and they bolt, leaving a trail of giggles as they scurry away. Kai turns back toward the fire.

"Was it something I said?"

The Matron waves a hand. "Pay them no mind. Some of them have never seen a male in the flesh."

"What?" I gape.

"Most of our clan went into hiding hundreds of years ago. This pocket world does not permit outsiders. You lot have been the only exception."

"What about husbands and fathers?" Kai asks.

"Sacrifices were made for the greater good. This was the safest choice for everyone. Those witchlings are our youngest. They were in their mother's wombs when we set up camp here. They have never known the outside world."

"I pity those poor fools," Marideth murmurs, staring after them.

"You shouldn't. Life is much simpler in here," the Matron says.

"This isn't life. This is shelter. They'll never know what it is to have their hearts broken and put back together. They'll never have anything to make their joy stand out. They'll never even be kissed."

"Safety doesn't come without a cost."

"But eventually your line will die out," I point out. The Matron nods.

"If things do not change, then yes, I suppose eventually we will. With limited access to red blood, we are weaker than we used to be. We must rely on nights like these to carry us through, and even then we face limits. This place will not hold forever."

"Why do you stay here?" I ask.

The Matron's voice is little more than a whisper, as if aloud, the words will conjure up something truly terrible. "The Seven."

Mar rolls her eyes as Zadyn and I take a seat across from them.

"The Seven?"

"Witch hunters."

The fire hisses, swallowing up the gathered logs and spitting out tiny sparks.

"Urban legend." Mar shakes her head dismissively, prodding the embers.

"The witches they massacred would disagree. How much do you know of your history, Blackblood?" the Matron asks, orange light glinting off the silver streaks in her hair.

"Only what I've read." I swallow, feeling a bit self-conscious. "Ienar created the Blackbloods and then destroyed them."

"Yes. When it became clear that he could no longer control your ancestors, he sought to extinguish their line along with the Blue-bloods, to prevent them from ever turning. He recruited seven of the world's most lethal hunters, and as a reward for their devotion, he bestowed each of their bloodlines with a drop of his power to pass through the generations. In exchange for a promise—that they would use their immortal lives and gifts to hunt down every Blue and Black-blood witch on this earth and destroy them."

Ice pricks the back of my neck.

"Our ancestors were hunted—tortured to gruesome extents and scattered so that their souls could not pass through the After and find eternal rest. They are the reason we remain here, between the folds of the outside world, outside of time and space. We hide to survive.

"After the Blackbloods were killed, our kind scattered. Tried to remain unseen. And for a time we were successful. But two hundred years ago, the killings began to resurge. We believed a new generation of the Seven to be behind it. So the elders convened, and this place was born. It was decided that any and all Blueblood witches seeking asylum would be welcome here, on the condition that in order to leave, their magic be relinquished. Magic is easily traceable, and this camp was meant to function as a sanctuary. Most covens decided to join us here. They left behind their families, their spouses, their mates in hopes of protecting them. But some chose to stay behind in the outside world and take their safety into their own hands."

"Your mother?" I turn to Zadyn.

"She chose to risk it. She refused to leave my father behind."

"So even after Ienar died, they continued to hunt Blues?" I ask, glancing between the Matron and Mar. "Are they still out there?"

"No one has seen or heard from them in over a century." Mar's silver eyes link with mine. "Who knows if they're still around."

"Some say that Ienar isn't truly gone," the Matron says. That cold fear begins to trickle down my spine and fold me into its claws.

"That's what the elders believe, at least," Mar clarifies.

I nod toward the Matron. "Is that what *you* believe?"

She heaves a loud sigh, directing her pale gaze toward the flames. "I have accepted that we may never know. And if we don't, then I take that as a good sign."

A thousand thoughts skid across my mind. "But Furi destroyed him. She killed him the day the Blackbloods fell."

"You will learn, girl, that just because something is killed does not mean it is dead." Her eyes fall on Zadyn, and my throat tightens. Sensing my concern, he slides closer on the bench, pulling me into his side.

The Matron studies him for a moment, angling her head. "What did you say your mother's name was, boy?"

The sound of excited squeals severs our conversation, drawing our gazes skyward. I glance around at the Bluebloods, gasping and pointing up at the parting clouds. Mar loops her arm through her grandmother's, leading her toward the crowd at the center of the clearing.

"Come on, I think it's starting." Zadyn slips his hand into mine and helps me off the bench.

"Where are we going?"

"I want to show you something."

The twinkling lights of the camp grow farther away as Zadyn tows me through the woods.

"I'm not so sure a hike is the best thing for you right now," I remind him, but he waves a hand, dismissing me.

Cicadas sing overhead as we duck beneath the moon-dipped trees. We help each other down a few boulders until we reach a long stretch of rock that ends in a steep drop. Stopping at the edge, we gaze across the chasm to the gentle waterfall on the other side.

"How did you even find this?" I ask over the calm rush of water.

"The guys and I went exploring earlier. Look," Zadyn takes my shoulders and steers my gaze to the sky. "It's so much better without the lights from the camp."

A shadow begins to creep over the moon's pearly face, bathing it in a warm red tone. We sprawl out on our backs and watch as it begins to turn a vibrant, bloody crimson.

A loud laugh bursts from me before I can contain it. Zadyn's head tips toward me. Probably out of deep concern for my mental health.

"This is crazy," I say.

"What is?"

"This world. Everything. Everything from the moment I arrived here has been too unbelievable. I'm still half-convinced that this is a fever dream and one of these days I'm going to wake up in my one-bedroom apartment to a mountain of debt."

"It does feel like a dream." He threads our fingers, planting our joined hands over his chest. And I get the impression he's not talking about the same thing I am. "But this is real."

His eyes rake over my face.

"What?" I beam at him.

"I just love seeing this world through your eyes."

I roll onto my side to plant a slow, lingering kiss on his lips. Which leads to another. And then another.

And as bad as things are, as bleak as they might get in the next few days, one thing is certain. Zadyn is my guiding light. And if anyone is going to get me through this, it will be him.

I don't know what time it is when we stop, but I know that we've missed most of the eclipse.

And I couldn't care less.

We've got more than enough magic right here.

93

SERENA

3 DAYS

"If we limit our stops, we should make it back in time for the coronation," Zadyn says as we head toward the antsy purple giant nestled inside the forest.

From the corner of my eye, I spot the Blueblood witchlings ogling Kai for a third time. Only now, they look sad. Kai glances over his shoulder as the huddle spits out a witch from the center. She stumbles and locks up as if she's just been tossed out to the wolves—blue eyes wide and terrified as Kai's gaze lands on her.

"I'll catch up," he mutters.

None of us moves. We can't help but watch as he walks up to the girl, who has now certainly stopped breathing.

He tucks a rogue strand of blonde hair behind her pointed ear and leans in. I don't know what he whispers to her, but her entire face transforms into something bright and beautiful as he bends to plant a kiss on her cheek. Tipping her chin up a degree higher, he stuffs his hands into his pockets and saunters back to us, smirking down at his own footsteps.

"You know you just made that witch's life right?" I ask, watching her friends swarm her with a rush of excited squeals.

525

"I know." Kai's tone holds no arrogance as he waves at them one last time.

They shouldn't have to live this way. They shouldn't have to hide. To be confined to this place, deprived of adventure, love, life. They shouldn't have to choose between their homes, their magic, and the outside world.

It isn't fair.

"Marideth?" We turn to see Calliope jogging toward us. She stops before her daughter. "A word before you go?"

Mar's feet remain planted, Dover quietly snarling beside her. Calliope's stern mask softens a fraction. "Please."

Mar waits one more moment before stepping away with her.

I reach up to pat Furi's side, and her tail goes wild, its spikes kicking up dirt as it thumps against the ground.

"I've never seen one in the flesh," the Matron murmurs, awe coloring her voice. She peers up at Furi, whose leg alone is twice her size. Furi's head swings down, her green eyes slowly blinking, as if bestowing her gratitude on the Matron for her help.

"She likes you," I say to her. "And she's usually a pretty harsh judge of character, so that's quite the compliment."

The Matron offers me a proud smile and lays a crinkled hand against Furi's leg.

"I don't know how to repay you for what you've done. For giving him back to me." My eyes slide to Zadyn, hauling himself up Furi's spikes to settle into the saddle. The Matron turns to face me.

"As I said, it was an honor to serve my queen." Her head dips in reverence before she moves to turn away. I rush to stop her.

"Can I ask you something?" She waits with patient eyes. "If it seemed like the entire world was shouting at you—telling you to do something you know in your heart can't be right—telling you *not* to do something, but you know you must, what would you do?"

"Nature is rarely ever wrong, dear girl. But then again, hearts are never misleading." She takes hold of my shoulders and leans in. Dropping her voice to a whisper, she says, "I think you know deep down that the harder you run from your fate, the faster it catches up to you.

You have no reason to shy from it. Turn and face yourself. Face the world that needs you to make it a better place."

She pulls back, her bony fingers squeezing my arms one last time before releasing me.

My mind flits back to those witchlings. I think of them—think of Mar—having to choose between their homes and their lives. And it makes me want to fight for them.

To fight for those who can't fight for themselves.

Suddenly, this role I never asked for, the one I have resisted and avoided, feels like an honor. And even though it scares me more than anything has in my entire life, I feel overcome with gratitude. Acceptance. Determination.

One day, I will fix this. I will make this world safe for them. Because I don't think anyone else will.

Or can, a small voice whispers in my head.

"Well, child," the Matron says as Mar makes her way back to us, "it would seem this is goodbye."

She holds my friend at arm's length, staring up at her with pride.

"I promise to stay away this time." Mar tries to smile, but I catch the wobble of her bottom lip. She throws herself into her grandmother's arms and holds fast.

"If we never meet again in this life, I will assume you are well and happy." The Matron's eyes close, savoring their embrace. "One last thing."

She pulls back and slips a hand into the pocket of her skirt. "That *thing* you showed up here wearing was a monstrosity. *This* was given to me by your grandsire, gods rest his soul."

Taking Mar's hand, she places a thick silver band inlaid with a round sapphire on her middle finger.

"Grandmother, I can't accept this—"

The Matron leans in and kisses her on both cheeks. Then she sweeps her thumb over Marideth's forehead, murmuring something under her breath.

Mar gasps, clapping a hand to her mouth as her eyes fill with tears.

"I fear you'll need it one day soon."

"Thank you." She throws her arms around her grandmother's neck, nearly knocking her small frame over. "Thank you."

"What was that?" I ask when Mar finally drags herself away.

"My magic." She breaks into a grin as tears glide down her ivory cheeks. "She gave it all back."

<h1 style="text-align:center">94
JACE</h1>

3 DAYS

My door blasts open, ricocheting off the marble wall. Serena stalks in and pins me against the mantel, one arm barred against my chest and a knife poised to my throat.

I could disarm her with my eyes closed and my hands bound. But I don't.

Instead, I wait, paralyzed by the heat of her touch. Desperate for one more second of her body pressed against mine—to breathe her in and get drunk off her scent.

So I allow it. I allow her to hold me there, eyes sharp as the dagger pressed to my neck.

"You know killing kings usually results in decapitation."

She shrugs, indifferent. "King *regent*. And not for much longer."

"Until Sorscha and Eaton's coronation."

"I'll take my chances."

"How do you intend to torment me without your head?"

"I'll think of something."

"I don't doubt it."

"Don't do that. Do *not* flirt with me," she snaps.

"I would never."

"Give me one reason I shouldn't drive this straight through your neck."

"I can't. You're going to do whatever you want to anyway, so I think I'll save my breath. But before you do—" I take her balled fist and place it at my nape, holding it there. "Just remember what this feels like. Remember who taught you how to hold a dagger, how to throw one. How to ruin someone with just a flick of your wrist."

The air around us is electric. Charged with adrenaline and desire and lines just begging to be crossed.

"I could ruin you with far less than that," she threatens.

"You already have."

I catch a rare flash of surprise in her stare. It's gone before I can blink.

"There," I whisper, unable to keep from looking at her lips. "Ready to die."

Her eyes flicker, some of the bloodlust receding. With a growl, she lowers the blade.

"You deceived me." Each clipped word is packed with icy venom.

"A necessary evil."

"Zadyn *died!*"

"I'm assuming he lived since you haven't acted on the urge to kill me yet."

"That is not the point. You're lucky I was able to bring him back. And don't think it didn't cost me." She shoves away from me, and I instantly mourn the loss of her nearness. "He never should have died in the first place. But thanks to you, he did. And whatever idiotic feelings I had for you died with him."

"Did they?" I reach for her wrist and angle her dagger back to my neck. "Then you should have no problem doing what you stormed in here to do."

The flames swell behind me. Orange and blue light flares across her face, and that look in her eye...

She *is* fire. She is heat. She is strength and blood and tears. Fury and grief. And sometimes it's like looking in a mirror.

"Just stop." She breaks away again, dropping the knife and holding up her hands. "Don't touch me."

My stomach churns.

"What you did—locking me up...I never in a million years expected you to do something like that. To banish me to the sidelines as people died out there. *Because* of me. As *you* went to battle. As Zadyn put himself at risk with that insane plan."

She takes a step closer, her glare eating through me. "If he had stayed dead, it would have been your fault."

"I was doing what I thought was best. We both were. He agreed that you needed to be stopped."

"Doing what was best? Best for who?!"

"For me!" I pound my chest, unable to contain the shout. Bounding off the wall, I back her up a step.

"Is that the answer you're looking for? Fine, then. I did it for myself. Because you are everything to me, and I will always be selfish when it comes to you. I don't care who has to die as long as in the end, you and I are still standing. I don't care if you hate me—at least you're alive to do it. You're here, in front of me, breathing. You can blame me, vilify me, yell at me all you want, but you know what? I am not sorry for locking you up. I love you beyond comprehension, beyond sanity—and I would do it again in a heartbeat, despite the cost—"

Her hand comes up to slap me across the face. The bite of her handprint clings to my skin as her chest heaves.

"Don't you *ever* say you love me. You don't. What you love is control. Even asking me to marry you. You didn't ask out of love, you asked out of fear. Because you didn't want to lose me. I am"—her voice trembles as tears brim in her wild eyes—"*so* disappointed in you. And I will never. EVER. Forgive you."*

That stings worse than a thousand of her hardest slaps.

And instead of falling on my knees and apologizing, instead of groveling and begging for the mercy of her forgiveness, instead of confessing all my deepest regrets and giving her the truth she deserves

---

* Cue: *you broke me* first by Tate McRae

—I double down, my face hardening as I draw my shoulders back and adopt that removed front I'm so well known for.

"Go on and hate me then. I don't really care. It will be better for both of us in the long run if you do."

"I wholeheartedly agree." Her lavender eyes sparkle with resentment as she backs away and reaches for the door.

It hasn't yet slammed before I grab the glass of whiskey off the table and hurl it against the wall to shatter into a thousand crystalline shards.

9 5

SERENA

2 DAYS

The last thing I feel like doing the next day is going to train with Jace. I was content to stay in bed, next to Zadyn, and make all kinds of mischief, but *he*, of all people, insisted. Said it was important to "air my grievances" with Jace.

I'm gonna air something, alright.

But there's a pit the size of Rhode Island in my stomach as we make our way to the training ring. Half of me hates him for what he did. The other half hates that I don't really hate him. Not even a little. Maybe not at all.

So here I am, the Julia Stiles to his Heath Ledger. I won't hold my breath for him to buy me a fucking apology Fender.

Zadyn and I pause in the threshold. Jace is already there, warming up, throwing punches into the padded post, the cuts in his muscled arms made even more defined with each artful thrust of his fist. He turns when he hears us.

"I'll see you later." I give Zadyn a slight smile, squeezing his hand. His eyes skirt from me to Jace before he disappears down the hall.

"So what? Are you two together now?" He approaches, a cocky look on his face.

"Maybe."

533

"Did he profess his undying love, and did it just suddenly occur to you that you felt the same?" he asks, his voice bleeding sarcasm.

"None of your business."

He coughs a snide, mocking laugh. "Okay."

Then he pauses, looking me up and down before glancing toward the hall. His nostrils flare, and he takes a menacing step toward me so fast I jump in response. His face pales a few shades, his body going rigid.

"What?"

He leans in closer, and I freeze. He's...smelling me. Then he grabs my hair and wrenches my head to the side, taking in the bite marks Zadyn left on my neck. I wince, shoving against him until he lets me go.

"You fucked him, didn't you?"

Instead of answering, I sink onto the ground to start stretching.

"Serena."

I roll my eyes at the sternness of his tone. As if I owe him any sort of explanation.

"Wasn't this what you wanted? For me to explore my relationship with Zadyn?"

Jace drops to a crouch before me, his voice low. "What I wanted, witch, was for you to get it out of your system."

"Why, so I could run back to you?" I glower at him. "Maybe it's you I need to get out of my system. Not him."

A nasty sneer covers his mouth. "Sounds like you're just looking for an excuse to fuck me."

"I don't plan to ever touch you again after what you did."

"Readjust your plans because we're about to get up close and personal." He pushes to stand and gestures to the empty training ring.

"You know exactly what I mean."

"I also know you don't mean what you say."

"Stop acting like you know me better than I know myself."

"Stop acting like you're a saint. Like you've never done anything questionable to protect the people you care about." His words are pointed. And I know exactly what he's referring to.

"You're never going to let it go, are you?" I shake my head.

"Let what go?"

"Kylian."

He doesn't say anything. He just stares down at me with the same bitterness that reminds me of the ruthless version of him I first met in Derek's throne room.

"It bothers you to no end." He scoffs, turning toward the center of the ring. I shove to my feet, stalking after him. "It's the root of everything that's spoiled between us. You stood there and told me to fuck Zadyn, but *Kylian—*"

He whirls to face me. "The thought of *anyone* else touching you bothers me. It makes me want to do terrible, horrific things even your worst nightmares couldn't contrive. It makes me want to burn this whole fucking world to the ground. But you and him? Together? No, witch, that doesn't bother me. It fucking *eats me alive,*" he says. "It burns me that after *everything*, after all he and his family have taken from me—"

"So this is about you. You and your vendetta against Vod."

"No, it's about the fact that *he*, of all people, got to have you when—"

"When what? When you never will?" I take a step closer, knowing full well the cruelty behind my words. His golden eyes flash, his chest heaving.

I know what the Trioris cost him—his parents, Derek. But I'm more than a piece of collateral in this mess. I'm a person, not a possession to be lost or gained or taken. By anyone.

"I hope that pride of yours keeps you warm at night." I knock his shoulder, brushing past him.

"That's right," he spits. "Push me away. It's what you do best."

"*You* are the one pushing me away, Jace." I turn back to him. "What happened to you? When did you go from being on my side to judging my choices to survive? When are you going to stop damning me for doing what I had to do? You were born a male and raised a fighter. You've never been powerless. Not really. So you don't know what it's like to have all of your power just erased in the blink of an eye. And the only one you have left is your power as a woman. Your body. And so you have to make the choice between your dignity and surviving. You don't know what it's like to bargain with your own flesh. To know that really, despite the blood in my veins, despite the absurd power I've found myself with, I am easily reduced to just a girl. Just a helpless, weak little girl. You have no fucking clue."

When he doesn't say anything, I know I've won. Too bad it doesn't feel like a victory worth celebrating.

It isn't hard to spar with him for the next two hours. Every punch I throw is packed with conviction. Every blast of my power has meaning, has weight.

Once again, Jace has given me a brick wall to shove against. He has pushed me, made me one second faster, one degree stronger.

I would be grateful if I could feel anything but pain when I look at him.

96

ZADYN

1 DAY

"Well, this isn't depressing at all," Kai mumbles, drumming his fingers on the high-backed leather chair.

It's been a quiet night. After dinner, all of us gathered in Sorscha's rooms—all except Jace, who's either been warned by Serena to stay the hell away from her, or he's decided to outcast himself.

I was just as responsible for getting myself killed as he was, but Serena is clinging to her anger like it's the last thing left on this earth. I wonder if that's because without it, there would be nothing standing in their way.

I know she's mine. But I also know that part of her is his. I either have to accept that, as Gnorr said, or walk away. And gods know I'm fully incapable of the latter.

The mood is somber, not even Kai wisecracking like his usual self. Two weeks is up tomorrow, and despite the coronation in the morning, no one seems remotely inclined to celebrate.

"So that's it?" Kai prods. "We're just giving up?"

The room is silent—heads low, spirits lower.

"We're not giving up, Kai," Serena says. "I'm just doing what I have to do."

She tries to smile, but I catch the crack in it. The chink in the armor. And I realize that she is just as scared as the rest of us.

Kai's brow ticks up. "Forgive me for saying so, but that doesn't sound extremely confident."

"I'm not sure what else we can do at this point," Serena answers, her voice filled with quiet regret.

"Anything is better than sitting here sulking." He pushes away from the chair, pacing over to the window. Rain slides down the glass in slow, heavy clumps.

"Zadyn has scoured that library. If there were something to find, he would have found it by now. Right?" She turns to me.

Sighing, I nod. "There was nothing there. I even checked with Gnorr. The deal is binding, short of death."

"So we kill him," Kai concludes. "Before he takes you."

"That would require catching him first."

Serena's head snaps around like a whip. Jace is leaning against the doorframe, arms crossed over his leathers.

"I know you don't want to see me right now, but I might have an idea."

"Pass. Your ideas suck." Serena turns back toward the group, folding her arms over her chest.

"Luckily, I care little for your opinion."

She snorts. "If that ain't the truth."

He gives her a dark look and moves to stand beside us on the settee. "We know he's coming. One way or another. So we set a trap."

"He's not a fucking mouse, Jace," Serena snaps. "He's a king. And a powerful one."

"You think I don't know that?" he retorts. "And what does he want? You. So we dangle the bait and watch him walk right into it."

It's my turn to interrupt. "We're not luring him out with Serena as bait."

"I can shield her. But if you've got a better suggestion, I'm all ears."

"He'll penetrate your shield like that." Kai snaps his fingers. "You don't know the extent of what he can do."

"Not if he's incapacitated. We outnumber him. All we have to do is get him alone."

"You think he's showing up here solo? He's going to have an army with him, Jace. Use your big-boy military brain," Serena goads.

He takes a deep breath, attempting to maintain his composure. "I'm *trying*. To *help* you."

"I don't *want* your help. In fact, I don't even want to see your face."

"Serena," Mar warns.

But she continues, "I don't want your plans, I don't want your help, I don't want *you*—period. So just get out."

He recoils as if she'd slapped him. He's even got the flushed cheeks to go with it. He opens his mouth and then closes it, grappling for words, his eyes a cocktail of misery and pain. Then without so much as a goodbye, he stalks from the room.

Kai blows out a long breath. "Harsh much?"

"It's better this way. Trust me." Serena leans forward, pushing her hands through her hair. "I'm not going to let Kylian get away with this. He is not coming for our home. And I fully intend to be the one to walk away from this fight. But just in case—"

She gets to her feet. Mar holds up a hand to stop her. "No. We are not going there."

"Absolutely not," Sorscha adds, shifting to the edge of her seat.

"Look, if I don't say this now, I might regret it."

Serena's lips curve into a sad smile.

"I used to think that living my life alone was the best way to protect myself. I thought the more you love, the more there is to lose. And I couldn't fathom losing anyone else that mattered to me. I was broken when I came here. Maybe I still am. But I also found strength I didn't know I had. Strength in all of you. Because now there is a reason to fight. I never realized how lonely my life had been, how empty it was, until I met you. Until you showed me that love is *always* worth the risk—worth the pain. So even if this all goes up in flames, you need to know that I don't regret a single moment of the time I've had with you. And I promise I will fight like hell for more of it."

We all just stare. And this girl doesn't think she could be queen?

"Cousin." Sorscha lifts a trembling hand to her mouth, springing out of her seat and throwing her arms around Serena's neck.

"Sorscha." Serena catches her and holds tight. "I need you to trust yourself and know how much you're worth. You're so strong, and brave, and you are going to make an incredible queen—"

"Hush! This is not goodbye. I refuse to allow it." She sniffles, tears leaking down her cheeks.

Serena smiles, planting a kiss on her forehead, which only makes Sorscha sob harder. "Thank you. For being my friend. For being the sister I always wished for."

"We are family," Sorscha manages to get out. "I would do anything for you."

A tear escapes down Serena's cheek. "Ditto."

She deposits the shaking princess into Eaton's arms and turns to embrace the rest of our friends. Even Cece, to whom she sincerely apologizes for breaking her nose.

"I refuse to take part in this ridiculous sob-fest." Mar's steely gaze remains fixed on the opposite wall, fingers locked around her crossed knees.

"I would expect nothing less, but I'm hugging you anyway. Don't worry, you don't have to return the favor." Mar stiffens as Serena bends to wrap her in a hug. "I want you to know I'm going to do everything I can to free those witches. So that they don't have to choose."

Marideth finally looks at her, a sad glimmer in her eyes.

"Be happy." Serena straightens and glances around at everyone. "All of you. No matter what happens."

"It's sounding more and more like you don't intend to be the one to walk away from this fight, savior."

"I promise you, Kai." Serena moves toward him, taking his hands. "I will fight and claw and kill my way back to all of you. If it's the last thing I do."

In their eyes, I see the echoes of their trauma. They forged a bond in Kylian's clutches, their loyalty so deep it's fused into their souls. I can read it as they cling to each other.

Serena looks at our friends like it might be the last time—which has me deeply concerned. But I don't say anything as she reaches for my hand. We've just made it to the door when Kai calls out, "Savior."

She turns.

"Give him hell."

Nodding, she says, "All the hell he deserves."

SERENA'S HEAD nuzzles against my bare chest. I drag the tips of my fingers down her arms, listening to the sound of her breaths.

"Do you still think we're doing the right thing?" she asks.

I hope so. But I don't know. Margot's message to Serena wasn't exactly comforting. Or clear.

"Kylian needs to be stopped. For various reasons." I tilt my head to look down at her. "But that doesn't mean you have to do this. Not if you don't want to."

"But the deal—"

"Fuck the deal, we'll figure something out." I push up to my elbows. "If we have to run until we can find a way to kill him, then you and I will go someplace. I'm not letting you go. Not now. Not ever."

Her lilac eyes blink up at me. "If I leave, he'll kill everyone I know."

"I can't lose you." My voice is no more than a whisper. It's my deepest fear. One that came far too close to becoming a reality the last time Kylian backed her into a corner.

She cranes her neck to peer at me. "Please don't make this harder than it has to be."

"Then stop trying to leave me."

She closes her eyes and sighs.

"Zadyn—" I cut her off with a kiss. She kisses me back for a moment, then breaks away.

Can I tell you something without you trying to convince me not to do this?

No promises.

She rolls her eyes but continues, *I know I'm supposed to be strong like my ancestors. Brave. But I'm scared. I just have this feeling that something bad is about to happen.*

My heart cinches as I drag her forehead to mine. *Then don't go.*

What did I just say? I need you to be objective for two seconds.

You want me to be objective? Fine. What do you think makes someone strong? Brave? It isn't being fearless. It's having fear. It's coming face to face with it and deciding to fight anyway.

So you see why I can't turn and run. I wouldn't be the person you fell in love with if I did.

When will you understand that no matter what you do, I will love you?

I won't be a coward, Zadyn.

I don't care what you are as long as you're alive.

He won't kill me. He wants me too much.

Serena—

"Please," she says out loud. "I just want to spend this night with you. I don't want to talk about Kylian. I just want you. So just be here with me. Okay?"

I rake my fingers through her hair, and she yields to my touch, her eyes closing. This time when we kiss, we don't stop.

97
SERENA

I'm dressed in a ballgown of the deepest ebony.

It's the kind of dress you dream of wearing as a little girl, with a full hoop skirt and elbow-length opera gloves. The kind that begs for twirl after glorious twirl. Little diamonds are woven into the velvet skirt, twinkling like stars each time I shift and they catch the light. The corset is wound so tight it borders on painful.

Beauty and pain. This world to a tee.

And the finishing touch? A silver sash wrapped around my waist and bowed at the back.

Making me a gift. An offering.

Conversation buzzes throughout the packed throne room. My friends surround me, hovering close by, our shared tension bubbling beneath the guise of this happy day.

The fanfare of trumpets sounds, swallowing the chatter of the crowd and commanding every eye toward the entrance. A line of royal guards in sleek black uniforms steps through the door in perfect synchronization, forming two parallel lines on either side of the aisle. At Max's command, they draw their swords with a loud swish, hoisting them into the air to form a tunnel. I catch Jace's eye through the arches, standing with the rest of Derek's small council near the

foot of the dais. A sharpness tugs at my gut, and I force myself to look away.

Sorscha and Eaton appear beneath the green vines snaking up the marble archway, looking resplendent and regal. They are sunshine personified, exuding power and confidence. Together, they make their way down the stretch of silver carpet beneath the gleaming tented swords, matching fur-lined capes dragging behind them.

Ceremonious words are recited on the dais, but they sound muffled and distant, like I'm listening underwater. I watch the figures up there like players on a stage, moving in slow motion. I finally snap out of it when Jace takes the crown of glistening diamonds from its velvet bed and places it on Sorscha's head.

She breaks into a winsome smile.

"Hail Queen Sorscha!" someone shouts. The room echoes the joyful chant.

When it's time for Jace to remove the crown from his own head, he stops in front of Eaton.

As soon as Derek's crown brushes his golden hair, all hell breaks loose.

SHADOWS SWALLOW US UP.

Black so thick it is completely opaque.

Screams surround me—horrified wails—and I know that something is very wrong. I whirl, reaching for Zadyn's hand.

But he's not there. I can't feel him. I can't feel anything at all.

"Zadyn? Zadyn!" Panic slicks my throat as I call his name.

This feels too familiar. Shouting into a crowd of terrified fae. Too far away from the people I love. My mind flashes to Jace.

Fuck. Why was I so awful to him? All my anger, all my resentment, is swiftly erased by the crippling fear of losing him.

Of losing them both.

Hysteria rakes through the crowd, so strong I can taste the fear.

But my shadows whisper to me, longing to mingle with the dark. They are drawn out by the likeness. They want to be friends.

I know who these shadows belong to.

The moment his name forms in my mind, my sight is restored.

The throne room is empty.

Except for me.

And Kylian.

9 8

SERENA

Long legs, sheathed in black pants, sprawl out before me. Kylian lounges on Derek's throne—making a fucking mockery of it. In his hand is Derek's silver and onyx crown.

"What have you done? Where is everyone?"

Eyes made of sea and smoke land on me. "They're fine. For now. I wanted our reunion to be private. Intimate."

He swings his legs onto the ground and stands in one streamlined move, tossing the crown onto the velvet cushion and adjusting the black jacket slung over his broad shoulders. He wears nothing underneath except that ridiculous eight-pack.

I take a step back as he ambles toward me.

"You've been ignoring my missives."

"What missives?"

"The letters I sent you?"

"What letters?"

"Silly of me to think they wouldn't be intercepted." He shakes his head. "Love letters, darling."

I would laugh if I weren't actually terrified.

A dull, distant roar draws my gaze toward the windowed-wall of the throne room. No, not a roar.

546

Boots. Marching in synchronization. And there they all are—the golden soldiers, the Stryga, the black-armored troops of Aegar—meeting with wild fervor on the fields.

My stomach sinks at the possibility of Jace and Zadyn out there. I have to get to them. But he has to die first.

I crouch into a fighting stance. "Don't come any closer."

"Time's up. Let's go home."

"You wasted a trip. I am home."

"When are you going to get it through your pretty little skull? You and I are fated. There are only so many times you can run from me before I tire of this game and catch you."

I blast him with a ball of fire. He waves a hand, blocking it with a swirl of shadows and continuing toward me, a dark smile blooming on his decadent mouth.

"We had a bargain."

"You already breached your terms. You sent your armies a week ago."

"Thank your captain for that. He's the one who struck first." He tsks. "Naughty."

"It doesn't matter. Deal's off, dick."

Sighing, he says, "Let's just skip past the part where you pretend to hate me so we can kiss and make up."

"I do hate you, though. With a burning passion."

He snickers. "I do enjoy the way you show it."

Whore, a nasty voice echoes in the darkest corner of my mind.

"What's that saying? The opposite of love isn't hate, it's indifference? Hating someone takes energy—it takes time and thought. Which means you think of me more often than you care to admit."

"You're delusional. Call off your armies."

"Come home with me."

I hike up my skirt and rip free the dagger sheathed at my thigh. Kylian's eyes sparkle—either at the flash of skin or the idea of a challenge. Probably both.

"So it's to be a fight then?" He makes a show of patting his pockets and cocks his head, fanning his heavy lashes.

"I'm afraid I left my lucky sword at home."

I clutch the blade in one hand and hurl out a wave of fire with the other. Kylian chuckles, shadows sprouting from his body, curling through the air like thick smoke. I swing my blade on reflex, my mind emptying of all Jace's training.

I'm on edge. Flighty. Unfocused.

I grit my teeth and eject a ring of fire around myself, but Kylian flicks his hand, and a wave crashes against it, dousing the flames entirely. When I call that fire again, it refuses to come. It's like my spark has been stolen. I try and try, but only steam rises in the air, and I know it's Kylian's doing.

I reach for my shadows, willing them to buy me some time. I won't get close enough to kill him this way. Without the element of surprise, I'm no match.

You lack control.

I start at his words in my mind.

But he's right. No matter how powerful my blood may be, I have no idea how to use it when it counts. Luck won't be enough this time.

I try anyway.

But when my shadows appear around my ankles, they flow toward Kylian. I try to rein them in, but they mingle with his—embracing like old friends. I stagger back a step.

How is he doing this? They're *my* shadows.

I can show you. The bastard smiles at me and shrugs his shoulders like this is just a harmless game.

Then I feel something sharp inside my head. Like claws sinking into my mind with lethal precision, taking hold of me, eager to shred straight through my consciousness.

I can't move. I can't breathe against the intensity. My head is screaming.

I can show you how to do things no one else could ever teach you. Like how to shatter a mind with barely a thought.

I grind my teeth, groaning beneath the paralyzing pain.

All that beautiful anger—that rage—I can help you control it. Turn it into something magnificent.

"I don't want your fucking help." My voice trembles under the weight of his attack. I grunt, trying to shove back against the riot in my head.

"Fine. I'll play fair. No magic," Kylian says in earnest, waving a hand.

The pain subsides as the razored claws retract. I suck in a loud gasp. He crooks a finger at me, inviting me to strike. When I don't move, he zaps in front of me faster than I can blink.

My reflexes kick in as I latch onto him and plunge my dagger into his side. I feel his flesh part around the knife, feel his hot blood leaking out around my shaking fist. He lets out a cruel laugh, sinking to his knees.

I rip the dagger free, angling it above him to strike again, but he's quicker. His hands fly up, redirecting the blade toward me as he rises to stand.

"Silly witch. That wasn't my heart. But you already knew that, didn't you?"

He backs me up a step. And then two. My arms quake as the stiletto nears my own heart. He smiles, barely exerting himself.

With a wild cry, I finally shove backward, ripping myself loose. I hear something tear, but I can't look away from him to see what. He clasps my dagger as I clamber backward, tripping over my damned hoop skirt.

Heart hammering, I pedal backward on my hands, suddenly overwhelmed. Suddenly helpless.

"Go ahead. Run. I'll even give you a head start to go find your little captain. Or your familiar. I can't quite keep track of your many trysts these days."

Like a coward, I do. Scrambling to my feet, I rush through the empty halls, terrified of what will happen when he finally does catch me, when I'm finally in his clutches. Because I know what I have to do.

And I don't think I can do it.

I careen down the corridor, breath coming in ragged hiccups. I don't know where I'm going, but I don't stop. His footsteps echo in my mind. I can hear that addictive, dark chuckle polluting my thoughts. I can feel his breath on the back of my neck.

I will never outrun him.

Spilling around a corner, my eyes lock on a curtained alcove off to the side of the hall. I stumble behind it, yank the heavy drape closed, and will my thundering heart to slow—to quiet.

"I can smell you, darling," Kylian calls. "Of course, this trail of blood you're leaving isn't doing you any favors."

I glance down, noting the warm sensation trickling down my inner arm. A deep gash peers back at me.

Fuck. I must have cut it trying to break away from him. I'm bleeding all over myself, all over the floor.

My back is pressed against the wall, my hand clamped over my mouth to stifle my heavy breaths.

I jump as the curtain flies back.

"Did you really think you could get away from me? I told you a thousand times—there is nowhere you can go where I will not find you."

And without hesitation, he kisses me. Fire bursts toward the surface of my skin, flaring up at the first touch of his mouth on mine.

I don't get the opportunity to fight him off. Because he's suddenly flying through the air.

Jace is there, a shadow of death, his entire aura shifting into something so innately violent it actually frightens me.

It frightens me more than Kylian ever could.

Zadyn springs forward out of nowhere, clamping blood ore chains around Kylian's wrists before he can react. Jace grips him by the collar and pulls his elbow back, a dagger poised to lodge itself inside that blackened heart.

And that's when it happens.

"Stop!"

My bond squeezes the strangled cry from my throat.

"He's my mate!"

99
SERENA

Jace goes deathly still.

His head angles toward me, one degree at a time.

"What did you just say?"

"He's my mate," I choke, crashing to the ground.

Jace stares at me, frozen, disbelief written all over his face. "No, he's not, he's—"

I witness the exact moment my words sink in. I see the change register in his eyes as they tighten and go cold. His hand goes slack, and Kylian crumples to the floor, gasping for air.

"That can't be true."

My shoulders sag as I shake my head. Jace sets his jaw, his knuckles turning white around the dagger's hilt.

It's hard to breathe, the air around us tight and thin, constricting further with each agonizing second that ticks by.

Does Jace even realize he's the one causing it?

My eyes fill with tears as he comes to stand over me, chest heaving.

"Tell me that this is some sort of sick joke."

A cracked sob bubbles from my lips. "I wish I could."

I reach for his hands like a beggar. And he rips them away—a dark angel with no mercy.

"I don't believe it. I *refuse.*"

"Serena." Zadyn says my name with a tenderness I don't deserve. I can barely meet his gaze.

"I'm sorry, Zadyn. It just—I'm so sorry."

I had prayed against all odds that it wasn't true. What I had been suspecting for weeks now. But what happened when Jace raised that blade to Kylian is undeniable. It was in that moment that I saw the truth of everyone's words. It clicked.

And I am so ashamed.

Kylian himself appears too stunned to remember that he's just been rendered powerless, staring at me as if seeing me for the first time. Like we're strangers. Like he hasn't threatened everyone I love, threatened me.

He doesn't seem afraid. But I'm guessing that's because he knows that even though he can't defend himself with magic, I will. Because of our bond.

Jace lifts his hand and drops his dagger at my feet. It clatters against the tile, the sound shrill and grating. With one last loathing glance, he storms away.

1 0 0

SERENA

TWO WEEKS AGO

Amber eyes inspect me from across the small table. I wait for the door to close behind Zadyn and Mar before turning back to the stranger wearing my mother's face.

"Say what you need to say."

She moves to the beverage cart, picks up a crystal decanter, and pours out two shots of golden brown liquor. Handing one to me, she sits.

"What is this?"

"Does it matter? You'll need it for what I'm about to tell you."

I glower at her before taking the glass and tossing it back.

She sighs, and begins, "The Fates are angry. You have been evading a destiny they took great care in mapping out."

I lean in, my brows slashing together. "Who are the Fates?"

"The weavers of destiny. They have great plans for you, but you must stop running. You must start facing what you are meant for."

"And what is it I'm 'meant for'?"

"When your ancestors died, they cast out their energy to preserve their line with the intention that you would return to finish what they started. That you would be this world's salvation. That you would defend and protect its inhabitants, as they did."

553

"Protect them from what? What are you saying?"

She flips over the first card she placed in front of me. *The Wheel of Fortune.*

"You are the queen this world has waited for."

My stomach turns to lead.

Not this again.

I shake my head as she presses on. "This is what you were made for. To free the witches and restore the balance."

"Free the witches? From what?"

"I am not at liberty to say."

Thanks, that's super helpful.

"Look, I'm not interested in being queen. All I care about is stopping—"

"Something is coming." Her eyes glaze as if looking through me—not at me—into some distant void. "If you hope to face it and live, then you must stop running and accept your birthright."

Her words strike a chord with me.

Something is coming.

Derek had said something similar that day in his study—the day he told me of his father's belief that I was the answer to Solterre's prayers.

A fresh wave of pain flares up at the memory of his face. I swallow it back as she continues, "The choice is yours. Choose well, and you may stand a chance at survival. Choose wrong, and the cost will be this world."

Cool. No pressure.

I pinch my temples between my hands. "What you're suggesting is insane. Becoming High Queen? No one will follow me. No one will listen."

"You are a dragon rider. You will make them listen."

"How?"

"Align yourself with Vod."

"Oh, like Derek tried to do by marrying Ilspeth? Look how well that turned out," I scoff. "I cannot team up with Kylian—he's the entire reason we're in this mess. He has to be stopped."

"I have seen what happens if you continue to pursue this notion that he is your enemy. You will err, and your mistake will set the wheels of destiny in motion."

"You expect me to just turn a blind eye to all he's done? All he's doing? If I'm supposed to protect this world, then this falls under the job description, don't you think?"

"You cannot see the entire picture," she says, her expression grave. "You cannot see what awaits if you keep resisting. Without him ruling at your side, you do not stand a chance."

"Ruling at my side? Kylian doesn't share anything! You expect him to scooch over and crack me off a piece of his crown?"

What does she expect me to do? Let Kylian trample all over us because it's part of some great master plan?

No. Abso-fucking-lutely not.

"If fulfilling my birthright means marrying Kylian, then people will die regardless. He's a tyrant who only cares about power. He does not care who has to die in order for him to get it. Aegar won't accept him without a fight, and I doubt the other kingdoms will kindly evacuate their thrones for *me*. This will only lead to more bloodshed, more lives lost."

"The other kingdoms will have no choice. Your mates are very powerful and very determined. If it's a throne you desire, they shall make sure you are seated comfortably."

It's like a record screeching to a halt.

"I'm sorry—my *mates*?"

As in plural? As in more than *one?!*

I blink. "I'm sorry, I think my brain just hemorrhaged. You said—"

"You didn't know?" She chuckles as if I just delivered the punch line to a joke.

"*No*—I—that's impossible."

"Rare, but not impossible. I've seen it before, multiple bonds. The Fates work in mysterious ways."

My eyes narrow in confusion. "The Fates? But I thought Adelphi—"

"Like most of the gods, Adelphi has not concerned herself with matters of our kind in centuries. The Fates now choose."

"But why would they do this?"

"They are like the gods. Old as time itself, always searching for entertainment, amusement, ways to feel alive. Seeing our struggles, watching our pain and our joy—I think it reminds them of a time they felt all of that too. A time that has been long forgotten."

"So they thought it would be *fun* to stick me with two mates and make me choose between them?"

"Not two," she whispers, a fascinated look in her eyes. "Three."

"Three?!" I practically shriek.

She nods. I burst into laughter. Even though I don't find it funny. Not at all.

"No. *No.*"

She reaches out a hand and flips over the second card laid before me. *The Lovers.*

"Choosing between them seems highly unlikely," she continues as if I'm not sitting here having an actual mental breakdown. "It would be like trying to sever one of your own limbs. A part of your soul is shared among them. Though I fear one choice has already been made for you."

"What do you mean by that?"

She flips the third card over, and on the back I read two words—so final and heavy.

The Tower.

Her oval-shaped nail taps the painted card as she goes on, "One among them is your true enemy."

I stop breathing.

"Where your paths cross, misfortune follows. Pain, heartache, even death." She peels the card off the table and balances it between two lithe fingers. "The two of you will try to fight it, but just as you were born to rule, he was born to destroy."

"Who is he?" I demand, teetering on the edge of my seat.

"You will know him by the suffering your bond brings," she explains. "The love between you may be strong, but it is blinding. It leads to irrational, desperate decisions with calamitous results." She leans in a touch closer. "I urge you to stay away from that one."

"But mates are meant to be together. That's the whole point," I argue. I may not know much on the subject, but that's a pretty universal concept.

"Just because two people are meant for each other does not mean they are good for each other. Or for the people around them. I think it's what you earthlings call *toxic*."

This is absurd. All of it. Three mates? One that just so happens to be my enemy?

"What if I can't stay away from him? What happens then?"

Her voice sends ice up my arms as she whispers, "You will tear each other apart, and those around you will pay the price."

My blood freezes over, my head reeling.

What does that even mean?

"I've said all I may say. Fight your urges and keep your distance. It will make it easier when the time comes. He is not for you."

The words trigger a distant memory. They're the same ones Furi spoke to me after Ilsa was killed.

He is not for you, Blackblood.

She had been talking about *Jace*.

My gut twists as the idea infests my mind. Because if that's the case, then…

Oh god.

She could be lying. Though I don't know what she would stand to gain from this, I do know my mother, and rest assured there is always a motive. I'm willing to bet her doppelgänger is no different.

"Why should I believe you?"

"I suppose whether you believe is up to you. I've done my part in warning you."

"Warning me?" I let out a bitter laugh. "With your vague little riddles and shady bullshit? *Something* is coming? I'd hardly call that helpful. Do you know who my mates are?"

She just looks at me, her silence confirmation enough.

"You know."

The pieces of the puzzle start to slowly click into place. The things I've been told, the warnings I've tried to ignore, the outside forces that always seem to be pushing and pulling me with no regard or respect for my free will.

"You know, don't you? Tell me who they are. Now."

"Oh, you know who they are. Deep down. You just refuse to accept it."

"I need to hear you say it. Out loud. Or I won't believe it."

"I cannot."

"If what you're saying is true, people's lives are at stake here!" I draw a deep breath, fumbling to reel back my frustration. "Please. I know you don't owe me anything, but I am begging you. Tell me who they are and how to fix this."

She hesitates, her gaze bordering on sympathetic. "There is no fixing this. You must accept that some things that are meant to be just *aren't* meant to be."

It's never been up to me, has it? It was all just decided upon by those who think they have the right. They don't.

She begins to gather the cards on the table, and I get the sense that we're done here. But I have way too many questions to pack it up and be on my merry fucking way.

"Just tell me something—anything. What is coming that we should be so afraid of? Tell me what I'm supposed to do—"

"Would that it were so simple. There are things I cannot reveal. Doing so would alter nature's course. There would be consequences."

"There already have been! I've already lost people I love. I can't lose any—"

"That is outside my realm of jurisdiction."

I bristle at the finality of her tone. "So that's it? You bring me here to drop a major bombshell, and then just shut the hell up?"

She draws up her spine. "I brought you here to keep you from making the biggest mistake of your life."

"How can you keep me from making it when I don't even know what it is?!" I hiss. "And since when has any version of you ever given two shits about my life and my mistakes?" I shout, my eyes stinging with hot tears.

She sits there shaking her head, a coldness creeping onto her lovely face. "Ungrateful."

I laugh in disbelief.

"I put much at risk to come here to give you this warning."

"Well, your problem, I guess," I snap, standing and striding toward the door.

"You'll be back when you're ready to face the truth." Her voice stops me. I turn back to her slowly.

"I'd like to send a message back to the Fates." I flatten my palms against the table and lean in close.

"This is my life. And I intend to do whatever the fuck I want with it. And if they try to come for the people I love, there will be absolute hell to pay. If they need a reminder of what it's like to feel pain, to feel loss—I am more than prepared to provide that for them."

Then I wrench the door open and tear into the hall.

101

SERENA

I find Jace in the forest, hacking a sword against the trunk of a weeping willow. The metal slams into the bark again and again, leaving behind deep, ugly gashes.*

"Jace?"

He doesn't turn as I approach. He just keeps on punishing the innocent tree.

"Jace, please just look at me."

"I can't. Not right now."

Another loud crack as his sword makes contact with the wood.

"I didn't choose this."

"Serena, please just *go away*."

"Not until you talk to me."

His sword meets the tree with such ferocity that the metal actually *bends*.

"Fuck," Jace curses, tossing the damaged blade into the grass and stalking away without a look in my direction.

"Stop." I grab his arm, pulling him to face me. "Talk to me."

"I can't talk to you."

---

* Cue: *I Knew It, I Know You* by Gracie Abrams

"Then yell at me! Just don't punish me like this."

"You want me to yell at you? Fine. What the fuck was that?" He points toward the castle.

"It's a long story."

"A long story?" His eyebrows leap up. He holds up a finger for every word that follows. "He's. My. Mate. It's three fucking words, seems like a pretty short story to me."

"I'm sorry, but it's true. Kylian *is* my mate—or one of them."

"There's more than one?"

I nod. He waits, the hostility in his eyes surrendering to desperate hope. Hope I am about to shatter with my next words.

I think about telling him the truth. Telling him that together we will cause destruction, heartache, death. But I know exactly what he will say. And I know he won't stop fighting for this until I give in.

And I can't.

So I do the only thing I can think of to keep us apart.

I lie.

"Kylian and Zadyn."

He hurls out a jaded laugh, rolling his eyes and crossing his arms behind his head. "You're fucking kidding me."

I force myself to swallow.

"You're telling me that what we feel for each other isn't a mating bond?" He gestures between us.

I shake my head, and he laughs again, the sound chilling and cold.

"No. No, I'm sorry, but that is *bullshit.*"

"Is it? Have you had that moment where it all clicked into place? Because I haven't. Not with you."

"No, I've had a thousand moments!" His voice blasts through the clearing, making me jump. "A thousand times I've found myself staring in awe of you, thinking, *It's her. It* has *to be her*—because never in my lifetime have I known what it was like to ache for someone the way I do for you. A thousand moments. A thousand moments, desperately fighting against a current that has always been bigger than me—stronger than me. So maybe you haven't had that big magical moment, maybe you haven't seen that flare go off. But *I* have. Every time I look at you, it's a flare—it's a fucking smoke signal telling me it's you."

My heart fractures.

"It's not me. It's not us, Jace. It can't be."

"Why not? I know you feel this too. Why are you denying it?"

"Jace, just let it go. Please."

"*Let it go?*" he spits. "If I could, don't you think I would have months ago when I got engaged to Sorscha? You think it's fun for me to choke on my own jealousy day after day? Do you think I enjoy this torment? You think I want to love you to the point of sickness?"

"We have never been good together! We've never been right."

The lie tastes like copper and ash on my tongue.

But the proof is there. We do hurt people—every time we've even *thought* about giving in to what's between us.

After the first time we kissed, the Stryga arrived, and Ilsa was killed. When Jace nearly died in the maze, I shattered my own glamour and exposed myself to Kylian. He comes to Vod for me—Derek dies days later. He tries to protect me by locking me up, and Zadyn dies...

How many more warnings do I need?

"We would know." He turns away, raking a hand through his dark hair. "If we weren't mates, we would know it."

"We *do* know. We don't belong together. We hurt people when we try to choose each other. Because we're trying to fit a round peg into a square hole. The universe has been driving us apart since day one."

"Fuck the universe, I want you!" His shout echoes through the forest, chasing a flock of birds from the branches above.

"I want you. I—I *love* you." His voice cracks as I stare at the ground, the ache in my chest growing sharper and sharper.

"Listen to me." His hands slide into my hair, fisting it tightly. "If you aren't my mate, then why does it feel like this? Why does it feel like I'm on fire every time I'm around you?"

"I don't know," I whisper.

"Tell me you don't want me."

"I—I don't want you."

"You don't love me."

"No. I don't."

He shakes me. "You're lying, Serena! What are you not saying? I am so tired of the secrets!"

"So am I!" I shove back. "You've kept your fair share of them, and look what's happened!"

"I lied because I care about you!"

Which is exactly what I'm doing now.

But he keeps pushing. "If you weren't my mate, you'd feel nothing when you looked at me. And you don't feel nothing. Do you?"

Of course, I feel something. Even knowing what I do, I feel compelled to be close to him, the same way I do with Zadyn. And Kylian.

What kills me most is the fact that there is still so much love between us. Love that I am crushing beneath a steel-toed boot.

"Stop fighting it. Stop fighting me. I don't care what the Fates say, I don't care what the gods say. I don't care if they made Kylian or Zadyn your mate, because in my bones I know that you are mine. I know that I could never belong to anyone else because I have always been yours. So don't you dare tell me I'm wrong. Don't you dare tell me it's over."

His mouth slams into mine. And before I can protest, I'm kissing him back so hard it hurts.

It isn't gentle. It isn't kind. It is fueled by desperate need, by grief, and stubborn defiance.

I break away, shoving out of his arms and sprinting off—my heart beating out of my chest and my cheeks streaked with stinging tears.

IT'S OFFICIAL.

I'm swearing off men.

Should have done it a long time ago. But my middle name is pushover.

I am a pushover for all three of them.

My mates. All of whom hate each other and will probably very soon end up hating me.

How is this supposed to work? What are holidays going to be like? Are they supposed to share me? How is that fair? Am I supposed to rotate beds every night for the rest of eternity?

Fuck this. And fuck you, universe. Fuck you, Fates.

I asked for *one*. One person to spend my life with. Not *three*.

I asked for a love as easy as breathing. Turns out knowing who you're meant to be with is just as complicated as spending thirty years blindly guessing.

So thank you. Batting a thousand here.

You are doing the right thing, Furi assures me.

Sure doesn't feel that way.

It makes sense now—Furi telling me to stay away from Jace and that I belonged to another. She had been talking about Zadyn. She hadn't known about a third mate until I did, let alone that it was Kylian.

I push open Zadyn's door to find him peering out the window. The fires from the attack are still going strong, eating their way through the hills below. He glances up, and the desire to rush to him and bury myself in his warmth slams into me.

"How's he taking it?"

"How you'd expect." I trudge into the room, hiding my face in my hands. "This is such a disaster."

The conversation with Jace keeps playing on a loop in my head. And it tastes like regret. But the fact is, bad things do happen whenever we get together or come close to it. And lately, being around him feels more nuclear than being around Kylian.

We were doomed from the start.

Zadyn's arms fold around me, easing some of the tightness from my chest.

"I had to lie to him. He won't let this go," I say. "I told him that we aren't mates. That I don't feel the same."

"And he believed that?"

"I'm hoping he will eventually."

"You and I both know that isn't going to work. Sooner or later the truth will come out. It always does."

"Then let it. Because it's better for him to hate me. It's better for everyone if we stay far away from each other. And as for Kylian—I don't even know what to do about that bucket of shit."

"Serena—"

"I'm so sorry for ruining the plan. You and Jace had the perfect opportunity to end this, and I choked. I felt the bond lock into place right as Jace was about to kill him, and ugh—this is so wrong. Kylian and mate do not belong in the same sentence. And Kai is going to hate me when he finds out, after everything Kylian put him through—"

Zadyn's hand shoots out to grip my face, smushing my cheeks together and shutting me up.

"Hey." Those rich brown eyes sweep me into their depths, putting a pin in my mini meltdown. "None of this was in your control. And we could have never predicted that Kylian would be your mate too."

"The signs were there," I admit. "I just didn't want to believe it. Could this situation get any worse?"

He offers me a soft smile, tucking my hair behind my ear. "You better knock on wood after the day we've had."

I appreciate the levity he's offering, but I can't match it.

"I'm in over my head, Zadyn," I whisper.

"Come here." He tugs me toward the bed. I resist for a second, then plop down, throwing my head into his lap. He smooths back my hair as we share the silence.

"I don't know where to go from here. All of this is so confusing. It's like I want him dead but—" I trail off not knowing how to phrase it.

"But you want him too."

I'm so sorry.

You've done nothing wrong. None of this is your fault.

I wish you'd stop saying that.

It's the truth.

"How are you not mad at me?"

"You expected me to be mad at you for Kylian being one of your mates?"

"Jace was."

"Because Jace is an asshole. And fuck him for not understanding. I swear, if he gives you any shit about it—"

"So protective." I smile at the fierceness in his voice.

"Of course I am, you're mine," he vows, playing with my hair. "Even if you're theirs too."

I frown at that thought.

How is this going to work?

It's certainly complicated, but you're not the first person this has happened to.

Well, if they've got a manual for this Ikea bullshit, it would be helpful right about now.

He laughs. *It's all up to you. You can choose which bonds to accept or reject. And if you don't want to decide, then that's fine too.*

If I reject Kylian and Jace, will these feelings go away?

Zadyn gives me a sad smile and shakes his head. *Probably not. They might lessen a bit. But, Serena, as much as I want you all to myself...you don't have to choose between us. In cases like these, I've never seen a central bond choose between her mates. It would be torture. No one would expect that of you.*

Not choosing—what would that even look like? I'm about as vanilla as they come. I don't think I could juggle a polyamorous quad.

It wouldn't have to be like that.

Well, however it would be—it seems unfair. To you. To all of you.

You don't have to figure this out overnight. And it's not unfair to me. Because if I get to love even some small part of you and have that returned, I promise you that will be more than enough. And if you ask either of them, I'm sure they'll tell you the same thing.

Not Jace.

Maybe not now. Look, I know how you feel about me. I have a direct link to your mind. I can feel everything you do. I'm not threatened by you wanting them too.

I sit up and gawk at him. *Are you like giving me a hall pass or something?*

It's not a hall pass. It's just acceptance. Do I enjoy the thought of anyone else touching you? Fuck, no. But the more you're around them, the harder it will be to fight your connection. You may hate Kylian right now, but a part of you will not stop thirsting for him. I know what it is to long for someone. I don't want that for you. And as your mate, your primary—I know what you need. I won't force you to choose between us.

My primary?

His eyes soften as he presses a kiss to the inside of my wrist. *It's what we call a familiar that doubles as a mate.*

I marvel at him. My best friend. My familiar. My mate.

He smiles that smile that's reserved only for me.

And while I'm still not fully convinced that I deserve him—I love him, I love him, I love him.

102
SERENA

"Plenty of room in here. Care to join me?"*

Kylian's voice floats down the hall, deep and rich. I roll my eyes, stopping just outside the iron bars of his cell.

"You've already lost, Kylian. Give it up."

"Give what up?"

"The other half of the star."

His eyes flash. "How do you know about that?"

"Doesn't matter, I do. Now tell me where it is."

"Say you'll come home with me, and perhaps I will."

"You're in no position to be making negotiations." I cross my arms.

"Aren't I?" He gives me a wicked smirk, staring up at me from the floor. "Haven't I been telling you all along that you belong to me? That you're mine and that we're fated?"

Shaking my head, I slide down the wall opposite him. "I still don't quite believe it."

"Did you figure it out before or after we slept together?"

My eyes narrow to daggers. "You do not *speak* of that."

"Well, darling? When was it?"

---

* Cue: *Million Dollar Man* by Lana Del Rey

"Probably when I couldn't bring myself to kill you. Even though I wanted you dead. Still do." For some reason, this makes him chuckle. "How long have *you* known?"

"About us?"

Us. The word rolling off his tongue feels sounds so foreign. So wrong.

"A while."

"How long is a while?"

"Since before you came to Vod."

"You mean before you *kidnapped* me."

"I had my reasons for doing what I did."

"They remain to be seen!" My hiss bounces off the walls.

Kylian stares at the ground, shaking his head.

"I have always been certain of my path. From the moment I stepped in front of those mirrors as a boy, I knew that one day I would be High King. I spent my life preparing to be the ruler I saw reflected there, the one I was expected to be. But one day, I saw something else. I saw a woman with lavender eyes on a throne at my side. I saw *you*. Flashes of a life together. Nothing clear. I didn't know who you were at the time, only that I had to find you and that I had to have you."

He pushes his raven hair back.

"When my mother reported the arrival of a witch in Aegar, I viewed it as the perfect opportunity to advance. If I could secure the last Blackblood witch and her dragon as part of my court, it would have made me unstoppable. But there was this nagging pull that I couldn't shake, urging me to come to Aegar and see you for myself. And when I did, I recognized you from the visions in the mirrors—except your eyes weren't quite right. I remember the moment you revealed yourself in the maze—I couldn't look away. I wanted you."

"No, you wanted to use me."

"I wanted *you*. Not for your power, but for me...I wanted you. That was the first time I considered the possibility that we were mates."

"And you kidnapped me anyway."

"I couldn't very well let you go. I saw the attachments you formed to your friends, your little kingdom. You would never have gone with me willingly. I tried to shove my personal interest in you down. But I couldn't deny what the mirror showed me—the two of us ruling side by side over everything. I saw the potential of greatness."

He pauses. "I also saw what would happen if we denied our fate— the destruction that would have followed."

"Right, because if you didn't get your way, you would have thrown a hissy fit and burned my kingdom to the ground." I tap my chin. "Oh, wait."

"No." The sudden intensity in his voice compels me to look at him. Really look at him. "I am not above killing when the end justifies the means, but that doesn't mean I crave destruction. If I didn't truly believe in the validity of my pursuits, I wouldn't have bothered with any of this. I wouldn't have ended those Guardians, I wouldn't have brought those creatures here, I wouldn't have poisoned my father—"

"I'm sorry—what?! You poisoned your own father?"

"Well, technically speaking, my mother did the poisoning."

I gawk at him. "What the fuck is wrong with you people?"

"Beside the point. Those mirrors showed me horrors far worse than the ones it showed you. Horrors not caused by my hand."

"Oh, really? Then what caused them?"

"It's still unclear. But this much is certain. If you refuse this—our bond—neither of us will walk away with our lives. Which is how I know I am not the villain in your story."

I dig my fingers into my temples. "You are, Kylian. You just don't see it that way."

"You've yet to reject me."

"Are you kidding? I don't know how many other ways I *can* reject you! You just can't take no for an answer."

His fingers close around the iron bars. "Listen to me, Dragon Rider. We are stronger together. But I cannot protect you if you won't allow me to."

"Protect me from what? What out there can be worse than you, Kylian?"

He sighs, pulling back.

"You're lying," I decide. "You didn't see shit in those mirrors. You are relentless, you know that? You will stop at nothing—"

"I'm telling the truth. Despite what you think, I am not the villain. I am not your enemy."

"Yes, you are. You are the devil. And to top it all off, you're my goddamned mate."

"Which is why I would die to protect you."

"You don't care about anyone but yourself."

"I care about *you*. Why do you think I've been so desperate to get you back?"

My mocking laugh echoes down the hall.

"So desperate that you threw the people I love right in the crossfires."

"You needed some kind of motivation. Can you honestly say you would have accepted me without the threat of your loved ones? If I had gotten down on one knee and asked nicely, would you have abandoned them and married me?"

"No."

"Then you see why my actions were necessary."

"You may think you had a good reason for doing what you did, but people died because of you. Ilsa, Derek—countless innocent lives taken because you let the Stryga loose. Your soldiers are ransacking our villages to get us to release you!"

"A small price to pay."

"You're a bastard."

"You don't have to believe me. You just have to trust that things are different now."

"Oh, don't tell me I've *changed* you. That you suddenly turned good and no longer care about ruling."

"Of course I still care. Ruling is my divine right. I was bred for this. I have been blessed by the gods with rare, powerful gifts for this purpose. And until recently, I never had trouble falling asleep with blood on my hands. They say the best rulers are the ones unhindered by emotion. Well, I'm living proof. But *you*—"

The sudden passion in that single word has me lifting my gaze to his. Those haunting eyes lock me in, cutting off all the circulation in my body.

"I never knew what emotion was. Not until I met you. You are the only feelings I have. You are my only sense of morality, you are my conscience, you are my *heart.*"

My stomach flutters.

"You know *nothing* about me," I whisper, fighting to cling to my anger.

"Our souls know each other. They always have," he mumbles, sounding tired.

I watch him, my fingers absentmindedly toying with his locket. It's oddly warm to the touch.

As much as I hate this, knowing he's my mate has eased some of my guilt. This is why I've been drawn to him. It's why I couldn't kill him. Why I couldn't resist him. Why I let him find me time after time.

I shake my head. "What am I supposed to do with you?"

"You don't plan on keeping me in here."

"How do you know that?"

His head tilts back against the wall. "Because you want me too much. And you need me in ways you don't even know yet."

"Don't flatter yourself."

"That isn't what I meant. You need me in a practical sense," he corrects. "We were paired together for a reason. Because believe it or not, you and I are evenly matched. There is no one else on this earth whose power could rival your own. That could come close to being able to shield you from what's coming. You may think me a tyrant. And that's fine. I don't need you to like me, I just need you to hear me when I say that all I have done, I have done for you."

"You'll forgive me for having a little trouble taking your word for it."

I study this male, this horrifying monster wrapped in exquisite packaging. I study the soulless, heartless creature that wears the most perfect skin I've ever laid eyes on. The beast who claims he's changed by true love.

Another fairy tale I can't marry with reality.

I hate him with all my heart, and yet somewhere within that loathing exists a strange and infinitesimal kernel of love.

My enemy. And my mate.

"If you don't believe me, then just end me now."

"I should."

I stand, unlocking the cell door. He stares up at me from the ground as I draw my dagger, tapping the point against my lips. With every step I take toward him, my locket hums with energy, heating against my chest. Kylian watches me, making no move to escape. I angle the dagger to his breast.

"Do it," he whispers. His fingers wrap around my wrist, driving the tip of the blade into his smooth chest. A drop of scarlet squeezes out.

"Do it and see that there is a heart there, despite what you believe. Do it and see that even devils bleed. Carve it out and mount it on your wall, because it is already yours."

Blood leaks out around the knife as he breathes harder, locking my hand in place, his eyes scalding mine.

My palm opens, and the dagger clatters to the ground.

And without a second thought, I kiss him.

1 0 3

SERENA

An aneurism.

That's what I'm choosing to blame that stupid kiss on. I wish I could take it back, if only to avoid swelling his already massive ego.

I swallow down the nerves bubbling up in my belly as I stride down the torchlit corridor. My locket warms with each step I take, the same way it did yesterday, proving my theory. I key open Kylian's cell and step inside.

"Drink."

His eyes drift open. I extend the waterskin to him and watch as he unscrews the cap and chugs it down within seconds. Every last drop. Without explanation, I crouch down, shoving my hand into his pocket.

"Well, hello to you too."

"I'm not here for you."

"Then is there something I can help you with?"

"The other half of the star." I look up at him. He doesn't answer. "There's no point in denying it. I know you have it on you."

"How, pray tell, did you come to that conclusion?"

574

"A little birdie told me." I tap my locket, which is now hot to the touch, humming with energy.

"What do you need it for?"

"Cut the shit. I know that together the stars make up a key and that key is the only way to close the portal. Now give it."

"There *is* no key. How many times do I have to tell you?" He fumes as I continue to accost him. "I know you think you know what you're doing, but I am telling you now, those stars *cannot* be joined."

"Why, because it would foil your plan? Oh, and pro tip—you telling me not to do something just makes me want to do it all the more. You need to learn a thing or two about reverse psychology."

"As usual, I have no idea what you're talking about."

"Look, I don't care what you say, I don't care what the Fates say, I don't even care what Arden said. I am closing that portal because I do not *trust* you."

He stares at me for a long time. "I would never hurt you."

"No, but you would hurt everyone I love, which is the same thing."

"Everything I do and have done has been to protect you."

I hurl a scornful laugh at him. "So we're still sticking with that line? Please."

"Ever since I realized you were my mate. I think deep down you know it's the truth. Mates cannot harm one another."

"Really? Because I drove a dagger into Zadyn's chest, thinking he was you."

He looks speechless.

"Give me the star."

He reaches up to knock my hands away, but then his eyes widen, and he slumps back into the wall.

"What have you done?"

"Just a little something to help you relax."

"Serena, do not do this. I am begging you."

"And did you listen when I begged you?" I snarl. "When I begged you to leave Kai alone? When I begged you to let me go? I'm just returning the favor."

"I gave you what you wanted. I left him alone."

"After I fucked you!" My voice clamors off the walls, throwing my own harsh words back in my face. He looks physically ill. Like I just slapped him.

"You could have stopped me with a single word. I wouldn't have—I thought it was what you wanted—"

I did.

And that sickens me to the core.

"Serena," he pleads again, his voice choked as the paralytic I slipped into his water spreads.

Fuck. Where is it? I've checked every pocket on him. He has to be hiding it somehow.

Use the shadows, Furi purrs. *Listen.*

I try to tune Kylian out and do as she says.

When I close my eyes, I can hear them moving—whispering. I can feel them slithering across my skin. I allow them to unfurl, their coils drifting into the cell with eerie grace, swirling around Kylian's neck like a noose.

When they recede, I can see the onyx pendant resting against his tanned chest, the one that was concealed moments ago.

Kylian strains through gritted teeth as I pull the gleaming chain over his head. It feels heavy in my hands. I crack it open and as expected, the star fragment shoots out into the cell, bounding off the walls emphatically.

"Bingo."

Kylian mumbles something that doesn't make sense. He tries to move, but only succeeds in trembling, the veins of his neck and arms bulging.

"Don't worry, you'll be able to move again in a few hours. I'd get comfy if I were you." I give his face a loud pat and lock the cell behind me, slipping the pendant over my head and disappearing into the darkness.

104

ZADYN

"**I** truly cannot tell if this is a joke or not." Eaton's cool eyes assess me.

Oh, how I wish it were.

"It's not a joke. Their bond snapped into place as we were about to take him out."

Marideth is pale as a ghost, sitting on the settee beside Dover, too stunned to speak.

"But you two are—" Sorscha trails off, confusion etched on her heart-shaped face.

"Also mates," I provide. "And yes, we are very aware of how fucked up this is."

I blow out a long breath, pinching the bridge of my nose.

"It's incredibly fucked up." Eaton slides onto the table, tugging Sorscha in between his thighs and snaking his arms around her belly. "But also incredibly useful."

"Please elaborate," I drone, massaging my temple. I can already feel the migraine taking root.

"She wouldn't let you and Jace hurt him, right? Why?"

"The bond stopped her."

"Exactly." Eaton leans his chin on Sorscha's shoulder. "It works both ways, as you well know, Rhodesie. He won't hurt her or put her life at risk."

I understand that. But it doesn't make me feel any better that she's down in his cell right now, unaccompanied. But she insisted, and I have to trust her.

"He imprisoned her and nearly starved her to death," Kai snaps from the corner, breaking his silence. It's the first he's spoken since he heard the news. He's just been staring out the window, unblinking, for the last twenty minutes. I was starting to get concerned.

"Maybe so, but did he ever cause her direct physical harm?"

It would explain why he lost it anytime someone laid a hand on her. Why he chose to use Kai as a whipping boy instead of taking his anger out directly on her. The bond was preventing it.

"The point is," Eaton continues, "we can use this to our advantage. She's got him by the balls now. He's going to want to please her—earn her trust, her favor, her love. So right now he's more likely to be compliant."

"I'm not letting her accept this bond just to lord power over him," I say, sinking into the high-backed leather chair.

"She doesn't have to accept it, but I wouldn't run and reject it, either. Their connection could serve as a huge advantage. Just don't let her do anything rash."

"I don't control my mate, Eaton."

"It's not the advantage you think it is," Kai says to the room. Gods, he looks so dejected. "He knows she won't actually kill him now. He has no reason to be honest with us. He's just going to bide his time until those shackles are finally off."

"I think Kai is right." Mar glances between us. "He won't say a word unless he's getting something in return."

"Well, we've got nothing to bargain with," Dover adds grimly.

The door opens, and Eaton's gaze shifts past me. "Hey, how skilled are you at seduction?"

I turn as Serena steps into rhe room, looking slightly keyed up. I'm on my feet to meet her in an instant.

"Out of the question," I snap at Eaton over my shoulder. Serena gives me a confused look as I drag my hands down her arms.

Sorry, I say to her. *Your body is your own to do what you like with, but I draw the line at weaponizing it to get what we need.*

She smiles at my protective tone.

"Is he cooperating?" Sorscha asks.

"He's wearing blood ore cuffs," Serena mutters. "He doesn't have much of a choice."

Mar twists around in her seat. "Did you confront him about his half of the star?"

"I did one better." She breaks into a feline smile and pulls a dark locket with a black chain from around her neck.

"Is that—"

"Uh-huh," she says, dangling it in the air.

Our friends form a huddle around us.

"How did you manage that?" Mar says, inspecting the chain.

Serena shrugs, planting her hands on her hips. "Last night, my locket started burning when I got close to Kylian, like it could sense its other half was near."

"And he just handed it over?"

"Essentially. With the help of a little mild poison."

Eaton snorts. "I see our time with the pirates was well spent."

I marvel at her. Is there nothing she can't do?

A smirk tugs at the corner of her mouth, and I want her. Right here and now. She meets the heat of my stare, sensing the shift.

Table or floor? She winks at me, and it's like an arrow to the heart.

Fucking hells.

Both, I reply. *And then maybe the wall, so it doesn't feel left out.*

Hmm, that sounds—

"He had it on him the entire time?" Dover interrupts. "That's convenient."

"Nicely done, Dragon Rider." Eaton gives her an approving nod.

She smiles, tucking the pendant into her pocket. "Well, people. We've got a key to repair."

105

SERENA

Y ou'd think carrying two halves of a star would be as easy as carrying a speck of dust on your jacket.

Wrong.

I can feel their pulses as if they were living, breathing things with individual heartbeats. Their timing is half a second off, throbbing around my neck and then again in my pocket. They strain toward each other with magnetic desperation—power so strong, it's dizzying. Draining to the point of exhaustion.

It's too *much* power.

"So what happens when we join them? Are they just going to shoot up into the sky?" I ask Mar.

"I hope not. But that's where this comes in." She reaches into her satchel and pulls out a shiny, metallic box with an ornate closure. "I need you to use Furi's fire to forge this."

"Forge it?" My eyebrows tilt up. "What the hell does that mean?"

"We are going to fortify this box so it can hold the star. And the best way to do that is for you to wield. Once the halves are joined, who knows what will happen. But until we know how to use it, we need to make sure it stays contained and secure."

"So forging first."

580

"Forging first."

My palms grow slick at the thought of wielding, my memory serving up a sample of that indomitable fire. The way it felt running through my veins, the pain—

Pain comes with the position, Dragon Rider, Furi says. *Luckily, it's nothing you aren't familiar with.*

I set the box down on the grass and head toward the cliff where she waits.

How is your fire going to fortify the box?

By suffusing it with magic, she answers, her scales shimmering beneath the pearly moon.

We're going to turn it into a magic box?

Her head swings toward me, and she lets out a huff, blowing my loose braid off my shoulder.

The strongest magical objects that exist in this world have been forged by dragon fire. It is the most efficient way.

That it may be, but it's also a fucking nightmare.

You're trembling, Blackblood.

I'm just not sure I can do this without killing myself, I admit.

You've done it before.

A little wave of sadness hits me as I glance toward my friends, scanning for the one person missing.

Jace was always there, talking me through it. Anchoring me. He's been MIA since he found out about Kylian.

I frown up at my dragon. Furi takes a definitive step toward me, her talons digging into the ground.

You do not need him. You stand on your own two feet now, on the shoulders of your ancestors. You need nothing and no one to bring this world to its knees.

Her words warm my heart, scaring away some of that anxious energy. I move closer and wrap my arms around the rough patch of her leg.

There, there, no need to slobber on me.

I laugh, releasing her. *Okay, let's do this before you really trigger the waterworks. Deep breath. Ready?*

Her head dips, nudging against my stomach. *Together.*

My hands find her snout, and her green eyes close in time with mine. Our breaths fall into a rhythm, and I block out all that exists outside of this bond. Her power latches on with a sharp bite, flooding me with an onslaught of heat.

It's terrible. Everything in me wants to recoil, to take a step back from the flames. But the flames are in me now. They *are* me. And I can't escape.

Steady, Blackblood.

I grit my teeth and shout to dust off the excess energy. But it's not enough.

The scorching pain intensifies, seizing my muscles, burning me alive where I stand. I'm roaring, my throat stripped raw, and I still can't even hear myself over the wild rush of fire. It's too much, it's killing me—

Take it, Blackblood! Now!

I can't! I can't stop, I can't move my hands!

You must. Let go. LET. GO.

I do. And that fire shoots from me so fast and urgent it feels like my soul is being ripped away with it. Furi's blue fire spits out of me like a laser beam.

"Serena!"

I whirl toward whoever called my name, and that fire slices across the clearing, spearing out over the wide ledge and into the ether. If there had been anyone in that line of fire, they would have been sliced clean in two.

"Get back!" someone shouts. "Now!"

Aim! Furi commands.

Right, that would help.

I adjust my hands toward the silver box on the ground. It instantly goes up in a glorious blaze, burning white and sparking colors I've never seen—never even heard of before.

It is done, Blackblood.

But her fire is still there, swallowing me. There's way too much of it.

I've severed the line, now you must do the same, Furi pleads.

This is me now—all me. And it's going to kill me. The very thing that makes me powerful is going to be the thing that ends me.

How's that for irony?

"Serena!" Zadyn's voice cuts past my screams. It's there in my mind and in my ears.

"Don't touch her, Zadyn! She's still wielding!" Mar shouts.

"I don't fucking care!"

My hands and knees hit the soil. I'm soaked in sweat and tears. Furi is whimpering like a kicked dog beside me. The blue fire is extinguished, but it's still in me. I'm still burning.

Zadyn skids in front of me on his knees, pressing his chest to the ground so my eyes can find his.

Hey, stay with me.

Please, I choke. *Don't come any closer. There's no reason this should kill us both.*

You're not dying. Not tonight, not even close.

A guttural cry spears through me. He taps the ground near my cheek, demanding my attention.

Look at me, Serena. I'm here. I love you. And you will stop this right now. *If you love me, you won't dare leave me behind, and I know you fucking do. This is not worth dying for. Nothing is, not even saving this entire gods-damned world. So let it go, sweetheart. Let it go and stay with me. I've got you.*

I try telling him I do love him, more than words, but fire doesn't quake in the face of love. It laughs.

He reaches for my hand and squeezes, grunting and gritting his teeth as the embers of my skin scourge him. But he holds fast and doesn't let go.

I've got you, he repeats over and over until I'm doing the same in my head—clinging to his words like a prayer, like my one last hope.

With a cry that splits the earth, I find the will to sever the chord. Sweet silence echoes through my mind. I'm not even aware that I'm falling until I feel the grass on my face. Zadyn's arms slide beneath me, cradling me in his lap.

Did it work?

Yes. It worked. You did it. You did so beautifully.

I let my eyes close for one glorious moment. He smooths my hair off my face, his fingers grazing my cheek with the lightest of pressure.

You're so fucking strong.

I laugh, because sitting here in a crumpled heap with no ability to even lift my head, I feel like the antithesis of strong.

You did well, warrior. Furi's voice twinkles with pride and relief. I turn my attention back to Zadyn.

"Can you help me up?"

"Maybe you should take a minute."

"No. We need to do this. Every minute counts."

He nods, fighting his concern, before snaking an arm around my waist and helping me up. He leads me toward Mar, Dover, and Kai—still crouched on the ground, eyes wide and…afraid.

My friends are afraid of me. I've terrified them.

"That was…" Kai shakes his head, words evading him for once.

"Let's just get this done." I spare him from having to finish that sentence.

"Alright, everyone take a point," Mar says, back to business.

She has constructed what she called a containment circle—a pentacle lined with raw diamonds. We stand in the field beneath the moonlight, my friends punctuating each point of the star.

"Magic like this is unpredictable. This is just another safety measure," Mar explains. "As long as we stay connected, nothing is getting in or out."

"You sure you're alright?" Zadyn asks. I nod, taking my place beside him.

"I'm okay. Walk me through this part again?"

"I'm going to say the words to seal the circle. You'll need to do it with me. Zadyn and I will hold onto your arms so your hands are free to release the stars. It's going to be bright, and it's going to be power-ful, but the circle should keep it from blasting us apart."

"Should?"

Mar shoots me a look before continuing. "Then on my word, you open that box. The second it's inside, you—"

"Close that sucker." I nod. "Sounds simple enough."

"No matter what happens, no matter what you feel, we are not going to break contact. Do you all understand?"

Mar glances around the circle. All of us nod.

"When you're ready, Mar."

Her eyes close, and she begins to mutter the words in Ancient Fae. I listen a few times before joining in. The stones begin to vibrate around us, growing brighter as if lit from within. Zadyn's hand is a vice on my arm, making sure I'm still here, that I'm still standing. Without breaking the chant, Mar bobs her head, giving me the signal. I flip open my locket first and watch my half spear into the center of the circle. Then I reach into my pocket for Kylian's onyx locket. The stone is hot to the touch.

Something makes me hesitate. Zadyn looks over at me, confusion etched on his face.

You alright?

I'm good, I assure him. And myself.

I rip open the locket, and out pops the other half of the star. The moment it's freed, it zooms toward its mate faster than I can comprehend, colliding in an explosion of light.

Blinding is an understatement of what they are together. The force blasts my hair back, challenging me to stay upright. The star grows like a giant, now doubled in luminosity, in size, in heat. But it doesn't leave the circle.

The sky above us seems to be shifting, the clouds rearranging themselves. No, not the clouds...it's the stars. The Aurea Dei is suddenly overhead, tugging at our star with brutal persistence.

"Get the box, Serena!"

My fingers slide over the cool, smooth lid and pry it open. The star rockets into the box so powerfully I fly backward, breaking the circle.

I open my eyes. The lid is shut, the star secured inside.

I look up at my friends. "Did we do it?"

Zadyn holds out his hand, flashing me that knee-weakening smile.

"I think we just got ourselves a key."

"HONEY, I'M HOME!" I sing, rounding the corner to Kylian's cell.

I'm pleased to see him looking miserable as fuck—his hair mussed, some grime covering his perfect face. His head rolls to the side, his corded arms draped over his drawn-up knees.

"You're awfully chipper for a poison-slinging viper. Happy to see me?" His sardonic words lack a bit of enthusiasm, as if his time here in solitary has taken its toll.

"My mood has nothing to do with you and everything to do with beating your ass. Finally." I flash him a smirk, closing my hands over the iron bars and pressing my face between them. "It's over, Kylian. You've lost."

I swear to god, his tanned skin turns ghost-white, his arms going slack as they fall to his sides.

"What in gods' names have you done?"

I bite my lip. "I joined the stars."

He's on his feet far faster than anything has a right to be, despite his haggard state. His clammy fingers wrap over mine through the bars, locking my entire body in place.

"No, you didn't," he whispers.

"Yes, I—"

"The stars don't make up a key for the portal, love." The blue fire in his eyes turns anguished as his face softens, something like pity swirled into his gaze.

"Then what..."

My whisper trails off, my stomach sinking lower and lower as Kylian opens his mouth and says, "You have no idea what you've done, do you?"

106

ZADYN

"What are you doing here?" Jace shoots me a dark look, lingering in the shadow of Serena's doorway.

I finish unbuckling my belt of weapons and toss it down on a chair. "She wanted us to meet in here."

"She told me the same thing." An awkward silence falls. "Yet she can't be bothered to show up," he adds under his breath, moving to the bar cart.

"Don't punish her for this."

His eyes cut toward me.

"Who should I punish then? You? Kylian? Trust me, I'm glad to." He pours himself a glass of dark liquor.

I rise from my seat, stopping beside him. "You and I have had to put our differences aside in her best interest before. Are you going to be selfish now when she needs you most?"

"She doesn't need me. Now she has you and her precious *Kylian.*" Jace tosses back the shot of whiskey.

Part of me feels sorry for him, but Serena was right to lie to him. And it's not as though she did it lightly. I can feel the toll it's taken on her. I feel everything she does, and since we've sealed the mating bond, it's been magnified.

587

Her denying their bond—it's as if she rejected it. And Jace is clearly feeling that strain too. I've never seen him look so dark. So grim. Like there's a literal shadow hanging over him.

I choose my words carefully. "She *does* need you. She needs all of us."

"Too bad." He shrugs, pouring out another drink. I clamp a hand over his wrist.

"She never wanted this."

"Still fighting her battles, I see." He gives me a cocky-ass smile and patronizing clap on the shoulder before redirecting his attention to the liquor.

I lean in closer, the leash on my temper slipping.

"She is hurting right now because of you."

"I fucking hope so."

I see red.

My knuckles crack against his jaw. I get one moment to revel in smug satisfaction before we're flying backwards, taking out the entire bar cart. He grabs hold of my collar and sends a sickening punch into my gut. I groan, curling around his fist as glass shatters and crunches all around us. He reaches for my throat, but I'm faster, twisting him beneath me and slamming his head into the floor. His elbow drives into my groin, and a second later, he lands a blinding punch to my left eye. My whole skull reverberates with the force, color spraying across my vision.

"What the hell are you doing?"

Both our heads snap up. Serena strides into the room, furious. Kylian is with her, leaning against the door, wearing an arrogant smirk.

Our fight is instantly forgotten.

"Get up," Serena demands.

Jace and I shove apart, brushing off as we get to our feet. She walks up to me and drags my face into her hands, smoothing over the tender spot Jace hit. "Jesus, your eye is a mess."

He watches from behind her, bitter jealously rolling off of him in waves.

"You cannot be doing this," Serena scolds. "We have bigger problems than the two of you getting on each other's nerves."

"What's this?" Jace sneers, nodding in Kylian's direction. "Taking out the trash?"

"You didn't really think she'd leave her mate down there to rot, did you, friend?" Kylian flashes him a condescending smile, shackled wrists folded over his bare chest.

Jace takes a step toward him, but Serena ducks into the line of fire.

"We are not doing this. Do you understand?" Her stare is unflinching as she meets Jace's fury head-on. He blinks, his anger fading to a simmer as he unclenches his fists. "We're all on the same side."

"Are you concussed?" he asks. Serena cocks her head. "I'm asking seriously. Because if you're not, then you are delusional for thinking we are on the same side." He gestures between us and Kylian.

"Kylian...had reasons for doing what he did. Reasons I do not by any means condone or respect. But I promise you we are on the same side."

"And which side is that?" I send a pointed look his way.

"The one that puts Serena's safety above all else." Hearing her name on his lips sends a spike of rage through me.

"You?" I bite. "*You* want to keep Serena safe?"

"Is that so shocking? She *is* my mate."

"This entire time you've been trying to bully her into compliance!" I shout, unable to stop myself. "You were so desperate for her power that you kidnapped her and tried to force her into marriage. She nearly died trying to escape you. Her kingdom—*our* kingdom—is up in flames because of you."

I point out the window to the hills his troops set on fire. They're still blazing, devouring the green fields and pastures, plaguing the nearby villages.

"Don't delude yourself into thinking you did all this in the name of love."

"It may not have started that way—" Kylian looks serious for once, all mockery emptied from his face. "But that is what it's come down to. Something is coming for her. That is why I have fought so hard for this union, fought to keep her at my side. Because at the end of the day, when she is found, you won't be the one to keep her safe." He takes a prowling step my way, then stops, rearing his head in Jace's direction. "And neither will you. *I* will be the one to keep her safe. Because I *can*."

Zadyn, please.

I glance at Serena, exhaustion weighing down her words, even in my mind.

You believe him?

She nods, her shoulders sagging, like standing—breathing—is full of painful labor. "We have a problem, guys."

"What's wrong?" I close the gap between us, taking hold of her arms. Her face houses every emotion, yet still betrays nothing.

"Allow me to explain," Kylian interjects.

"We're allowing you to live. I think that's generous enough," Jace snaps.

"Listen to what he has to say. Please," Serena begs.

"You made a grave error when you joined those stars. They were meant to remain separate," Kylian begins, sinking onto Serena's mattress. "Nice bed."

"Stick to the subject," I warn.

"That star was originally part of a constellation of seven—"

"The Aurea Dei."

"Very good, love. But did you know they aren't just any ordinary stars? Each one represents the gods. Their power, their essence, their entire being is tied to them. It is their lifeblood. The first star in the constellation burnt out when Zed was killed. Went out in a blaze of glory. But the second one that went dark did just that. There one minute, gone the next. That one is presumed to have belonged to Ienar."

Serena's shoulders tense.

"My ancestor, Garron Triori, was the most talented starsmith to ever live. So when Queen Arden sought him out, he was able to do what she asked of him. Harness a star."

"Oh my god," Serena breathes. "Arden and Garron stole Ienar's star from the constellation."

"Without it, he was weakened, reduced to nothing more than mere fae. Ienar and his Seven scoured the earth in search of it. Arden and Garron tried to destroy the star, but failed each time. So instead, they broke it in two to keep it hidden. One half was given to Arden to protect, and the other was Garron's."

"Get to the point," Jace threatens.

"The point is that those stars have been passed down my line with the knowledge that to join them would cause catastrophe. Until the day of our wedding, they had been locked in my family's vaults, never to see the light of day. Only those with Triori blood are permitted inside. When I was young, my father took me down there. He made me swear a blood oath never to join the two halves, never to speak of their existence."

"Yet here you are singing like a fucking canary," I point out.

"Serena is family," he says in earnest. "Besides, you three let the cat out of the bag all on your own. I'm free to speak of it as much as I desire now."

"So the stars don't make up a key?" Serena asks, all hope sinking from her voice. Kylian shakes his head. "Then what have I done?"

"I don't know for certain, but I know it isn't cause for celebration. There's something else." Kylian pauses. "My mirrors have been very helpful in guiding me, but the one thing they cannot see are the gods. It's like a complete blockage where they are concerned. I saw true destruction in those mirrors, fashioned around *her*. Someone is coming for her, and I cannot see who. Which basically tells me all I need to know."

"I don't see how that relates to the stars," Jace deadpans.

"Of course, you wouldn't. Simple-minded," Kylian hacks, disguising the slur as a cough.

Serena looks at him. "Real mature."

"I just find it coincidental, don't you?" Kylian muses, relishing the sound of his own voice. "Alright. Let's recap. We have an old, vengeful god hell-bent on recovering a star *my* ancestor and *her* ancestor managed to procure. War ensues, witches die, yada, yada, yada. Flash forward two thousand years, and here we are. And here *she* is, doing precisely what my father forbade me to do, and his father before him, and so on and so forth. My mirrors have been cautioning me, but refuse to provide context, and the one thing I know is that they can't see around the gods. I would say it's more than likely those dots connect. Are we following?"

The three of us link eyes. Kylian takes our grave silence as confirmation.

"I could be wrong, of course. It could be some *other* god looming in the mirrors, seeking the object Ienar was so desperate to wrestle from Arden's clutches. The same heirloom that, for all intents and purposes, is Serena's to inherit as the only living Blackblood."

"Ienar," Serena whispers. "But that would have to mean he's alive."

True fear gleams in my mate's voice as she backs into me. I band an arm around her waist, pulling her against my chest, the need to protect roaring in my veins.

"It's impossible."

"Is there proof? Were there remains?" Kylian questions.

"He couldn't have survived. Dragon fire kills gods, isn't that what you said, Zadyn?" She turns toward me, eyes desperate.

I nod, but my stomach feels leaden. "Ienar is dead. Furi made sure of that."

"No, she didn't. Because dragon fire doesn't work on fire walkers." Kylian sits up, his face grave. "Which is exactly what Ienar was."

No. No fucking way.

"You mean he got away? He's alive?" Serena croaks.

"I don't know what state he's in, love, but I do know that if he were dead, that star of ours wouldn't be shining."

Cold dread sinks into my bones.

Jace drifts closer, his brows knitting together. "If he's alive, then why hasn't he come for her? What is he waiting for?"

"I'm flattered you believe me to be omniscient, but as much as I hate to disappoint, I don't have *all* the answers. Everything I know, you now know as well."

"Why did you decide to give me Arden's half of the star?" Serena asks, stepping out of my grasp. "If it was such a risk, why take it out of the vaults at all?"

"I did it so that I could always find you."

"*What?*"

"The stars are drawn to each other like magnets. I've been tracking you from the moment you went through my mirror."

"Are you kidding me?! You've been following me?"

"Well, technically I had Mal follow you. And you did a number on him in Aeix, you little minx." He reaches for her, but she bats him away.

"Why didn't you just take me as soon as I fled?"

He drums his fingers on the bed and shrugs, peering at her from beneath dark lashes. "I relish a challenge."

"So the wanted signs and the cash reward on our heads were just for shits and giggles?"

"All part of the game, love."

"You gave her half of that star knowing it would put a target on her back," Jace confirms, his tone carefully measured.

"She did that herself when she ignored my pleas and joined the two halves. Apart, they are harmless."

"Do *not* blame this on me. I thought I was closing the portal when I joined them!"

"Yes, well, that was unfortunate and could have easily been avoided had you listened to me. I think we're going to need to work on our communication."

"You took her," Jace continues, hyper-fixated, a razor-sharp edge cutting into his voice, "*knowing* something was after her. That *Ienar* could be after her. That he might be fucking alive and here?!"

He seethes, his entire body now quaking with rage.

"The safest place for her was at my side. I was protecting her."

I blink, and Jace has Kylian by the throat.

"You did this!" he explodes. "You fucking stole her from her home, tracked her with that star, threatened everyone she cares about—and you're surprised she didn't trust your word? Your word is as good as shit!" His glare remains fixed on Kylian as he addresses us. "He's a liar and a manipulator. Don't believe a gods-damned word that comes out of his mouth."

Kylian grins, having gotten the rise out of him he was gunning for. "I have no reason to lie."

"You have every reason to lie now that you're powerless." Jace releases his throat with a shove.

"You can all sleep well at night knowing I would never harm my mate." He flings an arm around Serena's waist, tugging her onto the bed beside him. I bite back my fury as she scrambles out of his grasp.

"Funny that you don't classify kidnapping, imprisoning, and extorting into marriage as harm," I grit, clenching my jaw.

"As I'm sure she'll tell you—I never touched her. Well, I did, but it was consensual."

I glower at him, my fingers curling into fists at the thought of his gods-damned hands on my mate.

Jace turns bright red, all but convulsing. "Tell me how it was consensual when you had her chained up like a fucking whore in your bed!"

"Hey!" Serena shouts, demanding our attention. "It *was* consensual. You may never understand, and frankly I don't need you to. And you." She hits Kylian with a warning look. "Stop provoking them and tell us how to fix this."

He splays a hand over his chest, his brows inching higher. "Are you…asking for my help?"

"Yes," she answers begrudgingly.

"Then you should say please."

Her lavender eyes roll. "Please."

"I think you should say it on your knees, just there." He points to the ground beneath his feet.

"You fucker." A growl rips from my throat as I bound forward. Serena's hand on my chest is the only thing that stops me.

"It's fine," she hisses.

I twist away, taking deep breaths.

Stay calm, I tell myself. *The last thing we need is for you to shift and turn this into a bloodbath before we get the information we need.*

Slowly, she turns and lowers to her knees before Kylian. It makes me sick watching her supplicate herself to this bastard.

Jace makes a disgusted sound from across the room.

"Kylian, I am asking you, begging you"—Serena peers up at him from the ground, hands wrung like she's in prayer—"to please, please tell me how to fix this."

Kylian's gaze travels over her body, lazy and lingering. He waits a moment, and then, "It cannot be fixed."

She tosses her hands in the air, shoving to her feet.

"I just wanted to see you on your knees again."

"AGAIN?!" I whirl, lunging for him with bared teeth. Serena darts in front of me, attempting to shove me back.

"Why are you protecting him?!" I snarl, chest heaving. My claws threaten to poke right through the tips of my fingers, my spine seconds away from rearranging itself.

"Because he's an idiot, *clearly*, and has no idea how to keep from running his mouth. I truly don't think he can help it."

"Well, he'd better learn fast."

"Oh, relax, shifter," he tuts, crossing his legs. "You and I are going to be great friends."

The son of a bitch has the nerve to *wink* at me.

"Over my dead fucking body." I yank on the hem of my jacket, snapping it smooth. Jace snickers from behind us.

"Kylian, how do you know there's nothing we can do?" Serena keeps one hand on me, siphoning away my anger.

He sighs. "Unless you've been a secret starsmith this entire time, then what's done is done. They are joined and cannot be un-joined by you or me or anyone else in this room."

"So we're just supposed to wait and do nothing while he could be out there?" Panic floods her sweet little voice. "I might have brought him back or let him in or I don't even know what, but I can't just do nothing after I caused all of this!"

"Hey, this is not your fault. Do you understand me?" I pull her face into my hands, smoothing her cheeks and earning her tearful gaze.

"Waiting is the best thing we can do. And you, darling, should lie as low as you possibly can. Limit using your power in showy displays, anything that might attract attention." Kylian stands and walks toward her. "At least the star is in our possession."

"Right. Which means he'll be coming for it sooner or later," Jace huffs.

"I hope that I am wrong about this. Truly," Kylian says, all levity faded from his tone. "But I'm here. I am willing to do whatever it takes to keep you safe."

I loathe him with every fiber of my being. But the way he's looking at her, like he would leap in front of a bullet for her, is hard to deny.

"And what about your plans for world domination?" she murmurs, gazing up at him with a sliver of guarded hope.

He looks over Serena with hungry, faithful eyes.

"I've waited this long, haven't I? What's another minor delay at this point?"

EPILOGUE

Ilspeth Triori stepped out of the shadows and smoothed the crimson velvet pooling around her legs. Snow was drifting toward her in slow, white wisps that softly kissed the top of her raven hair. It was cold, she knew, but it had been years since Ilspeth had felt something as mundane as temperature.

Centuries, even.

Her heeled boots left prints in the snow as she made her way toward the mountain. Stopping before the massive gray boulder, she braced her hands on the cool, frosted rock, and with all of her strength, she pushed.

After a few moments, it finally gave way, clearing her path into the tomb.

A dark tunnel stretched before her—darker than night itself.

But she didn't need light. Because she wasn't afraid of the dark. She wasn't afraid of anything.

To be afraid, you had to be able to feel. And Ilspeth Triori could feel nothing at all. In fact, she was even beginning to forget *why* she felt nothing.

And that was perfectly fine.

The shadows led the way, black on black, coiling around her and

sweeping her deeper through the maze within the sacred mountain. With every step, she could feel the vibrations. The energy. The rumble of power so ancient it pre-dated this world.

She had felt the shift the moment it happened, all the way across the sea. And when she fastened her robe around her waist, climbed out of bed, and peered out the window, the constellation was closer to the earth than she'd ever seen. Like a string of jewels in a velvet bed of night.

She had come straightaway.

It had worked. It had taken thousands of years, but finally, she had delivered and made good on her promise of servitude.

There was a faint glow coming from the end of the fork. She followed it, already knowing what to expect when she stepped foot into the tomb.[*]

He was already awake.

He watched her approach, seated on the piled rock as if it were his throne.

She sank to her knees and bowed her head. The Dowager Queen of Vod *bowed*.

He stood and strode toward her, taking her shoulders and prompting her to rise.

He kissed her cheeks and smiled.

If Ilspeth could feel anything, she would have been lovestruck at the sight, as was the natural reaction to something so stunning. Had *always* been. A thousand years or two could not dampen it. Neither would another ten. It was a beauty time itself was not capable of eroding.

He took her hand, and together they stepped out into the blinding white storm.

They had plenty of work to do.

---

[*] Cue: *Eat Your Young* by Hozier

ACKNOWLEDGMENTS

Holy crap guys, we did it! We gave birth to book two. And I do mean "we" because without you and your support of Book Baby Number 1, this truly would not exist.

When you're writing a new novel and carving something from nothing, the process can be daunting and oftentimes discouraging. But as I sit here writing these acknowledgements, all I feel is excited and grateful to be on the other side of the mountain, sharing this story with you.

Now on to the thank you's.

Mom, you get the number one spot as always. Without you nurturing my creative side from the time I could walk, I wouldn't have been delusional enough to attempt half the things I have. You are my best friend and the one who constantly reassures me when I'm melting down. I love you so, so much.

To Josh, my biggest cheerleader after my own mother. Or maybe you're tied for first—I don't know, you're really coming for her job. Thank you for reminding me how cool this is, and for never letting me lose sight of my accomplishments. Love you.

To my brother—my little Longinus. Sorry for the uptick in spice. You can skip this one. Love you!

To my beta readers (Morgan, Cassy, & Elan)—I love you guys. I am so grateful to have such an amazing support system and group of cheerleaders in you. Your feedback has been invaluable, your friendship even more so.

To my ARC readers, street team, and every single person whose opinion I asked, every bookstore that carries my books, every single person reading this—I love you, and thank you for making my dreams come true.

Last but not least—thank you, Dad. I love you so much, always. See you in my dreams.

AFTERWORD

Did you enjoy reading *Chains of Fate & Fury*?

If so, please consider leaving a review on Amazon and Goodreads!

For news on events, signings, promotions, bonus content, and ARC opportunities, check out my website: www.marinalaurendi. com/books

You can also add me on Instagram and Tik Tok (@marinalaurendi) for bookish content, as well as tips on writing and self publishing.

For updates on new releases please follow me on Amazon!

ABOUT THE AUTHOR

Marina Laurendi is an American fantasy author, singer, songwriter, and creative. Because people did not throw tomatoes and beg her to stop, she decided to write a second book to go with her first, *Heir of Blood & Fire*. Hopefully, the tomato circumstances remain in check and she will write a third.

Visit www.marinalaurendi.com/ books to learn more.

ALSO BY MARINA LAURENDI

Heir of Blood & Fire: Blackblooded 1